UNDER ORDERS

It's the third death on Cheltenham Gold Cup Day

tha ...ley.
For ...rils
of ... ln't
usu ...38
rou ...he
fin ...urs
ear

Jus ...ry,
Ha ...e to
ma ...ses
ap] ...Are
rac ...d if
so, ...ous
gar

Ha ...per
int ...-or-
de; ...ery
lim

UNDER ORDERS

Dick Francis

WINDSOR
PARAGON

First published 2006
by
Penguin Books
This Large Print edition published 2007
by
BBC Audiobooks Ltd by arrangement with
Penguin Books Ltd

Hardcover ISBN: 978 1 405 61784 0
Softcover   ISBN: 978 1 405 61785 7

British Library Cataloguing in Publication Data available

Printed and bound in Great Britain by
Antony Rowe Ltd., Chippenham, Wiltshire

This book is dedicated to my late wife
Mary

and to the memory of
Dr Jara Moserova
my Czech language translator and friend for
forty years
who died the day this book was finished.

My thanks to

Andrew Hewson, literary agent
Alan Stephenson, Roehampton
Rehabilitation Centre
Professor Alex Markham, London
Research Institute
Dr Rosemarie Hutchinson, DNA specialist
Jonathan Powell, racing journalist
Edward Gillespie, Cheltenham Racecourse
Rodney Pettinga, Raceform Interactive
Catrina McDonald, RGN, nurse

And especially to my son
Felix
for everything

CHAPTER ONE

Sadly, death at the races is not uncommon.

However, three in a single afternoon was sufficiently unusual to raise more than an eyebrow. That only one of the deaths was of a horse was more than enough to bring the local constabulary hotfoot to the track.

*   *   *

Cheltenham Gold Cup day had dawned bright and sunny with a fine dusting of a March frost showing white between the grass. The forecast for the day was dreadful, with heavy rain due to drive in from the west, but as I stood in my ex-father-in-law's kitchen looking through the window at the westerly sky, there was no sign yet of the warm front that was promised.

'There you are, Sid,' said Charles, coming into the kitchen in his dressing gown over striped pyjamas, with soft blue velvet slippers on his feet. Rear Admiral Charles Rowland, Royal Navy (retired), my ex-father-in-law, my confidant, my mentor and, without doubt, my best friend.

I still introduced him to strangers as my father-in-law although it was now some ten years since his daughter, Jenny, my wife, had seen the need to give me an ultimatum: give up my job or she would give me up. Like any man at the top of his profession, I had assumed she didn't really mean it and continued to work day in and day out. And so Jenny left with acrimony and spite.

The fact that a crippling injury put paid to my chosen profession just a few months later was one of those little ironies from which there is no escape. Our marriage had been irreparably damaged and there was no going back. Indeed, by then, neither of us had wanted to go back but it still took many years and many hurtful exchanges before we were both able to move on. In time, Jenny and I had divorced and she had remarried, to a title and some serious wealth. Nowadays, we are civil to each other and I have a real hope that an arm's-length affection may be the end game of our tempestuous relationship.

'Morning, Charles,' I said. 'It's a good one, too.'

'Bloody forecasters,' he replied, 'never have the slightest idea.' He leaned towards the window to get a better view of the weather vane on the garage roof. 'South-westerly,' he remarked. 'That front has still to arrive. Better take an umbrella with us.'

I didn't doubt that he was right. A life at sea had given him the uncanny ability to predict the future simply by sticking a wet finger into the air. However, on this occasion, I think it may have been more due to his listening to the radio in his bedroom. His years afloat had also left him with a preference for all-male company, there being no female personnel on ships in his day, and a slow but determined approach to a problem. As he had often told me, it takes many miles to turn round an aircraft carrier and it is better to be sure in which direction you need to go before you start zigzagging all over the place and showing everyone what a blithering idiot you are.

We went to the races in his Mercedes, with raincoats and umbrellas stacked on the back seat.

As we drove west from his home in the Oxfordshire village of Aynsford across the Cotswold Hills towards Cheltenham, the sun began to hide behind high cirrus clouds. It had disappeared altogether by the time we dropped down from Cleeve Hill to the racecourse and there were spots of rain on the windscreen as we parked but the racing festival at Cheltenham is one of the world's great sporting occasions and a little rain couldn't dampen our spirits.

I had ridden so often round this course that I felt I knew each blade of grass as an old friend. In my dreams I still rode here, surging down the hill towards the home straight, kicking hard into the downhill fence when others would take a hold to steady themselves at this notorious obstacle. Here, many a partnership would come crashing to the turf if not foot perfect, but winning was the important thing and, while taking a hold might have been safer, kicking your horse hard could gain you lengths over the fence, lengths the opposition may not be able to regain up the hill to the finish line.

It had been a racing fall that had ended my riding career. It should have been easy. My young mount, stumbling while landing over the second fence in a novice chase, had failed to untangle its legs from underneath his neck and went down slowly to our right. I could have almost stepped off but chose to move with the falling animal and roll away from his flailing hooves. It was just unfortunate that a following horse, having nowhere else to go, had landed with all its weight on the outstretched palm of my left hand. But it was more criminal than unfortunate that the horse

3

had been wearing an old racing shoe, sharpened by use into a jagged knife-edge, which had sliced through muscle, sinew, bone and tendon, leaving my hand useless and my life in ruins.

But I shouldn't complain. I had been Champion Jockey for four consecutive years having won more jump races than anyone else, and would probably, by now, have had to retire anyway. At thirty-eight, I was well past the age at which even I thought it would be considered sensible to inflict the continuous battering on a human body.

'Sid,' Charles said, snapping me back to reality, 'remember, I'm the guest of Lord Enstone today and he asked me whether you'd be coming up to his box for a drink later.'

'Maybe,' I said, still half-thinking about what might have been.

'He seemed quite insistent that you should.'

Charles was pressing the point and I knew him well enough to know that this was his way of saying that it was important to him.

'I'll be there.'

If it were important to Charles, I would indeed be there. I owed him a lot and paybacks such as this were cheap. At least, that is what I thought at the time.

We joined the throng pouring into the racecourse from the car parks.

'Hello, Mr Halley,' said the gateman. 'What do you fancy for the big race?'

'Hello, Tom,' I replied, reading the name on his badge. 'Oven Cleaner must have a good chance, especially if we get much more of this rain. But don't quote me.'

He waved me through with a laugh and without

properly checking my badge. Ex-jockeys were a thorn for most racecourses. Did they get free entry or not? And for how long after they'd retired? Did it depend on how good they had been? Why wouldn't they go away and stop being an embarrassment, always carrying on about how much better it had been when they were riding and that the jumps were getting too easy and hardly worthy of the name.

If Tom had studied my badge more closely, he would have seen that, like me, it was getting a bit old and worn. I had simply not returned my jockey's metal badge when forced to retire and I had been using it ever since. No one seemed to mind.

Charles disappeared with a wave to make his way to the private luncheon boxes high in the grandstand while I walked unchallenged to the terrace in front of the weighing room next to the parade ring.

'Sid Halley!' I turned with a smile. 'How's the sleuthing business?'

Bill Burton, ex-jockey and now a mid-rank racehorse trainer whose waistline was getting bigger rather more quickly than his bank balance.

'Fine, Bill.' We shook hands warmly. 'Keeping me in mischief.'

'Good, as long as you keep your nose out of my business.' He said it with a smile that didn't quite reach his eyes.

We had ridden against each other regularly over many seasons and both of us knew that he had never been totally averse to a little extra cash for ensuring that his horse didn't get to the line first. He would adamantly argue that he would only 'stop' those who had no chance anyway, what crime was there in that? I could read in his face, I thought, that he had probably not changed his ways in moving from the saddle to the saddling box.

Shame, I thought. Bill was not a real villain but rumours were beginning to circulate that he was not fully honest either. As always, it was much easier to get such a reputation than to lose it. Bill couldn't see that he was never going to be the leading trainer as he had hoped, not because he didn't have the ability but because he would not be sent the best horses by the most knowledgeable of owners.

'Do you have any runners today?' I asked.

'Candlestick in the first and Leaded Light in the fifth. But I wouldn't risk your shirt on either of them.'

I wasn't sure whether he was warning me that they might not be trying their best. My doubts saddened me. I liked Bill a lot. We had been good friends and racing adversaries for many years.

He seemed to sense that I was looking deeper into his eyes than was prudent and briskly turned his head away.

'Sorry, Sid,' he said in my ear as he pushed past into the weighing room, 'got to go and find my jockey.'

I stood watching him disappear through the door and then looked up in the paper who his jockey was. Huw Walker. One of the sport's popular journeymen. He'd never yet made it to number one but had been consistently in the top ten over the past eight or nine years with numerous rides and plenty of winners. Son of a

Welsh farmer with, it was said, a fondness for fast women and fast cars in that order. I hadn't heard that he was ever suspected of 'pulling'—horses, that is.

In one of those strange almost supernatural moments, I looked up to find Huw Walker coming towards me.

'Hello, Huw,' I said.

'Hi, Sid. Did you get my message?' He looked far from his usual cheery self.

'No,' I replied. 'Where did you leave it?'

'On your answering machine. Last night.'

'Which number?'

'A London number.' He was clearly anxious.

'Sorry. I'm staying with my father-in-law in Oxfordshire for the Festival.'

'It doesn't matter. I can't talk here. I'll call you again later.'

'Use my mobile,' I said, and gave him the number.

He then rushed off, disappearing into the weighing room.

*   *   *

Even though it was still well over an hour to the first race, it was beginning to be rather crowded on the weighing room terrace, not least because everyone was getting close to the building to protect themselves from the rain that had begun to fall more intensely.

There was the usual mix of officialdom and Press, bloodstock agents and the media, trainers and their jockeys, both present and past. Here the gossip of the week was swapped and dirty jokes were traded like currency. Juicy rumours spread like Asian flu: who was sleeping with whom, and who had been caught doing so by a spouse. Divorce was rampant in the racing business.

I wandered among the throng with my ears open, catching up on events in racingland.

'Such a shame about that Sandcastle colt,' said someone in a group over my left shoulder. 'Didn't you hear, bought for half a million at Newmarket Sales last October as a yearling, put his foot in a rabbit hole yesterday morning and broke his hock so badly he had to be put down.'

I moved on.

'Useless jockey, flogged my horse half to death just to get a third place.' A large duffel-coated trainer, Andrew Woodward, was in full flow in front of a small group. 'Damn idiot got himself banned for four days. I'll give him excessive use of the whip on *his* bloody arse if he does that again.'

His fan club chuckled appreciatively but I believed him. Having once found his teenage daughter canoodling with an apprentice jockey in the feed store, he had held the hapless young man down over a hay bale and thrashed his bare buttocks raw with a riding whip. Some accounts say his daughter got the same treatment. It had cost Woodward a conviction for assault but it had won him respect.

He was a very good trainer but he had a well-deserved reputation as a hater of all jockeys. Some said that it was simple jealousy; he had always been too heavy to be a jockey himself. I had ridden for him a few times and more than once had received the lash of his tongue when results did not pan out as expected. He was not on my Christmas card list.

I drifted over nearer to the steps down to the parade ring where I had spotted someone that I *did* want to talk to.

'Sid, my old mucker!' Paddy O'Fitch was a fellow ex-jockey, shorter than I by an inch or two but a walking encyclopaedia on racing, especially steeplechasing. He spoke with a coarse Belfast accent and revelled in all things Irish, but the truth was that he had been born in Liverpool and christened Harold after the prime minister of the day. The surname on his passport was just Fitch. He had added the O' while at school. He had apparently never forgiven his parents for emigrating across the Irish Sea to England just two weeks before his birth.

'Hello, Paddy,' I said, smiling.

We shook hands, the camaraderie between us as ex-jocks being far greater than that between us when we were competing day by day.

After retiring from the saddle six years before, Paddy had turned his knowledge into a business. He wrote brief but wonderfully entertaining histories of racecourses and races, of racing characters and of great horses, and then sold them as slim booklets in racecourse car parks around the country. The booklets built up into an extensive history of the sport and soon were selling so fast that Paddy had employed staff to do the selling whilst he busied himself with the writing.

He had for years been the keeper of his own unofficial racing archive when, with due reverence from the Jockey Club, the post had been made official and he had been invited to coordinate all the material and documents held in various racing museums around the country. But it was the

9

histories that were his fortune. The slim, cheaply produced black-and-white booklets had given way to glossy colour, a new edition every month. Leather-bound holders for the booklets were a must-buy present for every racing enthusiast each December.

Paddy was a mine of both useful and useless information and, since I had taken up investigating as a career, I had frequently referred to him for some fact or other. In racing terms, Paddy could out-Google Google. He was the best search engine around.

'What chance do you think Candlestick has in the first?' I asked him casually.

'Could win. It depends . . .' He stopped.

'On what?' I prompted.

'Whether it's trying.' He paused. 'Why do you ask?'

'I thought I might have a bet.' I tried to make it sound normal.

'Bejesus! Now did ya hear dat!' He addressed no one in particular. 'Sid Halley's having a bet. And pigs may fly, I s'pose.' He laughed. 'Now if you told me dat you were having a third eye up ya arse, I might more believe ya.'

'OK, Paddy, enough,' I said.

'Now don't be telling ya Uncle Paddy lies, Sid. Now, why *did* ya ask about Candlestick?'

'What makes you think it may not be trying?' I asked instead of answering.

'I didn't say dat,' he said. 'I merely said dat it could win *if* it was trying.'

'But you must think it may not be, else why say it?'

'Rumours, rumours, that's all,' he said. 'The

10

grapevine says dat Burton's horses are not always doing their best.'

It was at this point that the first of the day's deaths occurred.

At Cheltenham, one end of the parade ring doubles as the winner's unsaddling enclosure and there is a natural amphitheatre created by a rise in the ground. A semicircular concrete-and-brick stepped viewing area rises up from the rail around the parade ring. Later in the day, this area would be packed with a cheering crowd as the winner of the Gold Cup returned triumphantly to be unsaddled. This early on a wet afternoon a few hardy folk stood under umbrellas watching the comings and goings at the weighing room and waiting for the sports to begin.

'Help! Help! Somebody help me!'

A middle-aged woman, wearing an opened waxed jacket over a green tweed suit, was screaming from the bottom of the stepped area.

All eyes swivelled in her direction.

She continued to scream. 'For God's sake, someone help me!'

Paddy and I ran over to the rail on the inside of the parade ring from where we immediately could see that it was not the woman but the man she was with who was in trouble. He had collapsed and was lying at her feet up against the four-foot high chain-link wire fence that kept the crowd away from the horses. More people had moved to help on her side of the fence and someone was calling for a doctor.

The racecourse doctor, more used here to treating injured jockeys, ran from the weighing room, speaking rapidly into his walkie-talkie.

11

There is nothing like a medical crisis to bring the great British public to stand and watch. The viewing area was filling fast as two green-clad paramedics came hurrying into the parade ring, carrying large red backpacks. The chain-link fence was in their way so, against the advice of the doctor, an enterprising group lifted the poor man over the top of it. He was laid on the closely mown grass, exactly where the afternoon's winners would later be.

The doctor and the paramedics set to work but quite soon it became clear that they were fighting a losing battle. The doctor put his mouth over the man's and breathed into his lungs. What trust, I thought. Would I put my mouth on that of a complete stranger? One of the paramedics took over from the doctor with a blue rubber bag that was connected to a tube down the man's throat while the other placed defibrillator pads on his chest. The man's body jerked as the voltage was applied but lay still and lifeless again afterwards.

They went on trying for much longer than I would have expected. They took it in turns to force air into the lungs or compress the chest. Almost half an hour had passed before they began to show signs of giving up. By then an ambulance had driven into the parade ring and a stretcher had been made ready. The man was lifted on to it but it was clearly all over for him. The urgency had fallen away from the medical movements. Another heart attack fatality, just one more statistic.

With the departure of the victim accompanied by his grieving wife, the crowds drifted away to the bars to get out of the rain, tut-tutting about the shame of it and the need to look after our bodies.

Sales of crackling at the pork-roast stall didn't seem to be affected.

*   *   *

I watched the first race from the Owners and Trainers Stand. The Triumph Hurdle is the blue riband event for four-year-old novice hurdlers over a distance of two miles and a furlong. The start was impressive as the twenty-five runners spread right across the course, resembling a cavalry charge to the first flight of hurdles. I found that I was paying particular attention to Huw Walker on Candlestick. The runners were still bunched together as they galloped fast past the grandstand for the first time. The climb to the highest point of the course began to sort them out and there were only half a dozen or so in with a chance as they swung left-handed and down the hill. Candlestick was third going to the second last where the leader got too close to the hurdle, hit the top and fell in a flurry of legs. Huw Walker pulled left to avoid the carnage and kicked Candlestick hard in the ribs.

It was one of those finishes that gives racing a good name. Four horses jumped the final flight abreast and the jockeys almost disappeared in a whirl of arms and whips as they strove to get the final effort from their mounts. There was no question that, this time, Candlestick was trying his best with Huw Walker driving hard for the line. His labours were well rewarded as they flashed past the post to win by a head.

Pleased, I walked back to the paddock to see the horse come back in, only to find that the trainer Bill Burton was looking like thunder. It seemed

13

that a win was not in his game plan. If he's not careful, I thought, he will confirm to all those watching that the rumours are true.

I leaned on the rail watching Bill Burton and Huw Walker unsaddle the sweating horse. The steam rose in great clouds from the animal's hindquarters but even this did not hide the animosity between the two men. They seemed oblivious of the thousands around them as they stood toe to toe beside the horse, shouting insults at each other. From where I was standing I couldn't hear the complete exchange but I clearly caught a few 'bastards' as well as some other, less flattering adjectives. The confrontation appeared to be heading towards violence when an official stepped between them and pulled Bill Burton away.

Huw looked in my direction, saw me, shrugged his shoulders, winked and then smiled broadly as he went past me to be weighed.

I was standing there wondering what to make of all that when I was slapped hard on my back. Chris Beecher, mid forties, balding and overweight. A journalist and a pain in the neck—and the back.

'How's that fancy hook of yours?'

He didn't seem to realise that it was one of those questions one shouldn't ask. Rather like enquiring if that strawberry birthmark on your face goes brown in the sun. Some things were best left alone. But Chris Beecher made his living hurting other people's feelings. Gossip columnist was his official title. Rumourmonger would have been more accurate. He was responsible for the Diary page in *The Pump*, a daily and Sunday newspaper that I'd been at odds with some years ago. Half of

14

what he wrote was pure fiction but there was enough truth in the rest that many believed it all. To my sure knowledge he had been the direct cause of two divorces and one attempted suicide during the previous twelve months.

My fancy hook, as he called it, was a highly expensive myo-electric false left hand. What the jagged horseshoe had started had been well and truly finished by a sadistic villain and I was now the proud owner of a state-of-the-art 21st-century hook. In truth, I had learned to do most things one-handed but I tended to wear the false limb as a cosmetic defence against people's stares.

'Fully charged and ready for action,' I said, turning and offering my left hand for a shake.

'Not bloody likely! You'll crush my fingers with that thing.'

'I'm good at picking up eggs,' I lied. In truth I had broken dozens of the bloody things.

'I don't care,' he said. 'I've heard stories on the grapevine of you hitting people with that and, by all accounts, they stay hit.'

It was true. I'd broken a couple of jaws. No point in fighting clean when I had a ready-made club firmly attached below my left elbow.

'What do you make of that little exchange between trainer and jockey?' he asked, with apparent innocence.

'Don't know what you mean.'

'Ah, come off it,' he said. 'Everyone must have seen that tiff.'

'What's the story, then?' I asked, equally innocently.

'Obvious. Walker won when he wasn't meant to. No stable money on the nose. Bloody fool.'

'Who?' I asked. 'Walker or Burton?'

'Good question. Both of them, I suppose. I'll be surprised if the Stewards don't have them in, or the Jockey Club. Fancy a beer?'

'Some other time. I promised my father-in-law I'd go and have a drink with him.'

'Ex-father-in-law,' he corrected.

'No secrets on the racecourse, not from you, anyway.'

'Now you're really joking. I couldn't beat a secret out of you if you didn't want to tell. I've heard that on the grapevine, too.'

He had heard too much, I thought.

'How's your love life?' he asked abruptly.

'None of your business.'

'See what I mean?' He tapped me on the chest. 'Who's Sid Halley screwing now? The best-kept secret in racing.'

He went off in search of easier prey. He was a big man who was used to throwing his considerable weight around. A bully who took pleasure from making people cry. I watched him go and wondered how he got to sleep at night.

But he had been accurate in one respect. Who Sid Halley was presently 'screwing' was indeed one of the facts I tried to keep from the racecourse. The racecourse was my place of work, my office. Apart from keeping my work and my pleasure separate, I knew from experience that I was vulnerable to threats being made against those I loved. Much safer for me, and for them, if their existence was unknown to my quarry.

16

CHAPTER TWO

I made my way up to the private boxes in the grandstand. It was not as easy as it used to be as so-called security seems to get stiffer each year. The friendly gatemen, like Tom down by the car park entrance who knew every trainer and jockey by sight and many of the owners too, were a dying breed. The new generation of youngsters, bussed in from the big cities, have no knowledge of racing. My face, once the ticket to every part of any racecourse, was now just another in the crowd.

'Do you have a badge for a box?' asked a tall young man with spiky hair. He wore a dark blazer with 'Event Security' embroidered on the breast pocket.

'No, but I'm Sid Halley and I'm going for a drink with Lord Enstone.'

'Sorry, sir.' He didn't sound sorry. 'Only those with passes can go up in this lift.'

I felt foolish as I flashed my out-of-date jockey's badge his way.

'Sorry, sir,' he sounded even less sorry and more determined. 'That doesn't get you through here.'

I was reprieved at that moment by the managing director of the racecourse, who I assumed was hurrying as usual from one minor crisis to another.

'Sid,' he said with genuine warmth, 'how are you?'

'Fine, Edward,' I replied, shaking his hand. 'But having a little difficulty getting up to Lord Enstone's box.'

'Nonsense,' he said, winking at the young man.

17

'Be a sad day for all of us when Sid Halley can't get everywhere on this racecourse.'

He put his arm round my shoulder and guided me into the lift.

'How's the investigation business?' he asked as we rose to the fifth floor.

'Busy,' I said. 'These days I seem to be working more and more away from the racecourse, but not this week, obviously.'

'Done a lot of good for racing, you have. If you need any help, just ask. I'll send you a pass that'll get you everywhere on this racecourse, even into my office.'

'How about the jockeys' changing room?'

'Ah.' He knew as well as I did that the jockeys' changing room was off limits to everyone except the jockeys riding that day and their valets, the men who prepared their equipment and clothes. Even Edward wasn't technically allowed in there on race days.

'Almost everywhere,' he laughed.

'Thanks.'

The doors opened and he rushed off.

*   *   *

Lord Enstone's box was bursting at the seams. Surely all these people don't have badges for this box, I thought, as I forced my way in. They could obviously talk their way past the spiky-haired young man better than I.

Those lucky few with boxes at Cheltenham on Gold Cup day invariably found that they had all sorts of dear friends who wanted to come and visit. That these 'dear friends' turned up only once a

18

year didn't seem to embarrass them at all.

A waitress offered me a glass of champagne. As a general rule, I held drinks in my real right hand but it made shaking hands so complicated, and I felt that I should use my left more to justify the large amount of money I had spent to acquire it. So I very carefully sent the correct impulses and the thumb of my left hand closed just enough around the stem of the glass. I had often shattered even the best crystal by not knowing how hard to grip with my unfeeling digits to prevent a glass from falling out. It could be humiliating.

Charles had spotted me across the throng and made his way to my side.

'Got a drink, good,' he said. 'Come and see Jonny.'

We squeezed our way out on to the balcony that ran the length of the grandstand in front of the glass-fronted boxes. The view from here across the racecourse and beyond to the hills was magnificent, even on a dull day.

Three men were standing close together at the far end of the balcony, their heads bowed as they talked. One of them was Jonny. Jonny was our host, Lord Enstone. Another was Jonny's son, Peter. The third I knew only by reputation. I had never actually met George Lochs. He was in his thirties and already a big player in the internet gambling business. His company, make-a-wager.com, while not being the market leader, was expanding rapidly and, with it, so was young George's fortune.

I had once been commissioned by the Jockey Club to do a background check on him, a routine procedure for those applying for bookmaking licences. He was the second son of a bookie's runner from north London. He'd won a free scholarship to Harrow where, apparently, the other boys had laughed at his funny accent and the way he held his knife. But the young George had learned fast, conformed and flourished. Except that he hadn't been called George then. He had been born Clarence Lochstein, named by his mother after the Duke of Clarence. Not Albert, Duke of Clarence, elder son of Edward VII, who supposedly died of pneumonia in 1892 although the rumours persist that he was poisoned to prevent his being arrested for being Jack the Ripper. Nor even after George, Duke of Clarence, the brother of Richard III, who was convicted of treason and drowned in a vat of malmsey wine at the Tower of London in 1478. Clarence Lochstein had been named by his mother after the Duke of Clarence pub at the end of her road in Islington.

There were rumours that Clarence/George had been asked to leave Harrow for taking bets on the horses from the other boys and, it was said, from some of the staff. However, he still won a place at the London School of Economics. Clarence Lochstein/George Lochs was a bright chap.

'Can I introduce Sid Halley?' said Charles, oblivious to the private nature of the men's conversation.

George Lochs jumped. Whilst his reputation had reached me, mine had also clearly reached him.

It was a reaction I was quite used to. It's a bit like when a police car stops behind you at traffic lights. A strange feeling of guilt inevitably comes over you even when you've done nothing wrong.

20

Do they know that I was speeding five minutes ago? Are my tyres legal? Should I have had that second glass of wine? Only when the police car turns off or passes by does the heartbeat begin to return to normal, the palms of the hands stop sweating.

'Sid. Good. Glad you could come.' Lord Enstone smiled broadly. 'Have you met George Lochs? George, Sid.'

We shook hands and looked into each other's eyes. His palm was not noticeably damp and his face gave nothing away.

'And you know my son, Peter,' he said.

I had met him once or twice on racecourses. We nodded in recognition. Peter was an averagely competent amateur jockey in his early thirties who had for some years enjoyed limited success, mostly in races reserved for amateur riders.

'Do you have a ride in the Foxhunters later?' I asked him.

'I wish,' he said. 'Couldn't convince an owner to put me up.'

'What about your father's horses?' I asked, giving his father a wink.

'No bloody chance,' said Peter with a half-hearted smile. 'Mean old bastard won't let me ride them.'

'If the boy wants to break his neck riding in races, that's his business, but I don't want to aid and abet him,' said Jonny, ruffling his son's blond hair. 'I'd never forgive myself.'

Peter pulled his head away from his father's hand with irritation and stomped off through the doorway. It was clearly a topic much discussed in the past.

21

'Charles, take young George here inside and find him a glass of fizz,' said Lord Enstone. 'I want to have a word with Sid in private.'

It was clear that young George didn't actually want to be taken off for a glass of fizz or anything else.

'Promise I won't listen,' he said with a smile, standing his ground.

'Dead right, you won't.' Enstone was losing his cool and with it his cultured RP accent. 'Jist gan' in there with Charlie, bonnie lad, I'm askin', OK?' Pure Geordie.

A few years previously, I'd also done a check on him for a horse-owning syndicate that he had wanted to join. Jonny Enstone was a builder. He had left school in Newcastle aged sixteen to become an apprentice bricklayer with J. W. Best Ltd, a small local general building company owned by the father of a school friend. Within two years he was running the business and, soon after, he bought out the friend's father. Expansion was rapid and, under the banner 'The J. W. Best built house you'll ever buy', Best Houses marched north, south and west covering the country with smart little three- and four-bedroomed boxes from Glasgow to Plymouth and beyond. Jonny Enstone had become Sir John, then Lord Enstone but he still had his hands on his business. He was famous for arriving very early one dark morning at a building site some two hundred miles from his home, and personally sacking anyone who was even a minute late at seven o'clock. He then removed the jacket of his pinstripe suit, rolled up the sleeves of his starched white shirt and worked the whole day in place of his fired bricklayer.

'Now, Sid,' RP fully restored, 'I need you to find out something for me.'

'I'll try,' I said.

'I'll pay you proper rates. I want you to find out why my horses aren't winning when they should be.'

It was something I was regularly asked to do. I inwardly sighed. Most owners think their horses should be winning more often than they do. It's a matter of 'I paid good brass for the damn thing so why doesn't it start repaying?'

'I think,' he went on, 'my jockey and trainer are stopping them.'

That was what they all thought.

'Move them to another trainer.' I was doing myself out of a commission.

'It's not as simple as that, young man. I tell you, my horses are not just not winning when they should, they're running to orders that aren't mine. I feel I'm being used and I don't like it.' I could suddenly see the real Jonny Enstone beneath the Savile Row exterior: powerful, determined, even dangerous.

'I'm in racing because I like to *win*,' he emphasised the word. 'It's not the money that's important, it's the *winning*.'

Why was it, I thought, that it was always those with plenty of it who believed that money was not important. To the hard-up punter, a place bet on a long-priced runner-up was much better than an ultra short-priced winner.

Peter returned with a fresh glass of champagne for his father as a peace offering, their earlier little spat obviously forgiven.

'Thanks, Peter,' said Lord Enstone. He took a

sip of the golden fluid.

'Who trains your horses?' I asked. 'And who rides them?'

'Bill Burton and Huw Walker.'

*   *   *

I stayed to watch the Gold Cup from Lord Enstone's box. The balcony was heaving with bodies pressed up against the front rail as everyone strove to get a view of the supreme challenge for a steeplechaser, three and a quarter miles over 22 fences, all horses carrying the same weight. The winner of the Cheltenham Gold Cup was a true champion.

I had ridden eight times in this race and I knew all too well the nervous anticipation being experienced by the jockeys as they paraded in front of the packed grandstands. This was one of only two or three really big jump races in the year that put the winning horse and jockey into the history books. For a horse to win this race more than once was the stuff of dreams. Winning it three times put the animal into the legend category.

Oven Cleaner, in spite of his name, was aiming to join the legends.

He was a big grey horse and I watched him canter down to the start with the others. I wondered if I would ever stop being envious of those doing what I still longed to do. I had not been born to the saddle and had never sat on a horse until I was sixteen when my widowed mother, dying herself of kidney cancer, had taken me to be apprenticed to a Newmarket trainer simply because I was very small for my age and I would soon be an orphan. But I had taken to riding like the proverbial duck to water. I found the bond between horse and rider exhilarating, especially when I realised that I could read their minds. When I discovered that they could also read mine, I knew I was part of a winning combination.

And so it had been until it all fell apart. A jockey feels a horse not through his feet in the stirrups nor through his arse on the saddle but through his hands on the reins connecting like power cables to the horse's mouth, transmitting commands and data in both directions. With only one hand, it was like a battery with only one end. Useless—no circuit, no transmission, no data, no go. At least, no go fast, which is what racehorses and jockeys are supposed to do.

I watched the field of the best steeplechasers in the world gallop past the stands on the first circuit and positively ached to be amongst them. It had been ten years but it felt like only yesterday that I had been.

Oven Cleaner cleaned up. In his trademark manner, he looked to all to have left his run too late but, to a deafening roar from his tens of thousands of faithful supporters, he charged up the hill to win by a whisker.

The crowd went wild, cheering and shouting and even throwing their soggy hats into the air. The big grey nodded his head in approval as he took the applause on the walk to the winner's unsaddling enclosure. He was a hero and he knew it. Grown men cried with joy and hugged their neighbours whether they knew them or not. The only unhappy faces were the bookies who would lose a fortune. Oven Cleaner was a national icon, and housewives had bet the housekeeping and children had loaded their pocket money on his nose. 'The Cleaner', as he was affectionately known, was a god amongst racehorses.

The cheering rose to a new height as the legend was led into the unsaddling enclosure by his euphoric lady owner.

Then the legend died.

*   *   *

Tears of joy turned to tears of despair as the much loved champion suddenly stumbled and collapsed onto the grass, pulling down his owner and pinning her leg under his half-ton bulk. The crowd fell silent, save for a group of celebrating punters at the back still unaware of the unfolding tragedy. The screams of the horse's owner, her ankle trapped and crushed, eventually cut through to them too, and they were hushed.

Oven Cleaner had given his all. His heart, so strong in carrying him up the Cheltenham hill to victory, had failed him in his moment of triumph.

Willing hands managed to free the poor owner but she refused to leave for medical treatment on her broken ankle, cradling the horse's head in her lap and crying the inconsolable tears of the bereaved.

I watched a vet examine the animal. He placed a stethoscope to the grey-haired chest and listened for a few seconds. He stood up, pursed his lips and shook his head. No paramedics, no mouth-to-mouth resuscitation, no defibrillator pads, no cardiac massage, just a shake of the head.

A team of men hurried in with green canvas

26

screens that they set up around the still steaming bulk. No screens, I thought, for the poor human victim who had died on the same spot not three hours before. But the screens were not really necessary. Whereas, earlier, the crowd had grown to watch the human drama, now they turned away, not wanting to witness the sad end of such a dear friend.

*   *   *

Deep gloom descended on the racecourse. It was not helped by an objection from the clerk of the scales because Oven Cleaner's jockey had failed to weigh in.

'How could I?' he protested. 'My bleeding saddle is still on the bleeding horse halfway to the bleeding glue factory.'

The 'bleeding saddle' in question had, in fact, been removed by the trainer when the horse had collapsed and had been placed out of sight under the cloth-covered table used for the presentations of the trophies. An uncommon amount of good sense broke out when it was agreed by the Stewards that the jockey, finally reunited with his saddle, could weigh in late.

I wondered what the rule would have been if the jockey had died instead of the horse. Could his lifeless corpse be carried to the scales? Dead weight. I smiled at the thought and received some stern looks for being so cheerful at a time of national mourning.

The fourth race on Gold Cup day is the Foxhunter Steeple Chase, often referred to as the amateur riders' gold cup. The favourite won but returned to almost silent grandstands. The will to cheer had gone out of the crowd, which politely applauded the winner's return.

'Where's that bloody jockey of mine?' Bill Burton was asking anyone and everyone outside the weighing room.

'Huw Walker?' I asked as Bill hurried towards me.

'Bloody unreliable bastard, that's what he is. Gone bloody AWOL. Have you seen him, Sid?' I shook my head. 'He's due to ride Leaded Light in the next but I can't find him. I'll have to declare another jockey.' He went back inside to change his declaration.

Leaded Light was beaten into second place in a close finish that should have had the crowd on their feet shouting. Such was the mood that the jockey on the winner didn't even look happy at having won. Many of the crowd had already departed and I, too, decided I'd had enough. I opted to wait for Charles at his car in the hope that he would also want to leave before the last race.

I was making my way past the rows of outside broadcast TV vans when a wide-eyed young woman came stumbling towards me. She was unable to speak but she pointed down the gap between two of the vans.

She had found Huw Walker.

He sat leaned up against the wheel of one of the vans looking at me with an expression of surprise. Except that his staring eyes were not seeing and never would again.

He was still wearing his riding clothes, breeches, lightweight riding boots and a thin white roll-neck top worn under a blue anorak to keep out the rain and the March chill. His anorak hung open so that I could clearly see the three closely grouped bullet wounds in the middle of his chest showing red against the white cotton. I knew what one bullet could do to a man's guts as I had myself once carelessly been on the receiving end, but these three were closer to the heart and there seemed little doubt as to the cause of death.

CHAPTER THREE

Charles and I didn't arrive back at Aynsford until after midnight.

As is so often the case, the police ran roughshod over everything with no care for people's feelings and, it seemed, with little or no common sense.

They cancelled the last race of the day and closed the racecourse, refusing to let anyone leave, not even those in the central enclosure who didn't have access to where Huw Walker had been found. Totally ill equipped to interview nearly sixty thousand people, they relented in the end and allowed the wet, angry and frustrated multitude to make their ways to the car parks and home but not before it was very dark and very cold.

In a way, I felt sorry for the policemen. They had no idea how to deal with a crowd of racegoers in shock and grief over a horse. Surely, they said, you are more concerned about the murder of a jockey than the death of an animal?

'Don't be bloody daft,' said one man standing near me. 'All jockeys are bent, anyway. Got what he deserved, I reckon.' Sadly, it was a common

29

view. If it wins, it's all the horse's doing. If it loses, blame the pilot.

I didn't get away quite so easily as I was a material witness and I reluctantly agreed to go to their hastily established incident room in one of the now vacated restaurants to give a statement. I pointed out that I hadn't actually been the first to find poor Huw. However, the young woman who had was so shocked that she had been sedated by a doctor. She was asleep and unable to speak to the police. Lucky her.

Huw had been seen in the jockeys' changing room before the Gold Cup but not after it. Bill Burton had been looking for him less than an hour later.

By the time they had set up their interview area and got round to asking me, it was clear they had received reports of the shouting match between trainer and jockey after Candlestick's victory in the first. Bill Burton, it appeared, was already their prime suspect.

I pointed out to Detective Chief Inspector Carlisle of Gloucestershire CID that Huw had obviously been killed by an expert assassin who must have brought a gun with him to the races for the purpose and that Bill Burton couldn't have magically produced a shooter out of thin air just because he had had a tiff with his jockey following the first race.

'Ah,' he said, 'maybe that's what we are meant to think while, meantime, Burton had planned it all along.'

Yes, I had spoken to Huw Walker earlier in the day.

No, he didn't say anything to me that could be of

use to the police.

Yes, I had seen Huw Walker and Bill Burton together after the first race.

No, I didn't know why anyone would want him dead.

Yes, I would contact them again if I thought of anything else which might be important.

I remembered the message on my London telephone and decided not to mention it. I wanted to listen to it first and the remote access system on my answer machine was broken.

*   *   *

The following morning, all the national dailies ran the ecstasy and agony of Oven Cleaner on their front pages. *The Times* ran the story over the first three pages with graphic photographs of his victory and the subsequent disaster.

Only on page seven was there a report of the discovery, late in the afternoon, of the body of jockey Huw Walker by Sid Halley, ex-champion jockey and now private detective. Even this item referred to the sad demise of the equine hero and, at first glance, one might have been forgiven for thinking that the two were connected. Somehow the impression was given that Walker's death was a bizarre after-effect of the great horse's passing, as if the jockey had killed himself in grief even though he had not himself ridden The Cleaner to victory. There was no mention of the three bullet wounds in Huw's chest. As any one of the three would have been instantly fatal, the police, at least, were not treating his death as suicide.

The *Racing Post* went even further, with an

eight-page spread of Oven Cleaner's career and an obituary to rival that of a prime minister.

'It was only a bloody horse,' declared Charles over his breakfast. 'Like that memorial in London for the animals in war. Ridiculous sentimental rubbish.'

'Come on, Charles,' I said. 'I've seen you almost in tears over your dogs when they die. Same thing.'

'Poppycock!' But he knew it was true. 'When are you off?' he asked, changing the subject.

'After breakfast. I have some reports to write.'

'Come again. Come as often as you like. I like having you here and I miss you when you're gone.'

I was surprised, but pleased. He had initially detested his daughter marrying a jockey. Not a suitable match, he'd thought, for the daughter of an admiral. A game of chess, which I had won, had been the catalyst to an enduring friendship that had survived the break-up of my marriage, had survived the destruction of my racing career, and had been instrumental in the blossoming of my new life out of the saddle. Charles was not one to show his emotions openly; command in the services was lonely and one had to learn to be emotionally robust in the face of junior officers.

'Thank you,' I said. 'I enjoy being here and I will come again soon.'

We both knew that I tended to come to Aynsford only when I was in trouble or when I was depressed, or both. Aynsford had become my sanctuary and my therapy. It was my rock in the turbulent waters I had chosen as my home.

*   *   *

I left promptly after breakfast and drove home to London along a relatively empty M40. The rain beat relentlessly on the roof of my Audi as I made my way round Hyde Park Corner and into Belgravia. I lived in a fourth-floor flat in Ebury Street near Victoria Station and, after five years, it was beginning to feel like home. Not least because I did not live there on my own.

Who Sid Halley was presently 'screwing', the secret I kept from Chris Beecher, was Marina van der Meer, a Dutch beauty, a natural blonde with brains, and a member of a team of chemists at the Cancer Research UK laboratories in Lincoln's Inn Fields searching for the Holy Grail—a simple blood test to find cancers long before any symptoms appear. Earlier detection, she said, leads to easier cure.

When I arrived at noon she was sitting in our large bed, wearing a fluffy pink towelling robe and reading the Saturday papers.

'Well, well, quite the little Sherlock Holmes!' She pointed to a picture of me in the *Telegraph*. It was the one they often used of me, smiling broadly as I received a racing trophy. That photo was now more than ten years old and pre the flecks of grey that were now appearing at my temples. I didn't mind.

'It says here that you discovered the body. I bet Colonel Mustard did it in the conservatory with the lead piping.' Her English was perfect with a faint hint of accent, more a rising and lowering of inflection than a specific style of pronunciation. Music to my ears.

'Well, he might have done, but he must have melted the lead piping into bullets first.'

'It doesn't say he was shot.' She looked surprised and tapped the paper. 'It even gives the impression it was natural causes or suicide.'

'Difficult to shoot yourself three times in the heart. The police kept that gem to themselves and I didn't tell the Press either.'

'Wow!'

'What are you still doing in bed, anyway?' I asked, lying down beside her on the duvet. 'It's nearly lunchtime.'

'I'm not hungry.'

'Fancy working up an appetite?' I grinned.

'I thought you'd never ask.' She giggled and shrugged the robe off her slender shoulders.

Chris Beecher, eat your heart out.

We lay in bed for much of the afternoon, watching the racing on the television while I should have been writing up reports for clients. We decided against a walk to St James's Park because of the incessant rain but, eventually, did huddle under an umbrella and make our way to dinner at Santini, the Italian restaurant on the corner. Marina had chicken while I chose Dover sole, off the bone.

We contentedly shared a bottle of Chablis and caught up on the week.

'Tell me more about the jockey who was killed,' Marina asked.

'He was nice enough,' I said. 'In fact, I spoke with him earlier.' I remembered Huw's message still sitting unheard on my machine.

'He won the first race,' I said. But I wondered if he should have. Had he been told to lose? Was that why he'd died? Surely not. That killing was expertly carried out. It was an assassination. As I had told the police, someone had to have come to the races with the wherewithal to commit murder in his pocket. Metal detectors were not usual at the entrances to racecourses, although Aintree used them after the Grand National was postponed one year due to a bomb scare.

The rain had stopped by the time we walked back to the flat hand in hand—her left, my right— dodging the puddles and laughing out loud. This was why I never took Marina to the races. This was a different world, one in which I could relax and act like a teenager, one in which I was increasingly happy and near to the point where I would seek to make it permanent. We stopped and kissed at least four times during the short fifty-yard stroll and went straight back to bed.

I had always preferred lovemaking to be gentle and sensual and it was clearly Marina's pleasure, too. After the violence of the previous day, I found solace in her tender embrace and we both seemed hugely satisfied by the experience. Afterwards we lay in the dark, touching occasionally, close to sleep.

As a rule, I removed my false arm prior to making love but we had been swept away with the passion of the moment so now I gently eased myself out of bed and went into the bathroom. The five or so inches remaining of my left forearm fitted snugly into the open end of a hard fibreglass cylinder built to be the same length as my healthy right. The plastic-covered steel myo-electric hand was attached to the bottom end of the cylinder. Chris Beecher had been correct, it was little more than a fancy hook. The fingers were permanently slightly bent and the hand was able to grip between forefinger and thumb by means of an electric motor that moved the thumb in and out. The motor was powered by a rechargeable battery that clipped into a recessed holder above the wrist.

Electrodes inside the arm-cylinder were held close to my skin near to where my real arm ceased. Initially I had had to learn how to open and close the hand using impulses I had previously used for bending my wrist. Try to move back the real hand that wasn't there and the false hand opened. Move it forward and the hand closed. Easy. Unfortunately there was a slight delay between the impulse and the action and, consequently, I had broken the eggs and almost everything else I gripped. Nowadays, the thought processes were second nature but I still tended not to stop the impulses soon enough and breakages were common. Hence I had learnt to live a mostly one-handed life to match my one-handed body.

One could sleep with the arm in place but I almost never did as it was hard and very uncomfortable to lie on, its unfeeling fingers having a tendency to dig in to real flesh. Once I had almost knocked a beautiful bedfellow unconscious when turning over in my sleep. A couple of pounds of steel and plastic was definitely not an aid to romance.

The open end of the arm-cylinder fitted over my elbow, a plastic cuff gripping tightly around the ends of what was left of my ulna and radius bones, the bumps on each side of the elbow. I was impressed by the strength of the join between the genuine me and the fake. I had recently discovered that the fit was so good that, if I locked my elbow straight and stressed my biceps, I could hang my

36

whole body weight by the arm. Not that I really fancied testing it with my life.

Removing it was consequently quite a challenge. I bent my elbow as far as it would go and gradually eased the plastic away from my skin. I placed it on the shelf over the washbasin. A tight-fitting rubber cosmetic glove covered the hand and wrist, protecting them from rain and beer spills. Shapes had been moulded into the rubber to represent fingernails and tendons, with bluish lines for veins. I preferred to wear it than not for the appearance it gave me of being two-handed. Lying there on the shelf, alone and disembodied, it looked gruesome and ghoulish. I covered it with a towel.

I padded in bare feet along the hallway to the kitchen to get some water and noticed the flashing light on the answering machine through the open door of the bedroom that doubled as my office. I pushed the button and the mechanical voice answered: 'You have six messages.'

The second was from Huw Walker.

'Hi, Sid,' he said in his usual jovial manner. 'Bugger! I wish you were there. Anyway, I need to talk to you.' The laughter had faded from his voice. 'I'm in a bit of trouble and I . . .' he paused, 'I know this sounds daft but I'm frightened.'

There was another brief pause.

'Actually, Sid, no kidding, I'm really frightened. Someone called me on the phone and threatened to kill me. I thought they were bloody joking so I told them to eff off and put the phone down. But they rang back and it's given me the willies. I thought it was all a bit of a lark but now I find that it ain't. I need your bloody help this time, mate, and no mistake. Call me back. Please call me back.'

There was another long pause as if he had waited in case I picked up at my end. Then there was a click and the next message played. It was from my financial adviser reminding me to buy an ISA before the end of the tax year.

There were, in fact, two messages from Huw, not one. Message four was also his.

'Where are you when I need you, you bugger?' His voice was slurred and he had obviously been drinking in the time between messages. 'Come on, pick up the bloody phone, you bastard! Can't you tell when a mate's in trouble?' There was a pause in which I could hear him swallow. 'Just a few losers, they says, for a few hundred in readies, they says. OK, I says, but make it a few grand.' He sighed loudly. 'Do as we tell you, they says, or the only grand you'll see is the drop from the top of the effing grandstand.' He was now crying. 'Should have bloody listened, shouldn't I?'

The message ended abruptly.

I stood in the dark and thought of him as I had last seen him; three closely grouped deadly holes in his heart.

Yes, he should have bloody listened.

CHAPTER FOUR

Archie Kirk called me at eleven o'clock on Sunday morning as Marina and I were still sitting in bed in our robes, surrounded by the newspapers.

'Thought you were meant to be a private detective.' He emphasised the word private. 'Not very private to be splashed across the front pages.'

The Sundays had taken up where the Saturdays had left off, with hundreds of column inches bemoaning the death of Oven Cleaner. One red-top rag even called for a national day of mourning and a memorial service in Westminster Abbey.

However, I assumed Archie was referring to the front-page banner headline in *The Pump* that read 'Sid Halley in Cheltenham Murder Mystery' above a three-column photograph of me looking extremely furtive. At first glance, anyone would have thought that it was me who had been murdered. *The Pump* and I had crossed swords in the past and maybe the headline was just wishful thinking by the editor.

Someone in their newsroom clearly had a source in the Cheltenham police who had reported that 'Sid Halley, ex-champion steeplechase jockey, has been interviewed by senior officers and is helping the police with their enquiries into the murder of jockey Huw Walker at Cheltenham races on Friday. No arrest has been made at this time.'

Clearly *The Pump* expected me to be hung, drawn and quartered by lunchtime. The piece went on to imply that all of the world's ills could be placed at my door. 'Sid Halley, crippled ex-jockey, is now searching the gutters for rats as a minor private dick. He should feel nicely at home amongst the low-life . . .'

'Ridiculous,' I said. 'They're fishing.'

'Nevertheless,' said Archie, 'enough people will believe it.'

Archie was always concerned for my welfare and now, it appeared, he wanted to protect my reputation as well.

He was some sort of civil servant but he didn't

belong to any specific department. Nominally, he answered to the Cabinet Office, but he appeared to work in his own way with little contact or regard for his superiors. He was the chairman of a small group who were tasked with attempting to foretell the future. Their remit was to try and work out the consequences of proposed legislation, to try and ensure that it would actually do what it was intended without any unpleasant side effects that had been overlooked. Officially they were called the Standing Cabinet Sub-Committee on Legislative Outcomes but they were referred to by the few who knew of their existence as the Crystal Ball Club. Archie tended to label them the Cassandra Committee after the Greek mythological heroine who was both blessed and cursed by the god Apollo with the ability to correctly predict the future whilst no one believed her.

'Any publicity is good publicity,' I quipped.

'Tell that to Gerald Ratner.'

I respected Archie and had grown to like him more and more as, over the past four years, I had become his very private ears and eyes.

Legislation in a democracy is, by its very nature, a compromise, a negotiated settlement somewhere in the middle ground. Whether it be a government-backed initiative or a private member's bill, there is usually some horse-trading to be done. Some amendments may be accepted, others declined, paragraphs may be removed, word orders may be changed. Laws passed by Parliament are often substantially different from those drafted.

Archie and his Crystal Ball Club tried to look at legislation from the perspective of the end user, the members of the general public who would be affected. History is littered with examples where law makers had grossly misjudged the reaction that their well-intentioned deeds would produce.

After World War I, no less than forty-five of the then forty-eight states of the US voted to amend the American Constitution to prohibit the importation, manufacture and sale of alcoholic beverages in the hope and expectation of reducing crime and corruption. Only the state of Rhode Island voted against. Fourteen murderous years later, during which time the federal prison inmate population increased by more than 350%, the same state legislators voted another amendment to the Constitution repealing their blunder, again in the hope and expectation of reducing crime and corruption.

In 1990, the United Kingdom Government of the day decided that in order to make local taxes fairer they would introduce a single flat charge, equal for all. What could be fairer, they thought? The Community Charge, as they called it, was soon dubbed the Poll Tax and resulted in violent demonstrations across the country. The law was repealed in 1993 but the damage had been done. The Government's reputation was terminally wounded. They lost the next election in a landslide.

Archie's team was set up to try and foresee just such problems. They spent much of their time on private member's bills, providing their political chiefs with a best guess at the effect that would be produced if a specific bill were to be passed into law. Many such proposed bills were the direct result of single-issue pressure groups that could be

41

very persuasive without necessarily revealing the whole truth behind their argument. The chance of a private member's bill reaching the statute book was largely dependent on whether the government of the day supported the measure and hence provided the parliamentary time. The grounds for such support were a combination of politics, practicality and expediency. Archie's job was to advise as to the practicality and expediency. However, political considerations sometimes outweighed everything else.

Over the years, I had quietly and discreetly investigated many pressure groups and their individual members. I tended to look for links to big business or organised crime, or both.

Never mind statistics, there were lies, damn lies and the spouting forth from single-issue pressure groups. Blinkered, fanatical and blind to counter-argument and reason. Facts they didn't like, they ignored or dismissed as lies. Sometimes they were just the foot soldiers in a bigger game, being used and manipulated by puppet masters working silently in the dark. Some were misguided and wrong. Others were plain crazy. A few had valid points but these were often lost in rhetoric and fury. Ask an animal rights supporter if he would rather have a new cancer drug tested on him first and he will say 'that's not the point'. But it's exactly the point. If his mother were diagnosed with cancer, he would demand treatment to cure her. He'd be the first to blame the government and the health services if it didn't exist.

'Are you still there?' Archie asked.

'Sorry,' I replied, 'miles away.'

'Well, what are you going to do about it?'

'About what?'

'About *The Pump*.'

'Oh.' I paused to think. 'Nothing. Their lawyers will have made sure they haven't libelled me, it's just absurd speculation.'

Laced with loathing, I assumed, but I didn't like them much either.

'Why don't you rant and rave like any normal man?' Archie asked.

'You wouldn't,' I replied. Archie was one of the most even-tempered men I had ever met. 'What good would it do? *The Pump* seem to have it in for me again and complaining will only make it worse.'

I had once shown *The Pump* to be completely wrong about someone who they claimed to be a saint but who turned out to be a bigger sinner than even I had realised. The Press doesn't like to be shown to be foolish. Stoking the fire in their belly would do nothing to make it go out.

'It's so unfair.' I rarely heard such anger in Archie's voice.

'Look, Archie,' I said, 'this is not worth getting upset about. Let it blow over.' Let the police find the killer, I thought.

'Can you come and see me tomorrow?' Archie asked, abruptly changing the subject.

'At home or in the office?' I asked.

'Whichever suits you.'

'Office, then. Ten?'

'Fine.'

I didn't bother to ask him what it was about. Archie was naturally a secretive man and on the telephone he habitually gave an excellent impression of a Trappist monk. He didn't trust telephones and, as an ex-member of MI5, he should know. Today he had been unusually effusive and was probably regretting it already.

*   *   *

Marina and I decided to walk down to the Goring Hotel for a glass of wine and a sandwich. As a jockey I had never been able to eat a large lunch, even on non-racing Sundays, and the routine of eating only an evening meal had survived the disaster.

We took the lift down and stepped out into the marble-floored lobby. I had chosen this apartment building partly due to the 24-hour manned desk facing the entrance with its bank of CCTV monitors. I had been attacked outside my previous home so I valued the peace of mind provided by the eclectic band of individuals who made up the team of porters/security men.

'Morning, Derek,' I said.

'Afternoon, Mr Halley,' he corrected.

Reassuring, reliable and discreet, no one set foot in the building without their knowledge and say-so.

Half an hour later, sustained by a shared smoked salmon sandwich and a glass of wine, we hurried back to the flat in watery March sunshine that did little to alleviate the biting northerly wind on our backs.

'Ah, Mr Halley,' said Derek as we walked in, 'guest for you.'

My 'guest' was sitting in the lobby and he was having difficulty getting up from a deep armchair. He was in his mid-sixties and was wearing dirty brown corduroy trousers and an old green sweater

44

with a hole in the front. A shock of grey hair protruded from under a well-worn cap.

In his right hand he held a copy of *The Pump*.

'Sid Halley!' His booming voice filled the air with sound and he took two quick steps towards me.

Oh no, not again.

I looked around for reinforcement from Derek but he had decided to stay in relative safety behind the desk.

But instead of trying to hit me, the man thrust the newspaper in my face. 'Did you kill my son?' he demanded at maximum decibels.

I nearly laughed but thought better of it.

'No, I did not.' Even to my ears it sounded very melodramatic.

'No, I didn't really think so.' His shoulders slumped and he sat down heavily on the arm of the chair. 'But *The Pump* seemed so . . . oh, I don't know . . . so believable.' He spoke with a strong Welsh accent and I quite expected him to add 'Boyo' to the end of each sentence.

'I've driven all the way here from Brecon.' He gulped and his eyes filled with tears. 'I set out to kill you. In revenge. But . . . the more I drove, the more stupid that seemed. It wouldn't bring Huw back and, by the time I'd gone half way, I realised that you wouldn't have done it. Huw always says . . .' he faltered, '. . . said . . . that you, look, are on the side of the bloody angels. God, what am I doing here?'

He began to cry, his shoulders jerking up and down with great sobs that he tried to suppress.

Marina squatted down next to him. 'Mr Walker,' her melodic tone brought his chin up a fraction,

45

'let's go upstairs and get you a cup of tea.'

She stood and pulled him to his feet and guided him towards the lift.

'Thanks, Derek,' I said.

Derek stood wide-eyed and uncharacteristically silent as the lift doors closed.

Marina fussed around Mr Walker like a mother hen and soon had him sitting on the sofa sipping strong sweet tea from a blue-and-white striped mug.

'What's your name?' she asked while stroking his hand.

He smiled at her. 'Evan,' he said.

'Well, Evan,' she smiled back, 'have you had anything to eat for lunch?'

'To tell you the truth,' he said, 'I haven't had anything to eat since Friday night. Since when the police came to tell . . .' He tailed off, the memory still too raw to describe. 'I don't feel like eating.'

Nevertheless, Marina disappeared into the kitchen.

'How did you know where I lived?' I asked.

'I didn't,' he said. 'The man from *The Pump* told me.'

'You just phoned them up and they gave you my address?'

'No, I didn't phone *them*.' He looked slightly disturbed. 'A man from *The Pump* phoned *me* at six o'clock this morning to ask whether I had seen their newspaper. Course I hadn't. Not at six in the morning. I'd fed the cattle but there's no delivery on Sundays and the shop doesn't open until nine.' He made it sound like a major failing.

He paused and looked at me. Was he thinking what I was thinking? Why did *The Pump* call him

46

so specifically to ensure he read their paper?

'So did you go and get a copy of *The Pump*?' I asked, prompting him to continue.

'Well, I did,' he said, 'but not from our local shop, see, it still wasn't open when I left. I stopped to get one in Abergavenny.'

Marina reappeared with a mountain of scrambled eggs on toast that Evan Walker devoured like a starving dog, hardly stopping to draw breath.

'Thank you,' he smiled again. 'Delicious. I didn't realise how hungry I was.'

'But why did you set off for London if you hadn't read the piece in the paper?' I asked.

'I didn't need to read it. The man from *The Pump* read the whole thing out to me over the phone. I was bloody mad, I can tell you. He kept saying what was in the paper was only the half of it. He good as told me you'd done it and no mistake. "Sid Halley murdered your son," he said, and he said you'd probably get away with it because you'd done a deal with the police. Then he gave me your address and asked me what I was going to do about it.'

'Did he give you his name?' I asked. I already suspected who had called him.

'No,' he paused to think, 'I don't think so.'

'Was it a man called Chris Beecher?' I asked

'I don't know, I didn't ask his name.' He paused again and shook his head. 'Right bloody idiot I've been. See that now, but at the time I was so bloody angry.' He dropped his eyes from mine. 'I'm glad that bloody drive was long enough for me to come to my senses.'

So was I.

He sighed. 'I suppose you'll call the police now?'

'How were you going to kill me?' I asked, ignoring his question.

'With my shotgun. It's still in the car.'

'Where?' I asked.

'Outside on the road.'

'I'll get it,' I said. 'What type of car and where are the keys?'

'Old grey Ford.' He patted his flat pockets. 'Keys must be in it.'

I went down and it was still there with the keys in the ignition, unstolen. Good job it was a Sunday, I thought, or he would have had at least three parking tickets by now. Amazingly, the shotgun was still there, too, lying in plain view on the back seat.

I picked it up, locked the car and turned to go back upstairs.

I am not sure why I noticed the young man in a car on the far side of the road take aim at me, maybe it was his movement that caught my eye. I strode straight across to him and lifted the business end of the shotgun I was holding in his general direction.

He had aimed not a gun but a camera that he now lowered to his lap. Experienced *paparazzi* would have gone on snapping, I thought—Sid Halley threatening a photographer with a loaded shotgun, just what *The Pump* would have loved for the front page.

'What are you after?' I shouted at him through the closed car window. 'Put the window down.'

He pushed a button and the window opened a couple of inches.

'Who sent you?' I asked through the crack.

48

He didn't reply.

'Tell Chris Beecher he shouldn't tell tall stories to Welsh farmers,' I said.

He just looked at me, then nodded slightly. It was enough.

I slowly lowered the shotgun. There were too many windows overlooking Ebury Street and I feared that net curtains would already be twitching.

The young man took one look at the lowered gun and decided that retreat was the best plan. He ground his gears and was gone.

I strode back through the lobby, grinning broadly, with the gun slung over my shoulder. Derek, who had watched the whole episode through the glass, now had an open mouth to match his staring eyes.

I winked at him as the lift closed.

So much for my secrets, I thought. Chris Beecher knew exactly where I lived. And he knew exactly who I was 'screwing'.

*   *   *

Evan Walker stayed for another hour before remembering that he had cattle to feed and 175 miles to drive home first. In the meantime, he managed to consume four more slices of toast with lashings of strawberry jam, and two more mugs of tea.

He talked about Huw and how proud he was of what his son had achieved.

'Glynis, that's my wife, and me, we were so pleased when he won the Welsh National at Chepstow. You should have seen us. Dressed to the nines, we were. My Glynis was so proud. Best thing that happened to us for ages. Glynis passed away last October, see. Cancer it was.' He was again close to tears. 'Stomach. Poor lass couldn't eat. Starved to death, really.'

'Do you have any other children?' I asked.

'Did have,' he said. 'Another boy, Brynn. Two year older than Huw. Knocked off his bike, he was. On his way to school. On his fifteenth birthday.'

Life is full of buggers.

'Glynis never got over it,' he went on. 'Visited his grave every week for eighteen year till her illness meant she couldn't walk down to the churchyard. Buried next to him she is.'

There was a long pause as he stared down at the floor.

'Suppose I should put Huw with them.'

Another longer pause.

'Just me left now,' he said. 'I was an only child and Glynis lost touch with her brother when he moved to Australia. Didn't even come back for her funeral although he could have afforded to. Successful businessman, apparently.'

Evan stood up and turned to me. 'It says in that damn rag that you're a private detective,' he said. 'I remember you as a jockey and a bloody good one too. I often wondered what Huw would do when he gave up riding . . . doesn't matter now . . . Anyway, what I meant to say was, will you find out for me who killed my son?'

'The police will do that,' I said.

'The police are fools,' said Evan forcefully. 'They never found out who killed our Brynn. Hit-and-run, you see. Never really tried, if you ask me.'

I noticed that Marina's eyes had filled with

50

tears. Just how much pain could a single man take?

'I'll pay for your time,' he said to me. 'Please . . . find out who killed my Huw.'

I thought of the desperate messages Huw had left on my answering machine.

'I'll do my best,' I said.

How could I say no?

CHAPTER FIVE

I lay awake for much of the night thinking nasty thoughts about what I would like to do to Chris Beecher and his young snapper and, sure enough, the Monday edition of *The Pump* had, on its Diary page, a photograph of Marina and me walking hand in hand along Ebury Street with the headline, 'Who's Sid Halley's new girlfriend?' The picture seemed to accentuate the fact that Marina was some four inches taller than I, and the brief paragraph underneath was hardly flattering with the words 'divorced', 'diminutive' and 'crippled' all making an appearance alongside 'murder suspect'. At least the photo wasn't one of me pointing a double-barrelled shotgun at the camera with the line 'Who's Sid Halley's new victim?'

So much for keeping my relationship away from the Press and a secret from those persons who might look for 'pressure points'.

I had created a reputation amongst the racing villainy that Sid Halley would not be put off by a bit of violence to his body. Such a reputation takes a while to establish and, unfortunately, quite a few had already tried the direct route. One such incident had resulted in the loss of my left hand. It had by then been useless for some time but I was still attached to it both literally and metaphorically. Its loss to a poker-wielding psychopath had been a really bad day at the office.

These days there were those who would stoop to different methods to discourage me from investigating their affairs. Consequently, I had tried to keep Marina's existence a secret and I was frustrated that I had been so glaringly unsuccessful. Perhaps I was getting paranoid.

Marina, meanwhile, seemed more concerned that the photographer had captured her with her mouth open and her eyes shut.

'At least they haven't got my name,' she said, trying to make me feel better.

'They'll get it. And your life story.' There were always those who would ring up a newspaper if they had a snippet of information. Too many people knew Marina at her work.

'Just take care,' I warned, but she didn't really believe that she would be in any danger.

'You work for the Civil Service,' she said. 'How dangerous can that be?'

There was nothing 'civil' about some of those I had separated from their liberty or from their ill-gotten gains. But that had been before I had encountered my Dutch beauty at a friend's party and invited her first to share my bed, then my life.

If I were honest, I would have to admit that nowadays I tended not to take on the sort of work that I had revelled in five years ago. Regular safe jobs provided by Archie Kirk filled most of my time. Boring but profitable. Hardly a threat to be heard, except from the tax man over my expenses—'a new suit to replace the one ruined due to lying in a wet ditch for two hours waiting for a certain Member of Parliament to complete an amorous assignation with a prostitute in the back of his Jaguar—you must be joking, sir'. I hadn't shown him the pictures.

Finding Huw Walker's killer might prove to be a little more dangerous.

*   *   *

Marina and I slipped out of the building through the garage in case there were more telephoto lenses awaiting our appearance through the front door. She took the tube to work while I walked along Victoria Street to Archie's office in Whitehall.

'*The Pump* have really got it in for you, haven't they?' he said by way of a greeting, the newspaper on his desk open at the Diary page.

'Ignore them,' I replied. 'Then they might go away.'

'Are they still going on about that other time?'

'The Press don't like being in the wrong,' I said, 'and they have very long memories. But that time there was an agenda. This time I think it is just one particular journalist and his warped sense of humour. He doesn't like me because I won't tell him anything for his gossip column. This is his way of getting back at me. Ignore it. I have broad shoulders.' Actually I didn't, but so what.

I stood by the window in Archie's office looking out at the traffic. Every second vehicle going down Whitehall seemed to be a bus. Masses of big red buses. Most were double-deckers but some were long single-deckers with a bendy bit in the middle. Almost all of them were nearly empty and I thought that much of the congestion in London was due to too many buses with too few passengers.

I turned and sat down on a simple wooden upright chair. Archie clearly did not want his visitors to become too comfortable and outstay their welcome.

I had found it difficult to determine quite how high up Archie was in the Civil Service hierarchy. To have a third-floor office on the corner of Downing Street with a spectacular view of the London Eye would seem to put the occupant into the 'considerably important' bracket. However, the threadbare carpet and the sparse furniture that would not have looked out of place in a hostel for the homeless tended to say otherwise.

Although I had been in this office several times, we normally did our business by meeting elsewhere, usually in the open air and well away from listening ears. Archie did not appear to have a secretary or an assistant of any kind. I had once asked him to whom I should speak if I needed something urgently and he was not available.

'Speak only to me. Only use my mobile, and don't talk about confidential matters on the telephone,' he had briskly replied. 'And don't use your mobile at all if you don't want anyone to later find out where you were at the time of the call. And never use the office switchboard.'

'Surely you trust the Cabinet Office switchboard?' I had said.

'I trust nothing and nobody,' he had declared. And I had believed him.

He cleared his throat.

'Have you heard about the Gambling Bill that's making its way through Parliament?' he asked, getting to the point.

'Of course,' I said. 'All the talk on the racecourse.'

The proposals in the Bill were, it seemed to me, designed to make it easier to separate a fool from his money, to provide easier access to casinos and to allow more and more internet gambling sites into every home. Not that I wanted to restrict anyone from having the odd flutter, even many odd flutters. The racing fraternity, however, was deeply concerned about the impact the Bill might have on their industry.

Twenty years before, racing had had almost a monopoly on gambling. Casinos existed but they were 'members clubs' and beyond the aspiration of the general public. Then came betting on football and on every other sporting activity. Next the National Lottery took a slice. Now the super-casinos planned for every town might prove the death knell for some of the smaller racecourses.

'Well,' he went on, 'we—that's my committee and I—are looking at the influences that organised crime may have on the way that licences are issued to new gambling centres. As you might know,' he sounded very formal, as though addressing a public meeting, but I was used to it, 'until recently, the issuing of licences for the serving and consumption of alcohol was the remit of a magistrate. Now that duty has been transferred to the local councils.'

It sounded to me as if he trusted the magistrates rather more than the councils, but it was only relative, I thought, since he trusted nothing and nobody.

'It is our expectation that gambling licences will be issued in the same manner under the control of a new Gaming Board. As always, the bloody politicians are rushing things into law without working out how they'll be implemented.'

As often seemed to be the case, I thought. Legislation tends to be shaped more by politics than by logic.

Archie went on. 'There are over three thousand bookmaking permits issued in this country and nearly nine thousand betting shop licences. There's already lots of scope for corruption and we feel this will only increase.'

Wow, I thought. More bookies than punters at some courses. I hope he didn't expect me to investigate every one.

'And that doesn't include the internet sites, which are breaking out like a rash,' he said. 'On-line poker seems to be the latest craze but racing is still the biggest market. Many of the new sites are based overseas and it will prove very difficult if not impossible to license and regulate them.'

He paused and seemed to have run out of steam.

'What do you want me to do?' I asked.

'I don't really know. Get your antennae working and listen. Ask the right questions. What you usually do.'

'How long do I have and how many days do you want to pay for?' I asked.

'Give it a month. Usual terms, OK?'

'Fine,' I said. We had an arrangement that worked well. In the month I might spend about half my time on Archie's work and I would charge him for twelve days plus expenses. I didn't know under which budget such work was included and I didn't ask. Cheques arrived promptly and, so far, they hadn't bounced.

Archie stood and offered his hand. My audience was over.

Work-wise, the last few weeks had been rather thin but now, like the buses in Whitehall, three had come along at once. Since Friday morning I had agreed to look into the running of Jonny Enstone's horses, find the murderer of Huw Walker, and now the minor matter of determining if there was likely to be major corruption in the issuing of betting permits and licences due to a change in the system. Piece of cake, I thought, but where the hell do I start?

I decided I could get going on the first two jobs at the same time and, I thought, maybe the third one, too. I went to see Bill Burton.

*　　　*　　　*

I collected my Audi from the garage under my flat and drove the sixty or so miles west along the M4 to Lambourn.

I had phoned Bill to make sure he would be in. 'Come if you like,' he had said. 'Can't think that it'll do any good.' He had sounded tired and lifeless, not like the strong Bill Burton who had once helped me through the double trauma of a marriage break-up and a career-ending injury.

It was nearly two in the afternoon when I pulled up the driveway and parked round behind the house near the back door. I could see through into his stable yard from here and all was quiet. A few

57

inquisitive equine heads appeared over the stable doors to inspect the new arrival.

I knocked, then, as is always the way in the racing world, I opened the door and walked straight into the kitchen, expecting Bill's children to run in to see who had arrived, as they always did.

'Hello! Hello, Bill, Kate,' I called out.

An elderly black labrador raised its head from its bed, took a look at me and decided not to bother to get up. Suddenly the house seemed very quiet. Dirty dishes were stacked in the kitchen sink and an opened milk carton sat on the kitchen table.

I called out again. 'Bill, Kate, it's Sid, Sid Halley.'

No reply. The labrador stood up, came and sniffed around my legs, then returned to lie down again on its bed.

I went through into the hallway and then into the den, a small sitting room where I knew Bill spent many an afternoon watching the racing on the television.

He was there, lying on a leather sofa. He was fast asleep.

I shook him gently and he sat up.

'Sorry,' he said. 'Didn't sleep too well last night.' He struggled to his feet. 'Fancy a coffee?'

'Love one,' I replied.

We went into the kitchen and he put the kettle on the Aga. There were no mugs left in the cupboard so he took a couple from the dirty stack in the sink, rinsed them briefly under the tap, and measured instant granules into them with a dirty teaspoon.

'Sorry,' he said again. 'Kate's not here. Left with the children on Friday morning.'

'How long will she be away?' I asked.

'Don't rightly know.' He sighed. 'We had a row . . . another row, but this was a big one. This time, maybe, she won't be coming back.'

'Where's she gone?' I said.

'Not sure. To her mother's I expect, or her sister's.'

The kettle started to boil and clouds of steam appeared above the spout. He didn't seem to notice. I stepped round Bill and took the kettle off the heat, closing the lid on the Aga. I poured the boiling liquid into the mugs.

'Haven't you tried to call her?' I asked. I sniffed the milk. It was off.

'I did call her mother's number,' he replied. 'I've never got on with my mother-in-law and she predictably put the phone down on me. I haven't bothered to try again. Kate knows where I am if she wants me.'

I put a steaming mug down beside him on the kitchen table. 'It'll have to be black, the milk's off,' I said, taking my mug and sitting down on a kitchen chair.

'Oh, there's more in the fridge,' he said but made no move to get it. He just sat down with another sigh.

'It hasn't been very good for a while, not since Alice was born, that's my youngest. Three she is now.' He paused briefly and smiled. 'We've been married twelve years. Bloody marvellous it was at first. I was the envy of the jockeys' room.'

I remembered. We had all fancied Kate who was the elder daughter of the successful trainer for whom Bill rode. We had all thought it had been strictly 'hands off' if he wanted to continue riding for her dad, so it had been a big surprise when Bill, twenty-eight at the time, had announced one day that he was going to marry Kate who was six years his junior. It had been the wedding of the year in Lambourn.

'We were so in love,' he went on, 'and I was proud as proud could be of my beautiful wife. We both wanted masses of children and she got pregnant as soon as we tried. She came off the pill on our honeymoon and "bingo" first bloody time.'

I knew—I'd heard this story numerous times before.

'That was young William. Then there was James and Michael, and finally we had Alice. Always wanted a girl.' He smiled broadly at the thought of his lovely little daughter.

'But since then, things have been going wrong,' he said. 'When I was riding it was easy. I went to the races, rode what the guv'nor told me to, and came home again. Or ended up in hospital. You know. Never had to bring work home. Easy.'

I remembered that, too. I agreed with him. It was easy if you were one of the top jockeys with plenty of rides, and plenty of money, as we both had been.

'This training lark is much tougher. Always kowtowing to the bloody owners. You try telling them that their horses are useless and only good for the knackers without upsetting them to the point of them taking my advice and having the bloody things put down. Then where would I be? No bloody horses and no training fees.' He stopped to take a gulp of his coffee, made a face and fetched the fresh milk from the fridge.

'Then there are the entries, the orders and the staff.' He sat down again, leaving a second opened milk carton on the table. 'You wouldn't believe how unreliable staff can be. They just pack up and leave whenever they feel like it, usually immediately after pay-day. Someone offers them a job with a bit more money and they're off. I had one lad last week told me he was leaving while we were in the paddock at the races. There and then. After the race he was gone. Didn't even turn up to take the horse back to the racecourse stables. I tell you, staff drive you nuts.'

He took another drink of coffee.

'Anyway, what with all the problems and the lack of money compared to when I was riding, Kate and I started to row. Usually it was about nothing, or something so small I can't even remember now. We would laugh about how silly we were and then go to bed and make it up. But recently things have been worse.' He stopped and looked at me. 'Why am I telling you all this?'

'You don't have to,' I replied. 'But carry on if it makes you feel better. I won't tell anyone.' Especially not Chris Beecher.

'I've heard that you can keep a secret,' he said, looking at my false hand. Far too many people, I thought, had heard that story.

'It all came to a head on Thursday night.' He seemed relieved to be able to tell someone. 'For some time now Kate has been coming to bed late, really late, one or two in the morning. Well, I have to be up at five thirty for the horses so I'm usually in bed by ten, ten thirty at the latest.'

He finished his coffee.

'Well, that doesn't do much for your love life, I can tell you. If I tried to wake up when she came to bed, she would shy away from me. It was as if she didn't want me even to touch her. So about ten o'clock on Thursday I said to her that I wanted her to come to bed now. She said something about wanting to watch some programme on the telly. So I said to her, "Why are you so frigid these days? You used to love sex. Is there anything wrong?"'

He paused and looked out of the window. The memory obviously hurt.

'I thought she might have a medical problem or something. I only wanted her to get back to the old ways. Then she said something I'll never forget.' He stopped and I sat and waited as his eyes filled with tears and he fought them back by swallowing hard a couple of times.

'She said that Huw Walker didn't think she was frigid.'

'Oh.'

'I thought she must be joking.' he said, 'but she started to goad me. Said that he was a much better lover than me and that he knew how to satisfy a woman. I still didn't believe it so I went to bed. But I couldn't sleep. She never did come to bed that night. She packed some things for her and the children and left while I was out with the first lot. I came back to find the house empty.'

He stood up and leant against the sink, looking out at the stables beyond.

'It isn't the first time she's left,' he went on. 'Third time since Christmas but before it was only for one night each time. I wish she'd come home.'

He stopped and began to cry.

'Is that why you were so angry with Huw on

Friday?' I asked, hoping he would continue talking.

He turned round and wiped his eyes with his shirt sleeve. 'I tried to be as normal as possible, so I went to the races—it was Cheltenham, after all. I hoped Kate would come home while I was out. And I still didn't really believe her about Huw Walker. I thought she had just said it to upset me.'

'What changed your mind?' I asked quietly.

'I was about to give him a leg-up on to Candlestick in the first when he turned to me and said, "Kate called me. Sorry, mate." I was stunned. I just stood there unable to feel my legs. Juliet, you know, Juliet Burns my assistant, she had to do everything. I stood in the paddock for the whole race.' He laughed sardonically. 'My first winner at the Festival and I never saw it.' His laughter died. 'I was still there when Candlestick returned to the winner's enclosure. I hadn't moved an inch. Juliet came and fetched me. Sort of woke me up. Then I lost it. God, I was so mad with that bastard! I could have killed him.'

The enormity of what he'd said hung in the silence.

He looked at me for several seconds that seemed much longer, then he looked down at his hands. 'When I heard he was dead, I was glad. But now, well you know, I don't really want that.'

But he is, I thought.

'Who would want him dead?' I asked.

'Don't know. I thought everyone loved him. Perhaps some jilted girl killed him.'

Unlikely, I thought. It was too clinical, too professional.

'Did he win or lose to order?' I asked.

Bill's head came up fast. 'My horses are always

trying to win,' he said, but he didn't sound totally convincing.

'Come on, Bill,' I said. 'Tell me the truth. Did Huw and you ever fix races?'

'Candlestick was sent out to do his best and to win if he could.'

It wasn't what I had asked.

'The Stewards had me in after the race. They were furious that I had been shouting at Huw in the unsaddling enclosure.' He laughed. 'They were particularly annoyed that all my effing and blinding had gone out live on the television. Apparently there had been more replays of that than of the race. Bringing the sport into disrepute, they said. Stupid old farts. Anyway, they accused me of being angry with Huw for winning on Candlestick. I told them it wasn't anything to do with that, it was a personal matter, but they insisted that I must not have wanted the horse to win. I told them that that wasn't true and I'd had a big bet on him. Luckily I was able to prove it there and then.'

'How?' I asked.

'On their computer. I logged on to my on-line betting account and was able to show them the record of my big bet on Candlestick to win.'

'How did they know that you hadn't had another bet on him to lose?'

He grinned. 'They didn't.'

'So had you?'

'Only a small one to cover my stake.'

'Explain,' I said.

'Well, I have an account with make-a-wager.com, the internet gambling site,' he said.

I remembered my meeting with George Lochs at Cheltenham.

'The site allows you to make bets or to lay, that is to take bets from other people. They're known as the exchanges as they allow punters to exchange wagers.' He was clearly excited. 'So I can place a bet on a horse to win. Or I can stand a bet from someone else who wants to bet on the horse to win, which means I effectively bet on it to lose. The Triumph Hurdle—Candlestick's race last Friday—is a race that you can gamble on ante-post, which means you can bet on the race for weeks or months ahead.' I nodded; one didn't need to be a gambler to know all about ante-post betting.

'Because you lose your money if the horse doesn't run, the odds are usually better. Prices are even better before the entries close because you're also gambling that the connections will choose to enter the horse for the race in the first place. Then lots of the horses that are entered never actually run.' He briefly drew breath. 'The entries for the Triumph Hurdle close in January, but I put a monkey on Candlestick to win at 30 to 1 way back in November.'

'So if he won, you'd win fifteen thousand,' I said. A monkey is gambling slang for five hundred.

'Right,' he said, 'but if he didn't win I would have lost my five hundred. So on Thursday morning, I bet on him to lose to cover my stake.'

'How exactly?' I asked.

'I took a bet of a monkey at sevens. So if the horse won I would win fifteen thousand minus the three and a half thousand I would have to pay on the other bet, and if he didn't win I was even. I would have lost my win stake but made it back on the lay bet. Understand?'

'Sure,' I replied. 'You stood to win eleven and a

half thousand against a zero stake.' And win he had.

'Piece of piss,' he laughed. 'Money for old rope. But you lose badly if the horse doesn't run so I only tend to do it if I am pretty sure my horse will actually run and it has a reasonable chance, which means the starting price will be a lot shorter than the ante-post price. On Friday, Candlestick's starting price was down to 6 to 1.'

'Do you ever make money if the horse loses?' I asked.

'Well,' he paused a moment as if deciding whether to continue. Discretion lost. 'I suppose I do sometimes, when I know a horse isn't too well or hasn't been working very well. Occasionally I will run a horse I really shouldn't. Say if it's got a cold or a bit of a leg.'

I remembered an owner who was surprised to hear from his trainer that his horse had 'a bit of a leg' when he expected that it had four full ones. 'A bit of a leg' was a euphemism for heat in a tendon, a sure sign of a slight strain. To run a horse in such a condition was quite likely to cause the horse to 'break down', that is, to pull or tear the tendon completely, requiring many months of treatment and, at worst, the end of a racing career.

Bill would know, as I did, that the powers-that-be in racing, while allowing trainers to bet on their horses to win, forbid them to bet on them to lose.

'So the Stewards only saw the win bet on your account?' I said.

'Bloody right,' he said.

'So how did you take the lose bet on Thursday?'

'There are ways,' he grinned again.

I wondered how big a step it was from running

66

an under-the-weather horse that was likely to lose, to running a horse that was fit and well that would also lose because the jockey wasn't trying. I was getting round to asking such a pivotal question when we were interrupted by the arrival of vehicles in the driveway, the gravel scrunching under their tyres.

'Who the hell can that be at this time?' said Bill, moving to look out of the window.

It was the police.

In particular, it was Chief Inspector Carlisle of Gloucestershire CID, together with several other policemen, four of them in uniform.

Bill went to meet them at the back door.

'William George Burton?' asked the Chief Inspector.

'That's me,' said Bill.

'I arrest you on suspicion of the murder of Huw Walker.'

CHAPTER SIX

'You must be having a joke,' said Bill. But they weren't.

The Chief Inspector continued, 'You do not have to say anything, but it may harm your defence if you do not mention when questioned something which you later rely on in court. Anything you do say may be given in evidence.'

Bill didn't say anything but just stood there with his mouth open.

They weren't finished.

One of the other plain-clothes policemen came

up and arrested him again, this time on suspicion of race fixing. Same rights. Bill wasn't listening. He went very pale and looked as though he might topple over. He was stopped from doing so by two of the uniformed officers who stood each side and held him by the arms as they led him to one of the cars.

Bill looked back over his shoulder at me standing in the doorway. 'Tell Juliet to feed the horses,' he said. A policeman wrote it down.

'I'll stay here until she comes,' I said.

'She lives down the road. Look after things, will you?'

'OK.'

He was bundled into the car and driven away. Seven policemen remained.

'You again, Mr Halley.' Chief Inspector Carlisle made it sound like an accusation.

'You again, Chief Inspector,' I replied in the same tone.

'What brings you here?' he asked.

I decided not to tell him that I, too, was looking for Huw Walker's killer. 'Visiting my friend,' I replied.

The policemen started to come in through the door.

'What do you think you are doing?' I asked.

'We're going to search this house,' said Carlisle. 'As Mr Burton has been arrested, we have a right of search of his premises. We would be most grateful if you would vacate the property now, Mr Halley.'

I bet you would, I thought. 'I believe that Mr Burton has the right to have a friend present during any such search and, as he told me to look after things, I intend to remain.'

'As you wish,' said Carlisle, not showing any obvious disappointment. 'But please keep out of our way.'

Instead, I fetched my digital camera from my car and took mega-pixel shots of the policemen as they systematically worked their way through the house. My presence was clearly an irritation to Carlisle who stamped around me and tut-tutted every time my camera flashed.

'Is that really necessary?' he finally asked.

'I thought you had to make a detailed record of the search,' I replied. 'I'm just helping out. I'll e-mail you a complete set of the pictures.'

'Do you know if Mr Burton owned a gun?' he asked. 'In particular, a .38 inch revolver.'

'No, but I think it most unlikely.'

I knew Bill would never give his children toy guns for Christmas or birthdays as he thought it would teach them to be violent. I couldn't imagine that he would own a real one.

By the time Juliet Burns and the other stable staff arrived at four thirty for evening stables, the police had removed all Bill's computer equipment from his desk, sealed it in large clear plastic bags, and loaded it into one of their vehicles. I was photographing them as they were bagging up his business record books when Juliet walked into the office.

'Hello, Sid—what the bloody hell's going on?' she demanded.

'And who are you, madam?' asked Chief Inspector Carlisle, coming into the office before I could answer.

'Juliet Burns, assistant trainer, and who the hell

69

are you, and what the hell are you up to?' She directed the last question at the uniformed policeman who went on filling his bag with papers off Bill's desk.

'I'm Chief Inspector Carlisle, Gloucestershire CID. We are searching these premises in the course of our investigations.'

'Investigations into what?' she demanded loudly. 'And where's Mr Burton?'

'He is helping us with our enquiries.'

I wondered if being taught 'police speak' was part of the training.

'Into what?' she asked again.

'Into a suspicious death at Cheltenham last Friday.'

'You mean Huw Walker?'

'Indeed.'

'And you think Bill did it? Ha!' She laughed. 'Bill wouldn't hurt a fly. You've got the wrong man.'

'We have every reason to believe that Mr Burton had a powerful motive for killing Mr Walker,' said Carlisle.

'What motive?' I asked. Their heads turned towards me.

Carlisle seemed to realise that he had given away too much information. 'Er, none of your business, sir.'

On the contrary, I thought, it was very much my business.

'Have you been speaking to Mrs Burton?' I asked him.

'That's none of your business, either,' he replied. But I could see that he had. He had known that Kate and the children were not in the house when he had arrived. There had been no female police officers in his party. He had expected Bill to be here on his own.

So I assumed Carlisle's 'powerful motive' was that Kate had told him that she was having an affair with Huw and that Bill had found out about it on Thursday evening. On Friday, Huw had turned up dead with his heart like a colander and Kate must have thought Bill was responsible. Not an unreasonable conclusion, I thought. No wonder she'd not come home. She believed her husband was a murderer.

Juliet stood with her hands on her hips. I hadn't seen her since she was a child but I'd known her family for years. She may have been small in stature but inside her petite frame was a giant of a woman trying to get out. Her mother had died bringing her into the world and she had been raised by her blacksmith father and her four elder brothers, growing up as the youngest in a household dominated by men. Childhood had consisted of wrestling in front of the television on a Saturday afternoon and playing rugby or football in the garden on Sunday mornings. And, of course, there was riding, plenty of riding, hunting in the winter and Pony Club gymkhanas in the summer. School had simply been a time-filler between more important pursuits. Now aged about twenty-five, I believed this was Juliet's first job as an assistant trainer after doing her time as a stable groom in and around Lambourn.

'Hey, you can't take that. It's the entries record,' she shouted at a policeman who was busy placing a large blue-bound ledger into a polythene bag.

'We can take whatever we like,' said Carlisle.

'They're also investigating race fixing,' I said.

Juliet stared at me with her mouth open.

'Bill was arrested on suspicion of race fixing,' I said. 'As well as for murder. I was here.'

'Bloody hell!' She turned to Carlisle. 'You'd better take all the bloody horses as well, then. They'll be accessories.'

Carlisle was not amused and politely asked us both if we would leave his men to their task.

Juliet and I went out to the stable yard where the lads were busy with the horses. The daylight was fading fast and bright yellow rectangles from the stable lights extended out through the box doors. Steel buckets clanged as they were filled with water from the taps in the corners of the yard and figures carrying sacks of straw or hay scurried about in the shadows. Life in the yard, at least, was continuing as normal.

'Evening, Miss Juliet,' said one lad coming up to us, 'I think old Leaded has a bit of heat in his near fore. Evening, Mr Halley. Nice to see you.'

I smiled and nodded at him. Fred Manley had been Bill Burton's head lad since Bill had started training, taking over the licence from his father-in-law, and had done his time in various stables around Lambourn before that. He had a wizened face from a life spent mostly outdoors with far too many early cold mornings on the gallops. He was actually in his late forties but looked at least ten years older. One of the old school: hard working, respectful and all too rare these days.

'OK, Fred,' said Juliet, 'I'll take a look.'

Juliet and Fred walked to a box midway down the left-hand bank and went in; I followed. Leaded Light turned and looked at the three of us. I had

72

last seen him giving his all up the hill at Cheltenham on Friday, beaten a short head in the two-mile chase. Now he stood calmly in his straw-covered bedroom with a heavy canvas rug hiding his bulk and keeping him warm against the March evening chill. He was also wearing a leather head-collar that was firmly attached to a ring in the wall to prevent him wandering out through the open door.

Juliet moved over to the left-hand side of the docile animal, faced away from its head, bent down and ran her hand slowly down the back of Leaded Light's lower leg. I watched her make such a natural movement, a movement repeated thousands of times a day in Lambourn alone. Every trainer, every day, with almost every horse. The feel for heat in the tendon is as regular a part of looking after a racehorse as feeding it. Her left hand on the horse's left front leg, feeling for the slightest variation in temperature. I looked at my own left hand. I could have plunged it into boiling water without it telling me a thing.

Juliet straightened. 'Mmm. He obviously gave himself a bit of a knock on Friday,' she said. 'There's a touch of heat there but nothing too bad. Thanks, Fred. We'll give him light work for a day or two.'

'OK, Miss,' Fred replied. 'Is the guv'nor not here? He asked me to find out about holiday dates for the lads.'

'I'm afraid he's a bit tied up this evening,' said Juliet, only fractionally hesitating.

I hoped not and nearly laughed. Unlike in the United States where handcuffs were de rigueur, Bill had been driven away without restraint. I assumed that he would not have been shackled, dungeon-like, to some police cell wall.

'I'll be doing the round tonight,' Juliet went on. 'Measure out the feed as usual, Fred.' He nodded and slipped away into the darkness.

She turned to me. 'Would you like to come with me?'

'Yes, indeed I would,' I said.

So we went round the whole yard, all fifty-two horses, with Fred fussing over each one like a loving uncle. Candlestick was there and looking none the worse for his exertions of the previous week. He lifted his head, gave us a brief glance, then concentrated again on his evening meal of oats and bran deep in his manger.

Fred went off to reprimand one of the lads he'd caught smoking near the wooden stables.

'Fire is one of the great nightmares for trainers,' said Juliet. 'Horses panic near flames and will often refuse to come out of their boxes even if some brave soul has opened the door. We have signs everywhere to remind the lads not to smoke in the yard and stacks of fire-fighting equipment just in case.' She pointed at the bright red extinguishers and sand-filled fire buckets in each corner of the yard. 'But there are always those who ignore the warnings and some silly buggers have even been known to court disaster by stealing a quick fag in the hay store. I ask you. Stupid or what?'

I was only half-listening. I was wondering if Bill Burton could have fixed races without the knowledge of his staff. In Fred's absence, I asked Juliet casually whether it was a surprise to her that Bill had been arrested for race-fixing.

74

'What do you think?' she replied. 'I'm astounded.'

She didn't sound very astounded and I wondered if loyalty to Bill was such that she wouldn't have told me if she'd seen him stick syringes in their bottoms, tie their legs up with hobbles, and give their jockeys wads of used twenties after losing.

'Can you remember rather too many short-priced losers?' I asked. It was the classic sign of malpractice.

'No,' she replied almost too quickly. 'Lots of favourites don't win, you know that. If they all did then the bookies would be out of business. Have you ever met a poor bookmaker?'

'OK,' I said. 'Not just short-priced losers but horses which occasionally didn't run as well as expected and lost when they should have won.'

'That happens all the time. Doesn't mean the race was fixed. Horses aren't machines, you know. They have off days, too.' She was getting quite stirred up. 'Look, what do you want me to say: "Bill and I worked out which horse would win and which would lose"? Don't be bloody daft. Bill's as straight as an arrow.'

I wondered if she believed it. I didn't.

*   *   *

It was past six by the time I left Juliet still arguing with Chief Inspector Carlisle.

'How am I to know which horse is running where tomorrow if you've taken the computers and the entries record?' she had demanded at full volume.

75

'That's not my problem, miss,' Carlisle had replied.

I left them to it. Carlisle looked likely to lose the battle and I thought he would find the situation easier to handle without me there. By then the police had removed so much material from Bill's house and office that they were running out of space in their cars.

I drove up the M4 towards London against the rush-hour traffic, the never-ending stream of headlamps giving me a headache.

So what next?

Jonny Enstone had asked me to investigate the running of his horses. The obvious place to start was to interview his jockey and trainer. But now one of them had been murdered and the other had been locked up on suspicion of having done it, and all before I could ask them the relevant questions.

I decided to go and see Lord Enstone himself.

'Delighted, Sid,' he said, when I called him using my natty new voice recognition dialling system in the car. With only one hand, it was prudent to keep it firmly on the steering wheel. In an emergency I could steer quite well with my knee but it wasn't to be recommended at high speeds on the motorway.

'Come to lunch tomorrow,' Enstone said. 'Meet me at the Peers' Entrance at one.'

'The peers' entrance?' I asked.

'At the House,' he replied.

Ah, I realised, at the 'House' meant the House of Lords.

'Fine,' I said. 'Tomorrow, one o'clock.' I disconnected, again by voice command.

*   *   *

Marina was busy in the kitchen when I got home and I was firmly told to 'go away' when I tried to nibble her ear.

'I'm experimenting,' she said, slapping my hand as I tried to steal a slice of avocado from her salad. 'Go and get me a glass of wine.'

I chose a Châteauneuf-du-Pape and opened it with my favourite cork remover. It consisted of a sharp spike that one drove through the cork. Then a pump forced air down the spike and the increased pressure forced the cork out of the bottle. Easy.

I had been severely chastised by a wine-loving friend for using it.

'You're pressurising the wine!' he had cried in horror. 'I'll buy you a Screwpull for Christmas.'

And so he had, and very fancy and expensive it was too, with multiple levers and cogs. I am sure it worked very well providing, of course, that one had two hands to operate it. I stuck to my tried and tested pump although I had to be careful to buy a bottle that had a 'cork' rather than a 'plastic'. It was impossible to push the spike through a 'plastic'.

I poured two generous glasses of my favourite Rhône red and handed one to Marina in the kitchen.

'It's not going well,' she said. 'Do you fancy beans on toast?'

'I just want you,' I said, kissing her on the neck.

'Not now,' she screamed. 'Can't you see that my soufflé needs folding. Go away. Dinner will be ready in about half an hour, if you're lucky. Otherwise we're going to the pub.'

'I'll be in my office,' I said, pinching another slice of avocado.

The flat had three bedrooms but I had turned one end of the smallest into an office the previous year. I sat at my desk and switched on my computer. Over the years I had become quite good at typing one-handed. I used my left thumb simply to depress the 'shift' key by rotating the arm at the elbow. I would never have made a typing-pool typist but I could still churn out client reports at a reasonable pace.

The computer slowly came to life and I checked my e-mails. Most were the usual trash trying to sell me stuff I didn't want or need. It never ceased to amaze me why anyone could think that this type of direct marketing sells anything. I deleted all of them without reading them. In amongst the masses of junk and spam, however, were three messages actually meant for me personally. Two were from clients thanking me for reports delivered and the third was from Chris Beecher.

It read: 'Lovely photo, shame he missed the gun.'

Not as far as I was concerned.

I declined to reply and deleted it instead.

I one-handedly typed www.make-a-wager.com into the machine and entered an alien world.

I had witnessed, as a child, the daily struggle of my widowed mother to earn enough to buy something to eat. Often she herself would go hungry to keep me fed. To gamble away such meagre resources would have been unthinkable. As I became successful and financially buoyant, even well-off, I had never felt the need to wager my hard-earned cash on the horses or on anything else. The rules of racing were meant to prohibit professional jockeys from having a bet but it wasn't the rules that stopped me, it was the lack of desire.

However, in races, I had gambled every day, with my life as the stake. I had enjoyed a long winning streak and, when it ran out, I had paid a heavy price but at least I hadn't broken my neck.

I entered the make-a-wager.com website like a child let loose in a toyshop. I was truly amazed at how many different ways there were to lose one's money. Without moving from my seat I could back horses racing in South Africa or Hong Kong, in Australia or America; I could have a flutter on football matches in Argentina or Japan, and I could bet that a single snowflake, or more, would fall on the London Weather Centre on Christmas Day. I could wager that the Miami Dolphins would win the next Super Bowl or that the number of finishers in the Grand National would be greater than twenty or any other number I might choose. I could gamble that the London Stock Market index would go up, or down, and by how much. I could put my money on Tipperary to win the 'All-Ireland' hurling in the Gaelic Games, or on the Swedish team Vetlanda to win at bandy, whatever that might be.

The choice was almost overwhelming and that didn't include the on-line bingo and poker that was readily available at just a further click of my mouse. I could bet to win or I could bet to lose. I could be both the punter and the bookmaker.

Was my computer the door to Aladdin's Cave or to Pandora's Box?

The website was an 'exchange'. Rather than simply being a method of placing a bet with a bookmaker, as was the case with those sites run by the high-street betting shop companies, an exchange was a site that matched people who wanted to have a wager between themselves. Like a couple of mates in a pub discussing a football match where one might say, 'I'll bet you a fiver that United win.' If the other thinks they won't then they have a wager between them. The barman might hold the stake, a fiver from each, and give both fivers to the winner after the game.

The make-a-wager.com website was like a very big pub where you could usually find two people with opposite opinions to make a bet between them, provided the odds were right. And find them they did. The site showed the amount of money actually matched in wagers and it ran into millions. The company that ran the site, George Lochs's company, acted like the barman and held the stakes until the event was over and the result known. George Lochs made his money by simply creaming off a 5% commission from the winner of each wager. It made no difference to him if all the favourites won: in fact, it was to his advantage as there would be more winners so more commissions. He couldn't lose, no matter what the result.

A nice little earner, I thought. No wonder such websites were, to use Archie's words, 'breaking out like a rash'.

Marina came in and cuddled my back. 'It's ready,' she said. 'I hope you like it. It doesn't quite look like it does in my cook book.'

'What is it?' I replied.

'Beef medallions with marsala and crème fraîche sauce, accompanied by a cheese soufflé and avocado salad. I think the soufflé was a mistake and it will be a complete disaster if you don't come and eat it *now*!'

We ate it on trays on our knees and it was delicious. Marina had prepared the medallions so that they were single-mouthful size and they were tender and juicy. I rarely ordered beef in a restaurant due to the inconvenience and embarrassment of having to ask someone to cut it up for me, so this was a real treat.

She kept apologising about the soufflé which, in truth, was not quite cooked through and didn't really go with the beef, but it didn't matter. This was the first time she had cooked a 'special' meal here and it was, I hoped, a sort of 'marking out of territory'. We finished the bottle of wine with a rich homemade chocolate mousse and coffee, and then went straight to bed.

Marina was poles apart from my ex-wife.

When I had first met Jenny, we had almost bounced around the room with happiness. Our courtship had been steamy and sensual with passion and laughter and fun. We had married quickly and without her father's blessing. Charles had not attended the service. We hadn't cared, we had each other and that was all we'd needed. We were so desperate to be together that I would travel halfway through the night to get back to her. I had once driven all the way home with a fractured ankle because I couldn't bear the thought of being alone in hospital without her.

It was difficult to say exactly when things had begun to go wrong. She hadn't liked what I did for a living and the demands it made on my body but it was more than that. A long time after we were divorced, she had finally said some of the things that she had bottled up for so long.

I could still recall the words she had used, 'selfishness' and 'pigheadedness' were merely two. She'd said, 'Girls want men who'll come to them for comfort. Men who'd say, I need you, help me, comfort me, kiss away my troubles. You can't do that. You're so hard. Hard on yourself. Ruthless to yourself. You'll do anything to win. I want someone who's not afraid of emotion, someone uninhibited, someone weaker. I want . . . an ordinary man.'

To me, I *was* an ordinary man. If you stick me with a needle, I bleed, I hurt. I may not wear my heart on my sleeve but raw emotion is there, slightly hidden from view, but there nevertheless.

Love for Jenny had come quickly, with huge energy and passion. It had then, inexorably, drained away to nothing, at least on her part. Worse still, where no love remained, bitterness and hatred had made a home. Joy and laughter were just a memory and an uncomfortable one at that. More recently, the loathing and disgust had lessened and those, in time, might also fade away to nothing. We might then again be able to meet as normal human beings without the urge to damage and to hurt.

Was I older and wiser now? I like to think that I had changed but I probably hadn't.

For a long time after Jenny, I had been afraid of starting any relationship. I feared that pain and despair would quickly follow the love and excitement. I'd enjoyed a few fleeting encounters but I had always been looking for the way out, a simple pain-free exit, a return to the solitary male condition I imagined was my lot. Forever the failed husband, fearful of making the same mistake again.

With Marina, it was very different.

Sure, I had fancied her at our first meeting, a dinner party at a mutual friend's house. Who wouldn't? She was tall, fair and beautiful. But my first attempts to ask her out had fallen on stony ground. She had confided in the friend that she wasn't sure about going out with a man so much shorter than she, and with only one hand to boot.

Fortunately for me, the friend had batted on my team and had convinced Marina that a single date wasn't going to be the end of the world so, reluctantly, she had agreed. I decided against an extravagant and expensive evening at the Opera and The Ivy, and had plumped for live jazz downstairs at Pizza on the Park.

'I hate jazz,' she had said as we arrived. Not a great start.

'OK,' I said. 'You choose.'

She had opted for a quiet pizza and a bottle of wine upstairs. We had sat in increasingly warm companionship for three hours and a second bottle before she took a taxi home, alone.

I remembered walking back to Ebury Street that night, not disappointed that I was alone but elated that I hadn't asked her to join me. I wasn't sure why.

She telephoned me in the morning (at least I had given her my number) to thank me for dinner and we had chatted for an hour. Eventually she had asked if I would like to meet for lunch, 'a lovely place' she knew, 'super food', 'wonderful ambiance'. Sure, I had said, why not.

She had arrived before me and was waiting on a bench outside the café in Regent's Park. We had sampled the 'super food': I had chosen an over-cooked hamburger whilst she had selected a hot dog with congealed onions and a line of bright yellow mustard. But I had had to agree that the ambiance was wonderful. We had strolled through the park to the lake and had fed the last bit of our lunches to the ducks that had had the good sense to decline. By the time we had walked back to my car, we were holding hands and making plans for the evening.

It had been more than a month later that she had first come willingly and eagerly to my bed. We had both been slightly wary and fearful of the encounter. Not to disappoint, not to repel; worse, not to disgust.

Our fears were unfounded. We had slipped delightedly into each other's arms between the sheets. Such a release of emotion. Such an understanding of love. Such joy. It had been an adventure, an expedition, a voyage of discovery and it had been hugely satisfying to both of us. We had drifted contentedly to sleep still entwined.

I had woken early as I always did, trained by a life of rising before dawn to ride. I had lain in the dark thinking not how I was to escape this encounter but how to make it permanent. Very scary.

And here we were, some eighteen months later. I loved her more and more each day, a situation that was wonderfully reciprocated. To love someone is a delight, to be loved back as well is a joy beyond measure.

I snuggled up to her back.

'I love you,' I whispered into her ear.

'You're only saying that because you want a bit of nookie,' she replied.

'No, I mean it.'

But we had a bit of nookie nevertheless.

CHAPTER SEVEN

With Jonny Enstone's reputation for promptness in mind, I arrived at the Peers' Entrance at one o'clock exactly. 'Peer' is a strange title really for a member of the House of Lords since the dictionary definition of 'peer' is 'a person of equal rank' and the Peers with a capital P were clearly not. Even amongst themselves there were five levels with Duke at the top and Baron at the bottom.

The tones of Big Ben were still ringing in my ears as I stepped into the revolving door, a time-warp portal rotating me from the hustle and bustle of 21st-century London on the outside to the sedate world of 19th-century quiet and formality on the inside.

The staff still wore knee breeches and silk stockings, their tailcoats and starched collars looking somewhat incongruous next to machine-gun-toting police in flak jackets, such are the necessities in our fear-of-terrorist-atrocity society.

Lord Enstone was already there and I noticed him glance at his watch as I arrived. He seemed to nod with approval and came forward to shake my hand.

'Sid, glad you could make it,' he said.

Glad I could make it on time, I thought.

'Let's go and find ourselves a drink.'

He waited as I went to pass through the security checkpoint.

'Anything metal in your pockets, sir?'

I obediently emptied keys and loose change into the plastic tray provided. What to do? Should I also remove the pound and a half of steel from the end of my left arm and put it in the tray? I had learnt from multiple experiences at airports that to do so usually caused more problems than leaving it where it was.

I stepped through the detector and, predictably, it went into palpitations.

'Sorry, sir,' said the security man. 'Please stand with your legs apart and arms out to your side.'

He waved a black wand up and down my legs and around my waist without success and was about to wave me on through when the wand went berserk at my left wrist. The poor chap was quite startled when he switched to a manual search and discovered the hard fibreglass shell that constituted my lower arm.

Lord Enstone had been watching this exchange with ill-disguised amusement and now burst into laughter.

'Why didn't you tell him?' he asked.

'He would ask me to take it off and it's such a bore. It's normally easier this way.'

The guard regained his composure and, with an embarrassed chuckle, he allowed me to pass. I thought about getting a gun installed to shoot through my middle finger. It was a common failing of security that, having discovered I had a prosthetic hand, they rarely checked it well enough to determine if I had a firearm or a knife built into it.

Jonny Enstone was in his element and clearly loved being a member of what has often been described as the best gentlemen's club in London (women were not admitted until 1958, and then reluctantly). We climbed one of the hundred or so staircases in the Palace of Westminster and strolled along bookcase-flanked corridors to the peers' bar overlooking the Thames.

'Afternoon, my lord,' said the barman.

Jonny Enstone obviously enjoyed being called 'my lord'.

'Afternoon, Eric. G & T for me, please. You, Sid?'

'G & T would be fine, thank you.'

We took our drinks over to a small table by the window and sat and discussed the state of the weather.

'Now, Sid,' said his lordship at last, 'how can I help?'

'Well, sir,' I started, opting for a formality that matched our surroundings, 'after our little chat at Cheltenham I was hoping you might be able to give me some more details of why you think that Bill Burton and Huw Walker were fixing the races in which your horses ran.' I purposely kept my voice low and he leaned closer to hear.

'Did you hear that Burton's been arrested for killing Walker?' he replied.

'I was there when it happened,' I said.

'Were you indeed!' He made it sound like an accusation in the same way that Carlisle had done.

'I went to ask him about your horses but never got the chance.'

'Fancy Burton being a murderer,' he said. 'One

87

never can tell.'

'He hasn't been convicted yet. Maybe the police have the wrong man.'

'No smoke without fire,' he said. I thought about some of the many rumours that surrounded his business dealings and wondered if there was fire there too.

'But about your horses and your suspicions,' I prompted.

'Doesn't really matter now, Sid. Took your advice and moved the lot this morning. New trainer, new start. No good crying over spilt milk. Walker's dead and Burton's been banged up for it. Little bit of race-fixing seems a bit trivial now, doesn't it, so I've cut my losses and moved on.'

'Who's your new trainer?' I asked.

'Another Lambourn man. Chap called Andrew Woodward,' he replied. 'Fine fellow, won't stand any nonsense. My type of man.'

He of the riding-whip reputation, a man prepared to run roughshod over other people's feelings. He was, indeed, Jonny Enstone's type of man.

'Sorry, Sid,' he went on, 'won't be needing your services any more. Send me the bill for your time—not that I've taken up much of it.' It was his way of telling me that my bill had better not be too big. He hadn't become a multi-multi-multi-millionaire by paying more for things than he could get away with. It was usually the poor who were more spendthrift with their money, one of the reasons they remained poor.

'Shall we go through to lunch?' he said, closing the matter.

There are two dining rooms. One for peers

alone, to discuss in private the affairs of state, and one for peers and their guests where such discussion was frowned upon, if not exactly forbidden.

Needless to say, we were in the second one, an L-shaped room with heavy oak panelling covered with stern-looking portraits of past lords of the realm. The upright dining chairs were covered in red leather and the carpet was predominantly red, and so were the curtains. Everything in the Lords' end of the Palace of Westminster was red. The commoners' end was green.

Jonny Enstone worked the room, stopping and speaking to almost every group as we made our way to what was obviously his 'usual' table at the far end. Why did I wonder that he liked this table for that very reason?

It was like walking into the pages of *Who's Who*. Faces that I was familiar with only from the television and newspapers smiled and said 'Hello'. Lord Enstone almost purred, he was so enjoying being part of 'the club', all the more so for having me in tow.

I decided on the soup and the mushroom risotto for one-handed eating while Lord Enstone chose the pâté and the rack of lamb. I rarely ate much for lunch and two large meals within twenty hours were not going to be good for my waistline.

We talked racing for a while and I asked what hopes he had for his horses.

'Well,' he said, 'I'll need to talk with Woodward but I hope that Extra Point might be ready for the big handicap at Sandown next month. He's still entered for the National but he's not fully fit, at least that's what Burton told me last week. I'll reserve judgement until Woodward has seen what he can do.'

'When did you start to question what Bill Burton told you?'

'I didn't really, not until last week.'

'What happened last week specifically?' I asked.

'It was something I heard—I can't remember exactly when, Tuesday or Wednesday, I think.' He paused. 'No, it was definitely Tuesday, after the Champion Hurdle. I was in the Royal Box having a drink with Larry—you know, Larry Wallingford.'

Larry Wallingford, or rather Lawrence, Duke of Wallingford was a regular on racecourses, a major owner of racehorses on both the flat and over the jumps, and a stalwart of the Jockey Club. I wondered when a boy from the wrong end of Newcastle had taken to calling dukes by their nicknames and most others by their surnames. Tomorrow, no doubt, Lord Enstone would tell someone that he had lunched with 'Halley, you know, Halley the crippled jockey'.

'Did the Duke tell you something specific?'

'No, no. It was a lady who was sitting with him. I didn't get her name. She said something about having been told by a friend that Burton's horses didn't seem to be always doing their best.'

'That doesn't sound much like evidence to me.'

'No, nor to me. But it was enough to make me ask around and to look at the results of my horses.' He stopped to take a sip of an excellent Merlot, the 'House' red.

'I have seven horses at present. I keep a detailed account of all their races and on Tuesday evening I went right through my records for the past two years. I had ninety-two runners over that time.

Fourteen winners but not one of them won when they started with odds of less than 5 to 1. Sixteen started favourite and only one of those won, and that was when the leading pair both fell at the last.' He took another drink. 'So I began to be suspicious and asked your father-in-law to get you to my box last week. I didn't want to go to the Jockey Club. Discreet enquiries were what I wanted.'

What he meant, I thought, was that he didn't want everyone to know that he had been a mug.

'Well, now I've moved the horses so that's that. End of story.'

'But it's not the end,' I said. 'Huw Walker's been murdered. Maybe he was shot because he was fixing races. Or perhaps for not fixing them when he had been paid to do so.'

'Maybe, but I don't want to get involved.'

'You may not have that luxury,' I said.

'I won't thank you for getting me involved with this business and it will be to your advantage not to.' He shifted in his chair and moved closer to me. 'Leave it alone, Halley. Let the police do their job. Do you understand me?' It was said with venom and there was little doubt that I was being warned off.

'Sure,' I said, 'but the police are still likely to talk to you because you had seven horses in Bill Burton's yard.'

He smiled, leaned back in his chair and spread his hands. 'I know nothing.'

Here was a member of the House of Lords, the highest court in the land, intent on obstructing justice. But honesty and integrity have never been prerequisites to remaining in the House of Lords.

A criminal conviction and prison sentence of twelve months or more results in expulsion from the House of Commons, but their Lordships remain immune to such inconveniences and can return to Her Majesty's Parliament on release from any length of stay in Her prisons. And they do, often.

Even a conviction for high treason does not disqualify members, save actually during their imprisonment. In the past this was not a problem as there was little chance of a return from the block and the axe.

And then there was the case of the 7th Earl of Lucan. A coroner's jury established that he had indeed battered his children's nanny to death with a length of lead piping in 1974 before disappearing for good. Even when, twenty-five years later in 1999, the High Court made a ruling that, body or not, Lord Lucan was officially dead, his son and heir could not sit in the House as it was deemed by their Lordships that there was no 'definite proof' that his father would not suddenly walk out of the jungle and claim his rightful place on the red leather benches.

However, the House does have some standards. Undischarged bankrupts cannot take their seats.

Clearly, to a Lord, being broke is a greater crime than being a murderer.

Lord Enstone and I finished our lunch mostly in silence and I was content to pass again through the revolving time-portal and back to the present.

*　　*　　*

I walked down Victoria Street towards my flat,

stopping twice on the journey. First, I went into an office equipment store to buy a new telephone answering machine. My trusty old one had served me well but had been overtaken by the electronics revolution. I decided on a fancy replacement that came complete with a vast number of megabytes in its digital memory, and one that could also tell me the dates and times when my messages were received. And, secondly, I popped into a betting shop.

I wasn't sure what to expect. I hadn't been in a betting shop for years, not since the law prevented them having any decent chairs or televisions, or any creature comforts like a coffee machine or a lavatory. Nothing that could persuade the itinerant gambler to linger.

Now we lived in more enlightened times when gambling was not seen as some shifty addiction of the low-life and was even to be encouraged in the form of the National Lottery, to 'provide for good causes'. That some of the 'good causes' were a touch suspect and others were simply an excuse for underfunding in the public services did not seem to deter the millions whose hopes each week far exceeded their true expectations. A few big winners gave the multitude faith, so much so that nearly a fifth of the population was seriously relying on winning the lottery to provide for their old age.

In spite of the change in the law, one would hardly describe the interior of this particular establishment as plush. The floor was covered in bare linoleum that had seen better days especially around the high traffic areas near the door and the betting window. There were a few stools and a counter that stretched down one side of the room at hip height, its surface covered with the detritus of past decision making, screwed up betting slips and scattered copies of newspapers.

Above the counter were pinned the pages from the *Racing Post* and, above them, a line of six television sets showed a mixture of betting odds and live action of both greyhound and horse racing.

On the other side of the shop were notice boards with brightly coloured posters extolling the benefits of wagering on the coming weekend's Premiership football matches with the odds for each game written large with a black felt-tip pen. A table with a coin-operated coffee machine sat in one corner with the all-important betting window in the other.

Business on the Tuesday afternoon after Cheltenham was slow, with just three others in the shop determined to take on the might of the bookmaker. Save for a few grunts during the actual running of a race, not a sound was uttered as they circled around one another from counter to betting window, then to a stool to watch their selections on a TV, and then back to the counter for deliberation on the next event. Race timings are so staggered to provide a contest from one venue or another every five minutes. And so it went on like a ballet, but without the grace.

I was the odd man out. First, I was in a suit and tie rather than the apparent uniform dress of extra-large replica football shirt hanging out over an extra-extra-large belly held in place by super-extra-large blue denim jeans with off-white training shoes beneath. Secondly, I was not gambling on every event, in fact I wasn't gambling on any of them. And, thirdly, I was talking. 'Well ridden,' I said to the second screen from the left as the jockey got up in the last stride to win by a short head.

'Do you come here often?' I asked a man as he sidestepped around me to the betting window.

'Not working for my wife, are you?' he replied.

'No.'

But he wasn't listening, he was busy counting out a wad of notes to hand over.

'I know you,' said one of the other two, the one in the Manchester United shirt. 'You're Sid Halley. Got any tips?'

Why did punters always believe that jockeys, or ex-jockeys, made good tipsters?

'Keep your money in your pocket,' I said.

'You're no bloody good,' he said with a smile. 'What brings you in here?'

'Furthering my education,' I replied, smiling back.

'Come off it, all jockeys are punters, stands to reason, they control the results.'

'What about the horses?'

'They'd run round in circles without a driver.'

'Do you really believe that jockeys control the results?'

'Sure they do. If I lose, I always blame the jockey. I have to admit though that I won more on you than I lost.'

I suppose it was a compliment, of sorts.

'What's your name?' I asked.

'Gerry. Gerry Noble.' He offered his hand and I shook it firmly.

'Shame you had to give up,' Gerry said. He

95

glanced down at my left hand then up at my face.

'One of those things,' I said.

'Bloody shame.'

I agreed with him, but life moves on.

'Sorry,' he said.

'Not your fault.'

'Yeah, but I'm sorry all the same.'

'Thanks, Gerry.' I meant it. 'Tell me, do you ever gamble on the internet?'

'Sure,' he replied, 'but not often. Too bloody complicated, never can understand all that exchanges stuff. Much easier to give the man my ready cash,' he nodded to the window in the corner, 'and then, win or lose, at least I know where I stand. Don't fancy using credit cards. I'd get into trouble too quick and too deep.'

'Do you come here every day?' I asked.

'Yeah, pretty much,' he said. 'I work an early shift, start at four in the morning, finished by twelve. Then I come here for a few hours on my way home.'

'Do you win?'

'You mean overall?'

'Whatever?'

'I suppose, if I was honest, I have to say I lose on the whole. Not much and some days I win big.' He smiled. 'And the wins give me such a high that I forget the losses.'

'But don't you hate to lose?'

'It's cheaper than cocaine.'

I stayed for a couple more races and helped Gerry cheer home a long-priced winner on which he had heavily invested.

'See what I mean!' he shouted, giving me a high five. 'Bloody marvellous!'

He grinned from ear to ear and I could see what he meant by a 'high'. I used to have that feeling, too, whenever I rode a big winner. As he said, it was indeed 'bloody marvellous'.

I had enjoyed his ready companionship.

'See you!' I called to him as I left, a simple goodbye said without any real expectation of seeing him again.

'You know where to find me,' he said, and went back to his deliberations.

* * *

When I got back to the flat, I connected my new answering machine to the telephone in my office. I recorded a greeting message and tested it by calling it from my mobile. I left myself a brief message and then tested the remote access feature. Perhaps I am a bit of a sceptic about electronics but I was pleasantly surprised that it worked perfectly.

I threw the old machine in the bin but not before extracting the cassette tape that still had Huw Walker's messages recorded on it.

I was hiding all the wiring beneath my desk when the phone rang. I thought briefly about letting my new machine do the answering but instead I clambered up and lifted the receiver.

'Hello,' I said.

'Sid! Great. I hoped you'd be there,' said a voice. 'I need your help and I need it fast.'

'Sorry,' I replied, 'who is this?'

'It's Bill,' said the voice.

'Bill! God, sorry! I wasn't expecting to hear from you.'

'They haven't banged me up for life yet, you know.'

'But where are you?' I asked him.

'At home, where do you think, Dartmoor?' He laughed but I could tell even over the telephone that it was a hollow laugh, the worry very close to the surface.

'They let you go?'

'Yup, insufficient evidence to charge me, at least for now. I'm out on police bail. I'm not allowed to leave the country and, more worrying, I'm not allowed on a racecourse.'

'But that's crazy,' I said. 'How can you earn your living if you can't go racing?'

'Doesn't really matter. The bloody owners are queuing up at the gate to remove their horses.' The forced cheerfulness had gone out of his voice. 'That bastard Enstone was the first off the mark. Had two LRT horseboxes here at seven this morning to collect them all. Taken them to that other bastard, Woodward. They're welcome to each other. His bloody lordship still owes me two months' training fees for seven horses. That's a lot of cash I could really do with but probably won't get now.'

I knew this was always a trainer's worst nightmare.

'Three other owners came later but Juliet was wiser by then and wouldn't let the horses go until their bills had been paid. She did well but didn't get it all because she didn't have the details, the damn police had taken so much away. I got back here about two thirty to find her having a stand-up row with one of the owners in the yard.'

'How did they all know so quickly about you?' I

asked. 'Your name hasn't been on the news.'

'That bastard Chris Beecher wrote a piece in today's *Pump*.' In Bill's eyes there were lots of bastards about. He probably didn't know that I was a real bastard, my window-cleaner father having fallen off a ladder to his death only three days before he had been due to marry my pregnant mother.

'You don't have to be a bloody rocket scientist to work out who he was writing about. And he had a copy of the paper couriered to each of my owners with the article marked round in red. Couriered! He's a bloody sod.'

Indeed he was.

'You didn't tell him, did you, Sid?' he asked.

'I wouldn't tell Chris Beecher if his trousers were on fire,' I assured him.

'No, I didn't really think it was you.'

'Did you get any sleep last night?' I asked him.

'None to speak of. I mostly sat in a room at the police station. They asked me a few questions about where I was last Friday. Bloody stupid. I was on the television at Cheltenham races, for God's sake! Yes, they said, they knew. Why did they bloody ask then?

'They also asked me about my marriage. Horrible things like did I beat my wife? I ask you, what sort of question is that? I said of course not. Then they asked me if I had ever smacked my children? Well, I have, the odd little clip around the legs when they've been really naughty. Made me sound like a bloody monster. They implied that it was just a small step from abusing children to murder. Abusing children! I love my kids.'

He yawned loudly down the receiver.

'Bill,' I said, 'you're exhausted, go to bed and sleep.'

'I can't,' he said. 'I've too many things to deal with here. And I want to go and find Kate. I tried calling her mother twice but she puts the phone down on me. I'm going round to her place in a minute. Sid, I love Kate and the children and I want them back. And I didn't kill Huw Walker.'

'I know that,' I said.

'Thank God someone believes me.' He paused. 'Anyway, Sid, I called you because I need your help.'

'I'll help if I can,' I said.

'I know the murder thing is the more serious but I didn't do it and I can't think that a murder rap will stick. There were far too many people who saw me all afternoon for me to have had the chance of getting a gun and finding a spot to do a bit of target practice on Huw's chest. But this race fixing stuff really worries me.'

I didn't ask him if that was because the allegations were true.

'What do you want me to do?' I said.

'You're an investigator. I want you to bloody investigate.'

'Bloody investigate what exactly?'

'Why my horses look like they've been running to order.'

'And have they?' I asked.

'Now look, Sid, don't you start. I promise you that as far as I was concerned all my runners were doing their best. I'll admit there were a few that I reckoned had no chance due to illness or injury but even those weren't sent out with orders to lose.'

'Bill, I'll not even think of helping you unless

you level with me completely.'

The tone of my voice clearly disturbed him. 'I am bloody levelling with you,' he said. 'I've heard the rumours, too, that my horses are not always trying, but it's not true, or, if it is, it's nothing to do with me. I promise you, on my mother's grave.'

'But your mother's not dead.'

'Details, details. It's true, though. I never tried to fix a race by telling the jockey to lose, or any other way either. Absolutely never.'

I wasn't sure if I believed him.

'Why do you think that it looks like you were?' I asked.

'The cops showed me a list,' he said. 'All Lord Enstone's horses. They won at long odds and lost at short ones. I told them not to be ridiculous, must be coincidence. But they said that I could go down to the slammer on coincidence and wouldn't it be better to come clean and tell the truth. I told them I was telling the bloody truth but they still refused to believe it. Then I sat in a cell for a couple of hours and did some serious thinking. Was someone else fixing my horses? Huw was riding them, so was he losing on purpose?'

'And what conclusions did you come to?'

'None,' he said. 'That's when I thought to ask you.'

'Where did the police get the list of Lord Enstone's horses?'

'Search me.'

'Was the list for the last two years?' I asked.

'I think it probably was. Why?'

'I think the police may have been given the list by the good lord himself.'

'Bastard!' he said with feeling. 'He's a friend of

101

mine—or he was.'

Jonny Enstone didn't have friends, I thought. He had acquaintances.

'Anyway, Sid, I need your help to get me out of this hole. I'm not guilty of either thing and I intend to prove it.' He certainly sounded defiant. 'Come over and let's talk it through.'

'I can't just come over, I live in London,' I said.

'Oh yeah, I forgot. Well, come tomorrow,' he said. 'I know, come and ride out for me in the morning.'

'Do you mean it?' I asked. I could still steer a straight course with one hand but invitations to ride out were rare.

'Of course, I mean it. A one-handed Sid Halley is streaks better than most of my lads. But you'd better come tomorrow since there may not be any horses left by Thursday.'

'Don't be ridiculous,' I said.

'I'm not.'

'OK,' I said, 'I'd love to.'

'First lot goes out at seven thirty. Come at seven, or six thirty if you want a cup of coffee first.'

'Right,' I said, 'I'll be there at six thirty.'

'Good. See you then.' He disconnected.

I called Marina at work and asked her to buy a copy of *The Pump* on her way home.

*   *   *

I woke at four thirty the next morning, took extra care attaching my arm, and was on the road by a quarter past five.

'Don't break your neck,' Marina had mumbled in my ear as I gave her a goodbye kiss.

'Try not to.'

I enjoyed driving through the empty London streets at this early hour, rush-hour gridlock merely a memory. I whizzed down the Cromwell Road with every traffic light in my favour and was soon on the M4 with the dawn appearing brightly in my rear-view mirror.

I had brought the answering machine cassette tape with me to listen to in the car but I could glean nothing more from Huw's messages. They were the pleadings of a frightened man, a man who had realised that he was in way over his head and that he couldn't swim.

I also had a copy of the previous day's *Pump* on the seat beside me, opened at Chris Beecher's column.

It has now been four days since the murder of top jump jockey Huw Walker at Cheltenham last week and *The Pump* can exclusively reveal that the police have someone in custody. But who is it? The police aren't telling but I can disclose that it's a racing man, a trainer, and that he has also been arrested for race fixing. I can further assist any amateur sleuth in trying to determine who this chief suspect is. Try using a Candlestick to give you Leaded Light to show you the way.

As Bill had said, it didn't take a rocket scientist to piece those clues together.

*   *   *

I made good time to Lambourn and pulled into Bill's gateway at twenty-five past six. I was really excited by the prospect of being back in the saddle on a Thoroughbred doing what came naturally to both horse and rider, travelling at speed with the wind in my hair.

So I was rather disappointed to find that I wasn't Bill's first visitor of the day. There was a police car in the driveway, with its blue light flashing on the roof.

Bugger, I thought! They've come to take Bill back in for questioning. A dawn raid.

I climbed out of the car and was met by a wide-eyed Juliet Burns.

'Bill's killed himself,' she said.

CHAPTER EIGHT

I stared at Juliet in disbelief.

'He can't have,' I said stupidly.

'Well, he has,' said Juliet. 'He's blown his brains out.'

'What? When?'

'I don't know,' she said. 'I found him in the den about half an hour ago and called the police. He usually comes into the yard to see me at a quarter to six. When he failed to turn up, I thought he might have overslept after all the excitement of the last two days.'

I didn't exactly think that getting arrested constituted 'excitement'.

'I went up to his room but he wasn't there and the bed was still made. So I looked for him in the

104

office and then in the den.' She shook her head. 'Pretty bad. I could see straight away that he was dead. The back of his head is missing.'

Her matter-of-fact description made me feel quite queasy but Juliet seemed perfectly fine and she had actually seen the carnage. Shock affects people in different ways and I suspected that Juliet was currently shutting out the trauma. In time, she might need help to cope but not yet.

I took her arm and sat her down in the passenger seat of my car. Then I went to the back door of the house. A young uniformed policeman politely informed me that no one was allowed in. He said that his superiors were on their way, together with the Scene of Crime Officer, and nobody, not even his superiors, could enter the house before the SOCO arrived.

'Ah,' I said, 'is it a crime scene then?'

'Maybe,' said the policeman. 'All suspicious deaths are treated as if they are crimes until we know otherwise.'

'Very wise,' I said and retraced my steps to my car. I sat down in the driver's seat.

'Juliet,' I asked, 'is Bill still in the den?'

'Yes, I suppose so. That policeman was here pretty quickly but no one else has arrived. I mean, there's been no ambulance or anything.'

'I expect the policeman will have called one.'

'Suppose so.' She appeared to be going into shock, staring straight ahead and hardly listening to what I said.

'Juliet!' I called loudly to her and she slowly turned her head. 'Stay here in the car and I'll be back in a minute and take you home.' She nodded slightly.

I picked up my camera from the glove box, jumped out of the car and, avoiding the policeman by the back door, made my way round the house to one of the windows of the den and looked in.

Bill was indeed still there although I couldn't see him very well as he was sitting in an armchair with its back towards the corner of the room between the two windows. I could, however, see his right hand hanging limply down. In the hand was a black revolver, now pointed harmlessly at the floor. I took some pictures.

I shifted round to the next window but it didn't give me a much better view of Bill. However, it did allow me to see and photograph a large red stain on the wall above and behind his chair. The room was well lit by the early morning sunshine and I could see that the stain was dry and there were no shiny droplets in the rivulets running down the cream paint. Bill had killed himself some time ago.

But why? Why would he kill himself after all that he had said to me yesterday? He had seemed then to be so positive and determined. Had he been rejected by Kate? Did that tip him over the edge?

And where did he get the gun?

I went right round the outside of the house looking in all the ground-floor windows. Nothing sccmed to be out of place or any different from what I remembered. Except, of course, everything in this house would now be different, the disaster in the den would see to that.

I stopped by the policeman standing guard at the back door and told him that I was taking Juliet Burns home and that his superiors could find her there.

'Don't know about that, sir,' he said rather hesitantly. 'I think she should stay here until the others arrive.'

'Well, I don't,' I said. 'She's going into shock and needs a hot drink and a warmer place than sitting in my car. And since you won't let us into the house, I'm taking her home.'

He thought for a moment and clearly decided that it was better to let her go home than into Bill's house. But he wasn't keen.

'All right, sir,' he said at last. 'But I need your name and a telephone number where Miss Burns can be reached.'

I gave him my name and my mobile number and drove away. Just in time, too. As we went down the road, a convoy of police cars passed us going the other way. Violent death had roused a posse from their beds.

Juliet's home was one of four identical little cottages standing in a line right up against the Baydon road on the south-western edge of Lambourn.

'Number 2,' she mumbled.

'Give me your key,' I said.

'It's under a stone in the window box,' she said. 'No pockets in my jodhpurs so I leave it there when I go to work.'

'You should put it on a string round your neck,' I said.

'Tried that but I still lost it. String broke.'

Use stronger string, dear Liza, dear Liza. But I didn't say so.

I helped her out of the car, found the key, and took her in.

Juliet went upstairs to lie down while I made her

a strong sweet cup of tea in her tiny kitchen. I took it up and sat on the edge of her bed as she drank it. She seemed to have recovered somewhat and the tea helped further.

'Why would he *do* such a thing?' she asked. 'Now I suppose I'll need a new job. Oh my God, the job!' She sat up with a jerk and started to get off the bed.

'Juliet,' I said, 'lie down. You don't have to be at work today.'

'But who will look after the horses?'

'I'm sure Fred will work out that the horses need to be fed and watered but they won't be going out this morning. They'll survive without you for a while. You are staying here and that's an order.'

I picked up her jacket from where she had dropped it on the floor and went to hang it in the wardrobe.

'That's OK,' she said. 'Leave it on the bed, I'll do it.'

'It's no problem.'

I opened the wardrobe and found some space for the jacket. Juliet always gave such an impression of being an out-and-out tom-boy that I was surprised to find that she had a row of dresses hanging there, many in their designer-named plastic covers. There was also a line of fancy shoes with colours to match the dresses. In a funny sort of way, I was pleased to glimpse her feminine side. I closed the wardrobe without comment and sat down on the bed.

'Juliet,' I said, 'I'll go back to the yard and sort out any problems that Fred has with the horses. I think you should rest here as long as you can. The police will be down to see you soon enough.'

'Thanks, Sid.'

I drove back to Bill's place, not to the main drive but round the back, to the far end of the stables. I hopped out and went into the yard to find Fred. He was there looking slightly agitated, checking his watch. It was already ten minutes after the allotted time for the horses to go out and there was still no sign of Bill or Juliet.

'Fred, hello,' I called to him.

'Oh, Mr Halley, good morning,' he said. 'I'm sorry but Mr Burton and Miss Juliet aren't here yet. I can't understand it—they should have been here about half an hour ago, at least.'

'They won't be coming, Fred,' I replied. 'The horses aren't going out this morning. Tell the lads to remove the tack and leave them in their boxes. Give them some hay and water.'

'But surely—'

'Just do it, Fred, please.'

He wasn't sure and kept glancing towards the gate through which he still expected Bill to appear at any second.

'There's been a bit of a disaster,' I went on. 'Death in the family. The police are in the house with Mr Burton. Just tell the lads that the horses are not going out this morning. No need to tell them why.'

They would know soon enough. It wasn't only Juliet who would need to find a new job.

'Right,' he said.

I left him to it and went back to my car. There was a task I had to perform before I went into the house to see the police, and it was something I was not looking forward to.

I drove out of Lambourn on the Wantage road

109

and turned into the drive of Kate's parents' house. They had moved here five years ago when Kate's father had retired and Bill had taken over the stables. But Arthur Rogers had enjoyed his retirement for only a few weeks before being diagnosed with pancreatic cancer and he had survived for barely two months after that. Daphne, his widow, now lived here alone and was one of the *grandes dames* of the racing world.

I stopped in front of the house and wondered if anyone would be up yet. I pushed the bell and heard a reassuring faint ringing somewhere deep inside. Daphne was indeed up but still in her dressing gown as she opened the door.

'Good morning, Sid,' she said with a smile. 'What brings you here this early?'

'Morning, Daphne,' I said, returning the smile. 'Is Kate here?'

'Why?' The smile disappeared.

'I have to see her.'

'Did Bill send you?' she asked. 'I always said that Kate shouldn't have married that man. He's brought disgrace on this family. Race fixing, indeed!'

Murder, it seemed, was acceptable.

'Is she here?' I asked again.

'Maybe she is, and maybe she isn't. Why do you have to see her?'

'Look, Daphne, it's important. Something's happened to Bill.'

'Something else? What's he done now?'

'Is Kate here?' I asked again in a more forceful tone.

'She's asleep. In the spare room.'

'Are the children with her?' I asked.

110

'No. They're in the attic rooms,' she said. 'Shall I go and wake them?'

'No,' I said, 'leave the children. Let me go and wake Kate.'

She looked at me quizzically but made no objection as I went past her into the house and up the stairs.

'It's the room at the front,' she called after me, 'over the front door.'

I knocked gently on the door and opened it a little.

'Is that you, Mum?' said Kate sleepily from inside. 'Who was that at the door?'

'Kate,' I said, speaking through the crack. 'It's Sid Halley. Can I come in?'

'Sid! What are you doing here? Did Bill send you?'

'Yes, Bill sent me. Can I come in?'

'Just a minute.' I heard her get up and open the wardrobe door. 'OK,' she said. 'Come in.'

She was wearing a tweed overcoat and pink slippers.

'Sorry,' she said with a laugh, 'I haven't got a dressing gown with me.' She looked tired and her eyes were red from too much crying. 'Where's Bill?' she asked.

'At home.'

'What are you doing here, then? I told Bill I'd be back by ten.'

'When?'

'When what?'

'When did you tell Bill you'd be back by ten?'

'Last night. Look, Sid, what's all this about?' She was beginning to be alarmed. 'Is Bill all right?'

'No, Kate,' I said, 'I'm afraid he's not.'

111

'Oh my God! What's happened? Where is he?'

'Kate, I'm afraid Bill's dead.' There was no easy way.

'*Dead?* He *can't* be. He was here last night.'

'I'm so so sorry.'

She sat down heavily on the bed, her overcoat swinging open to reveal a pink nightdress with little blue and yellow flowers embroidered around the top.

'He *can't* be dead,' she whispered. 'Everything was all right last night. He came round about eight o'clock and we talked for a couple of hours. He wanted me to go home with him then but the children were asleep so I said that I'd be home this morning.'

She looked at me. 'Was it a car accident?'

I nodded. Better, I thought, to have only one shock at a time.

A tear rolled down her cheek and fell on to her coat. A second followed and soon she was sobbing uncontrollably. She lay down on the bed and I put a pillow under her head and covered her with the duvet.

'I'll go and get you a cup of tea,' I said, and went downstairs to find that Daphne was still where I had left her.

'Is Bill dead?' she asked.

'Yes.'

'Thought so. Why else would you be here and so determined to see Kate. How?'

'Let's get some tea.'

She led the way to the kitchen and put the kettle on.

'How?' she asked again.

'I'm not really sure. He was shot.'

112

'Shot! I thought it must have been an accident.'

'No, I'm afraid not. He was shot in the head. It looks like suicide—but I'm not so sure it was.'

It was Daphne's turn to sit down. 'You mean it might be murder? It can't be. He was here last night.'

'How did he seem?' I asked.

'Oh, the usual . . . bloody-minded.' It was no secret that Bill and his mother-in-law did not get on, and that was putting it mildly. As she had rightly said, she had not approved of the marriage and thought that Bill was nowhere near good enough for her daughter.

'He came round here and begged Kate to go back to him. I thought she was better off without him and I told her so.'

Daphne could be a very stupid woman at times, I thought. The fact that it had been Kate who had cheated on Bill seemed to have passed her by.

'Grannie, why is Mummy crying?' Young William was standing in the kitchen doorway. How do you tell an eleven-year-old that his father's brains are all over the sitting room wall?

His carefree, little-boy days had ended. Today, as the eldest of the four, he would have to carry his share of responsibility for his brothers and his sister. Today, he would become a man. A challenging task for one so young.

I made the tea for us all and took one up to the spare room.

Kate was lying on her side, curled up like a foetus. She wasn't actually crying now. She was staring with unseeing eyes at the pillow next to her head.

I sat down beside her and laid my feeling, right

113

hand on her shoulder. 'Kate, I'm so sorry.' It seemed to be an inadequate starting point.

She rolled on to her back and looked at me. 'Where was the crash?' she asked. 'Was it last night? I must go and see him.'

She started to get up but I held up my hand.

'Kate,' I said, 'you must not go and see him. You must remember him as he was and not as he is now.'

'Oh God!' she wailed and the tears flowed again. There would be many tears in the days ahead. She sat up and clung to me, her head on my shoulder. I could feel the wet warmth of her tears on my neck.

And I cried with her. I cried in grief for my lost friend.

'Please tell me what happened,' she said when at last the sobs eased.

If I had not been there, she would have learned the grisly details soon enough. Just as soon as some caring but clumsy policeman, detailed to inform the next of kin, had arrived to notify her that her husband had put a .38 revolver in his mouth and blown off the back of his head. I had no doubt that the gun in question was the same gun that Chief Inspector Carlisle had been looking for two days ago, the same one that was used to make the holes in Huw Walker's chest.

'Kate, my love, I'm afraid Bill didn't die in a car crash. It seems that he may have shot himself.' I tried not to make it sound as dreadful as it was.

'You mean—he committed suicide?' She had leaned back to look at my face.

'It appears that he might have.'

'Oh, my darling. Why?' Her voice was a-quiver as a fresh round of sobbing sent a shudder through

114

her body.

'Here, drink your tea.'

She drank the hot sweet liquid. Best cure for shock there is.

'Why?' she said again. 'Why would he? It's my fault. I should have gone with him last night. Oh God, why didn't I go with him?'

'Kate, you mustn't blame yourself.' But I could see that she would. 'You need to be strong for the children.'

'Oh my God, how will I tell the children?'

'You'll find a way,' I said.

There was a gentle knock at the door and Daphne came in with all four of them, little three-year-old Alice in her arms.

I told Daphne to contact me on my mobile if she needed anything and left them to it. This was a family-only task.

I let myself out of the front door and was walking over to the Audi just as a police car swept up the drive and the same young policeman as before climbed out.

'Ah, Mr Halley,' he said, 'we've been wondering where you'd got to.'

'You only had to call,' I said, holding up my phone.

'My inspector's not pleased with me for letting you and Miss Burns leave the scene.'

'Tough.'

'I've been sent to inform the next of kin of Mr Burton's death.' Punishment for his failing, I thought. 'Is Mrs Burton here?'

'Yes, she is. But I've saved you the trouble. I told her myself, gently.'

'Oh.' He seemed relieved. 'But I need to make it

115

official so that I can report back.'

'She's telling her children now. So don't interrupt her.'

'Right,' he said rather indecisively. 'I'll just wait here for a while. I'm expecting a female officer any minute. Please will you go back to Mr Burton's house to see Inspector Johnson right now.'

'OK,' I said, and drove away.

*   *   *

The posse had made themselves at home in Bill's kitchen. Four men sat at the table. One of them stood up as I walked in through the back door.

'Yes, sir,' he said, 'can I help you?'

'I'm Sid Halley,' I replied.

'Ah, we've been looking for you.'

'You've found me, then.'

'I'm Inspector Johnson, Thames Valley Police,' he said. 'Where is Miss Juliet Burns?'

'At home in bed.'

At their request, I gave them both Juliet's address and my own, together with my date of birth. Strange how the police always want to know how old everyone is. They said I was free to go but I should expect to be contacted in due course by the coroner.

'Don't you want to interview me?' I asked.

'Why should I?' said Inspector Johnson. 'Looks like a pretty straightforward suicide. Done us a favour if you ask me.'

'What do you mean?' I asked.

'Couldn't bear the thought of going to prison for murder. Saved us all the time and money.'

'Are you sure it's suicide?'

'Forensics will find out. We're waiting for them now.'

'Just make sure they check that he did fire the gun,' I said. 'Residue on the hands and all that.'

'Everyone's a bloody detective these days,' he said. 'You've been watching too much television, sir.'

'Ask them to check all the same.'

'I'm sure they will.'

He had made up his mind that Bill had killed himself and I wasn't going to convince him otherwise at the moment. I hoped forensics might do so in due course.

*   *   *

I went to see Chief Inspector Carlisle in Cheltenham. I had phoned first to see if he would be there and he met me in the police station reception.

'Morning, Mr Halley.' It felt like afternoon but my watch showed that it was still only nine thirty.

'Morning, Chief Inspector,' I replied. 'Can I borrow some of your time?'

'As long as it's not a waste.' He smiled. 'Wasting police time is an offence, you know. Shall we go through to an interview room?'

'I'd rather go out for a coffee,' I said. 'I've haven't had breakfast yet.'

He appeared to consult his inner self and decided that it would be acceptable for him to have coffee with a 'public' and agreed to let me drive us the short distance down to the Queen's Hotel in my car. The previous week, this hotel would have been heaving with the masses from across the Irish

117

Sea, here for the racing festival. Now it was tranquil and calm. We found a quiet corner of the restaurant and ordered not only coffee, but toast and marmalade as well.

'Now, what do you want to see me about?'

'You are aware, I presume, that Bill Burton was discovered dead this morning.'

'Yes,' he said, 'Thames Valley rang me.' He made Thames Valley sound like a person not a police force. 'But how do *you* know that he's dead?'

'I arrived at the house just after he had been found by Juliet Burns.'

'You're making a bit of a habit of being around at critical moments.'

'Coincidence,' I said, and remembered that Bill had been told he could go down for coincidence. 'Do you think Bill Burton killed himself?'

'Why do you ask?' he said.

'Because I don't.'

'Ah,' he said, 'the loyal friend who believes his pal is innocent of all charges in spite of a load of evidence to the contrary.'

'Don't mock me.'

'Sorry,' he said. 'You're the last person I should mock. You've probably solved more cases than I have.'

I raised a quizzical eyebrow.

'Word gets round, you know. Never mind a criminal records check, most employers these days would like their staff passed by you. "Okayed by Halley" has become slang for reliable and honest.'

'Well then, don't mock me when I say that I don't believe that Bill Burton killed himself.'

We waited in silence as a waiter put the coffee

118

and toast down on the table.

'Tell me why you don't believe he killed himself.'

'He had no reason to do so. When I spoke to him last night he was positive and determined. Suicide was the last thing on his mind. He was hardly likely to ask me to come and ride out this morning if he was contemplating doing himself in.'

'Maybe something happened overnight,' he said.

'It did. His wife agreed to return home.'

'How do you know?'

'I've spoken to her. I went to tell her that Bill was dead. I thought it was better coming from a friend. I told her mother, too. They can both confirm that Kate was going to go home this morning. So he had every reason to live.'

'You're telling me he was murdered?'

'Yes.'

'Who by?'

'I don't know,' I said. 'Almost certainly the same person who murdered Huw Walker.'

'But why? What's the motive?'

'To stop the police hunt for the real killer. If the police's prime suspect is found with his head blown off, with the same gun as that used for the first murder grasped in his hand, the obvious conclusion is that he had been overcome with guilt for his actions and done the honourable thing.'

'Seems a reasonable conclusion to me,' he said.

'Bit too convenient, don't you think? And where was the gun? You failed to find it when you searched his house?' I was guessing, but it had to be so.

'True,' he said, 'but we didn't take the whole place apart brick by brick, and it may have been somewhere in the stables.'

'Nevertheless, I'm convinced he didn't kill himself—and, even if he did, he wouldn't have done it in the house for his wife to find—or, for heaven's sake, his children.'

'He might have done if he wanted his revenge on her for talking to the police about Huw Walker.'

The waiter came over and politely asked that, as breakfast was now finished, did we mind moving to the lounge so he could set up for lunch.

'I have something for you to listen to,' I said. 'Can we go out to my car instead?'

We went and sat in my car in the hotel car park.

I slotted the tape from my answering machine into the car tape player and let it run to the end of Huw's second message. Carlisle pushed the rewind button and listened to it all through again.

'You should have given this to me sooner,' he said.

'I only found it this morning.' He looked at me in disbelief, which I suppose was fair enough.

'Funny,' he said, 'I'd forgotten that he was Welsh. Makes him more of a man rather than just a body, if you know what I mean.'

I nodded.

Carlisle pushed the rewind button a second time and played the tape once more. I didn't need to hear Huw's voice. By now, I knew those messages by heart.

'Hi, Sid. Bugger! I wish you were there. Anyway, I need to talk to you. I'm in a bit of trouble and I . . . I know this sounds daft but I'm frightened. Actually, Sid, no kidding, I'm really frightened. Someone called me on the phone and threatened to kill me. I thought they were bloody joking so I

120

told them to eff off and put the phone down. But they rang back and it's given me the willies. I thought it was all a bit of a lark but now I find that it ain't. I need your bloody help this time, mate, and no mistake. Call me back. Please call me back.'

And the second one

'Where are you when I need you, you bugger? Come on, pick up the bloody phone, you bastard! Can't you tell when a mate's in trouble? Just a few losers, they says, for a few hundred in readies, they says. OK, I says, but make it a few grand. Do as we tell you, they says, or the only grand you'll see is the drop from the top of the effing grandstand. Should have bloody listened, shouldn't I?'

'When did he leave these messages?' asked Carlisle.

'I'm not absolutely sure,' I said.

'Didn't your answering machine tell you?' he asked.

'No, it came out of the ark,' I said, 'but, as you heard, there was another message between the two from Huw. I found out from that caller that he telephoned just before eight in the evening the day before Huw died. So one of Huw's calls was before eight p.m. and the other after.'

'So you didn't just find them this morning,' he said.

'Well, no, not exactly,' I said, suitably chastised.

Carlisle ejected the tape and put it in his pocket. 'I'll take this, if you don't mind,' he said.

I was sure he would take it even if I did mind.

'I'll give you a receipt for it when we get back to the station.'

'Doesn't sound like someone frightened of being killed by a jilted husband,' I said. 'More to do with fixing races.'

'Burton was arrested for that, too, remember.'

'Do you have an answer for everything?' I said.

'You pays your money and makes your choice.'

I drove back to the police station and pulled up in front of the entrance.

'Will you do me a favour?' I asked.

'Maybe,' he said.

'I asked the police inspector at Bill's house this morning to make sure that his forensic team check whether Bill had actually fired the gun or not—you know, residue on the hands. He seemed convinced that it was suicide and . . . well, could you check that the test is done?'

He nodded. 'Standard practice but I will ask.'

'And will you tell me the result?'

'Don't push your luck, Mr Halley.'

*   *   *

Pushing my luck is what I was about to discover I needed.

CHAPTER NINE

Impotence is frustrating.

I don't mean physical impotence, although that too must be exasperating. My current frustration stemmed from my impotence to get on with my investigations into Huw's death. I needed some Viagra for the mind.

I was also failing in my task for Archie Kirk, having done little to delve into the world of the internet gambler.

Today was now Friday, a whole week since the Gold Cup and two days since I had been to see Carlisle in Cheltenham. And there was still no word from him as to the result of the forensics.

I'd been to Sandown races the previous day and had spent a tedious time asking anyone and everyone why they thought Huw Walker had become a murder victim. Some suggested race fixing as a possible reason, most having seen the antics between Huw and Bill last week either live or on the television and misreading the cause, as I had done. No one had been able to suggest any names other than Bill Burton as the likely murderer, many easily believing that, by killing himself, Bill had as good as confessed. I spent the afternoon sowing seeds of doubt to this theory and spreading the word that Sid Halley, at least, believed that Bill had been murdered, too.

I sat in the little office in my flat playing with the make-a-wager.com website. Come on, I thought, how could this be a big earner for organised crime? Gambling had always attracted more than its fair share of dodgy characters and internet gambling was sure to be no exception.

There were two obvious ways for a bookmaker to separate honest men from their money fraudulently. First, to fix the result so that he can take bets in the sure knowledge that he cannot lose. And, secondly, to contrive to make people gamble on an event where the result is already known, but only to himself. Nowadays, with television pictures of every race beamed straight to the betting shops and to any home with a satellite dish, there is little scope for the second. In the good old days of the wire services, a couple of minutes' delay was easy.

The surest way has always been to fix the result. Not such an easy task in a race with plenty of runners, not unless nearly every jockey is in on the fix, which is very doubtful since the penalties for such behaviour are harsh. To be 'Warned Off Newmarket Heath' means to lose one's livelihood and to be banned not only from Newmarket Heath but also from all racecourses and all racing stables. It is quite a deterrent. Fixing races, if done at all, has to be subtle, but just a slight manipulation of the odds can pay huge dividends in the long run.

Suppose you knew that a well-fancied horse was definitely not going to win because you had paid the jockey to make sure it didn't, then you could offer considerably longer odds on that horse than its form would justify. You could even offer slightly better odds on the other runners, just a tiny fraction, mind, to encourage people to bet with you rather than someone else. Your extra losses on the winner would be far outweighed by the extra gains from the sure loser.

But make-a-wager.com was not a normal bookmaker. As an 'exchange', it didn't stand to lose if the punters won. As long as individuals were prepared to match bets, there would always be commissions to collect. Unless, of course, it was the site itself that was matching the bets, betting to win and betting to lose, especially betting to lose, laying the sure-fire loser with long odds to attract the market.

The internet sites all claim, of course, that they are squeaky clean and that their detailed computer credit card records make the system secure and foolproof. But organised crime is no fool. It's true that the system would show up any unusual pattern of gambling by individuals or groups, but the computer records themselves are under the control of the websites.

With the right results and a creative approach to the digital paperwork, make-a-wager.com could become make-a-fortune.com.

So it always came back to fixing the races.

I knew that Huw had been involved in fixing races, his voice from beyond death had said so. 'They', he'd said. 'Do as we tell you, they says.' Who were 'they'? He hadn't specified that 'they' were internet sites. I was simply putting that into the mix because of Archie. 'They' could have been a bookmaking firm, or even a gambling syndicate determined to improve the odds in their favour.

I used the internet to look up make-a-wager.com on the Companies House website. All UK companies have to be registered with Companies House and every year they have to submit their accounts. This information is in the public domain. So, as a member of the public, I downloaded it.

I discovered that make-a-wager.com was the internet site for Make A Wager Ltd, company number 07887551. I downloaded all the information I could find, including the annual accounts for the previous year. The company was doing very nicely, thank you, with a turnover in excess of a hundred million with a hefty operating profit of fifteen million. The increase over the previous year was staggering with more than a doubling of turnover and a trebling of profit. There was big money to be had in this business.

George Lochs was not listed as one of the five directors of the company but Clarence Lochstein was. So George/Clarence had never officially changed his name. But it was one of the non-executive directors listed that really caught my eye—John William Enstone.

I did another search and found that Jonny Enstone was quite a busy chap, with no less than fourteen different companies listed of which he was or had been a director. J. W. Best Ltd, his construction company, was there as expected, as was Make A Wager Ltd. I hadn't heard of the others but, nevertheless, I downloaded the list and saved it on my computer.

Marina called my mobile and said that she would be home a little late that evening. A colleague, she explained, was leaving to work in America, and she and others were giving her a farewell drink.

'Fine,' I said, 'I'll be here.'

I made myself some scrambled eggs for lunch and ate them with a spoon straight out of the saucepan. Such decadence! My dear mother would have had a fit.

I spent the afternoon doing reference checks on four short-listed candidates for the post of manager of a smallish educational charity. Such checks were the bread and butter of my one-man business. As Carlisle had correctly said, I had a reputation for sorting the wheat from the chaff. Fortunately, the reputation was self-perpetuating as referees seemed reluctant to give me wrong or misleading information in case I were asked to do a reference on them at a later date.

There are two reasons for giving someone a

glowing testimonial. One, because they actually are that good and, two, because they are useless and their current employer is trying to offload them on to someone else and thinks that a good reference will help. I knew that it was common practice for poor employees to be given a flattering reference on condition they looked for a new job.

On this occasion, in each of their three written references, all four of the candidates were described as hard working, reliable, loyal and as honest as the day is long. It was my usual practice to call the third listed referee first as I had found that this would often be the weak link if deceit were afoot. By the end of the day I had discovered that only one of the four candidates was as sound as his references would imply. Even he was not squeaky clean, having had to leave his present employment reluctantly due to a minor assignation of the heart with the wife of a senior colleague. Of the others, one was just about all right while the other two had serious honesty problems. One of these was suspected of theft from other staff but the evidence was circumstantial, and the other had threatened to sue her boss for sexual harassment unless she was given a good reference.

I would write my report and leave the charity to make its own decision.

*   *   *

It was almost eight o'clock by the time I printed out the report for the charity and shut down my computer. Typing one-handed, indeed with only one finger, was one of the many annoyances of having a false hand. Not being able to massage the typing-induced ache in my right wrist was another.

I thought about food and decided that as soon as Marina arrived home we'd go out for a local Chinese. Meanwhile, I opened a bottle of red wine and flicked on the television.

I was gently snoozing in front of some magnificent wildlife images of life on the Nile when the buzzer from the front desk woke me.

'Yes,' I said, picking up the intercom phone from the wall next to the kitchen door.

'You had better come down here, Mr Halley, at once,' said Derek.

There was something about the tone of his voice that made me drop the intercom phone and rush for my door. I charged down the flights of concrete stairs to the lobby and was met there not by a complete disaster but by a pretty scary sight, nevertheless.

A very pale-looking Marina was half-sitting, half-lying on the sofa in the lobby, bleeding. She was wearing the light fawn suede coat I had given her for Christmas and it was never going to be the same again. The front was covered in red splodges.

'Derek,' I said, 'go up to my flat, the door's open, and fetch me a large bath towel from one of the bathrooms. Wet it first.'

He hesitated for a second.

'Do it, please, Derek.' The urgency in my voice cut through his indecision and he went up in the lift.

I sat down beside Marina who was staring at me with wide frightened eyes.

'Fine mess you've got yourself into,' I said with a smile.

'Just the usual for a Friday night.' She smiled

128

back and I knew that she was fine on the inside. She was tough as well as smart. It was her beauty that worried me most. I could see that there were two places on her face from which the blood was flowing, one was a deep cut over her right eye and the other was a nasty split lower lip. Head wounds nearly always look worse than they are due to their profuse bleeding, but I could see that these two were bad enough for stitches and I hoped they wouldn't leave scars.

Derek returned with not just one towel but with a whole armful.

'Well done,' I said. I took one and applied pressure with it to the deep cut in Marina's eyebrow. It must have hurt like hell but she didn't flinch or complain one bit. She took another of the towels and held it to her lip, which had already started to swell quite badly.

'Darling,' I said, 'I think you are going to need some stitches in these cuts. We're going to have to go and find a doctor.' I had one in mind.

'Don't you want to know what happened?' she mumbled through the towel.

'You got mugged,' I said. 'What did they take?'

'Nothing.'

'You were lucky,' I said.

'You call this lucky!' She almost laughed. 'But I wasn't being robbed. I was being given a message.'

'What? What message?'

She removed the towel from her mouth and said, 'Tell your boyfriend to leave things be. Tell him to leave it well alone. Savvy?'

Wow, I thought, I really must have touched a nerve at Sandown yesterday.

Derek hovered around us and asked if he should

telephone for the police or for an ambulance.

'No ambulance,' I said. An ambulance meant casualty departments and a long wait to be stitched by the duty nurse who, on a Friday night, would be busy with her needle and thread on the fighting drunks. Speed rather than accuracy would be her tenet. No thanks.

'Did you see him?' I asked.

'No,' she said. 'He grabbed me from behind. Anyway, he was wearing a scarf or a balaclava.'

Police would mean masses of time and endless interviews with no real chance of catching the non-mugger. He wouldn't have set this up to get caught.

'No police,' I said. 'Come on, my darling, let's get you cleaned up and into the car. Time to go and see my doctor.'

'No, not yet. I want to go upstairs first.'

I picked up the rapidly reddening towels and went to take her left hand to help her up. She pulled it away.

'Are you all right?' I asked, concerned that she might have other injuries.

'Fine.' She smiled rather crookedly at me. 'You'll see.'

I thanked Derek who appeared to have taken this fresh incident in his stride. Never a dull moment when you lived with the Halleys.

We went up in the lift. The cuts were now merely oozing rather than gushing and some colour had returned to Marina's cheeks. Crisis over.

Marina went straight into our bedroom and picked up some nail scissors from her dressing table.

'Can you fetch me a clean plastic bag from the drawer in the kitchen?' she asked.

I found some small polythene sandwich bags and took one back to her.

'What are you doing?' I asked.

'I scratched his neck.' She smiled at me with her lopsided mouth. 'Maybe I have some of his skin under my fingernails.'

'Good girl. Perhaps we should involve the police after all?'

'No,' she said. 'I want you to get this bugger for Huw's murder, not just for punching me.'

She used the scissors to cut the elegantly long fingernails on her left hand which she placed carefully in the plastic bag. She then scraped the ends of her fingers and placed the resulting material and the scissors in the bag together with the cut nails.

'I can extract the DNA at the lab but we should go and do it now before it dries out too much. There might not be anything to find but it's worth a try.'

'After the doctor,' I said.

'No, before. This won't take long.'

'Are you sure you don't want me to call the police?' I said. 'They could run a check against the National DNA Database?'

'No police, Sid. I'm sure. We can always give them the DNA results later, if there are any. I really don't want to spend the next few hours at a police station being poked about by some police doctor. No thank you!' She picked up the plastic bag. 'Come on, let's go.'

*　　　*　　　*

In the world of racing, especially amongst jockeys, the need for medical services are frequent and crucial. A jockey with a broken bone needs immediate treatment for the injury, obviously, but he also needs to get back in the saddle in the shortest amount of time. A jockey not riding is a jockey not earning. They are paid by the ride. No ride means no cash. There is no sick pay for self-employed jockeys.

Hospital accident and emergency centres will lavish plaster of paris on the injured and tell them it must stay on for six weeks minimum. A whole industry has grown up that will get jockeys back in the saddle in half that time. Ballet dancers, footballers and all types of athletes have the same needs.

In the good old days, before jockeys had to 'pass the doctor' after every fall, many a race had been ridden with a broken collar-bone, or a fractured wrist. Losing a ride in one race may then result in losing the rides on that horse for good, especially if it had won.

My doctor, Geoffrey Kennedy, had managed to get me back in the saddle after injury in record time on many occasions. He knew not only how my body worked but my mind, too. He seemed to sense how much pain I could stand and how much I had been willing to endure in order to get back to racing. He had initially trained as a GP but had become a sports injury specialist after his brother, an international rugby player, had continuously complained to him about the lack of understanding of sports injuries at the local hospital. Geoffrey had opened a specialist clinic in north London and soon a line of A-list sportsmen and women were queuing up at his door. He was now semi-retired and the Kennedy Sports Clinic was thriving in the hands of a younger man, but we old lags still preferred to deal with the master.

Since my riding days had ended, Geoffrey had continued to patch up the damage caused by two-legged rather than four-legged opponents, sometimes willing to turn a blind eye where others might have called in the police.

I rang him while Marina changed out of her bloody clothes. Sure, he'd said, no problem. He would pack his sewing kit and meet us at the Cancer Research UK London Institute in Lincoln's Inn Fields. He wasn't doing anything except watching the television and it was a while since he had practised his sewing on a beautiful face. All you bloody jockeys are so ugly, he'd said, it'll be nice to work on a face without a broken nose. His skills would be appreciated, at last.

As I drove, Marina told me what had happened.

'I was almost home,' her voice sounded a little strange due to the swollen lip. 'I was passing those bushes outside Belgravia Court when I was grabbed from behind. He dragged me into that path between the bushes and I thought I was going to be raped.' She paused. 'I was quite calm but very frightened. It was like everything was happening in slow motion. He held me from behind and spoke into my car. I think he might have let me go if I hadn't scratched him. I reached over my head and felt the wool on his face. So I pulled it up from his neck and dug my nails in.' She laughed in the dark. 'He groaned. Serves him right. But he spun me round, called me something unprintable and hit

133

me very hard in the face. I think it was his fists. He had gloves on with shiny bits on them.'

Gloved fists with brass knuckle-dusters, I thought. That fitted; there was too much damage for fists alone.

'I went down on my knees and he ran off. It was quite a while before I could stand up and make it the twenty yards home.'

If I'd had a spare hand, I would have held hers.

Geoffrey beat us to the Cancer Research Institute from his home in Highgate but Marina kept him waiting as she electronically signed in to the building.

'Some experiments need constant monitoring,' she said, 'so the labs are always open. Some of the staff almost live here at times.'

'My, my,' Geoffrey said, seeing Marina in the light. 'That's quite a face. Is this a police job, Sid?'

'No,' both Marina and I said together.

'Walked into a door, did you?' Geoffrey said sarcastically. 'Correction. Two doors. Very careless.'

We went up in the lift with Geoffrey tut-tutting under his breath.

We walked down endless corridors with cream walls and blue vinyl flooring. Half of the corridor floor space was taken up with rows of grey filing cabinets interspersed by three-foot high cylinders with yellow triangular warning labels stuck on them: 'Liquid nitrogen—Danger of asphyxiation'. Marina punched numbers into another electronic lock that agreed with a beep to give us entry to her domain.

She flicked on the stark overhead fluorescent lamps and went to sit at one of the laboratory benches where she carefully removed the plastic bag from her pocket and put it in a fridge.

'That will keep it fresh for a while,' she said. 'OK, Doc, do your worst.'

Geoffrey worked for nearly half an hour, cleaning and tidying up the wounds, injecting some local anaesthetic, and finally closing the gaps with two rows of minute blue stitches. I had brought my camera up from the car and, much to Marina's annoyance, I took a series of shots as her wounds were transformed from an ugly bleeding mess to two neat lines, one horizontal in her eyebrow and the other vertical through her lower lip. With a rapidly blackening eye, she looked like one of those advertisements for wearing seat belts.

'There,' he said at last. 'I'll have to take them out again in about five or six days but you won't be able to spot the scars in a few weeks.'

'I thought stitches dissolved these days,' Marina said.

'Those are mostly used for internal stitching,' he replied, 'and staples are ugly and tend to leave scars. Nothing like good old-fashioned catgut stitches if you want to leave no trace, or this blue nylon as we tend to use these days And don't tie them too tight or they pull. These should be fine.'

'Thank you,' said Marina. 'Can I get back to work now?'

'Sure,' said the doctor, 'but those might be a bit sore when the anaesthetic wears off. And I should give you a tetanus shot, unless you've had one within the last ten years.'

'I have no idea,' said Marina.

'Well, you'd better have one just to be sure. I brought some with me.'

He stuck a pre-loaded hypodermic needle into Marina's bottom as she bent over a lab bench.

'What do you do here?' he asked. 'Reminds me of medical school.'

'This is a haematology lab,' she said. 'We look at blood to try and find a marker for various types of cancer. We take blood cells and cut the proteins into amino-acid chains using the enzyme trypsin. Trypsin is, of course, a protein itself.'

Of course, I thought.

'We look at the chains of amino acids which make up the proteins and see if there are markers which are certain cancer specific. We pass the chains through this mass spectrometer,' she pointed at a long grey cabinet that reminded me of a deep freeze. 'It determines the relative masses of each chain and if there is a variation we are not expecting this may be the marker we are looking for.'

I was completely lost but Geoffrey seemed to understand and he was nodding furiously as he moved around, inspecting the mass spectrometer from every angle.

'Glad to see my taxes are going to a good home,' he said.

'No, no!' said Marina. 'This institution and all the research we do here is funded by charitable contributions from the public to Cancer Research UK. We are not supported by taxation. It's very important to us that people know that.'

'Sorry,' said Geoffrey. 'I stand corrected.'

Marina nodded and took the plastic bag out of the fridge.

'Now from this little lot,' she said, getting back to her 'in lab' mode, 'what I want is a DNA profile.

DNA is the code for making cells. Proteins are the bricks from which the cells are built. The DNA strands are the architect's plans that show how the bricks go together to build the cell structures.'

'So people with different DNA have different cell structures?' I asked.

'Absolutely,' she said. 'Different DNA produce different-looking people due to slight differences in their architect's plans. Nearly all the DNA in each person is the same so we all have the same sort of cells—muscles, nerves, skin and so on. We all have two eyes and one nose. It's just the teeny-weeny differences in the codes which produce our different characteristics, like blue or brown eyes; blondes, brunettes or redheads; black or white skin; short, tall, everything. It's these minute differences that are distinctive to an individual and it is these differences that allow us to produce a DNA profile which is like a fingerprint, unique.'

Marina was on a roll. 'I can use restriction enzymes like EcoR1 to cut the DNA strands in this sample into what we call polynucleotides. Then I'll put them in an agarose gel matrix, a sort of jelly, for electrophoresis. The polynucleotides are charged so they'll migrate, or move, in the electric field. The amount they migrate is dependent on the size and shape of each polynucleotide. Imagine that the gel acts as a sort of sieve, the bigger the polynucleotide the less distance it will migrate.'

Geoffrey was still nodding. I wasn't.

'So in the gel matrix you get separation of polynucleotides into different bands. Then you bake the matrix on to a sheet of nitrocellulose paper to give a permanent pattern of lines where the bands are.'

'How does that help?' I was out of my depth here, I thought. Give me a poor jumping novice chaser over Aintree fences any day.

'Everyone has slightly different DNA so everyone has a different pattern. In criminal cases, they say that the odds of two different people having the same pattern is more than 60 million to one. Unless, of course, you have identical twins. They will have matching patterns because their DNA is exactly the same, that's what makes them identical. However, what I'm doing wouldn't be acceptable as evidence in court. The law requires much stricter systems for producing the profile to prevent cross-contamination. This one will be contaminated with my DNA for a start. I'll have to do another pattern of just my DNA so I can subtract my lines to leave those of our friend alone.'

'Our friend?' asked Geoffrey.

'The door,' I said.

'Door? What door?' Poor Geoffrey was getting very confused.

'The door Marina walked into, twice.'

'Ah,' the penny dropped. 'Yes, the door, our friend. Good. Well done.'

I wasn't sure if he understood or not but he seemed happy to wander around the lab as Marina worked away with the fingernails. She then scraped some cells from the inside of her cheek to do another profile of her own DNA alone.

'It will take several hours now for the polynucleotides to migrate in the gel matrix. We'll have the results next week.'

'What will they give us?' I asked.

'Nothing on their own,' she said, 'but if we get

more samples and one of them matches, then, bingo, we have our man.'

'So all I have to do is go around asking everyone for a DNA sample.'

'You don't *have* to ask,' said Marina. 'Just pluck out an unsuspecting hair. As long as the root follicle is still attached, there will be enough cells present to get a profile.'

'Is that legal?' I asked.

'No. Strictly speaking it's not,' she said. 'The Human Tissue Act makes it illegal to hold a sample for the purpose of producing a DNA profile without the consent of the donor.' She waved her hand at her work. 'All this has technically been illegal but I'm not telling.'

'Me neither,' said Geoffrey flamboyantly. 'Doctor/patient confidentiality, don't you know.'

*　　　*　　　*

Marina and I went back to Ebury Street while Geoffrey returned home to Highgate.

'See you next week to take the stitches out,' he had said as he got into his Volvo. 'Take care with that girl of yours. I'll send you my bill.'

He hadn't sent me a bill for years.

We arrived back home at about ten thirty, far too late to go out to eat, as I had planned.

'Package for you, Mr Halley,' said the night porter as we arrived. Derek had gone off duty.

The package was, in fact, a brown manila envelope about seven by ten inches. It had 'SID HALLEY—BY HAND' written in capital letters on the front.

'When did this arrive?' I asked the porter.

'About five minutes ago,' he said. 'It came by taxi. The driver said he had been paid to deliver the package and that you were expecting it.'

'Well, I wasn't.'

I opened the flat envelope. There was a single sheet of paper inside. It was a newspaper cutting from Monday's *Pump*. It was the picture of Marina and me walking down the road, hand in hand. This copy had some additions.

'Listen to the message. Someone could get badly hurt' was written across the bottom of the picture in thick red felt-tip.

And a big red 'X' had been drawn across Marina's face.

CHAPTER TEN

When in trouble, seek sanctuary.

I decided we should go to Aynsford.

Marina had become very agitated on seeing the newspaper cutting. She was sure that we were being watched and I agreed with her. She packed a few clothes whilst I rang Charles.

'What, now?' he asked. Charles was old-fashioned in that his house telephone stood on a table in the hallway and I could imagine him glancing at his long-case grandfather clock. It would have told him that it was after ten thirty, almost his bedtime.

'Yes, Charles. Now, please.'

'Physical or mental problem?' he asked. He knew me too well.

'Bit of both,' I said. 'But it's not me, it's Marina.'

140

'Marina?'

'I told you about her last week,' I said. 'She's Dutch and beautiful. Remember?'

'Vaguely,' he said.

Was he trying to make me cross?

'I suppose it's all right,' he said without conviction.

'Look, Charles, we won't come. Sorry to have bothered you.'

'No,' he said, sounding a bit more determined. 'Come. Does this Dutch beauty need her own room or are you two . . . together?'

'Charles,' I said, 'you're losing your marbles. I told you last week. We're together.'

'Right. So it's one room then?'

'Yes.'

Suddenly it didn't seem to be a good idea any more. Charles was being very reticent and I certainly did not want to abuse his hospitality. Perhaps bringing a new girlfriend into the house of my ex-father-in-law was not, after all, very prudent.

'Charles, perhaps it would be best if we didn't come.'

'Nonsense,' he said. 'I'm expecting you now. Looking forward to it. How long will you be staying?'

'Only for the weekend, I expect.'

'Jenny and Anthony are coming on Sunday.'

Ah, now I understood. Jenny, my ex, had always put her father in a spin. In the Navy, he had been at the centre of command and control but he could be reduced to a gibbering wreck by the cutting tongue of his only daughter. Just the thought of her imminent arrival had sent him into a fluster.

'What time on Sunday?' I asked.

'Oh, for dinner, I think. Mrs Cross has the details.'

Mrs Cross was his housekeeper.

'We'll be gone by then.'

It would save a scene that Jenny would have relished. Not my injuries this time but my girlfriend's. How delicious, she would think. The former Mrs Halley, the current Lady Wingham, would have had a field day.

'Oh, right. Good.' Charles, too, could see that it was an encounter best avoided.

'We'll be there in an hour and a half,' I said. 'Leave the back door open and I'll lock it when we get in. No need for you to stay up.'

'Of course I'll be up. Drive carefully.'

As if I wouldn't. Just because someone says 'drive carefully', does it make people actually drive more carefully? I suspect not.

We left the lights on in the flat and went down through the building to the garage. Marina lay down on the back seat of the car as I drove out on to Ebury Street. Anyone watching would have thought I was on my own and assumed that Marina was alone upstairs.

I jumped two sets of red lights and went round Hyde Park Corner three times before I was satisfied that we weren't being followed.

I drove, very carefully, along the M40 to Oxford and then cross-country to Aynsford, arriving there soon after midnight. Marina, having transferred to the front passenger seat, slept most of the way but was finally woken by the constant turning of the narrow lanes and the humpback bridge over the canal as we approached the village.

'Nearly there, my angel,' I said, stroking her

142

knee with my unfeeling hand.

'My bloody mouth hurts.'

'I'll get you something for that as soon as we get in.'

*   *   *

Charles was not only still up but he was still dressed, and in a dark blue blazer and tie.

No one could ever accuse Charles of being under-dressed. He had once worn his dinner jacket to a 'formal' dinner for his great-nephews. The formality of the dinner meant that the great-nephews had to use a knife and fork rather than their fingers, and Charles had looked a little out of place in Pizzaland in his bow-tie. He hadn't cared. Better to be over than under, he'd said, better than wearing a lounge suit to a Royal Naval 'Dining In' night, better than wearing a sweater to church.

He came out to meet us as I pulled up in front of the house and fussed over Marina. He was genuinely shocked that anyone could have hit a woman, especially one clearly so beautiful as Marina. Her face didn't look very beautiful at the moment with a badly swollen lip and two blackening eyes. I knew it would look worse in the morning.

'It's outrageous,' he said. 'Only a coward would hit a woman.'

Charles was a great believer in chivalry. He didn't care that many of his ideals were out of date. He had said to me once that, at his age, people expected him to have old-fashioned views so he didn't disappoint them.

Charles found some painkillers and a sleeping

143

pill for Marina and she was soon tucked up in bed. He and I retired to his small sitting room for a whisky.

'I hope I'm not keeping you up,' I said.

'You are,' he replied, 'but I'm happy to be kept up. What's this all about?'

'It's a long story.'

'It's a long night.'

'Do you remember Gold Cup day at Cheltenham?' I asked.

'Difficult to forget.'

'Huw Walker was murdered over something to do with race fixing. Murder seems to be a bit of an over-reaction for a little fiddle on the horses so I think there must be something more to it than that.'

'How can you be sure it was something to do with fixing races?' Charles asked.

'Because Huw left two messages on my London answering machine the night before he died and as good as said it was. He was frightened that someone might kill him for not doing as he was told.'

'I thought Bill Burton had killed him for playing around with his wife.'

I raised my eyebrows, both at the fact that Charles had heard the rumour and the way he expressed it.

'So someone told me,' he added. He had clearly used their exact turn of phrase.

'Look,' I said, 'I think Huw's murder was premeditated. Bill Burton didn't believe that, as you say, Huw was playing around with his wife until just before the first race that afternoon. Bill couldn't have suddenly magicked a gun out of thin

144

air. And Huw certainly left the first message on my answering machine hours before Bill had any hint that there was an affair going on between him and Kate. It wasn't Bill who Huw was frightened of. So I think we can discount the tidy solution that Bill killed him.'

'But Burton was bloody angry with Walker for winning on Candlestick. I saw it myself.'

'No, he wasn't. He was bloody angry because he had just found out it was true that Kate and Huw had been at it.'

'Oh.' Charles went over to the drinks tray and poured two more large single malts. It was indeed going to be a long night.

'Bill Burton was murdered as well,' I said. 'I'm sure of that, too. It was made to look like a suicide but it wasn't.'

'The police seem to think it was, or so everyone says on the racecourse.'

'I've been doing my best to cast doubts as to the accuracy of that theory. That's why Marina got beaten up. It came with a message to me to leave things be, to stop sticking my nose into Huw's death and allow Bill to carry the can.'

'So that the case will be closed and the guilty party will still be free?'

'Exactly,' I said.

'So are you?'

'Am I what?'

'Are you going to stop sticking your nose into Huw's death?'

'I don't know.'

I swallowed a mouthful of Glenmorangie's best 10-year-old and allowed the golden fluid to send a shiver round my body, the prelude to a comforting

145

warm glow that emanated from deep down. I realised that I had eaten hardly anything all day and that drinking on an empty stomach was a sure-fire way to a hangover. But who cared?

'No one has been able to stop you in the past.'

'I know,' I said. 'But this is different somehow . . . hurting Marina is out of order.'

'Hurting you is all right, I suppose?'

'Well . . . yes. I know how much I can take. I'm somehow in control, even when I'm not.' I paused. 'Do you remember that time when it all was too much? When Chico and I were almost flayed alive with the chains?'

He nodded. He had seen the damage first hand.

'Well, that was done to stop me investigating. At least they thought I would stop. They thought that I would have had enough, that surely I would get the message and run away. What they didn't understand was that I was going after them all the more, simply because of what they'd done to try and stop me. I really believe that nothing, short of actually killing me, would stop me if I thought it was right.'

'Didn't a man once threaten to cut off your right hand if you didn't stop trying to nail him for something?'

'Yes.' I paused.

I remembered the paralysing fear, the absolute dread of losing a second hand. I remembered the utter collapse it had caused in me. I remembered the struggle it had taken to rebuild my life, the willpower required to face another day. Sweat broke out on my forehead. I remembered it all too well.

'That didn't stop you, either.'

146

No, I thought, not in the end, although it had for a while.

'Nearly,' I croaked. My tongue seemed to be stuck to the roof of my mouth.

'You are surely not going to be stopped by a couple of punches to the face.'

'But it's not *my* face that's being punched. It's not *me* that's being hurt. I make the decision and someone else takes the pain, someone I love. I can't do that.'

'Shooting hostages never stopped the French Resistance killing Germans,' he said profoundly.

'It would have done if it had been their families.'

We finally went up to bed past two o'clock. By then, we had polished off the bottle and I had more than made up for the lack of calories in my missed dinner.

I slipped in next to Marina and kissed her sleeping head. How could I knowingly put this precious human being into danger? But how could I not? Suddenly, for the first time since I had started this caper, I was vulnerable to the 'we'll not get you, we'll get your girl' syndrome. What was the future? How could I continue? How could I operate if I were forever fearful of what 'they' might do to Marina?

I tossed this dilemma round in my whisky-fuzzed brain, found no acceptable solution, and finally drifted into an uneasy sleep.

*   *   *

Sure enough, I woke with a headache. My own fault.

Marina had a headache too, not hers. As I had

147

expected, her face looked worse than it had last night. And it was nothing to do with the daylight.

A giant panda has white eyes in a black face, Marina had the reverse. But the skin around her eyes was not only going black, it was going yellow and purple too. Her left eye was heavily bloodshot and the sticking plaster over her eyebrow gave her a sinister appearance. She looked like a refugee from a horror film. But these injuries were real and not the handiwork of a make-up artist.

She sat up in bed and looked at herself in the mirror on the wardrobe door that was cruelly at just the right angle.

'How do you feel?' I asked.

'About as good as I look.' She turned and gave me a lopsided smile.

That's my girl, I thought and gave her a gentle kiss on the cheek.

We both beat Charles to breakfast and found Mrs Cross busy in the kitchen.

'Good morning, Mr Halley.' I had never managed to get her to call me Sid.

'Morning, Mrs Cross,' I replied. 'Can I introduce Marina van der Meer—Mrs Cross.'

'Oh, my dear, your poor face!'

Marina smiled at her. 'It's fine, getting better every day. Car accident.'

'Oh,' said Mrs Cross again. 'I'll get you some tea.'

'Thank you, that would be lovely.'

I had coffee and dear Mrs Cross provided me, as always, with ready buttered and marmaladed toast.

Charles came in wearing his dressing gown and slippers and sat down at the long kitchen table. He rubbed his forehead and his eyes.

'When I was a midshipman I could drink all night and then be wide awake and full of energy for duty at six in the morning. What have the years done to me?'

'Good morning, Charles,' I said.

'Good morning to you, too,' he replied. 'Why did I allow you to keep me up half the night boozing?' He turned to Marina. 'Good morning, my dear, and how do you feel today?'

'Better than you two, I expect.' She smiled at him, which seemed to cheer him up no end.

'Morning, Mrs Cross,' said Charles. 'Black coffee and wholemeal toast for breakfast, please.'

'With or without Alka-Seltzer?' I asked.

'Without, I can't stand all that fizzing.'

We sat and ate our breakfast for a while in silence, Charles poring over the Saturday papers.

'It says here,' he said, pointing at the paper with a slice of toast, 'that the English are turning into a race of gamblers. It claims that more than nine million people in this country regularly gamble on the internet. Unbelievable.' He drank some coffee. 'It also says that on-line poker is the fastest expanding form of gambling. What's on-line poker when it's at home?'

'Playing poker on your computer,' I said. 'You join a poker table with others on their computers.'

'On their computers? Can't you see their faces?'

'No, just their names and those are simply nicknames. You have no idea who you are playing against.'

'That's crazy,' said Charles. 'The whole point of poker is being able to see the eyes of the other players. How can you bluff if you can't see who you are playing against?'

149

'The numbers playing it proves it must be attractive,' said Marina.

'How do you know that the players aren't cheating if you can't actually see the cards being dealt?' asked Charles.

'The cards are "dealt" by a computer,' I said, 'so the players can't be cheating,'

But what if the computer is cheating, I thought. What if the player only thinks he is playing against others who, like him, log on to the game from their own computers? What if the website has a seat or two at each table for itself to play against the visitors? What if the website is able to fix the 'deal'? Just a little, mind, so that the players don't really notice. Just enough to make the new players win. Just until they are hooked. It's a tried and tested formula: give away the cocaine just long enough to turn the users into addicts, and then charge them through the nose, as it were.

I had read that there were thought to be more than a quarter of a million gambling addicts in Britain. The resources needed to feed any compulsive habit increase at the same rate as the time and dedication to realising those resources decrease. The result is an insatiable appetite fed by unattainable provision. Something has to give and usually it's lifestyle, honesty and self-respect. All of these go out the window in the endless craving for the next fix. Gambling compulsion may be different from alcohol or drugs in the immediate damage it does to health, but, in the long run, as with all untreated addictions, it destroys sure enough.

'Still sounds crazy to me,' said Charles. 'Half the fun of playing poker is the banter between the players.'

'The difference is, Charles,' I said, 'you don't play poker where the winning and losing are important. You enjoy being with friends and the poker is an excuse to get together. On-line poker is a solitary experience and winning and losing is everything, whether it's fun or not.'

'Well, it's not for me,' he said and went back to reading his paper.

'Is it OK with you if I go to Newbury races?' I asked Marina.

'Yes, fine,' said Marina, 'but be careful. I'll stay here and rest. Is that all right with you, Charles?'

'Oh, yes, fine by me. I'll stay here, too, and we can watch the racing on the telly together.'

Marina pulled a face and I suspected that 'watching the racing on the telly' wasn't in her plans, but she would be too polite to say so.

*   *   *

After breakfast I called the Cheltenham police and asked for Chief Inspector Carlisle. Sorry, they said, he's unavailable at the moment, did I want to leave a message? When would he be available? I asked. They didn't know. Was he on duty? Yes, he was, but he was still unavailable. Could they pass him a message that he would actually get? Yes, they would. 'Good,' I said. 'Ask him to call Sid Halley. He has the number,' but I gave it to them again just in case.

He called me less than five minutes later. Good old Cheltenham police.

'I meant to call you yesterday,' he said, 'but things are a bit hectic down here at the moment.'

'Busy catching villains?' I said rather flippantly.

'Wish I were,' he sounded grave. 'Have you heard the news today?'

'No.'

'Well, that little girl that went missing from Gloucester in the week has turned up dead. At least, we've found a child's body and it's probably her. Still waiting for the official ID but there's not much doubt. Poor little mite. Don't know the cause of death yet but it has to be murder. How can anyone do such things to a 10-year-old? Makes me physically sick.'

'I'm sorry.' He had obviously had a lousy Saturday morning.

'I hate this job when it's kids. I'm glad they're rare. Only my third in twenty-five years.'

'What were you going to phone me about yesterday?' I asked.

'Forensics came back with the results. It was the same gun that killed Walker, and Burton definitely did fire it on the day he died. There was gunpowder residue all over his hands and on his sleeve.'

Oh, I thought. Oh, shit.

'So you believe that it was suicide?'

'That is the consensus of opinion in the Thames Valley force but it will be up to the coroner to decide.'

'Don't you think it was odd that he still had the gun in his hand? Surely it would fly out when he fired it?'

'It is not that unusual for a suicide to grip so tightly to the gun that it stays there. Like a reflex. The hand closes tightly at death and stays that way. Inspector Johnson said it was really quite difficult to prise the gun out of Burton's hand. Rigor mortis and all that.'

It was more information than I needed.

'Are you still investigating Huw Walker's death?' I asked.

'We are waiting for the inquest now.'

I took that to mean 'no'.

'How about if Bill Burton was already dead when he fired the gun?' I asked.

'What do you mean? How could he fire the gun if he was already dead?'

'Suppose you wanted to make murder look like suicide. First you shoot Bill through the mouth. Then you put the gun in his dead hand and pull the trigger again with his finger. Bingo, residue all over his hand and suicide it is.'

'But there was only one shot fired from the revolver?'

'How do you know?' I asked him.

'According to Johnson, there was only one spent cartridge in the cylinder.'

'But the murderer could have replaced one of the empty cartridges with a new one.'

'Then why wasn't a second bullet found?' Carlisle asked.

'Perhaps Inspector Johnson wasn't really looking for one.'

CHAPTER ELEVEN

I went to Newbury races still turning over and over in my head whether I should, or would, ask around about Huw Walker and Bill Burton again. It was

153

one thing to discuss the matter with Carlisle but somehow to continue to sow seeds of doubt over the guilt-driven suicide theory here at the races might be considered reckless and ill-advised after the previous evening's little message to Marina.

I waved my plastic hand at the man at the gate who waved back and beckoned me in like a long-lost friend. I parked in the trainers' and jockeys' car park, as usual.

A large Jaguar pulled up alongside my car and Andrew Woodward climbed out.

'Hello, Sid,' he said. 'How are things?'

'Fine, thank you, Mr Woodward.' I'd never called him Andrew.

'Good.' He didn't really sound as if he meant it. 'I'm told that I should consult you.'

'What about?' I asked.

'A reference. I'm appointing a second assistant at my yard. I've too many horses for just one now.'

I remembered that Jonny Enstone had transferred his allegiance and there were probably others too.

'What can I do for you?'

'Everyone tells me that I should get the applicants checked out by Halley.' His tone implied that he didn't agree. 'I reckon I'm a good judge of character and I think I've made up my mind but, as you're here, will you?'

'Will I what?'

'Will you give me an opinion of my chosen candidate?'

'I'll give you one for free if I know anything about him.'

'Her, actually. Girl called Juliet Burns. Used to work for Burton.'

'I know her,' I said.

Hasn't taken her long to look for a new job, I thought.

'Well, what do you think?'

'I don't know her very well, but I was a friend of her father and I knew her as a child. I've met her at Burton's place a couple of times recently.' I didn't tell him that one of them was immediately after she had found her boss with half his head blown away.

I recalled the evening she did the stable round. 'She seems to get on with the horses all right. I could do a more detailed check on her references, if you'd like.'

'I knew it would be a waste of time to ask you. Anyone could have told me that,' he sneered. 'I don't know what people see in you—you're just an ex-jockey.'

He turned to walk away.

'I know that two of your lady owners pay you no training fees and that you only use their names to market your yard.'

He turned back slowly. 'That's rubbish,' he said.

'You own the horses yourself.'

There was nothing illegal in it but it was a minor deceit of the betting public that was not approved of by the Jockey Club. I decided it would be prudent not to mention to him that I also knew he was having an affair with one of the ladies in question.

'You're only guessing,' he said.

'As you like.'

'How do you know?'

'I just know.' I didn't tell him that the lady owner he was not having the affair with had

155

supplied me with both bits of information because she was jealous of the other.

'Who else knows this?' he demanded.

'No one,' I said, 'not yet.'

'Keep your bloody mouth shut, do you hear, or you'll regret it.' He turned and strode away towards the racecourse entrance.

Damn, I thought. Why did I rise to that little insult? Why did I feel the need to show him that I was not *just* an ex-jockey? Why had I made an enemy of him when friends are what I needed to do my job? That was stupid, very stupid.

I spent a depressing afternoon avoiding Andrew Woodward and not mentioning Huw Walker or Bill Burton to anyone. Even the weather conspired to deepen my depression by turning from a bright crisp morning into a cold damp dull afternoon and I had no coat. I'd left it in London due to our hasty departure the previous evening.

Andrew Woodward won the big race and stood beaming in the rain as he received the trophy on behalf of one of his non-paying owners who had had the good sense not to be present.

Beaming, that is, until he saw me watching him. I had carelessly allowed myself to be in view and his expression of thunder showed that his antipathy towards me had deepened.

I'd actually been daydreaming about how I might pluck out one of his unsuspecting hairs to check on his DNA. He had very few remaining on the top of his head and kept those firmly out of sight beneath a brown trilby. It wasn't going to be as easy as Marina had suggested to acquire the necessary follicles, not from him anyway.

I retreated out of his eye-line and found myself

standing on the weighing room steps next to Peter Enstone who was dressed in breeches and boots.

'Hello, Peter,' I said. 'What are you riding?'

'Hi, Sid. I'm on a no-hoper in the last. A waste of space called Roadtrain.'

'Good luck.'

'Thanks.' He turned to go inside, into the warm.

'Oh, Peter,' I called after him, 'do you know how long your father has been a director of Make A Wager Ltd?'

I already knew the answer to my question from the Companies House website but I wanted to see if Peter knew of the connection.

'Oh, for years,' he said. 'Dad helped George set up the company. He's been a director right from the start. Non-executive.'

'Did he know George before the company was formed?'

'Absolutely. We've known George for ever. Sorry, Sid, must dash.'

He disappeared into the changing room, the holy of holies that I was no longer able to enter.

So Jonny Enstone and George Lochs/Clarence Lochstein go back a long way. How did they meet? I wondered.

I sought out Paddy O'Fitch. If anyone here knew the answer it would be him.

'Hi, Paddy.' I found him in the bar under the Berkshire Stand.

'Hello, Sid, me old mucker. D'ya fancy a Guinness?'

'No, Paddy, but I expect you do.'

I ordered a pint of the black stuff for him and a diet Coke for me. It was an unwritten rule that if I were seeking information it would cost me a drink, at least.

He took a long draught, finally appearing for breath with a creamy-white moustache that he wiped away on his left sleeve.

'Now, Sid,' he grinned, 'what is it ya'd be after?'

'Jonny Enstone.'

'Ah,' he said, 'the good lord. What's he done to ya?'

'Nothing. In fact, I recently had lunch with him.'

'Did ya indeed,' he said. 'Did he pay?'

'Absolutely. We were discussing business.'

'What business?'

'His, not yours,' I said with a smile.

'Come on, Sid,' he said, 'I'm the very model of discretion.'

Indiscretion is more like it, I thought. Paddy knew everything there was to know about racing and racing people but he liked others to know he did, so he was forever telling little secrets to anyone who would listen. He didn't do it with any malice, he just did it.

'How about George Lochs?'

'Ah,' he said again, 'young Lochs. Bit of a calculator on legs, he is. Real whiz kid.'

'What might connect George Lochs and Jonny Enstone?' I asked.

'What's this, a quiz?'

'Do you know?'

'Come off it, Sid. Ask me another. Dat one's far too easy.'

'What's the answer then?'

'It's make-a-wager.com.' He smiled broadly. He knew I was impressed. There was a swagger in his manner as he downed the rest of his pint.

'Fancy another?' I asked.

158

'To be sure,' he said. 'I'm not driving today. Got a lift.'

I ordered him another Guinness and I had another Coke. I was driving.

'So what about the good lord and young Lochs?' he asked, after testing the new pint.

'I only wondered how they met,' I said.

'Enstone helped Lochs set up his business. Years ago now. Must be seven or eight at least. Apparently, he put up some money to help start the company and so he became a director. Still is, I think.'

I nodded; I had learned as much from Companies House. 'But how did George Lochs know him to ask for the help in the first place?'

'What are ya up to?' Paddy looked at me quizzically. 'What are ya investigating? Is there a fiddle going on?'

'No, nothing like that, I'm just curious. I met them together at Cheltenham and thought them an odd couple.'

'Both bloody ruthless, if ya ask me,' he said.

'So you don't know how they met then?'

'I didn't say dat.' He smiled again. 'Rumour has it that Peter Enstone knew Lochs first and introduced him to his father. I don't know how Peter met him.'

'Oh, interesting.' I made it sound as though it wasn't that interesting. I finished my drink. 'Thanks, Paddy. See you at Aintree?'

'Absolutely. Wouldn't miss the National.'

'See you there, then. Bye.' I turned to go.

'Is dat all ya want?' he said. 'Was dat really worth a couple of Guinnesses?'

'Not everyone measures things so precisely,' I

said. 'Maybe I just wanted to buy a mate a couple of drinks. For old time's sake.'

'Don't be bloody daft,' he said and laughed.

*   *   *

I hung around for the rest of the afternoon managing not to run into Andrew Woodward. I saw in the racecard that he had a runner in the last so I decided to leave immediately after the race to avoid meeting him again in the car park. I hoped that he would still be busy unsaddling his horse.

Roadtrain, the mount of Peter Enstone, the no-hoper, the waste of space, won by ten lengths at a canter. I glanced at the Tote payout information. Roadtrain had started at odds of 10 to 1 in a five-horse race. If that didn't ring some alarm bells in the Stewards' room nothing would.

I decided not to wait around to find out and made my way with the throng to the exits, coming up behind an unsteady Paddy O'Fitch.

'Hello again, Paddy,' I said. 'Are you all right?'

'To be sure I am,' he said with a slur. 'But I tink I've had a bit too much. All your bloody fault, forcing drink down me throat.'

He wobbled and grabbed hold of an iron fence.

'Are you sure you'll be OK?' I asked again.

'I'll be fine just as soon as me bloody lift arrives.' He peered into the faces of those behind me making their way to the car park.

'Who's giving you a lift?' I asked.

'Chris Beecher. We're neighbours.'

Are you indeed? I thought.

'I'll leave you here, then.' I had no wish to see Chris Beecher today, or any other day.

'Right.' He sagged against the fence. I left him there, still scanning approaching faces with unfocused eyes. He'd be fine.

*   *   *

Marina was feeling much better when I returned to Aynsford, although the bruising around her eyes looked even worse than it had that morning. She and Charles were in the little sitting room and had already started drinking.

'Sun's over the yardarm, I see,' I said, giving Marina a kiss.

'Just a small sharpener before I change for dinner,' said Charles. He waved at the drinks cupboard. 'Help yourself.'

I poured myself a small Scotch with plenty of water. I was determined to take it easier that evening.

'Have you had a good day?' Marina asked.

'No, not really,' I said. 'I had a row with a trainer who I should have kept as a friend, and I was cold and miserable all afternoon. Did you?'

'Yes, as a matter of fact we did.' She smiled across at Charles, who smiled back at her.

'You two look as thick as thieves,' I said.

'We've been talking about last night,' said Charles.

'About the attack?' I asked.

'Yes,' said Marina, 'and also about your fears for me.'

I glared at Charles but he didn't seem to notice.

'Your Marina, here,' he said, 'is a truly lovely girl. I think I'm falling in love again.'

'You're too old,' I said.

161

'Sid!' said Marina. 'That's not very nice. I do believe you're jealous.'

'Nonsense.' But I was. However, not in the way she thought. I wasn't so jealous of Charles liking Marina, more the other way round. Charles was *my* friend, *my* mentor. He was *my* agony aunt, or uncle, and had been now for years. I felt that our conversations should have been in confidence. Not that I would keep secrets from Marina. I just wanted to be the one to tell her myself.

I shook my head and thought that I was being silly. These two people were, to me, the most precious things in the world. Why should I not want them to love each other? So why did I feel so resentful that they had been talking together without me there to act as the intermediary? I told myself to stop being such a fool, but I wouldn't listen.

'So what have you two decided?' I asked rather haughtily. I heard the tone of my own voice and I didn't like it. 'I'm sorry,' I said. 'I didn't mean it to sound like that.'

Marina looked at me. I could feel her stare. She could usually read me like a book and I was sure that all my inner thoughts were, even now, passing through the ether between us.

'We've decided nothing,' she said. 'That's for you to do.'

She spoke softly and comfortingly and I knew that she knew what had just happened. It didn't faze her one bit. She smiled at me and I felt like an idiot.

'It's all right,' she said.

'What's all right?' asked Charles.

'Everything,' I said standing up. 'Do you want a

refill?'

'Oh, yes, thank you.'

I poured a generous whisky and a splash of Malvern Water into his glass and he leaned back contentedly in his chair.

'More for you, my darling?' I asked Marina.

'Just a little.'

I looked deeply into her eyes. 'I do so love you,' I said.

'I love you more,' she replied.

Everything was indeed all right.

*   *   *

Mrs Cross had left us smoked salmon and cream cheese cornets as a starter and a beef casserole in the Aga for our main course. The cornets were small and one-mouthful size so they didn't need cutting. I silently thanked dear, thoughtful Mrs Cross. She always took the one-handed embarrassment out of eating. Marina cooked some rice and we ate in the dining room, formally at the table with silver cutlery and cut-glass crystal. I had never once known Charles to have a meal on his lap.

'So what did you two discuss today?' I asked while we ate the casserole.

'I'm sorry if I broke a confidence between us but I told Marina of our little discussion last night about what it takes to stop you investigating someone.' I realised that Charles had been more astute than I had given him credit for. I should have known better than to think he hadn't understood what had been going on over drinks. One doesn't rise to the rank of Admiral without being susceptible to vibes.

'As I understand things,' said Marina, 'you have a reputation. Villains know that beating you up won't stop you investigating them. In fact, quite the reverse. The more they hurt you, the more determined you become to continue.'

'Something like that.' It sounded rather implausible but I knew it was true.

'So the only way you protect yourself from violence is by not giving up even if you are assaulted. Any potential attacker now doesn't even bother trying because it won't stop you anyway, and will make things worse for them.'

'That's about it,' I said. 'But it has taken a few bad beatings for them to find it out. Times I would rather not remember.'

'But someone beating *me* up has now made you question whether you should go on asking questions about the murders. Is that right?'

'Yes.'

'Because that's what was said to me by my attacker?'

'Yes.'

'So what makes you think that I don't want the same protection? If you stop now because some vicious thug punches me a couple of times in the face, then every time anyone wants you to quit it will be "punch Marina" time.'

'She's right, you know,' said Charles. 'The same goes for me. If it's not "punch Marina" it may be "punch Charles". Neither of us want that burden. Neither of us want our love for you, yes, our love for you, to be a cause for us loving you less. Does that make sense?'

I couldn't speak.

'So let's have no more of this nonsense about not asking questions about the deaths of your friends.' Charles was in 'order giving' mode. 'They, or rather their families, they need you. So get on with it.'

'And,' added Marina, 'if I get beaten up again then all the more reason for carrying on. Let me have the reputation, too.'

'And me,' said Charles. 'Come on, let's have a toast.' He raised his glass of claret. 'Fuck the lot of them!'

I laughed. We all laughed. I'd never heard Charles use such 'below decks' language and certainly never in front of a lady. 'Fuck the lot of them,' we echoed.

*   *   *

I slept the sleep of the reprieved. Deep, dreamless, refreshing sleep.

We had all gone fairly early to bed but not before some further conversation over coffee for us all, plus a brandy for Charles.

'So what will you do now?' he had asked, with his nose deep in his balloon glass drawing up the alcoholic vapours into his lungs.

'As the controllers of my life, what do you two suggest?' I had asked with a grin.

'Well,' Marina had said, 'if the decision is to not heed the warnings about keeping quiet about the deaths, I suggest that you get yourself a bell, go and stand on street corners and shout about them. No point in doing things by halves. Go out there and make a fuss. Show the bastards who's the boss.'

'Good idea,' Charles had agreed with her.

'I'll sleep on it,' I'd said.

So I had.

I positively leapt out of bed the next morning with renewed vigour. The sun had even come back to echo my mood of optimism and I stood by the window looking out at the rolling Oxfordshire countryside, bright with a new day.

I had been brought up by my single mother in Liverpool as a city boy, playing football in the street outside our council flat and going to school at the end of the road. I remembered seeing my first cow when I was aged about twelve and being astonished by the bulbous shape and the enormous size of its udder. For me, milk came out of bottles, not cows. And apples materialised from cardboard boxes in the greengrocers, not from trees, and the very idea that pork chops had once been walking, oinking pigs would have sent me into giggles.

Then, during my race-riding years, I had lived first in Newmarket where I had been an apprentice jockey, and then near Lambourn, when my weight had increased beyond that for the 'flat' and I had converted to the 'jumps'. I had grown to enjoy the rural lifestyle but, after my hand disaster, I had soon moved back to the urban life in London, somehow needing a return to my childhood comfort of being surrounded by concrete, tarmac and brick.

Now, with Marina, I would look again for a change. Back to this calmer, less stressful environment of hills and trees and meandering streams. Back to where a chaffinch may sing from an orchard bough, or a pear tree may blossom in a hedge. 'Oh, to be in England now that April's

166

there'. Browning certainly knew what he was talking about.

Marina was still sound asleep and I decided to leave her that way. When the body is healing, sleep is the best medicine.

I quietly dressed, attached my arm, replaced its exhausted battery pack with one freshly charged, and slipped out and down the stairs. I wanted some time to think, and a wander through the village was just what I needed to energise my brain cells.

Mrs Cross was already in the kitchen busying herself with clearing up last night's dinner and making preparations for breakfast.

'Morning, Mrs Cross,' I said cheerfully.

'Good morning, Mr Halley,' she replied. 'And it is a lovely morning, too.'

'I know, I've seen. I'm going for a walk around the village. Back in about half an hour.'

'Fine,' she said. 'I'll have your breakfast ready on your return.'

'Thank you.' I unlatched the back door. 'Oh, Mrs Cross, Marina and I will be leaving right after lunch today.'

Before the ex-Mrs Halley arrives, I thought, but didn't say so.

'Right you are, sir,' she said.

'I wish you'd call me Sid.'

'I'll try, sir.' She would never change and I realised that I liked her all the more for that.

Aynsford was a peaceful west Oxfordshire village where the march of the metropolis had still to reach. The south of England was all too quickly becoming one joined-up housing estate with thousands and thousands of box-like town houses with postage-stamp gardens springing up around

167

every town. The green belt was doing its best to hold in the expansion of the urban stomach but, at the present rate, the belt would soon run out of holes and burst open altogether.

But, for now, Aynsford remained as it had been for decades, with stone cottages nestling around the Norman church, while the large and imposing old vicarage reflected the power and wealth that the clergy once wielded. Nowadays, the vicar was more likely to live in a small bungalow in a different village, such was the decline in the influence of the Church of England, the fall-off of congregations and the uniting of parishes. I saw from the church notice board that services were on alternate Sundays. It could be worse.

It took me only five minutes to walk to the far end of the village so I continued on down the lane between the high hedgerows to the little humpback bridge over the canal. I sat on the parapet and threw stones into the still, brown water.

Where do I go from here? I thought.

Could I really disregard what had happened to Marina? She had been adamant that I should go on. But we had been lucky. A couple of nasty blows to the face could so easily have been a knife between the ribs. Would I be able to live with myself if anything dreadful were to happen to Marina, or to Charles, as a result of my investigations? Conversely, would I be able to live with myself if I did nothing and stood idly by?

What would happen, I asked myself, if I did nothing more? The inquest on Huw Walker would eventually conclude that he had been murdered by person or persons unknown. That on Bill Burton would say that he had taken his own life while the balance of his mind was disturbed. It would be implied that his mind was disturbed due to the fact that his wife had left him, coupled with his overpowering guilt at having murdered her lover, his jockey. And that would be that, end of investigation, end of story. A miscarriage of justice.

I knew as well as I knew anything that Bill had not killed Huw. In my opinion, it just wasn't possible. So if I did nothing more, then the real killer of Huw, and of Bill, would literally get away with murder and the name of Bill Burton would forever be unfairly tarnished. Was I really considering leaving Bill's family that legacy?

In my heart, I knew that I would continue to search for the truth, but I didn't want to be too hasty. I needed to be comfortable with the decision; at ease, if not exactly relaxed, about the possible consequences. I promised myself that I would be less reckless in the future. That is, if I remembered.

*　　　*　　　*

By the time I made my way back to the house, both Marina and Charles were in the kitchen, munching on toast and marmalade.

'Beginning to think you'd left me,' said Marina.

'Never.'

'Where have you been?' she asked.

'For a walk,' I said. 'I went down to the bridge over the canal.'

'Didn't feel like throwing yourself in, I hope?' said Charles helpfully.

'Not today,' I said. 'Far too cold.'

Mrs Cross had made me scrambled eggs on an

array of inch squares of toast and I gratefully wolfed down the lot.

'My,' said Marina, 'that walk has given you quite an appetite.'

It certainly had and not just for food. I was now itching to get back on the trail of a killer.

After breakfast Marina and I went up to pack our bags, which we put in the car ready for our quick get-away after lunch.

'Are you sure you want to go back to Ebury Street?' I asked her.

'Sure,' she said. 'I am absolutely certain. I'm not going to hide for the rest of my life so I'm not going to do so now. And another thing, I want you to take me to the races in future.'

'OK, you're on.'

We went to join Charles for a pre-lunch drink in his expansive drawing room with its large open fireplace. He had lit the fire and was standing in front of it, warming his back.

'Ah, there you are,' he said. 'Have a glass of bubbles.' He gave us one each from a tray.

'Lovely,' said Marina.

'To you two,' said Charles, raising his glass.

'To all of us,' I said, raising mine.

'Now, when are you two going to get married?' asked Charles.

Marina nearly choked on her champagne.

'We haven't discussed it,' I said.

'You haven't discussed the date?' he persisted.

'We haven't discussed whether.'

'Oh, sorry. I'm a bit premature then.'

'You could say that.'

I am sure that Charles had been a great sailor but, as a diplomat, he still needed lessons.

'I just thought,' Charles went on, digging himself deeper into trouble, 'that you might want to get married from here.'

'We'll talk about it, thank you,' said Marina. 'It's a very kind offer.'

We all smiled at one another, lost for words.

Then, into this domestic tableau as we were discussing whether and where Marina might become the second Mrs Sid Halley, walked the first.

CHAPTER TWELVE

'Hello, Sid,' said Jenny. 'I wasn't expecting *you* to be here.'

You neither, I thought. Surely she wasn't due until much later? Not until after Marina and I had left for London.

'Ah, hello, Jenny,' said Charles all of a fluster. 'I thought you were coming for dinner.'

'Well, we are, but also for lunch. Mrs Cross knew. I spoke to her about it yesterday.'

I wished Mrs Cross had told us.

'Anyway,' said Charles, 'you're here now. Lovely to see you. Where's Anthony?'

'Getting our things out of the car.'

He went over and gave her a peck on the cheek. Charles and Jenny had never really enjoyed an intimate relationship. He had been away at sea for long periods during her early childhood and even the untimely death of Jenny's mother had not brought them close.

Jenny was looking at Marina.

171

'Oh, so sorry,' said Charles. 'Jenny, can I introduce Marina van der—' He tailed off.

'Meer,' I said, adding to Charles's state of unease.

'Yes, that's right, Marina van der Meer—Jenny Wingham, my daughter. Marina is Sid's friend,' he added unnecessarily.

Jenny's eyebrows lifted a notch.

Whilst Charles and I had become somewhat used to the state of Marina's damaged face, to Jenny, on first seeing the ugly black eyes and the still swollen lip, it must have appeared shocking.

'I hope Sid didn't do that,' she said.

'Oh, no,' said Marina with a nervous little laugh. 'Car accident.'

'Who was driving?' asked Jenny.

Unfortunately both Marina and I said 'I was' at the same instant into the sudden small silence.

'Really?' said Jenny sarcastically. 'Collided with each other, did we?'

Thankfully, Anthony arrived at that moment and the matter was dropped.

Sir Anthony Wingham, Baronet, was something in the city, something in banking. I never had been sure what, nor cared. He had inherited pots of cash which is why, I thought cynically, he had proved so attractive to my ex-wife.

Introductions were made and, as usual, Anthony was distinctly cold towards me. I couldn't think why. On our brief and infrequent meetings, he tended to treat me as the enemy. Jenny and I had been separated for many years before she had met him and, whilst it was true that we had actually divorced in order for her to be free to marry, he had absolutely not been the cause of our break-up

172

so I found his attitude somewhat odd. I certainly did not reciprocate it and shook his offered hand with a smile.

The coldness he showed me was more than made up for by the warmth and concern he showered on Marina.

'My dear girl,' he said in a most caring tone, 'what dreadful bad luck.'

That won't endear him to Jenny, I thought, and I was right. Jenny glared at him.

It transpired that they had always been coming to lunch but Charles had forgotten. Mrs Cross, habitually one step ahead of her employer in domestic matters, had laid the table for five and I found myself seated next to Jenny, opposite Anthony.

It was not a memorable occasion with dull, forced conversation. True sentiments were unspoken but communicated, nevertheless. Only Marina had no previous form in this family.

Inevitably, in such circumstances, the discussion tended to be predictable and about Marina: where do you live? what do you do? brothers and sisters? and so on. What I really wanted to ask Jenny and Anthony would have been more interesting: how much is your house worth? how much do you earn? how's your sex life?

'Where did you study?' Anthony asked Marina.

'I was at high school in Harlingen in the Netherlands. That's my home town in the Friesland province, in the north, near the sea. Then I went to university in Amsterdam. I did my doctorate at Cambridge.'

That shut Jenny up.

'And you?' Marina asked back. So diplomatic.

'I went to Harrow and Oxford,' replied Anthony. It rolled off his tongue, a much-repeated couplet.

'Harrow?' asked Marina.

'Yes, Harrow School. It's a boarding school in north-west London. I went there when I was thirteen.'

'So young to be away from home,' said Marina.

'Oh no,' he said, 'I went away to boarding school when I was eight.'

'Didn't your mother hate you going?'

'I don't think so.' He paused. 'I think she was too busy doing good works for charities or going off to the West Indies for the sunshine. I remember being happier at school than I was at home.'

So sad.

'Harrow,' I said. 'I know someone who was at Harrow. But he's younger, so he'd have been there after you.'

Anthony took that as an insult. 'I keep in touch with the old place,' he said. 'What's his name?'

'George Lochs,' I said. 'But when he was at Harrow he was called Clarence Lochstein.'

Anthony thought for a while.

'Sorry,' he said. 'Neither name rings a bell.'

'How would I find out about his time at school?' I asked.

'Not still doing that stupid investigating, are you?' said Jenny.

'Now, now, Jenny,' said her father. 'You know perfectly well that Sid does very well at it and he is much respected in racing circles.'

Jenny didn't actually say so but I could read from her expression that respect in racing circles didn't rate very highly with her. I was sure that she must have read somewhere about Huw Walker, and also about my having found his body at Cheltenham, but I was equally sure that she wouldn't say so in case it was interpreted by Anthony or Charles as her still having some interest in me or in what I did for my living.

'You could always contact the old boys' association,' said Anthony, bringing us back to Harrow. 'They have a resident secretary at the school, chap called Frank Snow. He's a retired housemaster and there's nothing worth knowing about Harrow that he doesn't know.'

'Thanks,' I said. 'I'll give him a call.'

Anthony suddenly looked somewhat irritated with himself, something to do with collaborating with the enemy, no doubt.

Finally, after soup, roast beef and then apple crumble, the lunch was over. Jenny had not failed to notice that Mrs Cross had cut my roast beef into fine strips that I could eat in single-mouthful portions, and that my Yorkshire puddings had been mini ones. She had said nothing, just rolled her eyes and smiled. But I knew that smile. It was more to do with irritation than with humour.

My injuries had been one of the major factors in our lost love.

Steeplechase jockeys get injured. It is an unfortunate but unavoidable consequence of the job. Horses do fall over. Sometimes they fall because they get too close to a fence, and sometimes they fall because they stand off too far from one. Occasionally they trip over other fallen horses that are already lying on the ground, and every so often they simply stumble on landing. The reasons may be varied but the outcome is pretty similar. Half a ton of horseflesh travelling at up to thirty miles an hour crashes to the ground and the jockey goes down with the ship. Eating grass at half a mile a minute becomes an occupational hazard, along with the bruises and the broken bones, the dislocating shoulders and the concussions.

Jenny found she couldn't live with both the deprivations required to keep my riding weight down, and the need to pick up the pieces when things didn't go to plan. Looking back, the injuries were always the catalyst for rows.

*　　　*　　　*

Marina and I made our escape soon after lunch, as we had planned.

Jenny came out to my car as I was loading our last few things.

'How did we ever come to this?' she said.

'To what?' I asked, but I knew.

'To trading insults whenever we meet, to scoring points over one another.'

'It doesn't have to be like that,' I said. 'Are you happy?'

She hesitated. 'Mostly. Are you?'

'Yes,' I said. 'Very.'

'Good, I'm glad. Life with Anthony is more predictable than with you.'

'Less exciting?'

'Yes, that too. If you call spending nights on hospital sofas exciting.'

We laughed. We laughed together. Something we hadn't done for a long time.

Marina, Charles and Anthony came out of the house.

'Take care of yourself,' Jenny said. She stroked my arm, the real one.

'Take care of yourself, too.' I gave her a kiss on the cheek and, just for a moment, there were tears in her eyes.

Marina gave Charles a hug, which seemed to embarrass him somewhat.

'Thank you so much,' she said. 'This was just what I needed. I can go back now and face the world.'

'It was nothing,' said Charles. 'Come whenever you want.'

'Thank you, I will.'

Anthony gave her a peck on the cheek and Jenny didn't seem to mind one bit. I shook hands with them both.

'Thank you again, Charles.'

He waved a hand.

I drove away. In the end, I was thankful that we hadn't avoided Jenny and Anthony.

*   *   *

The following day, Monday, Marina decided not to go in to work. We had both become rather obsessed with security and decided that, for the foreseeable future, I would take Marina to work and collect her every day in my car. I told the reception staff downstairs that on no account were they to allow anyone up to my flat without calling up on the internal phone system first to check with me that they were welcome. Absolutely, Mr Halley, they had said. They never would, anyway.

I called Harrow School and asked to speak to Frank Snow. They were sorry, they said, but

Mr Snow is only in his office on Tuesday and Thursday mornings. Would I like to leave a message or call back? I would call back. Fine.

I phoned Archie Kirk to give him an update on my lack of progress with the internet gambling. I had a few questions still to ask and would get back to him soon, I said. Good, he replied, and hung up. Never trust anyone, not even a telephone.

I sat for a while in my office tidying up my e-mail inbox. I was restless.

Marina came in and caught me playing cards on my computer.

'For goodness' sake, Sid, go out and investigate. I thought we'd been through all this. Yesterday you were gagging to find the killer so why this change of heart all of a sudden?'

I shrugged.

'I told you,' she said, 'I want the same protection as you, I want the same reputation.'

'Are you sure?'

'Yes. Now get a bloody move on and stop wasting time.'

'Right,' I said, standing up. 'Action stations.'

*   *   *

I decided to go and see Kate Burton and the children, and Marina came with me.

I had telephoned Daphne Rogers to find out if Kate was still staying with her. No, she'd said, Kate and the children went home two days ago. So I had called Kate at home and she was delighted that we were coming.

I drove into the familiar driveway and pulled up outside the back door. Immediately the children came running out to greet us. Life seemed to be back to normal, deceptively normal.

The children dragged us both into the kitchen where Kate was waiting. She looked little better than when I had seen her last. Her eyes showed the signs of a great deal of crying and she looked thinner, almost gaunt.

'Sid, how lovely to see you.' She gave me a kiss.

'Kate, this is Marina—Marina, Kate.'

'You poor thing, what happened to your face?'

'A car accident,' said Marina.

'How dreadful,' said Kate. 'Come and have a coffee.'

The children went out to play in the garden while the three of us sat in the same kitchen at the same table where, just a week previously, a mere seven days ago, I had sat with Bill. It seemed like a lifetime since. It was.

'I thought you might still be with your mother,' I said.

'I wanted to come back here as soon as possible. The police wouldn't let me in until Saturday. They were doing tests or something.'

And clearing up, I thought.

'How about the horses?' I asked.

'All gone,' she said, tears welling up in her eyes. 'The last ones went yesterday. Nothing else for it.'

I took her hand. 'How's the house?'

'Oh, fine. Have to sell it now, I suppose. I don't really want to stay here any more, not after what's happened. I wanted to come back to feel closer to Bill, but I haven't been into the den, and I don't think I want to. Just in case there's . . .'

In case there's a mess, I thought.

There was a long pause.

179

'I was brought up in this house. Only for the first three years after getting married have I ever lived anywhere else. Bill and I moved in here together when Daddy retired. It will seem strange to sell the place and leave permanently.' She paused again. 'How *could* he have done this to the children?' said Kate. 'I'm so bloody angry with him that I'd shoot him myself if he was still here.'

She started crying so I put my arms round her and held her close.

'Kate,' I said into her ear, 'I am absolutely certain that Bill didn't kill himself. And I'm sure he didn't kill Huw Walker either. And I intend to prove it.'

She pulled away from me and looked into my eyes. 'Do you really mean that or are you saying it to make me feel better?'

'I really mean it. I am sure that Bill was murdered.'

'Kate,' said Marina, touching her arm, 'I'm sure Sid will find out who did it.'

Kate smiled. 'I do so hope you're right. At first, I couldn't think why Bill would have killed himself. I am sure he would never leave the children in that way. It must have been a mistake or an accident but the police have kept telling me that he did it because he couldn't stand the guilt for having killed Huw.' She hung her head in her hands. 'How I so wish that I hadn't got involved with Huw.'

'Would it be all right, Kate,' I said, 'if I were to have a look in the den?'

'What for?' she asked, raising her head. 'I never want to go in there again. I locked the door when we got home and none of us have been in since. But, yes, I suppose it's all right. I mean, the police

180

haven't said we can't go in.'

'I want to go and look for something.'

'What?'

'Something that might show that Bill didn't kill himself.'

'Oh,' she said. 'Go on, then.' She got up and took a key from the top shelf of the Welsh dresser and gave it to me. 'But I'm staying here.'

'Fine.'

'And I'll stay with you,' said Marina.

'I may be a while,' I said.

'That's OK,' said Marina, 'take your time.'

I left them making themselves another cup of coffee and went through into the hallway, and then into the den.

It was much the way I remembered it. A leather sofa lay along the wall next to the door and the far end of the room was filled from floor to ceiling with bookcases containing racing books of all sorts, together with one shelf absolutely crammed full of videotapes. A large flat-screen television sat in one corner with video and DVD players beneath.

There was only one armchair where there used to be two. The other, I suspected, had been removed for forensic testing and then had probably been disposed of. Quite apart from the blood staining from the back of Bill's head, there would have been a pooling of fluids in the seat due to the natural processes that occur at death. I shivered, whether from cold or from the thought of too much knowledge, I wasn't sure.

There was a paisley-patterned rug covering about half the dark wooden floor and a few occasional tables dotted about.

I looked at the wall where I had seen the blood

181

last Wednesday morning. Someone had done their best to get rid of the redness from the cream paint but thorough redecoration would be needed to remove completely the brown deposit that remained.

I looked carefully at the stain. I could see, near the top, where the police must have dug the bullet from the plaster. It had passed right through Bill's skull and embedded itself in the wall, but not very deeply.

If Bill had not shot himself, then how did the gunpowder residue get on his hands? His hand had to have fired the gun. On the assumption that the gun wasn't forced into his mouth with *his* finger on the trigger, then there had to be a second shot. In my opinion, this would have had to have been fired after Bill was dead. The murderer would have put the gun into Bill's hand and used his dead finger to fire it.

So where is the second bullet?

I moved the remaining armchair into the place where I had seen Bill sitting when he died. I sat down on the chair. I was looking at the bookcases and the television. The bullet clearly hadn't gone into the television because the screen was unbroken, so I started with the books.

I removed the contents of each shelf in turn, checking both the books themselves and the wooden bookcase behind them. It took me ages and I turned up some surprising finds. One of the books was not a book at all but a secret hiding place. The centre of the book had been hollowed out and Bill had used the space to keep some gold coins. Behind a row of racing *Timeforms*, he had hidden a couple of men's magazines with well-thumbed pages, and there were two old-style fivers neatly pressed between the pages of Tolstoy's *War and Peace*. There were also a couple of old letters to Bill from people I didn't recognise, one concerning a horse for sale and the other about a holiday villa in Portugal. But no bullet, and no bullet hole.

I scrutinised all the surfaces of the bookcases and where they met the walls. I looked into the flap on the front of the video player to see if I could see any damage. I lifted the rug and looked at the wooden floor to see if a hole existed. I pored over every square inch of the leather sofa and inspected every thread of the cushions. I moved the sofa and the tables and looked under them all for a tell-tale bullet hole in the floor or a wall. I searched behind the curtains and in the pelmets, even though these had predominantly been behind Bill as he sat in the chair. I examined every nook and cranny that existed in that room. I missed nothing.

In the end, I had a few coins and a ball point pen from down the back of the sofa, a piece of a jigsaw puzzle and dust from underneath it, and some fine, gritty, sand-like material from the paisley rug. No bullet. No cartridge case. Nothing. Not a thing that could indicate that a second shot had been fired.

I sat down again in the chair, exhausted and fed up.

Was I wrong?

I had been so sure that a second bullet existed. I'd thought I just needed a quick search to find it and that would be enough to convince Inspector Johnson that I was right and he would reopen the case.

But now what?

Was there any other way of getting the gunpowder residue on to Bill's hand and sleeve?

I looked out at the garden. Had the second bullet been fired out through an open window?

I went back into the hall and let myself out through the front door. I spent some time looking but could find nothing. It was a hopeless task, I thought. If the bullet had been fired out here, it could have gone anywhere. But it would have been risky. Quite apart from hitting something that couldn't be seen in the dark, it would have been much noisier out here than with the windows closed. There would also have been the risk of someone hearing the noise and investigating before an escape could be made.

I didn't know the answer. Was I even asking the right question?

I went back inside the house and through to the kitchen.

Kate and Marina had been joined by the children who were sitting at the table, ready for their lunch.

'Any luck?' asked Marina quietly.

I shook my head.

'Would you like some lunch?' asked Kate.

'No, it's fine, thanks,' I said. 'We've taken up too much of your time already. We'll be off.'

'Are you sure? There's plenty.'

'Please stay,' said William.

'Yes, stay, pleeeeeeease,' chorused the others.

'OK,' I said, laughing.

Kids were a great tonic for the soul.

We stayed, squeezed round the kitchen table, and ate a hearty lunch of fish fingers, baked beans and mashed potato, with chocolate ice cream to follow. Wonderful.

After lunch, the children took Marina up to their bedrooms to show her their toys and I went for a walk round the stable yard. I had happy memories of many hours spent here, teaching young horses to jump on the schooling grounds beyond the hay barn.

I had ridden here first for Kate's father when I was about nineteen and had done so on and off until I had been forced to retire.

But my memories were of a place buzzing with activity, a living, energetic factory of thrills and excitement. Now it stood empty and quiet like a wild-west ghost town. The *Marie Celeste* of the racing world with straw still on the floor of some boxes and hay nets still hanging in others. It was as if the effort of clearing up had been too much and when the horses walked out, so did the staff.

I wandered around the lifeless buildings and wondered who would next occupy this establishment. Perhaps it was time for the timber stables to be torn down and replaced with warmer, fireproof brick.

I made my way back to the house. Beside the gate from the yard sat a red fire extinguisher and a red-painted metal bucket filled with sand. Some of the stable staff had put out cigarettes in the sand and left the stubs standing upright as if they had been thrown in like little brown darts. I was sure that if Bill had still been alive the lads wouldn't have dared dispose of their fag ends in the fire buckets.

I went through the gate, and then stopped. Fine, gritty, sand-like material.

I went back to the bucket and tipped the whole thing out on the concrete path. I went through it with my fingers and there it was, a lump of lead, slightly misshapen but still identifiable as a .38 bullet.

CHAPTER THIRTEEN

'You've found another *what*?' said Chief Inspector Carlisle.

'Another bullet,' I said.

'Where?' he asked.

'At Bill Burton's place. Can I come and see you to explain?'

He sighed. I could hear it down the telephone line.

'Do you have to? I'm up to my ears here. The Press are after me for failing to arrest a child killer. I'm exhausted.'

'I'll come now. It won't take long but it's easier face to face.'

What I really wanted was his undivided attention. I didn't want him looking at his computer screen and thinking of his other case while I prattled on to him over a wire.

'Oh, all right. I can give you half an hour, no more. How soon can you get here?'

Lambourn to Cheltenham, Monday afternoon.

'About fifty minutes max,' I said.

'OK. See you then. Bye.' He disconnected and I realised that he had his problems, too. The Press can be merciless on the police for not catching a killer, especially a child killer, whilst, at the same

186

time, accusing them of having too many powers. A no-win situation.

Marina was talked into staying with Kate and the children while I drove to Cheltenham.

I made it to the police station in forty-five minutes flat but Carlisle kept me waiting for fifteen minutes more before he hurried into the reception area. This time I accepted his invitation to join him in one of the interview rooms.

'Now, what is all this about another bullet?' he asked. 'Where is this bullet? Where did you find it? What is so important about it that brings you all the way here?'

Your undivided attention, I thought.

'All in good time,' I said. 'We are going to play a little game of "Let's suppose" first.'

' "Let's suppose"? I've never heard of that.'

'Well, it's quite simple really. You sit there quietly without asking any questions and I'll do the talking.'

'All right, if I must.'

I smiled. 'You must.'

He leant back and tipped the metal chair on to its back legs. My mother had always told me off for doing that, but I resisted the temptation to say so.

'Now let's suppose that Bill Burton didn't kill himself,' I said.

'That's up to the coroner,' said Carlisle.

'I said no talking—please.'

'Sorry.'

'Let's suppose Bill didn't shoot himself. There was indisputable evidence that he was shot, so someone else must have murdered him. But there was also gunpowder residue on Bill's hand and sleeve so he did fire a gun, probably the gun that killed him. Now, he could have shot the gun before he was murdered or his dead hand could have been used afterwards so that the residue would appear on his hand. Yes?'

'Yes,' said Carlisle, 'but—'

'No buts, not yet, we're still playing "Let's suppose".'

He closed his mouth and crossed his arms over his chest, a typical body-language movement showing displeasure and/or disbelief.

'Either way, there had to be a second bullet.'

'And, I *suppose*, you found it?' he said.

'Yes, I did.'

'Where?' he asked.

'I searched the den where Bill was killed,' I said. 'I searched every inch of that room and didn't find anything.' I took the misshapen lump out of my pocket and put it on the table in front of him. 'It was in a sand-filled fire bucket in the stable yard.'

Carlisle brought his chair back to earth with a clatter, and he bent forward to look first at the lump of lead and then up at me.

'What on earth made you look there?' he said. He picked up the bullet and rolled it around between his fingers. 'Perhaps Burton had a practice shot into the fire bucket outside in the yard first to make sure the gun was working. Perhaps he didn't want the thing to misfire when he put it in his mouth.'

'I thought of that, too,' I replied, 'but there are a number of things which don't add up. Firstly, you've proved that it was the same gun that killed both Bill Burton and Huw Walker and since it had fired perfectly well the week before, why did it need testing? Secondly, why would Bill replace the empty case in the gun with a fresh bullet so that there was only one fired cylinder? And, thirdly, there was a trace of sand on the rug in the den which tells us that the bucket had been brought there from the yard, so why would he bother to take the bucket back outside if he was about to make a bloody mess in the den anyway?'

'Hmm,' said the Chief Inspector. 'He might have tested the gun before he went to Cheltenham races. There's nothing on that bullet to say it was fired the day he died.'

'True,' I said, 'but what about the sand on the rug? Kate Burton told me they have a cleaner who comes in once a week on Mondays. Also, Bill would *never* have fired a gun in the yard close to the horses. If he'd wanted to test the weapon, he would have walked off into the fields to do it and fired into the ground.'

And, I thought, if he had wanted to shoot himself he would have gone into the same fields to do it.

'So what do you want me to do about it?' asked Carlisle.

'Reopen the case,' I said. 'You're a detective, so detect.'

'The case isn't shut.'

'All but. Order Inspector Johnson to start believing that Bill Burton didn't kill himself and that he was murdered.'

'I can't order him to do anything.'

'Why not? You're a chief, he's an injun.'

'It doesn't work like that and you know it. He's in a different police force. But I will speak with him about this.' He held up the bullet, then looked at his watch. 'Now, I must get on. I have a team of

189

over a hundred officers to brief in ten minutes.'

'Any luck with the little girl?' I asked.

'No,' he said gloomily. 'Poor little mite would have been eleven tomorrow. Breaks my heart to see the parents in such pain. Wish they'd bring back hanging for child murder. Give me the rope, and I'll do it.'

'Good luck,' I said and we shook hands warmly.

'I *suppose* I'll need it,' he said and smiled.

He wasn't a bad chap, for a copper.

*   *   *

I picked up Marina from Lambourn and we drove back to London against the rush-hour traffic.

'What did the policeman say?' she asked as soon as we had driven away.

'I think it's safe to say he wasn't wholly convinced by my argument,' I replied. 'Poor man is too wound up with this child murder. I think he'll probably speak with the man from Thames Valley Police but I don't hold out much hope that they'll put a team back on the case.'

'You'll just have to do it yourself, then,' said Marina.

'Did you have a nice afternoon with Kate?' I asked, changing the subject.

'Lovely,' she said. 'Those children seem very resilient after what has happened. Except William. He's a little quiet and moody.'

'How about Kate?'

'Poor girl. She blames herself. We had a good long chat over tea while the children watched television. She thinks everyone will blame her for Bill's death.'

190

'I expect they will,' I said, 'but I doubt that they'll do it to her face.'

'She said that she was seduced by Huw Walker, that she made no moves to get him.'

Huw almost certainly saw Kate as a challenge, I thought. 'I expect she's trying to shift some blame on to him for her own peace of mind.'

'It had obviously been going on for a while,' said Marina.

'I can't think how,' I said. 'Racehorse trainers are at home lots of the time and, when they are away, they're at the races where Huw would have been.'

'Well, clearly they did manage it, and often. Kate implied that Huw was great in bed.'

'You two really did have a good chat.'

'Yes, I like her. She also told me that recently Huw had been really worried about something. He wouldn't tell her what exactly but he'd said that it was all about power and not about money. Does that make sense?'

'Mmm. Perhaps it does,' I said. 'Maybe Huw was fixing races not because he enjoyed the financial rewards but because he felt it gave him even more power over Bill—screw his wife *and* his business.'

We drove down the Cromwell Road in silence.

'So what are you going to do now?' said Marina as we turned into Beauchamp Place.

'About what?'

'About the murders, of course.'

'Take a bell, and go and stand on street corners and shout.'

'Good boy.'

'It's dangerous.'

'Then we'll take precautions,' said Marina. 'You

191

take me to work, as agreed, and collect me and I'll be very careful not to talk to strangers.' She laughed.

'It's not a laughing matter.'

'Yes, it is. If you can't laugh, you'd go mad.'

We carefully checked every dark shadow in the garage and chuckled nervously at each other as we continually looked round like Secret Service agents guarding a president. However, I was right. It was definitely not a laughing matter.

We made it safely to our flat and locked ourselves in for the night.

*   *   *

In the morning I drove Marina to work. She had woken feeling much better and the ugly bruises to her face were, at last, beginning to recede.

I parked the car outside the London Research Institute in Lincoln's Inn Fields and we went inside and up to Marina's lab to see the results of our DNA work on Friday night.

'I have to bake the gel on to photographic paper to be able to see the results. I'll need some help. Rosie, probably. She spends all her time doing DNA profiles but mostly of fruit flies.'

'Fruit flies?' I asked.

'Yes. Parts of their DNA are not wildly different from that in humans. She's in a team that is trying to find out how cancers develop. Fruit flies are quite good for that and they reproduce quickly. No one minds if you kill a few fruit flies in an experiment. Less controversial than rabbits or monkeys.'

We went down the corridor to find Rosie who

was deeply disturbed by Marina's two black eyes. Rosie stared at me and was clearly asking herself if I were the guilty party but Marina introduced me in glowing terms and trotted out the car accident story again. I wasn't sure if Rosie was much reassured.

'Rosie, darling, can you help me with a DNA profile?' asked Marina.

'Sure. Do you have the sample?'

'I've already done the electrophoresis.' Marina gave her the square of gel.

'Right,' said Rosie, turning to the bench behind her and fitting the gel matrix into a machine. 'Ready in a few minutes.'

While she waited, she chased an escaped fruit fly around the lab. The fly was very small and difficult to see but she eventually trapped it in a clap between her hands.

'How do you do experiments on things so small?' I asked.

'We use microscopes to look at them. There,' she said pointing at a microscope on the bench, 'have a look down that.'

I leant over and looked down the double eyepieces. Fruit flies in all their glory, big, easy to see, and very dead.

'You see? They're not really that small, not compared to cells,' she said. 'Cells are so small, we need to use an electron microscope to see them.'

I decided not to ask how an electron microscope worked. I was feeling inadequate enough already as I couldn't have caught the fly between my two hands. I couldn't even clap, with or without a fly.

The machine behind her emitted a small beep and Rosie removed what looked like an early

Polaroid photograph from a small door in its side.

'This isn't from a fruit fly,' she said. 'Looks human to me. Anyone I know?'

'I hope not,' said Marina.

'So it wasn't a road accident?' said Rosie.

Rosie was a smart cookie, I thought.

'I'm going to have to go,' I said, 'or I'll get a parking ticket on the car.'

'Or it'll be towed away,' said Marina. 'They're dreadful round here.'

'Be careful, my love.' I gave her a kiss.

'I'll look after her,' said Rosie.

'Do that,' I said.

I went down and retrieved my car from under the gaze of a traffic warden with just one minute remaining of my time. He didn't look happy.

I drove round the corner and stopped to ring Frank Snow at Harrow.

'Yes,' he said, 'I'll be in the office on Thursday and you are welcome to come and see me. What is it about?'

'A former pupil,' I replied.

'We don't discuss former pupils with the media,' he told me.

'I'm not media,' I said.

'Who are you then?'

'I'll tell you on Thursday. See you about nine?'

'Make it ten.' He sounded unsure. 'Come for coffee, if you must.'

'Right,' I said. 'Coffee at ten on Thursday. Thanks. Bye.'

*   *   *

Instead of going back to the flat, I went to the

races. I needed a street corner to ring my bell and shout from.

Towcester Racecourse is set in the beautiful surroundings of the Easton Neston Estate to the west of Northampton. My spirits were high, as was the sun, as I turned through the impressive arched and pillared entrance into the car park. I chose my parking space carefully, not only to avoid another confrontation with Andrew Woodward, but also to make a physical ambush between car and racecourse entrance more difficult. I had been caught out like that once before.

I went in search of my prey. As always, he was in the bar nearest to the weighing room in the ground floor of the Empress grandstand.

'Hello, Paddy,' I said.

'Hello, Sid, what brings you all the way to Northamptonshire?'

'Nothing much. How come you're here?'

'Oh, I lives just down the road. This is me local course.'

I knew, that's why I had come. I was pretty sure he'd be here, and I was pretty sure he'd be in this bar before the first race.

'Now what can I do for ya, Sid?' he asked.

'Nothing, Paddy.'

I looked around the bar which was filling up with those looking for a drink and a sandwich before the entertainment began.

'Are ya going to buy me a drink?' said Paddy.

'Now why would I want to do that?' I replied.

'It's high time you bought me one.'

'Don't ya want to ask me anything?'

'No. What about?'

We stood for some time in silence and I could

tell that I would die of thirst before Paddy put his hand in his pocket so I ordered myself the ubiquitous diet Coke and stood there drinking it.

'Well, why are ya here then?' said Paddy.

'I'm meeting someone,' I replied.

'Who?' he asked.

'Never you mind.'

'What about?'

'It's none of your business.'

Paddy's antennae were almost quivering and he could hardly contain himself. He absolutely hated not being 'in the know' about everything. He finally bought a Guinness to calm his nerves.

Charles came through the door at the far end. I had called him on the drive north, had very briefly explained to him my little game and he had eagerly agreed to help. He had brought with him a distinguished-looking white-haired gentleman in a tweed suit and a dark blue bow-tie.

'Ah,' I said and walked over to greet them, leaving Paddy at the bar.

'Hello, Charles,' I said. 'Thanks so much for coming.'

'Sid,' he said, 'meet Rodney Humphries.'

We sat down on some chairs at a table. I checked to see that we were still in Paddy's view and caught a glimpse of him staring at us. We spoke with our heads bowed close together and, from Paddy's position, it must have appeared quite conspiratorial.

'Rodney lives down the road from me,' said Charles. 'He was keen as mustard to come.'

'Any excuse not to do the gardening,' said Rodney with a smile.

'Well, Rodney, if anyone asks you, which they

probably won't, you can give a fictitious name and say that you're a retired professor of ballistics.'

'Professor of ballistics, eh? I like that. Retired from anywhere special?' he asked.

'Anywhere obscure that no one could check up on.'

He thought for a moment. 'Professor Reginald Culpepper from the University of Bulawayo, in Rhodesia. In the good old days of UDI, which is when I was out there. That should do. No one will be able to check on that now that it's Zimbabwe.'

'Perfect,' I said, 'but I hope you won't need it.'

I watched Paddy out of the corner of my eye. He was a good sort and I felt a little guilty treating him in this way but it was important.

'Why don't you just tell . . . what's his name?' said Charles.

'Paddy, Paddy O'Fitch.'

'Well, why don't you just tell Paddy O'Fitch what you want him to know?'

'Because I want him to tell the right person what he knows and, unless he thinks it's a secret, he might not do that.'

'I don't understand,' said Charles.

'Secrets burn holes in Paddy's brain until they reach his mouth. The more secret a thing is, the more likely he is to tell someone. It's not that he's malicious, it's just that he absolutely loves to know something that others don't and he can't resist telling them.'

'So who's the right person?' asked Charles.

'A journalist called Chris Beecher.'

I could see Paddy moving over towards us. He obviously couldn't resist any longer.

'So Professor,' I said loudly, so Paddy would

hear, 'what is your expert opinion?'

Before Rodney/Reginald could say anything I made great play of putting my finger to my lips.

'Good afternoon, Admiral,' Paddy said, arriving at our table. He had known who Charles was, but there again, Paddy knew everything. Well, almost everything.

'Good afternoon,' replied Charles, getting up.

Neither Charles nor I made any move to introduce Rodney. Charles sat down again and the three of us waited in silence. Paddy eventually seemed to get the message and moved away.

'See you later then, Sid,' he said.

'Right.'

He went off towards the door but couldn't resist a backwards glance as he went through it.

'I bet you a pound to a penny that he will be hanging around outside to catch me when I leave.'

'But I still don't understand,' said Charles. 'Why do you need him to tell this journalist? Why don't you tell the journalist yourself?'

'If I went and told Chris Beecher something directly then he probably wouldn't believe me in the first place and, even if he did, he wouldn't write it in the newspaper because he would think that I only told him because I wanted him to. This way, if Paddy extracts the secret from me, which I will let him do eventually, and moreover if I tell him that under no circumstances to repeat it to anyone, he's bound to go and blabber it to his neighbour, who just happens to be Chris Beecher, and Beecher will put it in his newspaper solely because he thinks I don't want it there.'

'And what is this great secret?' asked Rodney. 'Or can't I know?'

'Yes,' said Charles, 'can I know too?'

'Sorry,' I said, 'of course you can know. In fact, you should know in case you are approached by Paddy or anyone else. It's not actually a secret at all and I want everyone to know. It just has to appear to be a secret to Paddy, and also to Chris Beecher. It's simply that I found a second bullet at Bill Burton's place and also that I *know* he didn't kill himself and the police are now looking for his murderer.'

'And are they?' asked Charles.

'Well, not exactly, but Chris Beecher won't know that.'

'I'm none the wiser,' said Rodney.

'It's a long story. Charles will fill you in. I want to go now so that Paddy can begin to needle me. If he asks you, say I asked you to look at a second bullet. Enjoy your day at the races.'

'I will. Do you have any tips?' Rodney asked.

'He'll tell you to keep your money in your pocket,' said Charles.

I laughed. He knew me too well.

I went out to the parade ring. As expected, Paddy came up to me as I watched the runners for the first.

'Who's the professor then?' he asked.

I looked suitably appalled that he knew he was a professor. 'None of your business.'

'Come on, Sid. What's he doing here?'

'I just wanted some advice. Nothing important.'

I hoped he didn't believe me. I moved onto the stands to watch the race and he followed, as I knew he would. He was now on a mission.

'So what advice could he give ya that I couldn't?'

'You don't know anything about ballistics.'

'Ballistics? What the bloody hell is dat?'

'Exactly! You know nothing about it. So I found someone who does.'

'What is it?'

'Look, Paddy,' I said, 'I told you, it's none of your business.'

He was about to ask again when thankfully he was cut off by the public address system. 'They're under starter's orders . . . they're off.'

I had always enjoyed riding here and I watched enviously as others did what I longed to do. Towcester is a 'park' racecourse set amongst rolling green hills. The fences are inviting and fair but the real challenge for a horse is the last mile to the finish, which is all uphill. The horses passed the stands for the first time and turned right-handed and downhill to start their second circuit, all twelve still packed closely together.

I noticed that Paddy had left my side and had made his way to the end of the stand where he was in earnest conversation with someone I didn't recognise, sadly not Chris Beecher.

On the far side of the course, one jockey kicked his mount hard in the ribs and they started to move away from the others in their bid for victory. Much too soon, I thought. Many a race had been lost here by horse and rider who have run out of puff on the long incline to the last fence and the finish line. It was an impressive break and soon the horse had established a lead of twenty lengths or more. None of the others seemed to have responded to the move, and I would not have done so either. Experienced jockeys know a thing or two, and going too soon at Towcester is one of them. It was not the way to win races.

At the second last fence, the leader was still in front but by a much-reduced margin that was diminishing with every tired stride. By the last he had been caught by the others and would not have won even if he had not come to grief in a bone-crunching fall.

Statistically, at every racecourse, more horses fall at the last fence than at any other, due mainly to tiredness. The last at Towcester has been the scene of more than its fair share of disasters, and today was no exception.

A close finish was fought out between two of the country's leading riders who had bided their time and made their runs late. A job well done. The crowd cheered them home with enthusiasm.

Paddy reappeared at my side.

'Now, what do ya want to know about bullets for?' he asked.

'How do you know I do?'

'Dat's what ballistics is all about,' he said proudly.

'So?'

'Your professor,' he said.

'It's none of your business.'

'So which bullets are ya interested in?' he persisted. 'Is it the one dat killed Huw Walker or the one dat killed Bill Burton?'

'Neither,' I replied.

'Well, what other ones are there, then?'

'Never you mind.'

I watched with relief as both the horse and jockey who had fallen at the last finally rose to their respective feet and walked away from the experience, bruised but not broken.

'So there are other bullets?' asked Paddy.

201

'I'm not saying another word,' I said.

'Aw, come on, Sid, me old mate, are there other bullets?'

'One other bullet.'

'Great!' said Paddy. He thought he was getting somewhere. 'Who was shot with it?'

'No one.'

He looked disappointed. 'Well, why is it important, then?'

'Did I say it was important?' I asked.

'Stands to reason,' he said. 'Why else would ya get a professor?'

'Look, I found another bullet and I wanted some advice about it, OK? Nothing important.'

'Where did ya find it?'

'Come on, Paddy, what is this—Twenty Questions? Leave it alone, will you?'

'But where did ya find it?'

'I said, leave it alone. I don't want everyone to know.'

'If ya tell me, I won't have to go on asking questions now, will I?'

'You could just stop asking questions anyway,' I pointed out.

'Bejesus, dat's not me nature.' He grinned at me.

'I found a bullet in a sand bucket at Bill Burton's stable yard, OK?' I said. 'I wanted it checked by a ballistics expert.'

'But why?' asked Paddy. 'What did ya want him to check about it?'

'I told you, Paddy, I don't want everyone to know about it.'

'But what did ya want him to check?'

I sighed. 'If it was fired from the same gun as

that which killed Bill Burton.'

He looked confused. 'So, what if it had?'

Eventually, I told him everything. I told him that I was certain that Bill Burton had not killed himself and that he had been murdered. I told him about the gunpowder residue on Bill's hand and sleeve and why there must have been a second shot fired. I told him about searching for the bullet and finding it. I made up a bit about having the bullet checked by my professor and about it having come from the same gun. I also told him that the police were now investigating Bill's death as murder and not as suicide. I hoped I was right.

I told Paddy everything twice to ensure he had all the details and then I told him not to tell anyone else.

'Ya can trust me,' he said.

I hoped I could do just that.

I went in search of Charles and Rodney and found them in the bar drinking champagne.

'So, have you passed your message?' asked Charles.

'Indeed I have. I only hope I didn't make it so much of a secret that Paddy doesn't actually tell. Now, what's with this fizz?'

'We got the winner of the second race, but this bloody bottle of bubbles cost us more than our winnings,' said Charles with a grin. 'Help yourself.'

I did and much enjoyed their company for a while, without Paddy snapping at my heels.

*　　　*　　　*

I left the races after the third in order to get back to Lincoln's Inn Fields to collect Marina at five

203

thirty.

She came bounding out across the pavement and into the car. Rosie was standing in the entrance and I waved to her as we drove away.

'Rosie is like a chaperone,' said Marina. 'She won't even let me go to the loo without her.'

'Good,' I said. 'Have you had a good day?'

'Much the same as always,' she said, sighing. 'In fact, I've had enough of this job. We heard today that somebody likes the results so much that the project, which was originally only for three years, is going to be extended for another couple of years at least. They want me to stay for the extension but I'm not sure if I will.'

'What will you do instead?'

'Don't know.'

'Something in London?'

There must have been some concern in my voice.

'I'm thinking of leaving my job,' she said, 'not you.'

She stroked my arm. That was all right then.

CHAPTER FOURTEEN

There was nothing about any second bullet or the Sid Halley theories on the Chris Beecher page of *The Pump* on Wednesday morning. I had bought a copy on my way back to the flat after taking Marina to work. Rosie had been waiting for her at the front door and Marina had rolled her eyes at me as she climbed out of the car. I had laughed.

I parked the car in the garage under the

building, went upstairs and searched the paper from start to finish. Nothing.

I was beginning to doubt my assessment of Paddy's character when Charles telephoned me.

'I've just had a call from someone who said that you had said that he could check with me the name of the ballistics professor you had consulted.'

'Really?' I said. 'And did you give them his name?'

'I couldn't remember it.' He laughed. 'So I made another one up. Rodney is now Professor Aubrey Winterton, retired from the University of Bulawayo—I could remember that bit.'

Aubrey Winterton/Reginald Culpepper, it didn't matter so long as no one was able to show that he didn't exist.

'And did this individual have an Irish accent?' I asked.

'No,' said Charles, 'he did not.'

'I wonder who he was.'

'I dialled 1471 to get his number and then I phoned back,' said Charles.

'And?'

'The number was for *The Pump*. I got through to the switchboard.'

'Thank you, Charles.' I was impressed. 'If you need a job, you can be my new assistant.'

'No thanks,' said Charles. 'I like to give orders, not take them.'

'Be my boss then.'

He laughed and disconnected.

Good old Paddy, I thought. I knew he wouldn't be able to resist telling.

Bejesus, dat was his nature.

I spent the morning writing a preliminary report for Archie Kirk.

I hadn't actually discovered any link between internet gambling and organised crime but I reported that I did believe there was potential for the craze of gambling on-line, and especially on-line gaming, to be abused by criminals.

The end user of the service, that is the gambler logged on to sites with his or her home computer, is placing a large amount of trust in the website operators to run their service properly and fairly.

For example, a game of roulette conducted on-line requires the player to place stakes on a regular roulette table pattern: numbers 1–36, 0 and 00, red and black, odd and even, and so on. The wheel, however, is a creation of the computer and does not actually exist, and neither does the ball. How can the player be sure that the computer-generated 'ball' will move randomly to fill one of the slots on the computer-generated 'wheel'? It would seem that without this trust between player and wheel the game would not profit, but players of current sites seem to accept this trust without question. I knew that the computers used were extremely powerful machines and, no doubt, they could be used to calculate, as the 'ball' was rolling, which number would provide for the lowest payout by the 'house' and ensure that the 'ball' finished there.

Similarly, in all games of dice or cards, the 'roll' of the 'dice' or the 'deal' of the 'cards' are computer images and consequently have the potential to be controlled by a computer and not be as random as the players might hope and expect.

I concluded that, as many of these operations are run from overseas territories, it remained to be seen if regulations there were sufficient. I believed that the current trend for self-regulation left much to be desired.

As to the question of internet 'exchanges', as used for betting on horse racing and other sports, I concluded that the scope for criminal activity was no more prevalent than that which existed in regular bookmaker-based gambling. The significant difference was that, whereas in the past only licensed bookmakers were effectively betting on a horse to lose, anyone could now do so by 'laying' a horse on the exchanges. It was potentially easier to ensure a horse lost a race than won it. Over-training it too close to a race or simply by keeping it thirsty for a while and then giving it a bellyful of water just before the off, were both sure ways to slow an animal down. Speeding it up was far more difficult, and far more risky.

The Jockey Club and the new Horseracing Regulatory Authority have rules forbidding those intimately connected with horses to 'lay' on the exchanges. However, I knew from Bill that 'there were ways', even though I had not yet found out how he had layed Candlestick in the Triumph Hurdle. Some trusty friend was all he had needed. Even untrustworthy friends would do it for a cut of the winnings.

The commission-based exchanges appeared to be such high-profit businesses, without there being any risk of 'losing' on a big gamble, that the temptation for them to meddle with results, and hence punter confidence, seemed to be minimal. But regulator vigilance was essential as there would always be those who would try to beat the system unfairly.

I finished the report by saying that my investigations of individual on-line gambling operations would continue and a further report would be prepared in due course.

I was reading it through when the phone rang.

'Is that Sid Halley?' asked a Welsh voice.

'Yes,' I replied.

'Good. This is Evan Walker here, see.'

'Ah, Mr Walker,' I said. 'How are things?'

'Not good, not good at all.'

'I'm sorry to hear that,' I said. 'Is there anything I can do to help?'

'Did Bill Burton kill my son?'

'No, I don't believe so, but I'm still trying to find out who did.'

'They won't let me have Huw's body for burial. Say they need it until after the inquest. I asked them when that would be and they said it could be months.' He sounded distraught. 'Can't stop thinking of him in some cold refrigerator.'

I wondered whether it was worse than thinking of him in the cold ground.

'I'll have a word with the policeman in the case,' I said. 'Perhaps he can give me a better idea of when you can have a funeral.'

'Thank you. Please phone me as soon as you find who killed him.'

I assured him that I would. And I'd shout it from the roof-tops, too.

*　　　*　　　*

I arrived to pick up Marina from Lincoln's Inn Fields at half past five.

I'd spent the afternoon doing chores around the flat and getting my hair cut around the corner. Such was my desperation to move my investigation forward that I had a crazy idea of collecting hair off the floor of all the barbers in London to test for a DNA match with Marina's attacker. Then I had remembered that Marina had said I would need the follicles too so cut hair was no good. Back to square one.

I had called Chief Inspector Carlisle at the Cheltenham police station but he was unavailable so I left him a message asking him to call me on my mobile, and he did so as I waited outside the Research Institute for Marina to appear.

'Sorry,' he said, 'but we can't release Walker's body for a while longer in case we need to do more tests.'

'What tests?' I asked him. 'Surely you've done all you need in nearly two weeks?'

'It's not actually up to us. It's the coroner who makes the decision when to release a body.'

'But I bet he's swayed by the police.'

'The problem is that in murder cases there have to be extra tests done by independent pathologists in case there's a court case and the defence require further examination of the body. In the past, bodies have sometimes had to be exhumed for defence tests.' He made it sound like a conspiracy.

'But you might not have a court case for months or even years.'

'The coroner has to make a judgement call and two weeks is definitely on the short side.'

'But surely there's no doubt as to the cause of Huw Walker's death?' I asked.

'Don't you believe it,' said Carlisle. 'I've known defence lawyers insisting that the victim died of natural causes just before he was shot, stabbed or strangled by the defendant. If it was up to me, I'd sentence some lawyers to the same term as their clients. Conniving bastards.'

I was somewhat amused by his opinion of the English legal profession but I supposed, in his job, all trials came down to conflicts of us versus them, with truth and justice as secondary considerations.

'So can you guess when Huw's father can have his son's body for burial?' I asked. 'He wants to make plans for the funeral.'

'Maybe a week or two more,' said Carlisle. 'The inquest into Burton's death will open next Tuesday in Reading. After what you told me on Monday, the inquest will be adjourned but, nevertheless, the coroner in the Walker case may then make an order which will allow his burial to proceed, though he won't allow a cremation.'

'I think Mr Walker is planning for a burial,' I said. 'He wants to put Huw in his local chapel graveyard next to his mother and brother.'

'That's good.'

'So you did take some notice of what I told you on Monday?'

'What do you mean?' he said.

'You said the Burton inquest will be adjourned.'

'Well, I did have a word with Inspector Johnson. He took a little convincing but at least he's considering it.'

'What?'

'That Burton may have been murdered.'

'That's great,' I said.

'Don't get too excited. He's only considering it because, as one of the first on the scene, you're bound to be called as a witness at the full inquest and he knows you'll raise it. So Johnson is considering it so that he won't be surprised by the coroner's questions. He is still pretty convinced that Burton killed himself.'

'Oh,' I said. 'And are you?'

'I don't get paid to think about other coppers' cases. But, if I were a betting man, which I'm not, I'd bet on your instinct over his.'

It was quite a compliment and I thanked him for it.

'I haven't yet been asked to appear at the inquest,' I said.

'Tuesday will only be the preliminaries. The Reading coroner will open and adjourn until a later date when the investigations are complete. You'll be summoned then.'

'Could you speak with the Cheltenham coroner's office about Huw Walker's body?' I asked.

'I'll enquire,' he said, 'but I won't apply pressure.'

'Fair enough,' I said. 'Any news on the bullet I gave you?'

'Same gun,' he said. 'Forensics came back with the confirmation this afternoon. No real surprise.'

'No,' I agreed, but I was relieved nevertheless.

*   *   *

Marina and I spent a quiet evening at home in front of the television eating ready-made and

211

microwaved shepherd's pie off trays on our laps.

'You know those street corners I was going to ring my bell on?' I said.

'Yes.'

'Well, tomorrow's *Pump* may have a certain ding-dong about it.'

'Are you saying that I should be extra-careful tomorrow?'

'Yes,' I said. 'And always.'

'Rosie hardly leaves my side.'

I wished that Rosie were a seventeen-stone body-builder rather than a five-foot two size six.

'I think I'll go and get *The Pump* now,' I said. 'Tomorrow's papers are always on sale at Victoria Station about eleven at night. They're the first edition that normally goes off to Wales and the west of England.'

'You be careful, too,' said Marina.

I was. I avoided dark corners and kept a keen eye on my back. I made it safely to the news-stand outside the station and then back to Ebury Street without incident.

There was no need to search this paper. You would have had to be blind to miss it. They must have been short of news.

Under a 'Pump Exclusive' banner on the front page was the headline 'MURDER OR SUICIDE?' with the sub-headline 'HALLEY ORCHESTRATES THE INVESTIGATION'. The article beneath described in detail everything I had revealed to Paddy. They 'quoted' Professor Aubrey Winterton as saying that the bullet definitely came from the same gun that had been used to kill Bill Burton. They even managed to state that Sid Halley was confident that an arrest was imminent.

212

I put that down to Paddy's tendency for exaggeration.

'That's what I call shouting from a street corner,' said Marina. 'Is it true?'

'Not about the arrest. And some of the rest is guesswork.'

No one could be in any doubt that I had blatantly ignored the message that Marina had received the evening she was beaten up. Even I had not expected my game to work so well that it would make the front page. I thought a paragraph in Chris Beecher's column or an inch or two on the racing page would have been all I could have hoped for. This much coverage made me very nervous but it was too late now; *The Pump* printed more than half a million copies a day.

I double-checked the locks, removed my arm and went to bed. Neither Marina nor I felt in the mood for nookie.

*   *   *

In the morning we took extra care going to the car. I had reiterated to the staff downstairs at the front desk that no one, repeat no one, was to be allowed up to my flat without their calling me first. Absolutely, they had agreed.

I dropped Marina at work, though not before taking a few detours to see if we were being followed. Rosie, the petite bodyguard, was waiting for Marina in the Institute foyer. She waved at me as I drove away.

I pointed the Audi towards north-west London and went to see Frank Snow.

Harrow School is actually in Harrow on the Hill,

213

a neat little village perched, as its name suggests, on a hill surrounded by suburban London. It seems strangely isolated from its great metropolitan neighbour as if it has somehow remained constant throughout its long history whilst life changed elsewhere around it. The village is mostly made up of the many school buildings with the Harrow School Outfitters being the largest store in the High Street.

I eventually found the right office under a cloister near the school chapel and Frank Snow was there, seated at a central table sticking labels on a stack of envelopes.

'For the old boys' newsletters,' he said in explanation.

He was a tall man with a full head of wavy white hair. He wore a tweed jacket with leather patches on the elbows and looked every inch the schoolmaster.

'Would you like a coffee?' he asked.

'Love one, thank you.'

He busied himself with an electric kettle in the corner while I wandered round looking at the rows of framed photographs on the walls. Many of them were faded black-and-white images of serious-looking, unsmiling boys in straw boaters. Others were more recent, in colour, of sports teams in striped jerseys with happier faces.

'Milk and sugar?'

'Just a little milk, please,' I said.

He pushed the pile of envelopes to one side and placed two steaming mugs down on the end of the table.

'Now, how can I help you, Mr Halley?'

'I was hoping you could give me some

background information on one of your old boys.'

'As I explained to you on the telephone,' he said, 'we don't discuss old boys with the media.' He took a sip of his coffee.

'As I explained to you,' I replied, 'I'm not from the media.'

It was not the most auspicious of openings.

'Well, who are you then?' he asked.

I decided against telling him that I was a private detective as I thought that might have been even lower on his scale than the media.

'I'm assisting the Standing Cabinet Sub-Committee on Legislative Outcomes in their consideration of internet gambling as part of the new Gambling and Gaming Act.'

If you can't blind them with science, I thought, baffle them with bullshit.

'I beg your pardon?' he said.

I repeated it.

'I see.' He didn't appear to.

'Yes. One of your old boys runs an internet gambling website and I was hoping you might be able to tell me about his time at Harrow.'

'I'm not sure that I can. Our records are confidential, you know.'

'Don't worry about the Data Protection Act,' I said. 'This is an official inquiry.'

It wasn't, but he wouldn't know that.

'I can assure you, Mr Halley, that our records have been confidential far longer than that piece of legislation has been on the statute book.'

'Of course,' I said. I had been put in my place.

'Now who exactly are you asking about?'

'George Lochs,' I said. 'At least, that's what he calls himself now. When he was at Harrow he was—'

'Clarence Lochstein,' Frank Snow interrupted.

'Exactly. You remember him, then.'

'I do,' he said. 'Has he been up to no good?'

'Why do you ask?'

'No reason.'

'What can you tell me about him?' I asked.

'I'm not sure. What do you want to know?'

'I heard that he was expelled for taking bets from the other boys.'

'That's not exactly true,' he said. 'He was sacked for striking a member of staff.'

'Really?' I said. 'Who?'

'His housemaster,' he said. 'As you say, Lochstein and another boy were indeed caught taking bets from the other boys and, it was rumoured, from some of the younger, more avant-garde members of Common Room.'

He paused.

'Yes?'

'It was in the latter days of corporal punishment and the headmaster instructed the boys' housemasters to give each of them a sound beating. Six of the best.'

'So?'

'Lochstein took one stroke of the cane on his backside and then stood up and broke his housemaster's jaw with his fist.' Mr Snow stroked his chin absentmindedly.

'You were his housemaster, weren't you?'

He stopped stroking his chin and looked at his hand. 'Yes, I was. The little swine broke my jaw in three places. I spent the next six weeks with my head in a metal brace.'

'So Lochstein was expelled,' I said. 'What

216

happened to the other boy?'

'He took his beating from his housemaster.'

I raised my eyebrows.

'No, not me.'

'And the boy was allowed to stay?'

'Yes,' said Mr Snow. 'His father subsequently gave a large donation to the school appeal which was said by some to be conscience money.'

'Do you remember the boy's name?'

'I can't recall his first name but his surname was Enstone.'

'Peter Enstone?' I asked.

'Yes, I think that's it. His father was a builder.'

Well well well, I thought. No wonder the Enstones had known George Lochs for ever. And, I thought, Lochs has a history of punching people in the face.

Frank Snow had little else of interest to give me. Harrow had done its best to keep the whole matter out of the Press and, at the time, had closed ranks. Lochstein was not even in the official list of old boys that Frank showed me.

We spent a companionable ten minutes or so together and he gave me a short tour of the photographs on the walls.

'These,' he said, indicating the black-and-white ones, 'are from before the First World War. Harrow was a pretty severe place then so I suppose they didn't have much to smile about. These others are the rugby teams I used to coach, the Under 16s. They were my boys and some of them still come in to see me. Makes me feel so old to see how they've changed. A few even have their own boys here now.'

I thanked him for his time and for the coffee.

He seemed disappointed that I didn't want to see more of the hundreds of pictures he had stacked in a cupboard.

'Perhaps another time,' I said, moving towards the door.

'Mr Halley,' he said.

'Yes.' I turned.

'I hope you do find that Lochstein has been up to no good.'

'I thought Public Schools stood up for their former pupils, no matter what.'

'The school might, but I don't. That one deserves some trouble.'

We shook hands.

'If you need anything further, Mr Halley, don't be afraid to ask.' He smiled. 'I still owe Lochstein a beating—five strokes to be precise.'

Revenge was indeed a dish best eaten cold.

*   *   *

On my way back to central London I made a slight detour to Wembley Park to take a look at the Make A Wager Ltd office building. I had their address from the Companies House website but nevertheless it took fifteen minutes of backtracking around an industrial estate to find it. I must get satellite navigation, I thought. Perhaps on my next car. I parked round the corner and walked back.

The office building was pretty nondescript. It was a simple rectangular red-brick structure of five floors with a small unmanned entrance lobby at one end. An array of mobile phone masts sprouted up from the flat roof and there were security cameras pointing in every direction.

A notice next to the entrance intercom stated that visitors for Make A Wager Ltd should press the button and wait. Visitors, it seemed, were not encouraged.

There was little to show that it was the headquarters of a multi-million-pound operation other than the line of expensive cars and big powerful motorbikes in the small car park opposite the door. I looked at the cars. The nearest was a dark blue Porsche 911 Carrera with GL 21 as its number plate. So George was in.

Shall I be bold? I asked myself. Shall I go in and see him? Why not? Nothing to lose, only my life.

I pressed the button and waited.

Eventually a female voice said, 'Yes?' from the speaker next to the button.

'Sid Halley here to see George Lochs,' I said back.

'Just a minute,' said the voice.

I waited some more.

After at least a minute, the voice said, 'Do you have an appointment?'

'No,' I replied. 'I was passing and I thought I would drop in to see George. I know him.'

'Just a minute,' said the voice again.

I waited. And waited.

'Take the lift to the fourth floor,' said the voice and a buzzer sounded.

I pushed the door open and did as I was told.

George/Clarence was waiting for me when the lift opened. I remembered him from our meeting in Jonny Enstone's box at Cheltenham. He was lean, almost athletic, with blond hair brushed back showing a certain receding over the temples. But he was not wearing his suit today. Instead he sported a dark roll-neck sweater and blue denim jeans. He hadn't been expecting guests.

'Sid Halley,' he said, holding out a hand. 'Good to see you again. What brings you to this godforsaken part of north London?'

Was I suspicious or was there a hint of anxiety in his voice? Or maybe it was irritation?

'I was passing and I thought I'd come and see what your offices looked like.'

I don't think he believed me, but it was true.

'There's not much to show,' he said.

He slid a green plastic card through a reader on the wall that unlocked the door to the offices on the fourth floor. He stood aside to allow me in.

'Have you been in this building long?' I asked.

'Nearly five years. At first we were only on one floor but we've gradually expanded and now we occupy the whole place.'

There were thirty or so staff sitting at open-plan desks along the windows, each with a computer screen shining brightly in front of them. It was quiet for a room with so many people. A few hushed conversations were taking place but the majority were studying their screens and tapping quietly on their keyboards.

'On this floor we have our market managers,' said George in a hushed tone. 'Have you seen our website?'

'Yes,' I said, equally hushed.

'You know then that you can gamble on just about anything you like, just as long as you can find someone to match your bet. Last year, we managed a wager between two young men concerning which of them would get his respective girlfriend pregnant quickest.' He laughed. 'We ended up having to get doctors' reports to settle it.'

'That's crazy,' I said.

'But most of our markets are less personal than that. The staff here look at the incoming bets and try to match them if the computer doesn't do it automatically. And there are always special events that need a human brain to sort out. Computers can be very clever but they like the rules to be absolutes. Just yes or no, no maybes.'

'Where are the computers?' I asked, looking around.

'Downstairs,' he said. 'The first and second floors are full of computer hardware. We have to keep them in climate-controlled conditions with massive air conditioners.'

'My computer's forever crashing,' I said.

'That's why we continually back up everything. And we have more than one main-frame machine. They check on each other all the time. It's very sophisticated.'

I could sense that George was bragging. He was clearly enjoying showing me how clever he was.

'Do you do on-line gaming as well as exchange wagering?'

'Yes, but not from this office. We have a Gibraltar-based operation for that. More cost effective.'

I suspected it was also more tax effective.

'Why the interest?' he asked.

'No real reason,' I said.

'Is there anything specific you came here to find out?'

'No. I'm just naturally inquisitive.' And nosy.

I wandered a little further down the office.

'Is this all the staff you have?' I asked.

'Nooo,' he said, amused. 'There are lots more. The accounts department is on the floor below here and there must be fifty personnel there. Then we have the technical staff who live amongst the machines on the lower floors. Then the ground floor has the company security staff, and a canteen.'

'Quite a set-up,' I said, sounding impressed. And I was.

'Yes. We operate here twenty-four hours a day every day of the year. There are always duty technicians on standby in case of problems with the machines. We can't afford for the system to go down. It's not good for business. Now, is there anything else you want, Sid? I'm very busy.'

His irritation was beginning to show through more sharply.

'No,' I said. 'Sorry. Many thanks for showing me around.'

And, oh yes, by the way, could I have a hair, please?

I followed him to the door and could see no convenient blond hairs lying on his dark sweater, and none helpfully sticking up from his head just waiting to be plucked out. This wasn't as easy as Marina had suggested, especially one-handed.

We stopped in the doorway.

'I see you're on the front page of *The Pump* today,' he said.

I hoped he couldn't see the sweat that broke out on my forehead.

'So I saw,' I replied, trying to keep my voice as normal as possible.

'Are you having any luck with your

222

investigation?' he said.

'I'm making steady progress,' I lied.

'Well, I hope you get to the bottom of it. I liked Huw Walker.'

'How well did you know him?' I asked.

Suddenly it was his turn to have a sweaty brow. 'Not very well. We spoke a few times.'

'What about?' I asked.

'Nothing much. About his chances, you know, in passing.'

'It's not very sensible for a man in your position to be asking jockeys about their chances in races, is it?'

He was beginning to get rattled. 'There was nothing in it, I assure you.'

I wasn't convinced that I could take his assurances at face value.

I applied more pressure. 'Are the Jockey Club aware that you ask jockeys about their chances in races?'

'Now look here, Halley, what are you accusing me of?'

'Nothing,' I said. 'It was *you* who told me that you had talked to Huw Walker about his chances.'

'I think you ought to go now,' he said.

He didn't hold out his hand. I looked into his eyes and could see no further than his retinas. Whatever he was thinking, he was keeping it to himself.

I wanted to ask him what he had been doing last Friday evening around eight o'clock. I wanted to know if he had scratch marks on his neck beneath the high roll collar of his sweater. And I wanted to know if he had ever owned a .38 revolver.

Instead, I rode the lift down and went away.

223

Back at Ebury Street, I parked the car in the garage. Instead of going straight up to my flat, I walked to the sandwich bar on the corner to get myself a late lunch of smoked salmon on brown bread with a salad.

I was paying across the counter when my mobile rang.

'Hello,' I said, trying to juggle my lunch, the change and the telephone in my one real hand.

A breathless voice at the other end of the line said, 'Is that you, Sid?'

'Yes,' I replied, then with rising foreboding, 'Rosie? What is it?'

'Oh God,' she said, 'Marina's been shot.'

CHAPTER FIFTEEN

'What?' I said numbly, dropping my change.

'Marina's been shot,' Rosie repeated.

I went cold and stopped feeling my legs.

'Where?'

'Here, on the pavement outside the Institute.'

'No,' I said, 'where on her body?'

'In her leg.'

Thank God, I thought, she's going to be all right.

'Where is she now?' I asked.

'Here, by the ambulance,' said Rosie. 'They're desperately working on her on the pavement. Oh God, there's so much blood. It's everywhere.'

Maybe my relief was premature. My skin felt clammy.

'Rosie,' I said urgently, 'go and ask the ambulancemen which hospital they'll be taking her to.'

I could hear her asking.

'St Thomas's,' she said.

'Go with her. I'm on my way there.'

She hung up. I looked at my phone in disbelief. This can't be happening. But it was.

Nature has evolved a mechanism for dealing with fear, or hurt. Adrenalin floods into the bloodstream and hence throughout the body. Muscles are primed to perform, to run, to jump, to escape the danger, to flee from the source of the fear. I could feel the energy coursing round my body. I had felt it all too often before when lying injured on the turf after a bad fall. The desire to run was great. Sometimes, when injured, the urge to flee was so overpowering that injuries could be forgotten. There were well-documented incidents of people who had been horribly maimed in explosions running away from the scene on legs from which the feet had been blown clean away.

Now, in the sandwich bar, this adrenalin rush had me turning back and forth not knowing if I was picking up my lunch or retrieving my dropped change or what. For quite a few wasted seconds I was completely disorientated.

'Are you all right, mate?' asked the man behind the counter.

'Fine,' I croaked, hardly able to unclench my teeth.

I stumbled out of the shop and fairly sprinted back to my car. I pressed the button that opened the garage and yelled at the slowly opening gate to hurry up.

I drove as quickly as I could to St Thomas's Hospital, which is on the other side of the Thames from the Houses of Parliament. 'Quickly' is a relative term in London traffic. I screamed at tourists outside Buckingham Palace to get out of the way, and cursed queues of taxis in Birdcage Walk. Bus lanes are for buses, and sometimes for taxis too, but not for cars. I charged along the bus lane on Westminster Bridge and didn't care if I got a ticket.

In spite of two jumped traffic lights and numerous near misses, I made it unscathed to the hospital's casualty entrance. I pulled the car on to the pavement and got out.

'You can't leave it there,' said a well-meaning soul walking past.

'Watch,' I said, locking the doors. 'It's an emergency.'

'They'll tow it away,' he said.

Let them, I thought. I wasn't going to waste time finding a parking meter.

Oh God, please let Marina be OK. I hadn't prayed since I was a child but I did so now.

Please God, let Marina be all right.

I ran into the Accident and Emergency Department and found a line of six people at the reception desk.

I grabbed a passing nurse. 'Please,' I said, 'where's Marina van der Meer?'

'Is she a patient?' asked the nurse in an east European accent.

'Yes,' I said. 'She was on her way here from Lincoln's Inn Fields, by ambulance.'

'Ambulance cases come in over there,' she said, pointing over her shoulder.

'Thanks.' I ran in the direction she had indicated, towards some closed double doors.

My progress was blocked by a large young man in a navy blue jersey. 'Hospital Security' was written on each shoulder.

'Yes, sir,' he said, 'can I help you?'

'Marina van der Meer?' I said, trying to get past him.

He sidestepped to block my way. 'No,' he said, 'my name's Tony. Now what's yours?'

I looked at his face. He wasn't exactly smiling.

'Look,' I said, 'I'm trying to find Marina van der Meer. She was being brought here by ambulance.'

'An emergency?' he asked.

'Yes, yes,' I said, 'she's been shot.'

'Where?' he asked.

'In the leg.'

'No, where was she shot?'

'In the leg,' I said again.

'No,' he repeated, 'where in London was she shot?'

'Lincoln's Inn Fields,' I said. What on earth does it matter? I thought.

'She may have gone to Guy's,' he said.

'The ambulance men said they were bringing her here.'

'You just wait here a moment, Mr . . . what did you say your name was?'

'Halley,' I said. 'Sid Halley.'

'You just wait here a moment and I'll see. Members of the public aren't allowed in this section—unless they come by ambulance, of course.' He almost laughed. I didn't.

He disappeared through the double doors and let them swing back together. I pushed one open and looked through. There was not much to see. The corridor stretched ahead for about ten yards and met another corridor in a T-junction. The walls were painted in two tones, the upper half cream and the lower blue. Perversely, it reminded me of the corridors in my primary school in Liverpool.

Tony, the friendly security guard, reappeared from the left and strode towards me. 'No one of that name has been admitted,' he said.

There was a clatter behind him and a trolley surrounded by medical staff was wheeled quickly by from right to left. I only had a glimpse of the person on it and I couldn't tell if it was Marina. Then a dazed-looking Rosie came into view.

'Rosie,' I shouted. She didn't hear.

Tony, the guard, started to say something but I pushed past him and ran down the corridor.

'Oi!' he shouted. 'You can't go in there.'

But I had already turned the corner.

'Rosie,' I shouted again.

She turned. 'Oh Sid, thank God you're here!' She was crying and seemed to be in a state of near-collapse.

'Where's Marina?' I asked urgently.

'In there,' she said, looking at some doors on the right.

There was a glass circular window and, with trepidation, I looked through.

Marina lay very still on a trolley with about six people rushing around her. There were two bags of blood on poles with plastic tubes running to needles on the backs of each of her hands. I could see a pool of blood down near the foot of the trolley—it was as though the blood was going straight through her.

'What are you two doing here?' asked a voice.

I turned to see a stern-looking nurse in a blue uniform with what appeared to be a green dishcloth on her head.

'You'll have to go back to the waiting room,' she said.

'But that's Marina in there,' I said, turning back to the window. If anything, the activity had intensified. One of the staff was putting a tube down her throat. Her face looked horribly grey.

'I don't care if it's the Queen of Sheba,' said the nurse. 'You can't stay here. You'll be in the way.' She mellowed. 'Come on, I'll show you where you can wait. You'll be told what's happening as soon as we know.'

Rosie and I allowed ourselves to be taken by the arms and led down the corridor. We went round several corners and were shown into a room with 'Family Waiting Room' painted on the door.

'Now stay here and someone will be along to see you.'

I mumbled 'thank you' but seemed to have lost control of my face. All I could see was the image of Marina so helpless and vulnerable on that trolley. 'Please God, let her live.'

I sat down heavily on one of the chairs. I'd again lost control of my legs, too.

'I'll send someone in with a cup of tea,' said the nurse. 'Now, wait here.'

I nodded. I don't think I could have moved even if I had wanted to. All I could think about was whether Marina was going to be all right. Rosie sat with her head in her hands. She had been awfully close to the action both on the pavement and in the ambulance.

After a few minutes a kindly woman in an apron brought us a cup of tea each. Strong, full of milk and with at least two sugars, just as I didn't take it. Delicious.

'What happened?' I finally said to Rosie.

She looked up at me. Her eyes were red from crying and she had a hangdog expression.

'I'm so sorry, Sid,' she said. 'We only went outside for a bit of air.'

'It's all right, Rosie. It wasn't your fault.'

But I could see that she thought it was.

'Tell me what happened.'

'It was all so fast,' she said. 'We were going to walk once round the square, but had gone only a few yards when a motorcyclist drew up and sat there on his machine looking at a map. He beckoned us over to him, pointing at the map. I couldn't hear what he said due to the noise of the engine. Marina went across the pavement to him and he just shot her. I think the gun was under the map.'

'Could you describe the motorcyclist?' I asked her. 'Would you be able to identify him again?'

'No, I don't think so,' she replied slowly. He was wearing a crash helmet—you know, one of those ones that covers the whole face. That's partly why I couldn't hear what he said.'

'How about the motorbike?' I asked.

'It was just . . . just a motorbike,' she said. 'I don't know what type.'

She paused and I could tell she was replaying the scene in her mind.

230

'At first I didn't realise she had been shot. I mean, I didn't hear a gunshot or anything. Marina doubled up and grabbed her knee and the motorcycle roared away. Then there was all the blood. It literally spurted out of her leg all over the place.'

I looked at her dark trousers and I could see that they were covered in Marina's blood.

'I did my best to stop it and screamed for someone to help. It seemed ages before the Institute's security men ran out. They called the ambulance but that took ages to arrive, too.'

The door into the waiting room opened and I jumped up.

'Are you with the girl that's been shot?' asked the head that appeared.

'Yes,' said Rosie and I together.

'Good. Wait here, please.' The head withdrew and the door closed.

I paced around the room. It took a huge effort not to run out of the door and back to the circular window.

'Why don't they come and tell us?' I said. But I knew the answer. They were busy doing their best. I prayed that their best was good enough.

'She lost so much blood,' said Rosie. 'I held her leg in both my hands and squeezed hard to stop the blood but it oozed between my fingers and ran all over the pavement. It was horrible.' She shuddered.

'You did brilliantly, Rosie. Without you, she would have probably died there on the pavement. At least here she has a chance.' I hoped so anyway.

The door reopened but it wasn't a doctor that came in but a uniformed policeman.

'Good afternoon,' he said, nodding to each of us in turn, and showing us his warrant card. 'Do either of you know the name of the young lady who was shot?'

'Marina van der Meer,' I said. 'Do you know how she's doing? I really need some news.'

'The doctors are still working on her, sir,' he said. 'I'm afraid I don't know anything further.' He took a notebook out of his pocket. 'How do you spell her name?' he asked.

I told him and he wrote it down.

And her age? And he wrote that down, too.

'And what is your name?' he asked me.

I told him that as well. Come on, I thought, where's the bloody doctor?

'And you, madam?'

Rosie's name went into the notebook along with our dates of birth, although why they were important, I couldn't imagine.

'Are either of you related to the young lady?' In other circumstances, his use of the term 'young lady' would have been amusing. He made Marina sound as if she were about fourteen. She was certainly older than he.

'I am,' I said.

'Are you her husband?' At least he hadn't asked if I were her father.

'No, I'm her . . .' What am I? I'm too old to be a boyfriend. I hate the term 'partner'. I used to partner horses in races. Significant other? No.

'. . . fiancé,' I said.

'Are you therefore her next of kin?'

I didn't like the sound of that. 'Next of kin' always seemed to go with 'inform' and 'death'.

'Her parents live in the Netherlands,' I said. 'I

have their address somewhere at home. She also has a brother. He lives in the States.'

'And you, madam?' said the policeman, turning to Rosie.

'I work with Marina at the London Research Institute. I was there when she was shot.'

His eyes opened wider. 'Were you? My superiors will want to take a statement.'

He turned away and spoke quietly into his personal radio. I didn't catch everything he said but I did hear him say 'witness'.

One of the medical staff came into the room. He was dressed in blue trousers and matching blue smock, with one of the dishcloths on his head.

'You're here with the girl who was shot?' he asked.

'Yes,' I said. 'She's my fiancée.'

'She isn't wearing a ring.'

'She will be next week.' If she lives, I thought. 'How is she doing?'

'Not good, I'm afraid. She's gone to theatre so I've handed her over to a surgeon. Sorry, I should introduce myself, I'm Dr Osborne; I'm the duty Accident and Emergency consultant.'

'Sid Halley,' I said. He didn't offer his hand. Germs and all that.

'Ah,' he said, nodding, 'the jockey. I thought I recognised you from somewhere. Well, your girlfriend has lost an awful lot of blood. In fact, I'm amazed she was still alive when she arrived here. There was no measurable blood pressure.'

'But she will be all right, won't she?' I was desperate.

'I'm afraid I don't know. Not yet. She was alive when she went to theatre, that's the best I can say.'

I could hear my blood rushing in my ears.

'The bullet missed the knee itself so the joint is fine but it tore open the femoral artery where it becomes the popliteal at the back of the knee, hence the blood loss. I think it was probably a small bullet and it didn't do much damage to the rest of her soft tissue. She was very unlucky.'

'But have you stopped the bleeding?' I asked frantically.

'Yes, I have for the time being but it's not that simple. I am worried about further bleeding into her internal organs.'

'Why?' I asked.

'We had to give her a great deal of blood and other fluids to replace what was lost, to fill the pipes up again, as it were.'

I nodded. I knew all about having to have blood.

'Well, we had to give her an awful lot due to the continuous bleeding.'

'Didn't you apply a tourniquet?' I asked.

'Something similar. We applied direct pressure to the leg but you have to release it every ten minutes or so otherwise the lower leg begins to die. Whenever we did, the arterial bleeding started again. So, we had to give her much more blood than her whole body normally holds.'

I'd been correct; it had been going right through her.

'This produces an added problem. Such a large transfusion severely dilutes some of the factors in the blood. It also causes a reduction in usable platelets. The combined effect is to reduce the ability of the blood to coagulate. It's called dilutional thrombocytopenia. The factors are essential to keep the arteries from leaking blood and causing diffuse bleeding at various points in the body, especially in the internal organs like the kidneys. Until her body can replenish the factors and the platelets naturally, she is living right on the edge. I have to be frank—I believe that any further bleeding might be more than she could take. It would require more transfusion which would further reduce the usable platelets, which in turn would lead to more bleeding and eventually to a complete collapse of her system.'

'But . . .' I swallowed, 'when will we know?'

'The next few hours are critical. If she survives that, then her chances are reasonable.'

'Reasonable' didn't sound reasonable enough to me.

'How long will she be in theatre?'

'Not long, I imagine,' he said. 'She's gone to have a better repair of the artery. It's risky but the surgeon and I thought it was better to fix the artery now so that it didn't rupture again, which might lead to catastrophic failure.'

'How do you fix an artery?' I asked.

'Using a graft,' he said. 'We take a piece of vein from her other leg and sew it into the artery to bridge the gap made by the bullet. The procedure is quite normal and is used all the time for heart bypass operations. The problem here is the need to keep blood loss to an absolute minimum.'

I wasn't really listening to the details. 'When can I see her?' I asked.

'After theatre she will be taken to intensive care. You'll be able to see her there but she'll be sedated and asleep. We will try to keep her blood pressure as low as possible for a while. Look, I'm sorry, but I must go now. I'm needed elsewhere.'

'Thank you,' I said. It was insufficient.

He went out, leaving Rosie, me and the policeman.

'She's in the best hands,' said the policeman kindly.

I nodded. I felt so helpless.

'I left my car on the pavement outside the hospital,' I said. 'I'd better go and move it.'

'Sorry, sir,' said the policeman. 'You're not to leave until you've given a statement to my super.'

His super turned out to be Detective Superintendent Aldridge of the Metropolitan Police who arrived with another plain-clothes officer in tow. They showed me their warrant cards.

'Thank you, constable,' said the Super, dismissing our uniformed friend.

'I'll go and check on your car, sir,' he said to me. 'What's the registration?'

'It's probably been towed away by now.' But I gave him the registration anyway, and the keys.

The Superintendent wanted a blow-by-blow account of everything both Rosie and I had done all day. It was tedious and my mind was elsewhere.

'I'm going to find out how Marina's doing?' I said finally with exasperation.

'All in good time, Mr Halley,' said the Super.

'No,' I said. 'Now.'

I stood up and walked to the door.

'Please sit down, sir.' He said it with a degree of stiffness in his tone.

'No,' I said, 'I'm going to see my fiancée.' The term was beginning to grow on me.

I didn't really blame the police. All too often the villain of the piece is the husband or the wife, the

boyfriend or the girlfriend. It always seemed to me
that to do one of those tear-jerking press
conferences appealing for the murderer of a loved
one to give themselves up was tantamount to
holding up a banner with 'I DID IT' blazoned
across it.

If he wanted to arrest me, let him. I had a
cast-iron alibi in the sandwich man. And I wanted
to see my girl.

But that wasn't as easy as I'd hoped.

I went to the reception desk and asked if Dr
Osborne was available.

Sorry, he's busy.

Could they tell me where Marina van der Meer
was? Or how she was?

Sorry, she's no longer in this department.

Could they tell me how to get to the Intensive
Care Unit?

Sorry, ask at the main reception desk.

There was a large notice pinned to a board
above the desk. It read: 'Our staff have the right to
work free of verbal or physical abuse from the
public.' I understood the anger that can be present
in such places. It is anger born out of fear,
frustration and hurt.

I swallowed my own anger and left the A & E
Department in search of the main reception desk. I
found that I had acquired a shadow in the form of
the Superintendent's sidekick.

'Making sure you don't leave the hospital, sir,'
he said.

'Fine,' I replied. 'You lot must know where
Marina is. Do me a favour and get on your blower
to find out.'

He punched numbers into his mobile phone and

talked briefly.

'Can you turn that phone off, please,' said a man in the corridor. 'Mobile phones are not permitted in the hospital.'

'I'm a policeman,' said the officer.

'And I'm a doctor,' said the man. 'Mobile phones can interfere with medical equipment so turn it off.'

'OK,' said my shadow but he listened for a few moments longer.

'She's still in the operating theatre,' he said to me. 'We have a guard outside.'

Marina needed a guard inside, I thought, a guardian angel.

'I'm going to the Intensive Care Unit to wait for her.'

My shadow nodded and we went together to the main reception desk to get directions.

*   *   *

I sat on one of the chairs outside the door to the Intensive Care Unit, opposite the lifts. My shadow sat alongside me and time passed very slowly.

I looked at my watch. Unbelievably it had been only fifty-five minutes since Rosie had rung me in the sandwich bar. It felt like hours.

I thought about Marina's parents. I had only met them a few times. They had stayed with us in London last year at Easter, and we had been over to stay with them in Holland during August so Marina could show me where she was brought up. I should give them a call. I ought to let them know that their daughter was fighting for her life. I hoped she was still fighting. But it would have to wait. I didn't have their number with me and I wasn't leaving to get it.

Who else should I call?

Perhaps I should tell Charles. I'd welcome his support.

Charles! For God's sake! If they, whoever 'they' might be, were trying to pressurise me into stopping my investigation by shooting Marina, they might try and shoot Charles, too. Marina was shot a little over an hour ago. Lincoln's Inn Fields to Aynsford takes about an hour and a half by car, maybe less by a traffic-weaving motorbike.

'I've got to make a phone call,' I said to the policeman. 'Now! It's urgent!'

There was a big 'No Mobile Phones' sign on the door to the unit.

Too bad, I thought, this is an emergency.

I moved down to the end of the corridor next to the window and switched on my mobile. Come on, come on. SIM not ready.

At last it was and I dialled Charles's number. Thankfully he answered at the fourth ring.

'Charles,' I said, 'this is Sid. Marina's been shot and I'm frightened that you might be next. Get out of the house. Take Mrs Cross with you and then call me.'

'Right, on our way,' he said. 'Call you in five minutes.'

Thank goodness for military training. But it was not the first time I'd had to do that and, on the previous occasion, I had been right to warn him. I remembered and, apparently, so had Charles.

I waited near the window and the five minutes seemed to be an eternity.

He called.

'We're safely in the car and well away from the house,' he said. 'Is Marina . . . ?' He couldn't finish.

'I'm at St Thomas's Hospital,' I said. 'It's touch and go. She's in theatre but it's not too good.'

'I'll drop Mrs Cross and then come on.'

'Thanks, I'd like that.'

'I think I'll call my local bobby and get him to watch the house.'

I didn't think anyone had a local bobby any more.

'Fine,' I said. 'I'm in the Intensive Care Unit waiting for Marina to come out of the operating theatre. It says ICU on the hospital notice boards.'

'I'll find it,' said Charles, and I was sure he would.

I went back to sitting with my shadow.

Where had Marina got to? She should have been here by now. Had something gone wrong with the operation? Was she not coming to Intensive Care because she was already dead? Should I go to the morgue? Oh God, what should I do?

I played things over and over in my mind. I was becoming convinced that she had died. What was I doing, sitting here on a chair next to a policeman?

One of the lifts opened. I jumped up but it wasn't Marina. It was Superintendent Aldridge and Rosie. The poor girl looked about half her normal tiny self and absolutely exhausted.

'I've spoken to the hospital,' the Super said to me. 'Miss Meer is still in surgery but she should be coming here shortly. I was told to tell you that nothing's changed.'

I was hugely relieved.

My shadow had stood up on the arrival of his boss, and Aldridge sat down next to me on one

240

side with Rosie on the other.

'Now, Mr Halley, I know all about you.'

I looked at him quizzically.

'There's not a copper alive who doesn't, not a detective anyway.'

I wasn't sure whether it was flattery or not. Every detective also knew all about the Kray twins.

'So?' I said.

'Was this shooting of Miss Meer anything to do with your investigations?'

I knew it was a question I would be asked. But I hadn't expected it to be asked quite so soon.

I was saved from the immediate need to answer by the appearance through the door of another dishcloth-wearing medic.

'Mr Halley?' he asked.

I stood up. My heart was thumping in my chest.

'My name's Mr Pandita,' he said. 'I've been operating on the lady with the bullet wound in her leg.'

'Marina van der Meer,' I said.

'Quite so,' he replied. 'She's now been transferred here.' He cocked his thumb towards the double doors behind him.

'How is she?' I asked.

'The operation went well. Now it's a matter of time.'

'What chances are we looking at?' asked the Superintendent.

'Reasonable,' said Mr Pandita.

'How reasonable?' I asked.

'She's a fit young girl and obviously a fighter, otherwise she would have died in A & E, or even before. I give her a better than fifty-fifty chance. I don't think there will be any brain damage.'

Brain damage!

'Why would there be?' I asked numbly.

'If there was a lack of oxygen to the brain for more than a few minutes,' he said, 'then there would be damage. Even though her body was very short of blood for a while, her heart didn't stop at any stage so she should be all right in that department. But her heart must have been pumping next to nothing round her so there's always a risk.'

'Can I see her?' I asked.

'Not just yet,' he said. 'The nursing staff are with her, making her comfortable and setting up all the monitoring equipment. Soon. But she'll be asleep. We've given her a sedative to keep her blood pressure low. I'll tell the staff you're here and they'll come and get you when they're ready.'

I nodded. 'Thank you.'

He disappeared back through the door and I sat down.

I looked again at my watch. It was only three thirty. How could time pass so slowly?

'Where were we?' said Superintendent Aldridge. 'Ah, yes, did this shooting have anything to do with any of your investigations?'

'What do you mean?' I asked.

'I am presuming this wasn't a random shooting,' he said, 'and that Miss Meer was specifically targeted by the gunman.'

'But he would have had to wait there for ages,' I said. 'It was only by chance that Marina came out when she did.'

'Assassins can wait for days or weeks to get a single opportunity if they are determined enough,' he said.

And, I thought, if it was the same person who had attacked Marina in Ebury Street, he had had to wait for her then, too.

'So, I ask again,' he said, 'do you think this has anything to do with your investigations?'

'I don't know,' I replied. 'If you mean do I know who did this, then the answer's no. If I did, I'd tell you, you can be sure of that.'

'Do you have any suspicions?'

'I always have suspicions,' I said, 'but they're not based on anything solid. They're not actually based on anything at all.'

'Anything you say might be useful,' he said.

'Do you remember the jockey who was murdered at Cheltenham races two weeks ago?'

'I remember that horse—Oven Cleaner—died,' he said. 'Now, that was a shame.'

'Yes, well, a jockey was murdered on the same day. Then a racehorse trainer appeared to kill himself. Everyone, and especially the police, seem to think he committed suicide because he'd murdered the jockey.'

'So?' he said.

'I believe the trainer was in fact murdered by the same man who killed the jockey and that it was made to look like suicide so that the police file on the jockey's death would be conveniently closed. And I've been saying so loudly and often for the last ten days to anyone who'll listen.'

'What has any of this to do with Miss Meer being shot?' he said.

'Last Friday, I was warned that, if I didn't keep my mouth shut, someone would get badly hurt. And now they have.'

CHAPTER SIXTEEN

They finally allowed me in to see Marina around four.

First I had to don the regulation outfit of blue smock, with matching dishcloth hat. And I had to wear a mask over my mouth and nose. I wondered how she would know who I was, but I needn't have worried, she was deeply asleep.

She looked so defenceless lying there, connected to the machines, with the tube still in her mouth. Her breathing was being assisted by a ventilator and the rhythmic purr as the bellows rose and fell was the only sound. A rectangular blue screen showed a bright line that peaked with the beat of her heart. Go on heart, I said to the machine, keep pumping.

I sat to one side, opposite the ventilator, and held her hand.

There were other patients in the unit but partitions rather than curtains separated the beds and these provided a fairly high degree of privacy.

I spoke to her.

I told her how much I loved her and how dreadfully sorry I was to have brought all this on her. I told her to fight, to live, and to get better. And I told her that I would get the man who had done this. And then we'd see. Maybe I'd take up gardening as a career, though one-handed gardening might be a problem.

And I asked her to marry me.

She didn't reply. I told myself she was thinking it over.

A nurse came to tell me that there were some people to see me outside. Not more police, I thought. But it was Charles, and he had brought Jenny with him.

'Hello, Sid,' she said. She leaned forward and gave me a peck on the cheek. 'How is she?'

Charles and I shook hands.

'She's doing OK—at least, I think so. The nurses seem optimistic, but I suppose they would. Certainly her colour is much better than earlier.'

'Jenny picked me up from Paddington,' said Charles. 'I called her on the way up on the train and she wanted to come. You know, to give support.'

Or to gloat, I thought. But maybe that was unfair of me.

'I'm glad you're here,' I said. 'Both of you.'

I looked past Charles and was astonished to see Rosie still sitting on one of the chairs opposite the lifts.

'Rosie,' I said, 'why don't you go home?'

She turned and looked at me with sunken eyes. She was clearly in no state to leave the hospital on her own. There was no sign of the Superintendent or his sidekick. What were the police thinking of, I thought, to leave her here without help?

'Charles, Jenny, this is Rosie,' I said. 'Rosie works with Marina. She was there when Marina was shot. She saved her life.'

Jenny sat down next to Rosie and put her arm round her shoulder. The human contact was too much and Rosie burst into tears and sobbed, hanging on to Jenny as though her life depended on it.

'We'll look after Rosie,' said Charles. 'You go

245

back to Marina. We'll be here when you need us.'

He ushered me back to the unit door and almost pushed me through. It was such a comfort to have them there but I felt a little guilty at leaving them out in the corridor.

'Sorry, just you,' said the nurse when I asked. 'And only then because she's your fiancée.'

I stayed with Marina for what seemed like a long time. Every few minutes, a nurse would come to check on her and twice Mr Pandita, the surgeon, came in too.

'She's doing fine,' he said on his second visit. 'I'm more hopeful.'

'More hopeful' didn't sound wonderful but a lot better than 'less hopeful'.

'It's been more than two hours now since she left theatre,' he said. 'Her blood pressure is still low but that's a good thing. It reduces the chance of internal bleeding. We will leave her sedated overnight and attempt to bring her out in the morning.'

'Bring her out?' I asked.

'From the induced coma,' he said. 'Only then will we really know.'

We stood at the foot of the bed looking down at the unconscious figure.

'I think I'll go and get something to eat,' I said. It was a while since I'd left my uneaten lunch on the floor of the sandwich bar, and even longer since dinner the previous night. 'Then I'll come back, if that's all right?'

'There are no visiting times on this ward. We run a twenty-four-hour service here.' He smiled. At least I think he smiled. Due to his mask, I couldn't see his mouth but there was a smile in his eyes.

*　　*　　*

Charles, Jenny and Rosie were still there when I came out.

They had made themselves at home and were surrounded by the remains of bacon rolls and chicken mayonnaise sandwiches with salad. Empty polystyrene coffee beakers stood in a row on the bottom of an upturned waste bin that had doubled as a table.

Rosie looked much better for having had something to eat and other people to take her mind off the horrors of earlier.

'Hello,' said Charles, looking up from a newspaper. 'How's she doing?'

'The official bulletin is "more hopeful".'

'That's great,' said Jenny.

'I'm starving,' I said. 'I see that you've all had something but I need some food. Where's the hospital canteen?'

Charles stood up, put all the trash in the reinstated bin, and gathered up his newspaper.

'A policeman came and gave me these,' he said, holding out my car keys. 'He said to tell you that your car is in the hospital administrator's parking space to the left of the front door.'

'Fantastic,' I said.

'He also told me to tell you that he was only just in time to stop the bomb squad blowing it up.'

I laughed. The first time since . . .

'He also wants you to move it as soon as possible as the hospital administrator could arrive at any time and demand his space back.'

'I'll drive it home now and put it in the garage,' I

said. 'We could get something to eat there, and I could put on a clean shirt.' It seemed like a very long time since I'd dressed to go to Harrow.

'The policeman didn't really want to give me the car keys but I told him I was your father-in-law.'

'And I told him I was your wife,' said Jenny.

That must have confused him.

*   *   *

My car was where it was promised and I drove the four of us back to Ebury Street. Rosie didn't want to go home on her own and Jenny and Charles were happy to have her stay with us.

'Hello, Mr Halley,' said Derek at the desk. 'Delivery for you.'

He held out an envelope to me. I just looked at it as he put it down on the marble top.

'Did it come by taxi?' I asked him.

'Yes,' he said. 'About an hour ago.'

'You didn't get the number of the taxi, I don't suppose?' I asked.

'No, sorry.'

'Could you identify the taxi driver?'

'I doubt it,' he said. 'Flat number 28 have been moving today and there have been a load of people through here. Not only the removal men but the gas and electricity, to read the meters and so on.'

'Do you have security film?' I asked, pointing at the bank of monitors.

'Yes, but we only have cameras in the garages and round the back. There are none in reception.'

Dead end.

I looked at the envelope. It was white, about four inches wide by nine long, with 'SID

HALLEY—BY HAND' written in capital letters on the front, as before.

'This is the same as I received last time,' I said to Charles. 'After Marina was attacked.'

'You ought to give it to the police,' he said. 'Don't touch it.'

'The envelope's been handled by the taxi driver and by Derek,' I said.

'And Bernie,' said Derek. 'He took it from the taxi driver.'

Bernie was another of the team of porters/security.

I used Derek's pencil to turn the envelope over. It was stuck shut. It looked like a birthday card.

'I'll open it,' I said.

I used another sheet of paper to hold the envelope down on the desk and used the pencil to slit it open. Only touching the sides I withdrew the contents. It was a card but not a birthday card. It said, 'Get Well Soon' on the front, along with a painting of some flowers. I used the pencil to open it.

There was some writing, again in capital letters:
'NEXT TIME SHE'LL LOSE A HAND. THEN SHE'LL BE A CRIPPLE, JUST LIKE YOU.'

Charles drew in his breath sharply. 'Not much doubt about that, then.'

'What does it say?' said Jenny, coming closer and reading it. 'Oh!'

'Don't let anyone touch this. I'm going to get something to put it into for the police,' I said.

'Can you get fingerprints off paper?' said Charles.

'I'm sure you can,' I said.

'You can also get DNA from saliva,' said Rosie.

249

I turned to her. 'So?'

'If someone licked that envelope to stick it shut then they will have left their DNA on it,' she said.

I stared at her. 'But won't it have dried out by now?' I asked.

'The DNA will still be there.'

'Could you get a profile from it?' I asked.

'I can get a profile from a single fruit fly you can hardly see,' she said, smiling. 'This would be a piece of cake.'

'Shouldn't you leave that to the police?' said Jenny.

'There's plenty of stick for both of us,' said Rosie. 'I would only need a tiny bit of the envelope. And I really want to do it.' She looked at me.

'So do I,' I said. 'I'll fetch some scissors and two plastic bags.'

Derek had stood listening to it all.

'Like something out of Agatha Christie,' he said. 'Death on Ebury Street.'

'No one's died yet,' I said. At least not here. But I thought of Huw Walker and Bill Burton.

We went up to my flat and I raided the refrigerator to find some food. I made a plateful of ham and mustard sandwiches and found some bananas lurking in a fruit bowl behind the kitchen television. The others kindly let me have first go but then they also tucked in with relish.

I went into my office to find Marina's parents' number. I tried to call them but there was no answer. I wrote down their address to give to the police, just in case.

I went back into the sitting room. Rosie was on a mission and she wanted to go off to Lincoln's Inn

Fields straight away with her bag containing its piece of envelope.

'What's the hurry?' I asked. 'It takes hours for the stuff to move in that gel anyway.'

'Not with the machine in my lab,' said Rosie. 'I can get results much quicker than Marina could. The whole thing would take me less than an hour.'

I knew that Rosie was desperate to do something that, in her eyes, would compensate for what she saw as her failure to keep Marina from harm and I wasn't going to stop her. I was also interested to know if there was DNA on the envelope and if it matched our previous sample. It wouldn't, however, give us the answer to the puzzle.

'Do whatever you like,' I said. 'I'm going to change and then I'm going back to the hospital. I'll call the Superintendent after I've gone and tell him to collect the card from reception. I don't want to spend another age being interviewed.'

'I don't mind going with Rosie to her lab,' said Charles. 'We'll come on to the hospital after.'

'And I'll go with Sid,' said Jenny.

*   *   *

I left the car in the garage and we took two taxis. It was a long time since I'd been in a taxi alone with Jenny.

'Just like old times,' I said.

'I was thinking the same. Funny old world.'

'What do you mean?' I asked.

'Here I am, going with you to see the woman who's taken my place and I am desperate that she should be all right.'

'Are you?' I asked.

'Of course. I liked her last Sunday. You two go well together.'

I looked out as we passed Big Ben and absentmindedly checked my watch.

'I do want you to be happy, you know,' she said. 'I know we're divorced but it doesn't mean I don't care for you. I just couldn't live with you. And . . .' She tailed off.

'Yes?' I said. 'And what?'

She didn't answer. I didn't press her. I really was glad she was here and I didn't want to have a scene.

We arrived at the entrance to St Thomas's and I started to get out of the cab.

Jenny put her hand on my arm, the real one. 'I'm not sure how to put this,' she said. 'And obviously it's not the reason I want her to get better but,' she paused, 'Marina . . . takes away my guilt.'

I sat back in the seat and looked at her. My dear Jenny. The girl I had once loved and ached for. The girl I thought I knew.

'Are you getting out, guv'nor?' asked the driver, breaking the trance.

'Sorry,' I said.

Jenny and I climbed out of the taxi, paid, and went into the hospital.

*   *   *

Dr Osborne in Casualty had said that the first three hours would be critical, but he had said that over four hours ago and Marina had survived so far. Every passing minute must surely improve her chances.

When we arrived at Intensive Care, Jenny said she would wait on the same chairs outside by the lifts, and read. I noticed that she had borrowed a book from my flat. I was surprised to see that it was an autobiography by a leading steeplechase trainer, someone I had ridden for regularly, and someone Jenny and I used to argue about.

I put on the regulation blue uniform and went in to be met by the police guard that had belatedly appeared in the unit. Yes, a nurse agreed, she could vouch for Mr Halley; he's Miss Meer's fiancé. Pass, friend.

Marina looked the same as when I'd left her.

I sat down as before and held her hand. It seemed natural to talk to her so I did, albeit softly.

I told her about all sorts of things. I told her about leaving my car on the pavement and how the bomb squad had been called out to check it. I told her that Charles had come up to London and how he had arrived with Jenny. I told her about Rosie and that she might be staying the night but not to worry because Charles would be there too as a chaperon. I didn't tell her about the card and its violent message. I was pretty sure that she couldn't hear me but I didn't want to distress her, just in case.

'And do you know,' I said to her, 'Jenny says you take away her guilt. Her guilt for leaving me. Now there's a shock, I can tell you. I've never thought she felt guilty for a moment. The irony is that I had felt guilty, too, because I hadn't given up riding when she wanted me to.'

I stroked her arm and sat there for a while in silence. For all its intensiveness, the Intensive Care

Unit was a calm, quiet place with subdued lighting and almost no noise. Just the hum of the ventilator pump and the slight hiss of escaping air.

'But I don't feel guilty any more,' I said.

'Guilty about what?' said a voice.

I jumped. Mr Pandita, the surgeon, had entered the cubicle silently behind me.

'For God's sake,' I said, 'you nearly gave me a heart attack.'

'There are worse places to have one,' he smiled. 'I have a friend who had a heart attack at a hotel where hundreds of cardiac surgeons were having a convention. They almost fought over him as he toppled off a bar stool.'

'Lucky him.' I nodded at Marina. 'How's she doing?'

'Fine,' he said. 'I think I would refer to her condition now as serious but stable. It's no longer critical. I do believe your girl is going to live.'

I could feel the welling in my eyes, I could sense the tightening at the bridge of my nose and the pressure in my jaw. I cried the tears of relief, the tears of joy.

'Provided we can bring her out of the unconsciousness safely tomorrow then she should make a complete recovery. But we'll keep her sedated for the night just to be on the safe side.'

'What time in the morning?' I asked.

'We'll stop giving her the sedative in the drip around seven. We'll remove the ventilator, and then we'll see. Everyone is different but, if I was a betting man,' he smiled again, 'I'd say she should be awake by noon at the latest. That is, of course, if her brain wasn't starved of oxygen, but I think that's unlikely. There were no reports that she had stopped breathing at any time.'

'Should I stay here the night?' I asked.

'You're welcome to if you want,' he said, 'but it's not necessary. She's over the danger time. There shouldn't be much change overnight and we can always call you if there is. The best thing you can do is to go home and get a good night's sleep and be here for her tomorrow. She won't be feeling too well, I'm afraid. The sedative tends to make patients feel rather sick.'

'Thank you, doctor,' I said.

'Actually I'm a mister.'

'What?' I said. 'Off the street?' I smiled at him.

'Not quite,' he said. 'It stems from the time when surgeons were all barbers. They were the only people with sharp enough blades. Can you imagine? "A quick shave, sir, and I'll whip out your appendix on the side." In those days, doctors saw it as a failure to have to cut open their patients, and most surgery proved fatal. It was the option of last hope. So surgeons weren't doctors and they were called mister. And it's stuck. Now you progress from being a mister to a doctor and then finally back to a mister.'

'For jockeys, mister means an amateur.'

He laughed. 'Well, I don't think I'm an amateur.'

'No,' I said. 'I think not. You saved her life.'

He waved a hand. 'All in a day's work. Bye now.'

He moved on. There were probably others more needful of his skills.

I waved at the silent policeman as I went back out to Jenny. I thought it would be too soon for Charles and Rosie to be there but they appeared out of the lift at the same moment as I came

255

through the door.

'Great news,' I said. 'The official bulletin is now that Marina is no longer critical and she is expected to make a full recovery.'

'Thank God,' said Charles.

Rosie clasped her hands to her face but it did nothing to stem the rush of tears down her cheeks. Her shoulders shuddered with sobs at the same time as her mouth opened in laughter. The release of tension was tangible for us all.

'That's all right, then,' said Jenny.

Yes, indeed, it was very much all right.

'I only have three bedrooms,' I said when Jenny said she wanted to come back to Ebury Street with the rest of us. 'So who are you going to share with?'

I thought for a moment that she was going to say she'd share with me, but good sense prevailed.

'I'll go home later,' she said, 'and I'd better give Anthony a call. He may be wondering where I've got to.'

'Haven't you called him?' Charles said.

'No. I'm often out when he gets in from the office. And other times I wait in and he doesn't come home for hours. He goes for drinks or dinner with a colleague. He doesn't usually phone me. It's the way we are.'

How sad, I thought.

*　　　*　　　*

We went straight down to the street and set off back to my flat in a black cab.

'Well?' I said to Rosie.

'No match,' she said.

'Oh,' I said. 'We're looking for two people then.'

'Yes,' said Rosie. 'And this one's a woman.'

'Are you sure?'

'Absolutely.' She sounded rather hurt that I'd questioned her. 'I got a good profile off that piece of envelope and it didn't match the first one at all. Men and women have different chromosomes and different DNA. It's easy to tell from the two profiles that it was a man who punched Marina last week, and a woman who licked the envelope tonight.'

A wife, perhaps, or a girlfriend? Could anyone stick that envelope shut without knowing the contents? I doubted it. A man had attacked Marina outside my flat last week; Marina had his skin under her fingernails. And this week the message came with the saliva of a woman. Maybe I was searching for even more than two people.

'So what are we going to do now?' said Charles.

'No idea,' I said. 'I thought I could at least discount the female half of the population from suspicion, but now . . .'

'It can't be that bad,' said Charles.

'Almost,' I said. 'And there is one thing that really bothers me. Is race fixing sufficient motive for murder?'

'Money is always a motive for murder,' said Jenny.

'But we're not talking big money here. Huw Walker was offered a few hundred a time to fix a race. He told me that himself.' And Chief Inspector Carlisle has the tape, I thought.

'If really big money was involved then you would be likely to offer the jockey a bit more than a few hundred. That's not much more than his riding fee,' I said.

'It might seem a lot to a jockey from the valleys,' said Charles.

'Maybe,' I said, 'but Huw had been around a long time and had been used to earning good money.'

We arrived back at my flat, piled out of the taxi and went inside.

'I come back to the race fixing,' I said when we were all safely settled and I had provided sustenance in the form of more ham sandwiches and a bottle of wine.

'Who could gain sufficiently for it to be worth the risk of killing a jockey in broad daylight with sixty thousand members of the public close to hand? The era of an individual running a big betting coup is past. Drug dealing has killed the ability for the crooked gambler to pull off the big con.'

'Why?' said Jenny.

'Because drug dealing produces such huge amounts of cash that banks and governments have introduced a whole raft of money-laundering checks. These days, it's almost impossible to pay for anything in cash without six pieces of identification and a reference from the Pope. Gone is the time when you could sidle up to a bookie with a hundred thousand in readies to stick on number two at Cartmel in the three-thirty. He'll likely tell you now to get lost or place the bet by credit card.'

'And you're not going to do that if you're doing something dodgy,' said Charles.

'Exactly,' I said. 'Far too easy to trace.'

'So what could be the motive for the murder?'

said Rosie.

'That's the million dollar question,' I said. 'Kate Burton, that's Bill's wife, told Marina that Huw Walker had said to her that the whole race fixing thing was more about power than money.'

'But money gives you power,' said Jenny.

'Indeed it does,' I said, 'but if you have enough money, there may be the urge to have power merely for its own sake.'

'Sounds too complicated for me,' said Charles. 'Power to me means a broadside of twelve inchers.'

Charles could usually apply a naval sea battle analogy to most situations.

'So what's the order of the day tomorrow?' asked Jenny. 'Please say I'm needed again. Today, for all its trauma, has been the most exciting day in my life for years.'

She looked at me and smiled. I don't think she truly realised what she had just said.

'I'll go to the hospital early,' I said. 'They're taking Marina off the sedative at seven and I want to be there when she wakes. As far as I'm concerned, you can all come. In fact, I'd love it if you did—so long as you don't mind more sitting around in the hospital corridor.'

'I should go to work,' said Rosie.

'I'm sure no one would mind if you took a day off, especially after today's events.'

'My flies would,' she said. 'They don't stop turning from larva into pupae and then into flies just because someone gets shot.'

'Give them a day off,' said Charles. 'I'm sure that Marina will want you there when she wakes up.'

'I'll see how I feel in the morning.'

'I'll need to get some food in tomorrow morning before I go to the hospital,' I said. 'Marina will want more than ham sandwiches when she gets home.'

'I suspect she'll need lots of rest, too,' said Charles.

'Nonsense,' said Jenny. 'What she'll need is shopping. Trust me, I'm a woman. Things get better with shopping. And the more expensive, the better. Retail therapy and all that.'

'You're absolutely right,' I said. 'And she's been nagging at me for ages to take her to Bond Street to buy her some designer dresses. Armani, I think she wants.'

'Blimey,' said Jenny. 'You never treated me to anything so grand. I hope you've got your gold card ready.'

'They can't be that expensive,' I said.

'Don't you believe it,' said Jenny. 'You won't get any change from a couple of grand for each dress. Then there's the matching shoes and the handbags. You'll need one of those big gambling coups yourself just to pay for it all.'

'Really,' I said. But I wasn't paying attention. My mind was replaying the image of a long line of designer dresses with matching shoes that I had seen in Juliet Burns's wardrobe.

CHAPTER SEVENTEEN

'What time is it?' Marina said softly into the silence.

Her condition had steadily improved during the

night and she had been moved to a new room with a view of the Thames and the Houses of Parliament. I was standing looking out of the window, and I hadn't noticed her open her eyes.

I glanced at Big Ben across the river. 'Twenty past ten.' I turned and smiled at her.

'What day?' she said.

'Friday. Welcome back to the land of the living.'

'What happened?'

'You got shot.'

'That was careless. Where?'

I mentally tossed up. 'In your leg.'

'Oh.'

'Can't you feel it?'

'All I feel is sick,' she said.

'My darling love,' I said. 'I was warned that you might feel bad due to the sedative they gave you.'

I rang the bell for a nurse who duly appeared.

'She's awake,' I said rather unnecessarily. 'Can she have anything for the nausea?'

'I'll see what the doctor says.' She disappeared.

I sat down on the chair by the bed and held Marina's hand. Only yesterday I had been required to wear a mask. Now I leaned forward and kissed her.

'You had us all worried for a while,' I said.

'All?' she asked.

'Charles and Rosie are outside, and Jenny too.'

She raised her eyebrows. 'And will I survive?'

'Yes, my dear, indeed you shall.'

'What damage is there?' she said.

'None that will be permanent,' I said. 'But you emptied most of your life-blood on to the pavement outside the Institute. If it hadn't been for Rosie's attempts at stopping the bleeding, you wouldn't be here.'

'Which leg?' she asked.

'Can't you tell?'

'Both of them hurt.'

'They had to take a piece of vein out of your left leg to repair the artery in your right, which was damaged by the bullet.'

'Clever stuff,' she said, smiling. There was nothing wrong with her brain.

The nurse returned with a couple of pills for her to take. 'These will only be any good if you can keep them down so only a little water.'

'But I'm so thirsty,' said Marina.

'Just little sips,' said the nurse bossily, 'or you'll bring them up again and it'll be worse than ever.'

Marina pulled a face and winked at me as the nurse poured a thimbleful of water into a glass and gave it to her to take the pills.

We waited in silence for her to leave, then laughed.

I marvelled at how a human being can be at death's door one day and then seemingly fine and dandy the next. All to do with the need for oxygen to make things happen, and the blood supply to deliver it around the body. Cut off the current and the bulb goes out. Turn it on again and the light shines brightly. Only it's not that simple with a brain. Once off, it stays off, because the brain also controls the switch.

'I'll go and get the others,' I said.

'What am I wearing?' said Marina, trying to sit up a little to look down at the off-white regulation-issue hospital nightgown.

'They're not going to worry about what you're wearing,' I said.

'Well, I do,' she said. 'And what's my hair like?'

'It's fine,' I said. 'You're beautiful.'

In truth, she appeared washed out and tired with the two lines of stitches from last week still prominent in her face. But, all things considered, she looked great.

I went to fetch Rosie, Charles and Jenny. They came in and gathered round Marina's bed, fussing over her and being equally astonished at how quickly she was mending.

The bossy nurse reappeared. 'Only two visitors at a time,' she said.

'OK,' I said. 'They won't be long.'

I stood back by the window and looked at Marina. I had been badly frightened at how close I had come to losing her. Fear, relief, desperate fear again and finally overwhelming relief—the emotional rollercoaster of the last twenty hours had left me mentally exhausted and physically drained.

Now I began to notice a subtle change in me. The feeling of wellbeing and joy at finding that Marina would fully recover was slowly ebbing away and being replaced by a growing anger. I was annoyed with myself, of course, for not having taken the previous warning even more seriously than we had. But this was a mere bagatelle compared to the fury that was rising in me towards the person, or persons, responsible for this.

Mr Pandita arrived, wreathed in smiles.

I found that I had consciously to relax my right hand to shake his. I had been clenching my fist together so hard that my fingernails had been digging into the flesh.

'I see she's doing fine,' he said. 'But don't tire

263

her out too much.'

'Hello,' said Marina. 'I assume we've met.'

'Yes, sorry. I'm Mr Pandita and I'm the consultant general surgeon here. I operated on your leg.'

'So it's your fault I bloody hurt so much?' said Marina.

'Not all mine,' he said. 'You were pretty badly hurt when I first saw you.'

'Yes,' said Marina, suitably admonished. 'Well, thank you.'

Mr Pandita nodded then turned to me. 'I think she should stay here for a while longer. That leg needs to be rested in order to allow the graft to heal. I don't want her back on the table with a rupture or an aneurysm. You were lucky, young lady,' he said to Marina. 'The bullet missed your knee and your femur. A couple of days' bed-rest here where you can be monitored and then you should be ready to go home.'

Luck is relative, I thought. Marina had been unlucky to be shot in the first place and unlucky that the bullet had torn open an artery, but prompt action by Rosie, first-rate medical care, and her own strong constitution had won the day, not luck.

Mr Pandita ushered all of us away to allow Marina to rest.

'Come back later,' he said to me. 'Give her at least a couple of hours to sleep.'

*   *   *

Rosie went back to work and Charles took Jenny off to lunch. I had urged him to stay with Jenny in London for a few days.

'But why?' he'd said.

'Where you live is common knowledge,' I'd replied. 'And I don't want you to get any visits from a gun-toting motorcyclist.'

'Oh!' he'd said. 'Well, perhaps for a day or two. Or I could stay at my club.'

I had inwardly laughed at his dilemma. The Army & Navy Club had much more attraction for Charles. It had a decent bar for a start. Jenny was always complaining about the amount of whisky he drank so he was unlikely to get much of it at her place. They had decided to discuss it over some lunch.

Suddenly I felt quite lonely as I walked back across Westminster Bridge in the watery March sunshine. I called into the betting shop on Victoria Street but my friend from before, Gerry Noble, wasn't there. Perhaps I was too early for him. I was disappointed and I hung around for a while in the hope he might turn up. He didn't, so I asked one of the staff behind the counter if they knew if he was coming.

'Gerry Noble?' said the man. 'I don't know their names. I take their bloody money not their life histories.'

'A big guy. Wears a Manchester United shirt,' I persisted.

'Look,' he said, 'they could all wear bloody leotards for all I'd notice. As I said, I'm only interested in their money.'

Clearly, he enjoyed his work and I was wasting my time.

Instead I continued my walk back to Ebury Street and then busied myself clearing up.

So how could Juliet Burns afford to have a wardrobe full of designer clothes with shoes to match?

I was mulling over this little teaser when my mobile phone rang.

'Mr Halley?' said a voice.

'Yes.'

'Superintendent Aldridge here,' said the voice.

'How can I help you?' I asked.

'Glad to hear that Miss Meer is making steady progress,' he said.

'Yes,' I said. 'Miss van der Meer is awake and doing fine this morning.' I emphasised the 'van der' and there was a moment's pause while he took stock.

'Exactly,' he said. 'Excellent news.'

'Are you still providing her with a guard?' I asked him.

'We are, but I don't really think it's necessary.'

'How so?' I said.

'The gunman clearly didn't mean to kill her in the first place as he shot her in the leg. He was obviously trying only to wound her. In a way, she was very unlucky to be so close to dying. If you wanted to kill someone, you wouldn't try to sever their femoral artery. Much too chancy. So I don't really believe that she is in any danger in the hospital. And there's also that card you left for me. I don't think "next time" means the following day. I'm afraid the guard will be withdrawn this afternoon at the change of shift.'

Reluctantly, I agreed with his assessment.

'Did you get any fingerprints off the card?'

266

'It's still with forensics but they weren't very hopeful. The card appears clean but they are still testing the envelope.'

'Is there anything you need from me?' I asked him.

'Not at the moment. But be sure to let me know if you think of anything.'

'So what do you do now?' I said.

'What do you mean?'

'Where are you going to send your task force to find this gunman?'

'I don't have a task force,' he said. 'This wasn't a murder and I have limited resources.'

'But it was a shooting in broad daylight in a London street.'

'Mr Halley, have you any idea how many shootings take place every day in London streets?'

'No.'

'Well, it would surprise you. There's about one shooting a day that results in injury or death. And there's a gun crime somewhere in London on average every five or six hours. There were more than a dozen armed robberies last week in the Met area alone, and there's a murder at least every second day.' He paused for effect. 'I'm sorry,' he said. 'If Miss *van der* Meer had died I might have had a few officers in a team to help find the gunman. Thankfully, she didn't, so I don't get the resources. We are too busy trying to catch some other poor sod's killer.'

'But it may be the same person who killed Huw Walker,' I said.

'Who?'

'The jockey at Cheltenham.'

'Oh, yes,' he said. 'Perhaps I'll give

267

Gloucestershire police a call.'

'Ask for Chief Inspector Carlisle,' I said, but he too was busy with another case. A child killer had more fascination for the media than the death of a 'crooked' jockey.

'Right,' he said, and disconnected.

I'd better investigate this myself, then.

*   *   *

Marina was sitting up in bed looking much better when I returned to see her at four thirty. I had brought with me a suitcase of things for her but I needn't have bothered.

She was already wearing a pretty pink nightdress and a matching cotton dressing gown. Her hair was clean and neat and she had applied some makeup. And, I noticed, the stitches had been removed from her eyebrow and lip.

'You look wonderful,' I said, giving her a kiss. 'Where did you get the nightie?'

'Rosie had it sent over from Rigby and Peller. Isn't she fantastic?'

'Absolutely,' I agreed, sitting down on the chair beside the bed. Rosie was beating herself up unnecessarily for allowing Marina to get shot. It wasn't her fault and no one but she thought so.

'A policeman did come to see me this morning,' said Marina. 'He asked me if I could describe the man who shot me.'

'And can you?' I asked.

'No, not really. It all happened so fast. I remember him looking at a map and beckoning me over to him. He was wearing black leathers and a black helmet, you know, one of those with a full

268

front and a dark visor. That's why I couldn't see his face. That's about it.'

'Are you sure it was a man?'

'You think it might have been a woman?'

'It's possible,' I said.

'No.' She paused. 'I'm pretty good when it comes to spotting women, even if they're wearing motorcycling leathers.'

'Are you sure?'

'Yes. It was a man. If it had been a woman I would have looked at her bottom.'

'What for?' I said.

'To see if it was smaller than mine. Silly boy.'

'Do you do that all the time?'

'Of course,' she said. 'All women do it.'

And I thought I was the one who looked at women's bottoms.

'What else did the policeman say?' I asked.

'He asked if I would recognise the motorbike.' She laughed. 'I told him it had two wheels but that didn't seem to help. I don't know what type it was. I wouldn't know if I'd had all day to examine it.'

'But it was blue,' I said. I didn't know.

'No, it wasn't,' she said. She stopped with her mouth open. She closed it. 'It was red. How funny, I didn't remember before.' She paused for quite a while. 'It also had a big red fuel tank with yellow flashes down the side. And the rider had more yellow bits on his trousers, along his thighs.'

'Could you draw the shape of the yellow flashes?' I asked.

'Absolutely,' she said. 'They were like lightning bolts.'

'Good girl,' I said. 'I'll get you some paper and a pencil.'

I went off in search of them and eventually managed to borrow a pad and pen from the nursing station. Marina set to work and had soon produced some drawings of the lightning type flashes on the fuel tank and on the motorcyclist's leather trousers.

Just as she finished, a nurse came in and told me it was time to go. 'The patient must get some rest,' she said, and stood in the open doorway waiting for me to leave.

'See you tomorrow, my love,' I said to Marina, giving her a kiss.

'OK,' she said, yawning. She did look tired but so much better than yesterday.

I made my way down to the exit. What a difference a day makes. I didn't notice anyone at the hospital reception desk who was desperately looking for the Intensive Care Unit as I had been just over twenty-fours hours ago. But then I wouldn't. A crisis doesn't make you grow a second head or anything; the turmoil is on the inside. Invisible.

*   *   *

When I had been riding, Saturday morning had always been a 'work day' in Andrew Woodward's yard and I assumed that nothing would have changed. On a 'work day' the horses would do 'work'. A large string of them would be out on the exercise grounds early, galloping hard to increase their stamina and speed. Preparing a horse for racing was all about developing stamina and speed. High protein oats, minerals and oils are transformed into strong, firm muscle through regular and demanding training gallops.

First lot in the Woodward stable had always gone out at half past seven sharp. Horses need to be made ready with saddles and bridles, with protective bandages on their lower legs, and with their coats and tails brushed. There was much to do for the trainer and his assistants prior to the 'mount up' order being given; at ten past seven they would be busy and preoccupied with the horses and the stable staff.

Which is why, on Saturday morning at ten past seven precisely, I let myself in through the front door of Juliet Burns's tiny cottage.

Lambourn is set in a hollow of the Berkshire Downs, appropriately close to the Bronze Age White Horse figure carved into a chalk hill at Uffington. Locally, and for good reason, the area is known as The Valley of the Racehorse. At about two thousand, there are almost as many racehorses living in the village as there are people. And the majority of the human residents earn their living either directly or indirectly from their equine neighbours.

I wasn't sure what made a village into a town but, if any village deserved it, it was Lambourn. Not many villages I knew had at least a dozen shops, several restaurants, two fish-and-chip bars, four pubs, a leisure centre and a fully equipped hospital, even if it was only for the horses. But still no town hall.

There was only one betting shop. In spite of a roaring trade, it apparently wasn't very profitable. There were too many winners.

I had lived here myself for five years during my racing career and my face was almost as well known in this community as Saddam Hussein's was in Baghdad. If I were ever to take up burglary as a career, the one place I would not choose to start would be Lambourn.

Thankfully Juliet had not heeded my advice to increase the security of her cottage. Her front door Yale key was under the stone in the window box, just as before. I turned the lock, put the key back under the stone, and stepped into the cottage.

I stood very still in the hallway listening for the slightest sound. The house was silent, and from outside there were no shouts from nosy neighbours who might have witnessed my arrival. I closed the door.

I padded silently up the stairs. It would be just my luck if she was still here, ill in bed. I risked a peep into her bedroom. The bed was empty and unmade. I put my right hand down on the sheet; it was cold.

I hadn't put on gloves as I wasn't worried about fingerprints. I didn't intend stealing anything and I'd been in this house only last week anyway. My right-hand dabs must have already been everywhere.

I reckoned I had at least twenty minutes before Juliet could possibly come home. I thought that she would probably be going out to the gallops with the horses, either seated on one of them or in Andrew Woodward's old Land Rover. That would give me well over an hour to look around, but I didn't want to take the chance that she might pop back after the string had left the yard. I gave myself twenty minutes to be out of the place. Better safe than arrested.

I went across to her wardrobe and opened the

door.

Altogether, I counted a dozen outfits hanging there, many of them in the designer-named plastic covers so thoughtfully provided to keep the dust off. There were short floral cocktail dresses and long slinky evening gowns, skirts with matching jackets and brightly coloured trouser suits, and they didn't look like fakes or copies to me.

It was an impressive list with four Giorgio Armanis, two each from Versace and Gucci, and a scattering of others, all of them from well-known designers that even I had heard of. There were rows of shoes from Jimmy Choo and a shelf of handbags from Fendi. It was a veritable treasure trove. I did a simple mental calculation using some information about prices that I had obtained from Jenny.

I knew that good assistant trainers were hard to find these days and that they could command quite high salaries, especially compared to only a few years ago, but I again wondered how Juliet Burns had obtained the means to have nearly thirty thousand pounds' worth of clothes and accessories in her wardrobe.

I remembered the morning I had brought her back here, the morning when Bill had died. She had been very keen for me to leave her jacket on the bed and not to hang it up. But at that time, I hadn't realised what I'd been looking at.

I took my camera out of my pocket and took some shots through the open wardrobe door. I didn't want to disturb things more than I needed to. If, as I imagined, these dresses were Juliet's pride and joy then she would know exactly in which order they were hung up, and the exact position of every shoe and handbag. I didn't want her to know I'd been here. Not yet, anyway.

I closed the wardrobe door carefully and looked round the rest of the bedroom. There wasn't much that I hadn't seen on my previous visit. I looked in the drawers in her dressing table but there was nothing unusual. I discovered no hidden cache of jewels, no boxes of bearer bonds.

There were bedside cabinets on either side of the double bed. In one I found a pair of men's boxer shorts and a rolled up pair of men's socks. In the other there were some condoms hidden in a Jimmy Choo shoe-box, together with a couple of raunchy paperbacks. I smiled. So much for the tom-boy exterior.

I went into the bathroom. Two toothbrushes stood in a beaker on a glass shelf but otherwise there was nothing of interest. I looked in her bathroom cabinet but there were only the usual things: tampons, painkillers and sticky plasters. I took care to put everything back as I had found it.

I made a last check of the bedroom and noticed Juliet's hairbrush on her dressing table. Amongst its mass of black bristles were some hairs that had conveniently been pulled out with the follicles still attached. I took a photograph of it.

I had a plastic bag in my pocket that I had brought with me, just in case. I very carefully removed at least a dozen of the hairs and placed them in the bag. I put the brush back in the same position I had found it and went downstairs.

I glanced at my watch. I had already used up ten minutes, half my time.

I searched the kitchen but there was nothing of interest there. The small fridge in the corner

274

contained some skimmed milk, a pack of bacon, a bunch of black grapes that looked past their best, and a row of six eggs in the door. No champagne, no caviar, and no incriminating hypodermic syringes full of dope.

The waste bin under the sink was empty and I didn't dare go outside to rummage through the dustbin. There were too many eyes that might have been watching. Such a shame. I had discovered all sorts of secrets in people's dustbins.

I went through to the small sitting room. A laptop computer sat on the floor next to the sofa. Computers can be funny things. They have a habit of remembering everything done to them so I was particularly wary of leaving any tell-tale signs that might indicate to Juliet that I had been there.

I opened the lid of the machine. It was on but in 'hibernation' mode. I woke it up and was busy sifting through the recent document list in Word when there was a noise from the front door. I froze. I racked my brains for a credible story to tell Juliet to explain why I was kneeling on her sitting room floor going through the private files on her computer.

The noise came again. A metallic clink. And again.

I quickly moved behind the sitting room door and looked through the crack by the hinges into the hallway. A letter came through the letter box in the front door and the cover closed with a metallic clink. The letter joined some magazines already on the mat. The postman! I heard him move away. I chanced a look out of the sitting room window and could see him going next door.

I started breathing again and my heart-rate

began to return to normal.

I looked at my watch. My time was up.

I went back to Juliet's computer. How I would have loved to have had all day to search through the digital maze inside it. No wonder a suspect's computer is the first thing the police seize after an arrest. These days, personal computer records are the window on a person's life. Try as we might to delete the stuff we don't wish others to read, our computers still remember it and they can be coaxed and persuaded into giving up our most intimate secrets. In most circumstances, a wife cannot be forced to give evidence against her husband, or vice versa. There is no such protection for a defendant against his computer. Far from being a friend, the machine on the desk can be a villain's worst enemy.

I sent Juliet's laptop back into hibernation and returned it to its original spot on the floor.

Then I opened the front door wide and took a quick look either way down the road. The postman was a good hundred yards away by now and moving further away with every step. There was no one else visible so I quickly pulled the door closed behind me and walked steadily to my car. I had parked on the grass verge fifty yards further out of the village with the car facing away from Juliet's cottage. I climbed in and sat in the driver's seat. My hand was shaking. I was getting too old for this cloak and dagger stuff.

I checked for the umpteenth time that I had not left behind my camera or the bag containing the hairs. Satisfied that I had them both, I set off for London.

By the time I got back, I was tired. At six that morning, the journey from my flat to Lambourn had only taken about an hour, but the return had been a nightmare. Three hours of stop-start in heavy traffic due to major road-works on the approach to London. The M4 had been one long queue from well before Slough.

I changed out of my housebreaking clothes of black jeans, dark sweater and loafers into grey trousers, blue collared shirt and black leather slip-on shoes. I snapped a recharged battery into my arm and made myself a cup of strong coffee to recharge the rest of me.

Marina phoned. 'Please come and get me out of here,' she said. 'I can't stand daytime TV.'

'I'll be in later,' I said, 'and I'll bring you a book.'

'I want to come home.'

'Bed-rest, that's what the doctor said.'

How strange, I thought. All my riding life, it had been me who had tried to ignore well-intentioned doctors' advice with Jenny sounding just as I had done now. I had been the one who had been caught working out on an exercise bike after being told by my surgeon to rest in bed after he had removed my spleen. And I had been the one who had once tried to chip away a plaster cast with a kitchen knife before my ankle bones had fully mended.

I told her to stay put for the moment and I would see what could be done.

At lunchtime I took the tube to Lincoln's Inn Fields with my precious parcel to give to Rosie. I had phoned her at home and she had agreed to give up some of her Saturday afternoon to analyse the hairs.

While she went upstairs to her laboratory I took my camera round the corner into Kingsway to a photographic shop. They had one of those machines that will convert digital images into prints while you wait, so I made two sets of all the pictures stored on the camera memory card. There were some of the police search of Bill Burton's house after his arrest and the ones through the window of the den on the day he died. There were several of poor Marina's face being stitched up, six images of a wardrobe full of designer gear and, finally, a crisp close-up shot of a hairbrush with hairs amongst its bristles.

There was no sign of Rosie when I returned so I sat in the reception area under the gaze of the ever-present Institute Security and read leaflets about why it was so vital to give money for cancer research, and why early diagnosis of cancer was so important. By the time Rosie reappeared, I had not only emptied all the cash in my pockets into a Cancer Research UK collecting tin, but I was beginning to examine my body for lumps and bumps in intimate places.

'Jackpot!' she called, as she emerged from the lift. She was almost jumping up and down with excitement. 'In fact, double jackpot.'

'Why double?' I asked.

'I tested all the hairs in the bag separately,' she said. 'They're from two different people. Most of them are from the woman who licked the envelope the other night.'

'And?' I said.

'One of them is from the man who attacked Marina last week.'

CHAPTER EIGHTEEN

'You're a bastard,' said Chris Beecher. 'You used me.'

He was right, on both counts.

It was Saturday afternoon and I had telephoned him while I watched the racing from Kempton on the television.

'You didn't have to run the piece,' I said.

'Wish now we hadn't. Wasn't so much of a scoop after all, was it?'

'How do you know?' I said.

'Worked it out, didn't I?' He was a bright chap. 'No bloody police reaction, was there? Bloody Paddy O'Fitch. Why do I ever listen to him?'

'Can I come and see you?' I asked.

'What do you want me to write for you this time, you bastard?'

'You can write what you like,' I said. 'However, I may have a real scoop for you after all.'

I despised the creep but he was the best man for what I had in mind.

'On the level?' he said.

'On the level. But I might need your help to get it.'

'OK, so fire away.'

'Not on the telephone. And not until tomorrow.'

'It may have disappeared by then or some other bloody paper may have it.'

'Rest easy,' I said. 'This will be your exclusive,

279

but all in good time.'

'I don't work on Sundays,' he said.

I laughed. 'Liar.'

In the end we agreed to meet in the Ebury Street Wine Bar at seven the following evening. I needed to do some thinking before I talked to him, and also I wanted to have the day free to bring Marina home.

*   *   *

I went to St Thomas's about four. I could sense that all was not well in Marina's world. I stood by the window looking out across the Thames.

'At least you've got a nice view,' I said, trying to lighten the mood.

'I can't see it,' said Marina. 'The bed is too low. All I can see is the sky. And the nurses won't let me get up. Not even to go to the loo. I have to use a bedpan. It's disgusting.'

'Calm down, my darling,' I said. 'You shouldn't be pushing your blood pressure up at the moment. Give the artery in your leg a chance to heal.'

The sooner I got her home, the better. I was also sure that her security would be better there, too.

'OK, OK, I'm calm,' she said. She took a few deep breaths and laid her head back on the pillow. 'And what have you been up to that has kept you from me until four in the afternoon.'

Ah, the real reason for the fluster.

'I've been with another woman,' I said.

'Oh,' she said pausing for a moment. 'That's all right then. I thought you might have been working.'

We giggled.

'I went to Lambourn this morning,' I said.

'What, to ride?'

'No, I went to Juliet Burns's cottage.'

'What on earth for?' she asked.

I pulled out the pictures of Juliet's wardrobe. 'Look at these,' I said.

She studied the six photographs. It wasn't easy to tell what they were of unless you had seen it live, as it were.

'So?'

'They're pictures of Juliet Burns's wardrobe, in her bedroom.'

'So you were in her bedroom, were you?'

'She wasn't there at the time.'

'So what's so special about Juliet Burns's wardrobe?' she asked.

'It contains at least thirty thousand pounds' worth of designer dresses, Jimmy Choo shoes and Fendi handbags.'

'Wow!' she said. She took another look at the pictures. 'I take it you don't think she obtained them through hard work and careful saving.'

'I do not.'

'But how did you know they were there?' Marina asked.

'I saw them when I took Juliet home the morning she found Bill dead.' I suddenly wondered whether she had, in fact, 'found' him dead.

'How come?'

'I hung her jacket up in that wardrobe. But I didn't realise what I was looking at until Jenny told me yesterday how much designer clothes cost.'

'It doesn't make her a murderer,' said Marina.

'There's more.' I told her about the hairbrush

and the hairs and about Rosie having done a DNA test on them. And I told her about the card that had been waiting at Ebury Street for me and also about its hand-written message.

She went very quiet.

'Well, whoever licked the envelope on Thursday is the same person that left the hairs on the hairbrush, and that has to be Juliet Burns herself.'

'I take it that she didn't actually invite you into her bedroom this morning,' Marina said.

'No,' I said. 'She was at work.'

'So what now?' she asked. 'Shouldn't you tell the police about the clothes and the hairs and all that?'

'The police are too busy with other things,' I said. 'As far as I can see, they aren't even investigating your shooting. I was told they don't have the resources. The Gloucestershire police are spending their time trying to find a child killer and Thames Valley believe that Bill killed himself anyway.'

'Another policeman came to see me this morning,' said Marina.

'What did he want?' I asked.

'Just to know if I had remembered anything else,' she said.

'And have you?' I asked.

'Not really,' she said. 'I told him about the flashes on the motorbike fuel tank and gave him the drawings. He didn't think it helps much. Apparently masses of bikes have flashes on their fuel tanks.'

And lots of riders have flashes on their trousers, I thought.

'Oh, yes,' she said, 'and another thing.'

'What?'

'The policeman told me that you had told him that I was your fiancée.'

'Never!'

'Yes, you did. I asked the surgeon and he said, yes, definitely, Mr Halley told everyone he was my fiancé. Everyone but me, it seems.'

'It was the only way they would let me in to see you.'

'Oh. You didn't mean it then.'

'I did ask you to marry me, on Thursday night,' I said. 'But you didn't answer.'

'That's not fair. I was unconscious.'

'Excuses. Excuses.'

'If you really meant it, then ask me again.'

I looked deeply into her eyes. Did I want to spend the rest of my life with this person, for richer for poorer, in sickness and in health, until death do us part? Yes, I did, but I worried that, unless I found the gunman soon, death might us part rather more quickly than we would like.

'Do you want me to kneel?' I asked her.

'Absolutely,' she said. 'Get down to my level.'

I knelt on one knee beside the bed and took her left hand in my right.

'Marina van der Meer,' I said smiling at her, 'will you marry me?'

She looked away from my face.

'I'll think about it,' she said.

*   *   *

I spent all of Saturday evening researching the running of horses from Bill Burton's yard.

How did we manage before computers?

I was able to find out more in one evening using

283

digital technology than I would have done in a week using the old-fashioned small-printed pages of the form books.

The *Raceform* database with its almost instant access to a whole mass of statistics proved invaluable as I delved into the running of all Bill's horses over the last five years.

I was not so much looking for a needle in a haystack, as looking for a piece of hay in a haystack that was slightly shorter than it should have been. Even if I found it, I might still not be sure it was what I was looking for.

The classic tell-tale signs of race fixing have always been short-priced losers followed by long-priced winners. A horse is prevented from winning until the betting price lengthens, and then a big gamble is landed at long odds when the horse is really trying. But the ability to use the exchanges to bet on a horse to lose has changed all that. The classic signs no longer exist. Indeed, I asked myself, what signs might exist?

Tipsters and professional gamblers use patterns in performance as tools to select where a horse will tend to run well, and where less so. A course may be close by to the home stables and many horses do better when they don't have to travel long distances to the races. Trainers who use uphill training gallops may have more success with uphill finishes such as at Towcester or Cheltenham.

There are many other reasons why horses run better or worse at different venues. Some racecourses are flat and others are undulating, some have gentle curves while others have sharp ones. In America all tracks are left-handed, so the horses run anticlockwise, but in England some are left-handed and others right-handed, and at Windsor and Fontwell the horses have to run both right- and left-handed in the same race as the tracks are shaped like figures of eight.

The serious gambler needs to know where a trainer, or even a particular horse, does well and where not. And Raceform Interactive allows the user to look for hitherto unseen patterns in performance, to ask his own questions and use the huge data available to answer them. Could the system, I wondered, be used to look for dodgy dealing in the Burton yard? Could it show me that Huw Walker had been developing a pattern of fixing races?

I tried my best by asking what I thought were the right questions but my computer refused to serve up the hoped-for answers. Either there was no pattern to find or else the pattern was so long established that variations to it didn't show up over the past five years. And there had been no convenient, dramatic change to Bill Burton's results when Juliet Burns had arrived in his yard three years ago.

Another dead end.

I went into the kitchen to make myself some coffee.

So what *did* I know about the race fixing allegations?

I knew that Jonny Enstone believed his horses had been running to someone else's orders. He had told me so himself over lunch at the House of Lords. And the police had shown a list to Bill when they'd arrested him, which they said showed that the horses had not been running true to form.

I went back to my computer. Now I asked it to

look only at the running of Lord Enstone's horses. I spent ages giving every Enstone runner a user rating depending on whether it had run better or worse than its official rating would suggest. I then asked my machine if there was anything suspicious? Give me your answer do! Sadly, it was not into suspicion. Hard facts were its currency, not speculation.

However, the *Raceform* software did throw up a pattern of sorts.

I was so used to getting negative results that I nearly missed it. According to the data, Enstone's horses tended to run fractionally above their form at the northern tracks, say north of Haydock Park or Doncaster.

I brought Huw Walker into the equation. I thought that Huw might not have ridden them in the north, but the machine told me that that wasn't the case. There was no north/south divide by jockey. Every time in the past year that an Enstone horse had run north of Haydock Park, it had been ridden by Huw Walker.

Which is more than could be said for races run further south. Huw had been sidelined with injury for five weeks the previous September and eight of Lord Enstone's horses had run in the south during that time. They didn't appear to have run appreciably better for having had a different pilot.

What made running in the north so special? And was the improvement in their running really significant?

My eyes were growing tired from staring at on-screen figures. I looked at my watch. It was past midnight. Time for bed.

Early on Sunday morning, I called Neil Pedder, another trainer in Lambourn. His yard was down the road from Bill's.

'What's special about the racecourses north of Doncaster or Haydock?' I asked him.

'I wouldn't know,' he said unhelpfully. 'I hardly ever send runners up there.'

'Why not?' I asked. There are eighteen racecourses north of Haydock and Doncaster out of a total of fifty-nine in Great Britain. That was nearly a third of tracks that Neil didn't send runners to.

'Because it means the horses having to be away overnight,' he said. 'Haydock or Doncaster is as far from Lambourn as you can realistically send a horse on the morning of the race and still expect it to perform. So I won't send my horses north of there unless the owner will pay for the extra costs of an overnight stay, and most of them won't.'

Why, I wondered, did Jonny Enstone's horses run slightly better whenever they had to stay away overnight?

'Who goes away with the horses when they have to stay away?' I asked.

'It varies,' said Neil. 'If I absolutely have to send a horse away overnight, I will usually send at least two, sometimes three of my staff with it. Especially if it goes in my horsebox. There will be the lad who does the horse, then a travelling head lad and my box driver, though the driver often doubles up as the travelling head lad.'

'Don't you go as well, on the race day?' I asked.

'That depends.'

287

'On what?' I asked

'On whether the owner will be there, or if the race is televised, or if I have other runners somewhere else. I won't go if I can help it. It's a bloody long way up there, you know.'

'How about your assistant trainer, would he go?'

'Maybe, but it's doubtful.'

'But there doesn't seem to be any standard practice?' I said.

'No, everyone does things differently. I know one trainer, who will remain nameless, who enters lots of horses up north. And he always goes. He doesn't like what he calls "interfering owners" coming to the races so he sends their horses where he thinks they won't be able to come and watch them, and also it gets him away from his wife for a night or two each week.'

And into the arms of his mistress. I had investigated the same nameless trainer for one of his owners who had thought that his trainer was up to no good because he could never get to see his horses run. He'd been convinced that the trainer had been swapping the animals around and running them as ringers. The truth had proved to be less exciting, at least for the horses. The owner in question had subsequently switched stables.

'Thanks, Neil.'

'Any time.' He didn't ask me why I wanted to know. He knew I might tell him in due course, or maybe not at all. Asking didn't make any difference and Neil knew it.

Next I called Kate Burton.

'Oh, Sid,' she said, 'how lovely of you to call.'

'How are things?' I asked.

'Pretty bloody,' she said. 'I can't even organise

Bill's funeral because the police won't release his body.'

That was interesting, I thought. Perhaps after all the police are taking more notice of my murder theory than they were letting on.

'And Mummy is being absolutely horrid.'

'Why?'

'She keeps going on and on about Bill being arrested for race fixing, and the disgrace he's brought on the family. I tell you, I'm fed up with it. The stupid woman doesn't understand that race fixing is the least of my worries.' She paused. 'Why is suicide so shameful?'

'Kate,' I said, 'listen to me. I am absolutely certain that Bill didn't kill himself. He was murdered. And I'm becoming equally convinced that he was not involved with any race fixing.' *Raceform* didn't show it.

'Oh God,' she was crying, 'I do so hope you're right.'

'Believe it,' I said. 'It's true.'

We talked for a while longer about the children and the future of the house. I managed to steer the conversation around to the stable staff.

'What has happened to them all?' I asked her.

'Gone off to other jobs. Mostly in Lambourn,' she said.

'What about Juliet?' I said.

'She's with Andrew Woodward now,' said Kate. 'It's a good job, and she's done really well to get it. I'm so pleased for her. I like Juliet Burns.'

Jesus had liked Judas Iscariot. They had kissed.

'How about Fred Manley?' I asked. Fred had been Bill's head lad.

'I'm not sure. He may have retired.'

'I doubt it,' I said. 'Fred is actually a lot younger than he looks. He's not yet fifty.'

'I don't believe it!' said Kate. 'I always felt so sorry for him having to carry such heavy loads at his age.' She laughed. It was a start.

'Do you know where he lives?' I asked.

'In one of those cottages on the Baydon road. Next door to Juliet, I think.'

Wow!

'Do you have his phone number?'

'Yes.' There was a pause. 'But it's in the den.'

'Ah.'

'Well,' she said, taking a deep breath, 'I have to go in there sometime. I suppose it had better be now.'

I heard her lay the phone down and I could hear her footfalls on the wooden floor as she walked away. And again as she came back. She picked up the phone. There was a breathlessness in her voice as she gave me the number.

'Well done, Kate,' I said. 'Be strong and believe what I told you.'

'I'll try.'

'Good,' I said. 'Oh, and one more thing, Kate. Could you do me a favour?'

'Of course,' she said. 'What do you want?'

I explained at some length what I needed without giving away the whole truth.

'It sounds a bit strange,' she said after I told her, 'but if that's what you want, I suppose it's no problem.'

'Thanks,' I said. 'It will probably be tomorrow afternoon. I'll call you.'

I tried Fred Manley's number but got his wife.

'Sorry, Mr Halley,' she said. 'Fred's not here just

now.'

'When will he be back?' I asked.

'He'll be back for his dinner, at one.'

'I'll call again then.'

'Right you are,' she said and disconnected.

It was a quarter to ten.

Provided Marina received the 'all clear' from Mr Pandita during his round this morning, she would be free to come home around midday.

I spent an hour cleaning the flat and washing up the dishes that were stacked in the kitchen sink. I was genuinely excited by the prospect of Marina's homecoming. I was about to leave for the hospital when the phone rang. It was Charles.

'Do you really think it's necessary for me to stay in London?' he asked, clearly hoping to be given the green light to go home to Oxfordshire.

'Are you still at Jenny and Anthony's?' I asked back.

'Yes,' he said. 'I'm desperate for a decent single malt. I'm fed up with carrot juice and bean sprouts, I can tell you.'

I laughed. 'It'll do you good.'

I thought about what I was planning to do.

'I think it might be safer for you to stay away from Aynsford for a while longer,' I said. 'A few more days.'

'I'll go to my club then,' he said. 'I've been with Jenny now for two nights and everyone knows that guests begin to smell after three. I'll move into the Army & Navy tomorrow.' The lure of the bar had become too great.

*   *   *

I arrived at St Thomas's to find Marina dressed and sitting in a chair.

'They've cleared me for release,' she said. She made it sound like the parole board.

'Great,' I said.

A hospital porter arrived with a wheelchair and he pushed Marina along the corridors and down in the lift to the patient discharges' desk near the main entrance. I retrieved the car from where I had parked it, legally this time, in the underground car park, and we were soon a distant memory at the hospital. Today's dramas had taken over.

'Stop fussing,' Marina said as I shepherded her into the Ebury Street building and up in the lift to our flat. 'I'm fine.'

I knew she was fine. I was fussing because I was worried about her security.

At one o'clock, with Marina settled on the sofa with the Sunday papers, I telephoned Fred Manley, and spoke to him for nearly an hour.

'Don't let your dinner get cold,' I said.

'No problem, it's keeping warm in the oven.'

He told me all about the systems that Bill had used, and about who went away with horses that needed to stay overnight at the northern tracks. In the end he told me more than I could have hoped for.

'Thanks, Fred,' I said. 'That's very helpful.'

'What's it for?' he asked.

'Oh, just some research I'm doing about training methods. I was about to ask Bill about it when he died.'

'Damn shame that was. Mr Burton was a good man and a fine employer. I knew where I stood with him.'

'Have you found another job?' I asked him.

'Not yet,' he said. 'To be honest, I'm thinking of leaving racing. It's not like it used to be. The fun's gone out of it. Nowadays, it's all about blame. If a horse doesn't win, the owners blame the trainers and the trainers blame their staff. There are bound to be more losers than winners, stands to reason. Mr Burton, mind, he never blamed his lads but nearly all the other trainers do. Mr Burton had one owner that used to rant and rave at him for the horses not winning. We all could hear it from the house. But Mr Burton never used us as his excuse. Proper gentleman, he was, unlike that owner.'

'Do you know which of the owners it was?' I asked.

'Sure,' he said. 'It was that lord. You know, the builder.'

'Lord Enstone?' I said.

'Yeah, that's the one. Lord Enstone.'

Finally, I let him go and have his dinner. I hoped it wasn't completely ruined.

Marina and I spent a quiet afternoon cuddled up on the sofa watching a rugby international on the television. Marina kept her leg up on a footstool as instructed by the surgeon and we eased the hours with a bottle of Chablis.

*   *   *

I arrived at the Ebury Street Wine Bar at a quarter to seven to be sure to be there before Chris Beecher. I had left Marina still on the sofa and had doubled-locked the flat on my way out. I didn't expect to be away for long.

The wine bar was very quiet when I arrived so I

chose a table where I could sit with my back to the wall with a good view of the door. I knew a politician who always insisted on sitting the same way in restaurants and for the same reason. It was difficult for anyone to creep up without being spotted.

I wondered why I was giving Chris Beecher a scoop after what he had done to me. After all, it was he who had sent Evan Walker after me with a shotgun, and it was he who had shown Marina's face to the world. But now I needed him. I needed his large readership. I needed his bloody-mindedness. And, above everything else, I needed his rottweiler tendencies. Once he had a good bite, I knew he wouldn't let go.

He arrived at ten to seven and was surprised to see that I was there ahead of him.

'Hiya, Sid,' he said. 'What are you drinking?'

I hadn't yet ordered.

'Are you buying?' I asked.

'Depends,' he said. 'Is it a good story?'

'The best,' I assured him.

'All right, I'm buying.'

I had a large glass of the wine of the month while he had a pint of bitter.

'So what's the angle?' he said, after having a good sip.

'All in good time. You have to earn this story. I need you to set something up for me.'

'Shoot,' he said. I rather wished he wouldn't use that turn of phrase.

I explained in detail what I wanted him to do and when.

'Why?' he asked.

'You'll find out,' I said. 'That will be the story.

Are you on?'

'Yes, I'm on.'

'Good. You can make the call now.' I gave him the number.

He spoke into his mobile phone for quite a time before hanging up.

He smiled at me. He was enjoying the conspiracy. 'All set,' he said. 'Tomorrow afternoon at one o'clock. Where you said. We'll meet in the kitchen.'

'Great,' I said. 'I'll be there by twelve to set things up. You should arrive by twelve thirty at the latest.'

'Right,' he said. 'Now don't be talking to any other papers in the meantime.'

'I won't,' I said. 'And you keep mum, too.'

'You bet.'

*   *   *

On Monday morning, Marina's leg was sore so she stayed in bed while I spent some productive time calling Bond Street boutiques.

Charles rang at nine thirty to tell me he was leaving Jenny's to set course for the bar at his club and that I should call him there if I needed him.

'Thanks for telling me,' I said, 'but could you come round to Ebury Street first, to sit with Marina for a few hours?'

I could sense the hesitation in him.

'I've got an excellent bottle of Glenfiddich that could stand some damage,' I said. 'And a side of smoked salmon in the fridge for lunch.'

'I'll be there in thirty-five minutes,' he said.

'Perfect.'

295

I spent the thirty-five minutes telling Marina what I was going to be doing this afternoon.

'Darling, please be careful,' she said. 'I don't want to find myself a widow before we even get married.'

'I thought you were still thinking about it.'

'I am, I am. All the time. That's why I don't want to lose you before I decide. Then all this thinking would be a waste.'

'Oh, thanks.'

'No, I mean it, my darling, please be careful.'

I promised I would. I hoped I could keep the promise.

Charles arrived and took up his post as guardian of Marina.

'I don't need anyone,' Marina had complained when I told her Charles was coming.

'I'd prefer it,' I'd said. And, I thought, it would give Charles a purpose in life. To say he was bored with his time in London was an understatement.

'Now rest that leg and I'll be back later,' I said, and left them.

*   *   *

I arrived in Lambourn at ten to twelve and drove round the back of Bill Burton's now-empty stables and parked my car where, until recently, he had kept his horsebox. Kate had told me that it had been repossessed by the finance company at her request.

I'd called Kate earlier that morning to tell her that it was definitely this afternoon that I needed the favour. Fine, she'd said, see you later.

I removed a large hold-all from the boot of my

296

car and carried it through the empty and lifeless stable yard to the house. Kate was in the kitchen giving some early lunch to Alice, her youngest, Bill's much-wanted daughter.

'Hello, Kate,' I said, giving her a kiss.

'Hi, Sid. How nice to see you. Do you want some lunch?'

'Just coffee would be lovely. Do you mind if I go and set up?'

'Help yourself—though I'm not really sure what you're doing.'

I had purposely not told her everything. It would have been too distressing.

'My visitor is coming at one o'clock,' I said.

'OK.' I think she realised that asking who the visitor was would be pointless, so she didn't. 'I'll be going shortly to do some shopping in Wantage, and will have Alice with me. I have to pick the other children up from school there at three so I won't be back until three thirty at the earliest. Is that OK?

'Better make it four,' I said. 'Or even four thirty, if that's not too late.' I wasn't sure how long my little plan would take.

'OK. I'll take the children to see Mummy for tea. Black or white coffee?'

'White, please.'

'I'll bring it through.'

Setting up took me about twenty minutes and just as I finished, Chris Beecher arrived. I heard his car on the drive.

'Your visitor is here early,' said Kate as I went back into the kitchen. 'We're off now, and we may see you later. If you finish early, put the key through the letter box when you go. I've another

297

one to get in with.'

'Right,' I said. I gave her a kiss. 'And thank you.'

Chris and Kate passed each other at the kitchen door and briefly paused to shake hands without formal introductions. I watched Kate strap little Alice into her car seat and then drive away.

Chris watched with me. 'Does she know what you're up to?' he asked.

'Not exactly. She thinks you're my visitor.'

'Ah.'

Chris and I went through everything again to be sure we had the sequence right.

'And once you start talking,' he said, 'you don't want me to say anything, is that right?'

'Yes,' I said. 'Please try not to say or ask *anything*, however keen you might be. But don't stop listening.'

'No chance of that.'

I went into the sitting room to wait, and Chris went back to the kitchen. I couldn't hear a car on the drive from where I was, but at one o'clock sharp I detected voices in the kitchen. Our real visitor had arrived, and then I could hear Chris laying on the charm as he guided our visitor through the house.

I waited. When I was sure that they would be in the right place, I left the sitting room and walked across the hall. The house was old fashioned and it had locks with big black keys on all the internal doors. I went silently through one of the doors the other side of the hall, then closed and locked it behind me. I put the key in my pocket. Our visitor was facing the window, sitting in the big armchair.

We were in Bill Burton's den. The scene of his death.

298

I walked round until I was in front of the chair. 'Hello, Juliet,' I said.

CHAPTER NINETEEN

Juliet looked at me, then at Chris and back to me again.

'Hello, Sid,' she said. 'What are you doing here?' She shifted in the chair and looked slightly uneasy.

'I arranged it,' I said.

'But, I thought . . .' She turned to look at Chris again. 'I thought you said you wanted to interview me for the newspaper.'

Chris didn't say a word.

'He did,' I said, 'because I asked him to.'

Chris had called her on the telephone from the wine bar to ask if he could write an article about her for *The Pump* as a rising assistant trainer. He had told her that he was doing a series of such pieces on the future stars of racing and she would be the first. He had told her he wanted to meet her at the place where she had started her career, at Bill Burton's. I had assumed that her vanity would overcome any reluctance, and I had been right. Juliet had been really keen and had readily agreed.

So here she was.

I hoped that she was feeling a little uncomfortable to be back in the room where Bill had died. I was.

'Why?' she said.

'I wanted to have a little chat,' I said.

'What about?' She was keeping her cool but her eyes betrayed her anxiety. She looked back and forth from me to Chris with a little white showing around her irises.

'And what's that for?' she asked, pointing at the video camera on a tripod that I had set up facing her. I had brought it with me in the hold-all together with a separate tape recorder and microphone. Just to be on the safe side.

'To make sure we have a full record of what we say in our little chat,' I said.

'I don't want a little chat with you,' she said, and stood up. 'I think I'll leave now.'

She walked over to the door and tried to open it. 'Unlock this immediately!' she demanded.

'I could,' I said slowly, 'but then I would have to give these to the police.'

I withdrew the photographs of the contents of her wardrobe from my pocket.

'What are those?' There was a slight concern in her voice.

'Photographs,' I said. 'Sit down and I'll show you.'

'Show me here.' She stayed by the door.

'No. Sit down.'

She stood for a moment, looking first at me and then at Chris.

'All right, I will, but I'm not going to answer any questions.'

She moved back to the chair and sat down. She leaned back and crossed her legs. She was trying to give the impression that she was in control of the situation. I wondered for how long she would believe it.

'Show me the photographs,' she said.

I handed them to her.

She looked through all six prints, taking her

time. 'So?' she said.

'They are photographs of the inside of your wardrobe.'

'I can see that. So what?' She didn't ask how I had got them.

'Your wardrobe is full of designer clothes, shoes and handbags.'

'So? I like smart things. What's wrong with that?'

'They're very expensive,' I said.

'I'm an expensive girl,' she replied, smiling.

'Where did you get them?' I asked.

'That's none of your bloody business,' she said, growing in confidence.

'I think it is,' I said.

'Why?'

'Because assistant trainers don't usually make enough to buy upwards of thirty thousand pounds' worth of clothes,' I said. 'Not unless they're selling information about the horses they look after or are up to other acts of no good.'

She slowly uncrossed her legs and then recrossed them the other way. 'They were given to me by a rich admirer,' she said.

'Oh,' I said, 'you mean George Lochs.'

That shook her. She quickly sat forward in the chair, but then recovered her composure and leaned back again.

'Who's he?' she asked.

'Come on, Juliet, that won't do! You know perfectly well who George Lochs is. He gave you all that stuff in your wardrobe.'

'Now what makes you think that?' she said.

'I called the Jimmy Choo boutique in Sloane Street this morning and I asked if they kept a record of everyone who buys their shoes. The manager said they did, but he wouldn't tell me who was on the list.'

Juliet smiled slightly. But she had relaxed too soon.

'So I called their boutique in New Bond Street and said that I was phoning on behalf of Miss Juliet Burns who was abroad and had lost a buckle off a shoe and wanted to have a replacement sent out to her. They told me that they had no record of a Miss Juliet Burns having bought any shoes from them.'

I walked round behind the chair and bent down close to Juliet's ear.

'I told them that maybe that was because I had bought them for her myself. And who was I, they had asked. George Lochs, I'd said. Well, of course, Mr Lochs, they said, how nice to hear from you again. Now, which pair was it? So I described the turquoise pair you can see in the photographs and they knew it straight away.'

I didn't tell her that I had also called Gucci and Armani, saying I was George Lochs. They, too, had all been so pleased to hear from me again.

'So what if George did buy them for me,' Juliet said. 'There's no crime in that.'

'Were they payment for services?' I said.

'I don't know what you mean.'

'Was he buying sex?'

'Don't be ridiculous,' she said, offended. 'What do you think I am, a prostitute?'

No. I thought she might be a murderer but I didn't say so. Not yet.

I changed direction.

'Don't you think someone did a great job at

cleaning up this room?' I asked.

'What do you mean?' Juliet said.

'This is where Bill Burton died. Look,' I pointed, 'you can still see the stain where his brains splattered on the wall.'

I caught sight of Chris's horrified face. I nearly laughed. He'd had no idea.

'How could I forget,' said Juliet, far less troubled.

'Did you know I found a second bullet?' I asked.

'I read it in the paper,' she said. 'But I don't know what you're talking about anyway.'

'I'm talking about the fact that Bill Burton was murdered and you know more about it than you're telling.'

'That's nonsense,' she said. 'I've had enough of this. I'm not saying another thing until I see a lawyer.'

'A lawyer?' I said. 'Why do you need a lawyer? You're not under arrest and I'm not the police.'

'Am I free to go then?' she asked.

'Absolutely,' I said. 'Any time you like.'

'Right.' She stood up. 'I will.'

'But then I'll have to tell the police about the DNA evidence.'

'What DNA evidence?' she snapped.

'Your DNA evidence.'

'You're bluffing,' she said.

'Can you be sure?' I asked. 'Sit down, Juliet, I'm not finished yet.'

She slowly descended back into the chair.

'Take a look at this.' I handed her the photograph of her hairbrush.

'How did you get these photographs?'

'I visited your house,' I said, 'while you were at

303

work.'

'Is that legal?' she asked.

'I doubt it,' I replied. 'Have a close look and tell me what you see.'

'A hairbrush,' she said.

'Not just any hairbrush, it's your hairbrush,' I said. 'Anything else?'

She looked again at the picture. 'No.'

'Some hairs?' I asked.

'Everyone has hairs in their hairbrush.'

'Yes,' I said. 'But not Juliet Burns's hairs. Did you know that you can obtain a DNA profile from a single hair follicle?'

She didn't say anything.

'Well, you can.'

I again went round behind her so that both our faces would be in the video recording.

'And,' I said, 'I bet you don't know that it was also possible to get your DNA from the saliva you used to lick the envelope of the "get well" card you left for me last Thursday.'

It was a bombshell. She jumped up. Her mouth opened and closed but no sound came out. She looked for a place to run and went over again to the door and wrestled with the knob. Another good thing about old houses is that they are well built. The door didn't budge a fraction as she threw herself against it.

She looked at the windows as a route of escape.

'Don't even think about it, Juliet,' I said.

She didn't appear to be listening, so I shouted at her. 'If you run away I'll hand the whole lot over to the police.'

Her gaze swung round to my face. 'And if I don't?' she said. Her brain was still ticking under all the external panic.

'Then we'll see,' I said. 'But I make no promises.'

'I didn't shoot your girlfriend,' she said, still standing by the door.

I could see Chris desperately wanting to say something. I shook my head fractionally to stop him.

'I know that,' I said. 'Marina was shot by a man. But you do know who it was, don't you, Juliet?'

There was no reply.

'Come and sit down again.' I went over and took her arm, and led her back to the chair. 'That's better,' I said as she sat down.

I sat down on a stool facing her, but not in the way of the camera.

'And the same man murdered Huw Walker, didn't he?' I said.

She sat very still, looking at me. She said nothing.

'And also Bill Burton?'

Again no response.

'In this very room. And you were here at the time.'

'No,' she said, her voice little more than a whisper. 'That's not true. I wasn't here.'

'But you didn't find Bill in the morning like you said, did you?'

'No.'

She began to cry and buried her head in her hands.

'There have been lots of tears,' I said. 'The time has come, Juliet, to stop the crying and tell the truth. The time to put an end to this madness. To do no more damage.'

She rocked back and forth. 'I never thought he would kill Huw Walker, or Bill,' she said.

'Who was it?' I asked.

Still she didn't reply.

'Look, Juliet, I know you've been sleeping with someone. I found some of his clothes in a drawer beside your bed and his hair was also in the hairbrush. So I have his DNA and it matches that of the man who attacked Marina the first time, in Ebury Street. You won't be able to protect George Lochs even if you won't tell us he's the murderer.'

She sat up and looked at me again. 'George?' she said. 'You think it's George Lochs?'

'He bought you the clothes,' I said.

'You don't know, do you?' she said, almost sneering.

'Know what?'

'George is gay. He'd never sleep with me. I've got the wrong bits.'

It was my turn to stand with my mouth open. 'Why, then, did he buy you the clothes?' I asked.

'As thank-you presents.'

'For what?'

She didn't answer. I stood up and walked round behind her.

'Did George give you something every time you told him a horse wasn't going to win?'

'What do you mean?' she asked.

'I mean that it was you that was fixing the races, wasn't it? It never was Bill. And George Lochs would have loved to have had the information so that he could adjust the odds on his website.'

'Why would I fix races?' she asked.

'That I don't know yet,' I said, 'but it has to be you that was doing it.'

'But how could I?' she said.

'Because it was you that was responsible for helping the lads prepare the horses ready for running. Fred Manley told me that you had wanted that particular job and had badgered Bill until he gave you the task. Fred said that you also insisted on "putting them to bed" the night before they ran.'

I went back round in front of her.

'And it was you that insisted on helping to groom each runner early in the morning of the race. You plaited their manes and polished their hooves. You took a pride in their presentation.'

She nodded. 'We won lots of "best turned out" awards.'

'But it also gave you the opportunity to keep the horses thirsty. You threw away their water the night before a race and again in the morning. You only then had to ensure that the horses had a good drink just before the race. If the water in their bellies didn't slow them down, then the lack of water for nearly twenty-four hours beforehand would have done so.'

She hung her head again.

'And when horses ran at the northern tracks, you didn't go with them, did you, so you paid Huw Walker to make sure they didn't win. But they still ran slightly better in the north because Huw was only trying to stop them winning, second was fine, but your little water trick slowed them right down. Some of them in the south finished last.'

Chris was now the one with an open mouth. He was almost rubbing his hands with glee at the scoop he would have.

'But why,' I asked, 'did you only stop Lord

307

Enstone's horses? And then not every time they ran? Did you really do it for a few dresses?'

'I don't even like the dresses. I never wear them. I should have got rid of them. They only clutter the place up. They were George's idea. He loves designer wear and thinks everyone else does too. He bought me something whenever he made a good profit from a race where one was stopped. He could make an absolute fortune out of some races, sometimes more than a hundred thousand, especially if we stopped the favourite.'

'We?' I asked. 'Who are we?'

She didn't answer.

'Juliet,' I said, 'I need to know his name or I will call the police and I won't tell them that you've helped me. Quite the reverse, in fact. And, be sure, they will find out who it is anyway. We have his DNA, and his fingerprints must be all over your cottage. It will only be a matter of time before he's caught, and it will be your fault if he does any harm to anyone else in the meantime.'

'Will . . . will I go to prison?' she asked in a faltering voice.

I don't think she had been listening to me. 'Probably,' I said. 'You certainly will if you don't cooperate. I'll do a deal with you. I'll do my best to keep you out of prison if you tell us everything, but I can't promise. At the very least, I will try to ensure you don't get charged with murder.'

Her head came up fast. 'But I didn't kill anyone.'

'So who did?' I asked.

'Peter did.' She said it so softly I hardly heard her.

'Peter?' I said. 'Peter Enstone?'

'Yes.'

*   *   *

Suddenly everything came out. Juliet unburdened the great secret that had been eating away at her. Chris still sat silently in the corner, listening intently. He had by now produced a notebook and was scribbling furiously as Juliet spoke.

She told us the lot.

She started at the beginning with her first meeting with Peter Enstone when she had been working at Bill's for only a few weeks. It was very clear that she had fallen head over heels for Peter and soon they were lovers.

'He said that no one must know, especially his father,' she said. 'It was all very exciting.' She smiled.

Peter's father, Lord Enstone, was a social climber par excellence. I expect that the daughter of a blacksmith with no family means was not what he would have had in mind as a suitable match for his son. No wonder Peter had wanted the affair kept quiet.

'Peter said wouldn't it be funny if we were able to influence the running of his father's horses just by wanting to. We used to sit in bed some afternoons watching the racing, holding the television remote and pretending that we were using it to control the horses like robots. Turn up the volume to make it go faster, turn it down to go slower. Push the off button to make it fall. Silly, really.'

She stopped.

'Look,' she said, 'can I have a drink of

something?'

'Water OK?' I asked.

'Fine.'

I gave the key to Chris who unlocked the door and went out to the kitchen to fetch some. Juliet sat silently waiting for his return while I stood guard at the door, but I think her desire to run had gone. Chris came back and I relocked the door and put the key back in my pocket in case I was wrong. Juliet drank half the glass then sat holding it in both hands on her lap.

'Go on,' I said, sitting down again on the stool in front of her.

'I remember saying to Peter that there was a way to control the horses for real,' she continued. 'But I only said it as a joke. I remembered my father telling me of a betting coup at the local point-to-point where a horse was stopped by giving it a big drink just before the start. He always said that water didn't show up on any dope test.'

She took another drink of the evil stuff.

'Peter became very excited by the idea. He doesn't like his father. He hates the way he still tells him what to do even though Peter is over thirty. And he didn't have a happy childhood. Lord Enstone tells people that Peter's mother died but that isn't true—well, it is now, but it wasn't the reason for her leaving his father. She died a long time after that. By then, she had divorced Peter's father and had claimed mental and physical cruelty to do so. I hate him.'

'So when did you start to fix the races?' I asked.

'A few months after I first met Peter,' she said. 'God, I was nervous the first time. I was sure everyone would know what I was doing but it was

310

really very easy. The lads would always do what I said, so I'd send them off to do something while I poured the water away. I would then feed the horses. As you know, oats and the horse nuts make the horses thirsty so they drink during and after eating. I simply took away their water. It was dead easy.' She smiled again.

It was not a new trick but she was undoubtedly pleased with herself for having managed to do it without being detected—at least, until now.

It seemed like more unnecessary mental and physical cruelty to me. She was no better than Peter's father. Worse even, as a horse has no means of escape. I could feel the anger rising in me again. Anger at the callous nature of this person who had been trusted to look after the horses, but had been the cause of great distress for them instead.

'But soon it stopped being a game,' she said. 'Peter became obsessed with being in control of his father's horses. It gave him such power to know when they would do well and when they would not.'

Huw had told Kate it was more about power than money.

Juliet was almost gabbling now. Now she had started there was no stopping her. 'Lord Enstone liked his horses to run up at Newcastle or Kelso and at the other northern tracks when he was up there at home for the weekends. I couldn't go up there with them, but Peter was specially keen that the horses should be stopped when he knew his father was going to be at the races with all his mates—so he would be shown up when the horse lost. So he paid Huw Walker to stop some. I told him it was stupid to get someone else involved, but he was absolutely determined. He said he needed Huw to get at the horses in the north.

I wondered how long it would take Juliet to work out that Peter had probably only bedded her to get at the horses in the south.

'Then it all started to go wrong,' she said. 'Huw Walker said he was afraid that people would say that he was fixing races. He wanted out, but Peter told him that if he didn't do as he was told then he would fix him good and proper, so much so he would get warned off by the Jockey Club.'

'But surely that would have been the same for Peter?' I said.

'As you know, professional jockeys are not allowed to bet but Peter placed bets on the other horses in the races that Huw was going to fix and used an account that could be traced back to Huw. Peter had it as a hold over him. Unless Huw did as he was told, Peter said he would anonymously tell the Jockey Club where to look to see Huw's name on the account.'

'Why didn't Huw report Peter to the Jockey Club himself?' I asked.

'When Huw threatened just that, Peter said that no one would believe him, that they would just see it as an attempt to shift the blame, and they would be more likely to warn him off for life. I don't know whether they would have, but it frightened Huw enough.'

'How many races did Huw fix?' I asked.

'Only a few,' she said. 'Maybe eight or ten, all in the north.'

A little greed had been his undoing.

'He had wanted out after only two,' said Juliet.

A very little greed, indeed.

'Then Huw said he would tell Peter's father what we were doing if we didn't stop, or at least stop involving him. Peter went mad and threatened to kill him. I didn't think he meant it, but . . .' She stopped.

'Peter shot Huw at Cheltenham,' I said.

She nodded. 'I didn't know anything about it at the time, I swear, but Peter told me afterwards that it was during the Gold Cup when everyone was watching the race either live or on the big screens near the paddock. He said no one noticed him and Huw going off for a chat.'

And some shooting practice, I thought.

'And I suppose the crowd noise at the end of the race would have drowned out the noise of the shots,' I said, 'but it was still a hell of a chance.' Perhaps he'd used a silencer, I thought.

'I know,' she said, 'but Peter was desperate. He's terrified that his father would find out about the race fixing and go and change his will just before he drops off the perch.'

'Is he likely to drop off the perch?' I asked.

'He's got cancer,' she said. 'Didn't you know? It's prostate cancer and he's had some treatment but it isn't working. Peter doesn't think he'll last much longer, a year maybe, and he's shitting himself in case the old man cuts him off without a bean for fiddling with his horses.'

So it was about money, after all. It usually was.

'And how about Bill?' I said.

'Peter started a rumour some time ago that Bill Burton was involved in race fixing.'

'Why?' I asked her.

'He said that it would keep the heat away from

313

us if anyone started asking too many questions.'

Seemed to me to be like waving a red flag, bringing needless attention.

'Peter was so excited when Bill got arrested,' she said. 'He reckoned that the only thing better than getting away with something was to have someone else convicted for it.'

Peter Enstone wasn't the nicest of people.

'He was annoyed when the police released Bill. He said that it meant that they didn't really think he'd done it.'

'But why did Peter kill Bill?' I asked. 'He'd done nothing to deserve that.'

'He wanted to get the police to think that Bill had killed himself after killing Huw. So they would stop looking for Huw's murderer.' She looked at me. 'And it would have worked, too, if you hadn't stuck your damn nose in.'

'Did you see him do it?' I asked her.

'No, absolutely not,' she cried, 'I didn't know that he was going to kill him. I'm not a murderer.'

I still wasn't sure about that.

'So what happened that night?' I asked her.

'Peter rang me to say that he had to talk to Bill urgently,' she said, 'about his father's horses going to another trainer.'

'But the horses had already gone to Andrew Woodward,' I said.

'I know, but Peter told me that he was going to help Bill get them back.'

I wasn't sure I believed her.

'So what happened?' I asked again.

'I tried to get Bill on the phone but he'd gone out,' she said.

To see Kate, I thought, at Daphne Rogers'

place.

'Peter picked me up from home,' she continued, 'and we spent ages in the driveway waiting for Bill to come back, which he finally did at about half past ten.'

'Then what did you do?' I asked.

'Bill was a bit surprised to see us, I can tell you. "What on earth are you doing here at this time of night?" That's what he said. He was all smiling and joking. He asked us in for a drink so we went into the den. Bill poured himself a Scotch and Peter asked me to go and make him a coffee in the kitchen as he was driving.'

To get her out of the way, I thought.

'I was in the kitchen waiting for the kettle to boil,' she said, 'and there was a loud bang and the next thing I know Peter comes out to the kitchen all frantic like and hyper. He said that would sort out the police. I asked him what he'd done.'

She began to breathe more quickly at the memory.

'He didn't reply,' she went on. 'He just stood there laughing and saying that that would show them. So I went into the den and saw Bill.'

Or what was left of him, I thought. She glanced up at the faint stain on the wall.

'I couldn't believe that he had killed him.' She held her head in her hands. 'I was bloody mad with Peter. I didn't want Bill dead and I had absolutely nothing to do with it. It wasn't my idea and I'm not taking the bloody blame for it.'

'Why didn't you go to the police?' I asked her.

'I wanted to, I wanted to,' she said. 'I told Peter that I was going to call the police right there and then but he said the same thing would happen to me if I did. I thought he was joking but I didn't do it. I was really frightened of him that night.'

With good reason, I thought. I also wondered if that was the first ounce of truth she had told for a while. I wasn't at all sure that I believed her account of how Bill died.

'Did Peter say how he managed to shoot Bill in the mouth?' I asked.

'Peter said that when he pulled out the gun Bill was absolutely terrified of him,' she said. 'He was pleased about that and he has talked about it over and over again since. Peter says Bill was scared shitless. Apparently Bill just sat there shaking with his mouth open, so Peter just shot him through it.'

'So what happened next?' I prompted.

'I was in a complete panic but Peter was dead calm,' she said. 'I don't know why but he kept saying he wanted to fire another shot so that it looked like Bill had killed himself but there had to be no second bullet found. He wanted to fire it out the window but I thought he might hit one of the horses in the stables.'

Her love of the horses was clearly deeper than her love for her boss.

'I suggested firing it into one of the fire buckets,' she went on, 'so I went to get one from the yard.' She looked up at me almost with pleading eyes. 'I know I shouldn't have done that. I am really sorry . . .' She tailed off and began to cry. 'I didn't mean for Bill to get killed, I promise.'

Did I believe her? Did it matter? It was a jury who would ultimately decide if she were telling the truth or not.

'So what did you do then?' I asked.

'Peter drove himself home and I just sat here in

316

the kitchen all night,' she said. 'I didn't know what to do. I kept thinking I should call the police but I was worried they would want to know why I had been at the house in the middle of the night, in order to find Bill, so I waited until it was the time I usually came to work in the mornings and then I phoned them.'

I remembered the shocked condition that Juliet had been in when I'd arrived at the house that morning. She had clearly been working herself up into that state for quite a while. I also remembered her saying, 'How could he have done such a thing?' At the time, I had thought she had meant Bill; now I knew she had been talking about Peter.

'But why did you target Marina?' I said.

'Peter said it was no good attacking you to get you to stop. He said that you wouldn't be put off by a bit of violence. I said that perhaps he should kill you.'

Thanks, I thought. For that I would not try too hard to keep her out of prison.

'Why didn't he?' I said.

'Peter said that would defeat the object. Then the police would know for sure that Bill's death wasn't suicide.'

Good old Peter.

'He said the way to you was through your girlfriend.'

It nearly was.

'Peter is not very bright,' I said.

'He's cleverer than you,' she said, loyal to the last.

'If he was,' I said, 'he would have killed you before you had the chance to tell me what you have.'

317

'But he loves me,' said Juliet. 'He wouldn't harm me.'

She wasn't very bright either.

'As you like,' I said, 'but if I were you, I'd watch your back. You can't testify against him if you're dead.'

She sat there looking at me. I don't know if she believed me or not, but I had sown a seed of doubt.

I jerked my head at Chris to come out with me into the hall. I removed the key from my pocket and unlocked the door. Juliet remained sitting in the chair looking at her hands. I wondered if she was beginning to regret talking to us. As an afterthought, I took the video camera and the tapes out into the hall with me.

'I simply can't believe this!' exclaimed Chris as I shut the door of the den behind us. 'How the hell did you work it all out? And what now?'

'First you had better get on and write your piece,' I said. 'If Juliet is charged, you won't be able to publish. It will be *sub judice.*'

'Blimey,' said Chris, 'you're so right. What will you do with her now?'

'I'd like to strangle the little bitch,' I said.

'You can't,' he said. 'You've only got one hand.'

I smiled at him. It had broken the tension.

'I suppose I'll give these to the police,' I said, indicating the tapes. 'Then I'll let them get on with it.'

'What's on those tapes will surely be inadmissible in a court,' he said.

'Probably, but I reckon the police will be able to get the same information from Juliet as I have done. Even if they don't do the same deal.'

'Well, don't give it to them until my piece has

318

appeared in print,' he said.

'Your article might prejudice a court case,' I said.

'I don't care,' he said. 'I want to expose Peter Enstone as the bastard he is. And I also want to make his upstart father squirm with front-page headlines.'

I wanted it, too.

CHAPTER TWENTY

In the end, Juliet accepted an invitation from Chris Beecher to be put up in a swish hotel for a night or two. He made out that it was for her own safety, but he and I both knew that really it was to allow time for him to write his piece and get it published before the police or the courts stuck their noses in and put a stop on the story.

I went back to London to relieve Charles from his guard duties in Ebury Street and found him snoring on the sofa.

'Right little Cerberus, aren't we?' I said to him, shaking his foot. I was not best pleased. 'I thought I left you on guard and you're bloody asleep.'

'What?' he said, rubbing his eyes.

'Never mind.'

All appeared well, however, and there was no point in making a fuss. And I had offered him my bottle of single malt for lunch, so what did I expect?

Marina was in the bedroom resting her leg as instructed and watching an afternoon game show on the television. A huge basket arrangement of pink and white carnations sat on her dressing table.

'Lovely flowers,' I said.

'Yes, aren't they? Colleagues at the Institute sent them,' she said. 'Rosie probably organised it.'

'And how do you feel?' I asked.

'Bored, but mending,' she said. 'Did your plan work well?'

'Yes,' I said, and told her all about my little chat with Juliet.

'So, Peter Enstone shot me,' Marina said finally.

'Yes, I think he did. Unless he organised someone else to do it and that's very unlikely.'

'And where exactly is the little swine now?' she asked.

'According to the *Racing Post*, he was in Scotland, riding at Kelso races this afternoon. That's why I was so keen to talk to Juliet today, while he was out of the way. I don't know where he will go from there. I think he lives in London somewhere.'

Marina shivered. 'I don't want him coming here.'

'He won't get past Security downstairs, even if he does,' I said. 'And I'm not having you left alone anyway.'

'Sid,' Charles called from the hallway. He put his head round the door. 'I think I'll go back to my club now, if that's all right.'

I felt guilty for having been angry with him.

'Of course, Charles,' I said. 'And thank you so much for coming over and spending the time with Marina this afternoon.'

'Humph,' he muttered. He was not greatly soothed. 'See you then.'

His head disappeared for a moment but then came back round the door. 'I forgot,' he said. 'Jenny asked me to ask you, Marina, if you would be up to going out for lunch with her tomorrow? If yes, she said that she'd pick you up from here at twelve thirty in the car.'

'I don't know,' I said. I was worried about what reaction the next day's edition of *The Pump* might produce.

'I'd love to,' said Marina. 'I'll be fine. Don't fuss.'

'OK,' I said, 'but I am going to organise a security guard to go with you, and no arguments. He will sit quietly in the corner of the restaurant and not disturb you, but I would be happier.'

'Fine,' said Marina. 'Charles, tell Jenny that would be lovely and I will see her tomorrow at twelve thirty.'

'Right,' he said, and disappeared again.

I went out to see him off and make my peace with his wounded pride.

'I'm sorry,' I said. 'I didn't mean to sound so cross when I found you asleep.'

'No, it's all right,' he said. 'It is me who should be sorry. During the First World War soldiers in the British Army could be executed for falling asleep on guard duty.'

'That's a bit extreme, isn't it?' I said.

'Not at all. One dozing sentry could have allowed a surprise attack that might have killed hundreds.'

'Thankfully, nothing like that happened here.'

We shook hands warmly and I walked him to the lift.

'I'll pop round tomorrow,' said Charles, 'to see

the girls when they get back from lunch.'

'That would be great,' I said. 'But take care. Mount Vesuvius has nothing on the eruption that's going to occur tomorrow morning when *The Pump* comes out. Don't get in the way of the molten lava. It might be dangerous.'

'I'll be careful,' he said. 'I've dodged more than my share of molten metal in my life.' He had been a junior officer on IIMS *Amethyst* during the Yangtze incident.

I decided that, much as I loved him, I should no longer place Marina's security in the hands of a septuagenarian retired naval admiral with a penchant for single malt whisky, so I called a fellow private sleuth who worked for a firm that had a bodyguard department and asked for their help.

Certainly, Mr Halley, they said, they would happily provide a bodyguard for Miss Marina van der Meer, starting at eight o'clock the next morning until further notice. Great, I said, and gave them the address.

As I put the phone down, I began to wish I had asked for their help immediately. I could imagine the presses at *The Pump* busy churning out tomorrow's copy with its banner headlines. Poking a stick into a hornets' nest had nothing on this. I shivered. Too late now.

And tomorrow's newspaper would be available at about eleven this evening, round the corner at Victoria Station. I looked at my watch. Five hours to go.

I spent much of the evening making duplicates of the videotape from my little chat with Juliet. I had made one copy at Kate's using her video

322

recorder in the sitting room. Chris had taken it with him as he was pretty certain that, without the actual tape, *The Pump*'s lawyers weren't going to let him write anything about the Enstones.

'All your bloody fault,' he'd said.

'How come?'

'You remember that last time when the paper went after you?' he'd said. 'You know, all that stuff a few years ago.'

I'd nodded. How could I forget.

'Well, nothing gets in now unless it's passed by the libel lawyers and they're pretty tight after you took us to the cleaners.'

I hadn't. They had got off lightly.

Now I made six further copies on to VHS tapes between performing my nursing and domestic duties around the flat. I steamed some salmon fillets in the microwave for dinner and Marina and I ate them in front of the television with trays on our laps.

Marina's salmon remained only half eaten as she watched the tape with growing fascination.

'I really don't think I want to meet this Peter,' she said.

'You already have,' I said. 'He was wearing motorcycle leathers.'

'Oh, yes. So he was.' She rubbed her knee.

My phone rang. It was Chris Beecher.

'It's all in,' he said. 'Front page! They allowed me to do the lot.' He was very excited.

'Good,' I said, 'you've done well.' It was under seven hours since we had left Lambourn.

'Where's Juliet?' I asked him.

'Bricking herself in the Donnington Valley Hotel,' he said. 'She has tried to call me on my mobile at least fifteen times but I won't answer. She leaves messages saying she doesn't want to be named. Bit late now!' He laughed. 'If she wanted it off the record, she should have said so at the beginning, not after the event.'

'Will she stay there?' I asked.

'What would you do?' he said. 'I don't reckon she'll go back to her place. I think we can safely say that young Mr Peter is not going to be best pleased with her in the morning. If I were in her shoes I'd stay put in the hotel and keep my head down.'

In her Jimmy Choo shoes, I thought. Young Mr George is not going to be too pleased with her, either.

'Right then,' I said. 'Now that I know that the story will definitely be in the paper tomorrow, I'll get these other tapes off to their new homes.'

'Yes,' Chris said, 'and . . . thanks, Sid. Guess I owe you one.'

'More than one, you bugger.'

He laughed and hung up. He wasn't a bad soul, but I still wouldn't be sharing any of my secrets with him in the future. Not unless I wanted to read them in the paper.

I spent some time packing the six videotapes into large white padded envelopes and then went round to Victoria Station to await the papers. I made sure that the door was properly locked and told Marina not to open it under any circumstances, even if someone shouted that the building was burning down.

At ten minutes past eleven, I watched a bale of *Pumps* being thrown out of a delivery van. It was tied up with string but the paper's headline was clearly visible.

'MURDERER' it read across the whole width, above a large smiling photograph of Peter Enstone. The picture editor obviously had a sense of humour. He had chosen to show an old shot of Peter in bow-tie and dinner jacket receiving the prize for Best Young Amateur Rider at an annual racing awards dinner.

I waited impatiently while the news-stand staff cut the strings and stacked the papers on a shelf. I suddenly felt very vulnerable as I picked up seven copies and stood there, in the open, paying for them. I could clearly feel the hairs rising on the back of my neck.

I turned round and looked behind me but, of course, there was no one there. Just some late-night revellers making their unsteady way to their trains home.

With the papers safely tucked under my arm, I went swiftly back to the flat to find that all was well, and not a fire to be seen. I let myself in and locked the door behind me. Marina and I sat at either end of the sofa and each read a copy of *The Pump*.

Chris Beecher had done a great job. Everything was there. Juliet's story was largely quoted word for word and there were pictures of Huw Walker and Bill Burton, and one each of Jonny Enstone and George Lochs. I was pleased to note that my usual *Pump* mug shot was not included. Indeed, there was hardly a mention of me by name at all, except as the partner of the girl who had been shot in London.

It was a true hatchet job with the comment section of the paper getting in on the act to criticise Enstone senior for having produced such a monster.

I was still packing the relevant pages of *The Pump* into the padded envelopes at a quarter to midnight when the buzzer of the internal phone sounded outside the kitchen door. The porter/security downstairs informed me that my pre-ordered late-night courier service had arrived.

I took five of the envelopes downstairs with me in the lift. I was slightly taken aback to find a motorcyclist in reception dressed in black leathers and wearing a full-face helmet, but he turned out to be the real thing, a courier and not a gunman. He took the packages and assured me they would be delivered during the night.

'The first three can arrive any time you like,' I said. 'The fourth must arrive after five o'clock when you'll probably find him feeding his cattle. And the fifth should be delivered last, on your way back.'

'Right.' His voice was muffled by the helmet that he seemed determined not to remove. He stuffed the packages in a bag and swung it onto his back.

'Don't go to sleep and fall off your bike,' I said.

'I won't,' he mumbled, and left.

What would be his route, I wondered. New Scotland Yard first, I expected, for Detective Superintendent Aldridge, then on to Thames Valley Police headquarters in Oxfordshire to drop the one for Inspector Johnson. Then down to Cheltenham to deliver the one for my friend Chief Inspector Carlisle. Next to South Wales, to Brecon, to find Evan Walker's farm for package four.

Finally, on his way back, the motorcyclist's last stop was to be at the House of Lords. Package five was for his lordship. The videotape was in case he didn't believe what he read in the newspapers.

*   *   *

The bodyguard I had arranged for Marina arrived promptly at eight and turned out to be a six-foot-two ex-Marine with biceps bigger than my thighs. The biceps, along with an impressive pair of pecs and assorted other bulging muscles that I didn't even know existed, were squeezed into a bottle-green T-shirt that looked to be at least two sizes too small.

He dismissed my suggestion that he should sit in reception and wait for Marina to come down when she went out to lunch. No good, he said. He wanted to have 'the target' in sight at all times.

I said I would rather he did not refer to Marina as 'the target' and he couldn't have her in sight at all times as she was still in her dressing gown and was about to have a shower. He covered his disappointment well.

In the end, he settled for a chair outside the flat door, opposite the lift.

'But how about the windows?' he asked. 'Someone could come through one.'

'We'll take our chances,' I said. After all, as I pointed out to him, we were on the fourth floor. But he still wasn't happy.

However, it was a great relief to see him there when I left for Archie Kirk's office at nine to deliver the last of the videotape packages. And, in the interests of my own security, I telephoned for a taxi that was waiting for me at the front entrance of the building with its engine running for a quick getaway.

'Well, you have caused a bit of a stir,' Archie said as I arrived.

I needn't have bothered to bring the pages of *The Pump* as he already had a copy open on his desk.

'Is it all true?' he said.

'Perfectly,' I said. 'And the full interview with the girl is on this tape.'

I handed the sixth package to him.

'Thank you.' He took it. 'Good job that truth is now a defence against libel.'

'Hasn't it always been?' I asked.

'Good God, no,' he said. 'In the past, one could be guilty of criminal libel even if you were telling the truth. Just to ruin someone's reputation was enough despite the fact that they may have deserved to have it ruined. The European Convention on Human Rights has stopped all that. No one can now be convicted for telling the truth.'

Tell that, I thought, to the mothers of the cot death babies sent to prison for murder due to the erroneous evidence of a so-called medical expert.

'I will leave it to you to decide who gets the information on the internet gambling and gaming,' I said. 'I realise it was not really what you wanted but it's a start and I will do a bit more digging before you get my final report.'

'What do you think will happen?' he asked.

'About the murders,' I said, 'or the gambling?'

'Both.'

'I hope the police pick up Peter Enstone pretty quickly. I don't think Marina, that's my girlfriend, is very safe with him on the loose. Then, with luck, there will be enough evidence to remand him in custody, and then to convict. I think there should be.'

'And make-a-wager.com?' said Archie.

'I think it will be far more difficult to prove anything against George Lochs. He's a very sharp cookie indeed and he will have covered his tracks very carefully. However, punters like to have confidence when they gamble and all this is going to severely shake their trust in his website.'

'And I'm sure you could help to further undermine that trust,' he said, spreading his hands wide.

'Indeed, I could,' I said with a smile. 'And I think I just might. Especially the trust required for on-line gaming. If I can show that he has been involved with some dodgy dealings with race fixing, it is only a small step for people to believe that he has also been fixing the games on his website. I think the earnings and value of Make A Wager Ltd are about to take a major dip in the market.'

'George made a wager, and lost,' he said.

I left Archie still chuckling at his little joke and took another taxi back to Ebury Street. My Charles Atlas look-alike was still on guard outside the door. I wondered if he ever went to the lavatory.

*   *   *

Jenny arrived on the dot of twelve thirty as promised. In spite of being announced from downstairs and being met by me at the lift, she was still keenly scrutinised by the bodyguard who insisted on looking in her handbag before he would allow her into the flat.

'But I know this person,' I said. All too well.

'Sir,' he said, sounding a little patronising, 'most

people are murdered by someone they know.'

I decided against mentioning that Indira Gandhi, the former Indian prime minister, had been murdered by her bodyguards.

After an inspection of the bag had revealed nothing more lethal than half a packet of menthol cigarettes, Jenny was allowed to proceed. At least he hadn't performed a full body search.

'What's that all about?' she said.

'The man who shot Marina is still on the loose,' I said. 'And I don't want him having another go.'

'Oh,' she said. 'Was going out to lunch such a good idea after all?'

'Absolutely,' I said. 'We can't hide away for ever. And I've arranged for Muscles out there to go with you.' She opened her mouth. 'It's all right. He won't sit at the same table. You can tie his lead to a lamppost.'

Marina was ready and itching to get out of our cramped home if only for a couple of hours.

'Take care,' I said as they squeezed into the lift with the muscles. They were both giggling as the doors closed. Would I ever have thought that Jenny, my ex-wife, and Marina, my future one, would be giggling together? Not in a thousand years.

I went out on to the balcony to watch them leave. The muscleman was too big to fold himself into the back seat of Jenny's little town runabout so he rode up front while Marina sat behind. The girls were still laughing but I was happy that Muscles, at least, was taking their security seriously as he scanned every nook and cranny for potential danger. None transpired, and they drove off safely.

I was just sitting down at my computer to answer

a couple of e-mails when my phone rang. It was Chief Inspector Carlisle.

'Did you get the tape?' I asked him.

'Yes, thank you,' he said. 'Very interesting. But you should leave that sort of questioning to the police. You may have damaged the case by locking her in the room like that.'

'But the police weren't interested,' I said. 'You were too busy elsewhere and Johnson from Thames Valley believed Bill's death was suicide. If I hadn't questioned her, no one would have.'

'Breaking into her house was not very wise either.'

'I didn't break in. She had previously shown me where she left the key, so I simply used it.'

'A technicality,' he said.

'Cases hinge on technicalities,' I said. 'Anyway, have you caught him yet?'

'Who?' he said.

'Peter Enstone, of course.'

'Not yet, but we are now officially looking for him. An APB has been put out jointly by the Met Police, Thames Valley and us.'

It sounded a bit like 'Hawaii Five-O'.

'What does APB actually stand for?' I asked.

'All Points Bulletin,' he said. 'It means that various agencies like the police, immigration service, customs and so on get a list of names of people to be apprehended. It should prevent him leaving the country.'

'If he hasn't already done so,' I said. 'When did this APB get put out?'

'Only about an hour ago, I'm afraid. The Met went to his home at nine this morning but he wasn't there. His neighbour apparently told the officers that Enstone had just popped out for a newspaper and would soon be back. So the officers waited for him. They waited for an hour but he didn't come back.'

God help me, I thought. Of course he didn't come back. He would have arrived at the newsagents to find his smiling face on the front of *The Pump* and he would have done a runner.

'Where else are you looking for Enstone?' I asked.

'Where do you suggest?'

'How about Juliet Burns's house,' I said.

'Ah, Juliet Burns,' he repeated slowly. 'And where is she exactly?'

'Last I heard she was at the Donnington Valley Hotel in Newbury,' I said, 'but that was last night. I expect she may be in need of your protection.'

'I'm sure we can find a secure cell for her somewhere.'

'Don't be too hard on her,' I said. 'She did help me in the end.'

'She had better help us, too,' he said, 'or I will personally throw away the key to her cell.'

The buzzer sounded on the internal telephone so I went into the hallway to answer it, still holding my mobile.

'Just a moment,' I said to Carlisle.

'Yes,' I said into the internal system.

'Charles Rowland down here for you, Mr Halley,' said one of the porters.

'Fine,' I said. 'Send him up.' He was early, no doubt eager to have another go at my whisky.

I replaced the internal phone receiver and spoke again to Carlisle. 'I must go, my father-in-law has arrived. You will call me if you catch Peter

Enstone, won't you?'

'Certainly will,' he said, and we hung up.

I went out to the lift to meet Charles, but it wasn't Charles in the lift.

It was the smiling man from the front page of *The Pump*.

Only he wasn't smiling now.

He held a black revolver very steadily in his right hand and he was pointing it right between my eyes.

Damn, I thought. That was bloody careless.

CHAPTER TWENTY-ONE

'I've come here to kill you,' Peter said.

I didn't doubt it.

'Inside,' he said.

We were standing outside my front door near the lift and, typically, there was no sign of my neighbours when you needed them.

We went in through the door and he locked it behind us. He took the key out of the lock and put it in his pocket.

He didn't once allow me to get close to him. Never close enough to give me the chance of wresting the gun out of his hand before he had time to use it.

'In there,' he said, waving the gun towards the sitting room. He seemed to be looking for something.

'She's not here,' I said, assuming it was Marina he was after.

He ignored me.

'This way,' he said, again waving the gun, this

333

time directing me back into the hallway.

We proceeded to go all round the flat until he seemed satisfied that we were alone. I could see the clock in the bedroom. It was only ten to one, it would be at least an hour before Marina and Jenny came back. Would I still be alive by then?

'Go in there,' he said, pointing at the bathroom.

I went.

He turned on the light and the extractor fan began to emit a whine. I wished it could extract me from this situation.

The bathroom was a small room about six foot six square. It was built in the interior of the building and consequently had no windows. A bath ran down the wall on the right with a lavatory next to it and there was a wash-basin opposite the entrance. But Peter was most interested in what was behind the door attached to the left-hand wall—a shiny chrome three-bar centrally-heated towel rail about three feet long. There were three yellow towels neatly hanging on it.

'Catch,' he said and threw me a pair of sturdy-looking metal handcuffs that he had brought with him in his pocket. I caught them.

'Put one on your right wrist and the other round the bracket of the towel rail where it is attached to the wall. Shut them tight.'

I managed it with some difficulty. My only real hand was now firmly attached to the heating system. Not a great improvement.

'Now put your left hand out towards me,' he said.

I wondered if and when I would not do as he said.

He seemed to sense the thought in me and

334

raised his gun higher, taking deliberate aim at my head. I could see right down the barrel. I speculated about whether I would have time to see the bullet coming before it tore into my brain. I decided that I didn't want to find out. I put my left hand forward.

He lifted the sleeve of my shirt and removed the battery from my false arm and put it in his pocket. He was very careful never to move the gun line away from my eye and I was equally careful not to make any sudden movement that might encourage him to pull the trigger.

'Now take that thing off,' he said, stepping back.

'I can't,' I said.

He held the gun in his left hand and grasped my left wrist with his right. He pulled. I pulled back. I stressed my arm to prevent the false bit from coming off. He pulled harder. The arm didn't shift.

'You won't remove it, it stays on permanently,' I said. 'You see those little rivets on either side? They're the ends of the pins that go right through what's left of my real arm to hold it in place.'

I wasn't really sure why I told him the lie. The rivets were actually holding the sensors in place on the inside, the sensors that sat against my skin to pick up the nerve impulses that made the hand work. It was only a small act of defiance, but it was something.

He gave the arm one last violent tug but I was ready for him and the fibreglass shell didn't budge.

He stood back and looked at me. Then he said, 'Put the arm out again.'

I did so.

He took the battery out of his pocket and clipped it back into place. I moved my thumb in and out.

'Grab hold of the towel rail,' he said. 'There.' He pointed.

'What?' I said.

The gun came up a fraction.

'Just do it,' he said.

I placed my unfeeling fingers around the boiling hot rail and closed the thumb. He leaned forward and removed the battery, dropping it on the floor. Without the battery the thumb wouldn't move. The hand and arm were locked in place.

I was standing in my bathroom with my back against a hot towel rail with both hands firmly attached to it at either end.

Peter Enstone seemed to relax a little. He had been as frightened of me as I was of him.

'What does it take to stop you?' he said.

'Honesty,' I said.

'Don't be so bloody self-righteous,' he said. 'You have ruined my life.'

'You ruined it yourself,' I said.

He ignored me.

'Do you know what it's like to hate your own father?' he said.

'No.'

I had never even known my own father.

'And do you know what it's like to spend your life trying to please someone only for them to despise the very ground you walk on?'

I didn't say anything.

'Do you?' he shouted.

'No,' I said.

'It becomes your whole existence. Looking for things he will like but only finding things he hates. And all the time he thinks you're an idiot, an imbecile, a helpless child, with no feelings.'

I stood there looking at the monster. This man was no helpless child.

'Then I found a way of breaking out of the cage,' he said. 'I found a way to control his emotions. To make him happy, to make him sad, and especially to make him angry with someone else for a change.'

He came closer to my face. I could almost have leaned forward and kissed him. Provided, that is, I wanted to kiss the devil.

'And now you have taken all that away, and worse still, he will now know that it was me that was controlling him. He's going to be so angry with me again.'

He's not going to be the only one, I thought. He sounded like a petulant schoolboy caught with his hand in the biscuit tin.

'Do you know what it's like to have someone angry with you all the time?'

'No,' I said. Actually I did. People were often angry with me for exposing their misdeeds. I had always rather enjoyed it, but I decided not to say so, not now.

'I'll tell you,' he said. 'It eats away at your soul. When you're a child, it's frightening. I spent my whole childhood being frightened of him, every single minute. He would beat me for being naughty, and the harder I tried to be good, the more he saw me as naughty. "Hold out your hand, Peter," he would say. Then he would hit me with a wooden bat. Then he would smile and say it was for my own good.'

He went quiet for a moment and stared off into space; I could tell he was reliving incidents

337

elsewhere.

'He used to hit my mother as well,' he said. 'He drove her away. At first, she used to protect me from him but then she left. She deserted me and he killed her.' He paused then went on. 'Well, he didn't actually kill her, but as good as. She was desperate to get away from him and she agreed to everything he said so long as he would leave her alone. He saw to it that she left with nothing, no money, no home and no chance of ever seeing me again. I was twelve.'

She obviously hadn't had a very good solicitor, I thought. Times had changed.

'He never spoke about her. It was as if she had never existed. I found out much later that she had been absolutely destitute and had even been begging in the street.' He made it sound like the most shameful thing in the world. I had occasionally seen my own mother beg. It had sometimes made the difference between life and death for us both.

'She tried to get him to give her some money to live on but he refused. When she tried to take him to court to get access to me, his lawyers blocked her. They just tore to shreds the hardly qualified Legal Aid lawyer that my mother had to resort to.'

Definitely not a good solicitor.

'She walked straight out of her lawyer's office and under a number 15 bus. Funny,' he said, 'ever since I found that out, I've never been able to ride on a number 15 bus, just in case it was the one.'

He sat down on the edge of the bath. The longer he talked, the greater the chance that Muscles would come back with the girls and save my skin, but I would probably need to survive for another hour if the cavalry were to arrive in time.

'The inquest said it was an accident, but I reckon she did it on purpose. My father killed her as sure as if he'd been driving the bus himself.'

He had tears in his eyes. I wasn't sure whether it was for the loss of his mother or for the reaction the incident may have produced in Jonny Enstone. Peter's relationship with his father was highly complex.

'When I got older and bigger, he stopped hitting me. I told him that if he hit me again I'd hit him back. So he's changed his tactics from physical to mental abuse. He puts me down at every opportunity. He belittles everything I do. He tells his friends that I am useless, and that I can't be his true son as I am no good at business. I hate him. I hate him.'

Why then, I thought, don't you go and shoot him instead of me?

'And then when I find I am good at something, you go and wreck it. At last I discovered that it's me that has the power, it's me that's in control, and it's me that people are frightened of.' He looked up at my face. 'Everyone except you. You're not even frightened now.'

Yes, I was. But I didn't say so. I stood there in silence and watched him.

I began to sweat. In spite of the insulating effect of the towels against which I was leaning, I was getting very hot. I was worried that he should think that my skin was damp due to fear. But did it matter? Yes. It did to me.

'You should be frightened,' he said. 'I am going to kill you. I've got nothing to lose now, thanks to you. I'll get done for the other two murders so why not for three. Three life sentences are just as long as two. And in all those years ahead, I will have the satisfaction of knowing that it was me that beat Sid Halley. I won. I might be in jail but you will be pushing up the daisies. And then one day I'll be out, but there'll be no bringing you back from the dead.'

He smiled. I began to be more than frightened. I became angry.

Why, I thought, should this little worm use his father as his excuse for his actions? Yes, his father was an ogre and a bully, but Peter was thirty-two years old and there are limits to how much and for how long you can blame the parents.

The rage rose inside me as it had done in the hospital. I raged, also, at my predicament. Damn it, I didn't want to die. I wanted to live. I wanted to marry Marina. I especially didn't want to die like this, trussed up and at the hands of Peter Enstone.

'I think I've talked enough,' he said suddenly, standing up. 'I get fed up with all those silly films where the gunman spends so long telling his victim why he's going to kill him that someone finally arrives to stop it. That's not going to happen here because I'm going to kill you now, then I'm going to wait and kill your girlfriend when she gets home. She can keep you company in hell.'

He laughed.

He leaned forward until his face was just six inches away from mine.

'Bye, Sid,' he said. 'Now be a good boy and open your mouth.'

Instead, I hit him.

I hit him with all the pent-up anger and frustration of the last three weeks.

I hit him with the stump of my left arm.

The look on his face was more of surprise than hurt. But I had put every ounce of my considerable strength into that blow and he went backwards fast. The edge of the bath caught him behind the knees and he went over it. There was a satisfyingly loud thud as the back of his head hit the far rim of the bath near the taps. Thank goodness for old-fashioned values, I thought. This bathtub was not one of the modern flexible cheap plastic things; it was solid cast-iron and very hard.

Peter was lying face up in the bath but he was half turned, with his chin pushed into his chest. He groaned a little but he was unconscious. But for how long?

Now what?

My left forearm hurt.

I had been gradually easing it out of its false case for some time and the seal around the elbow had finally separated as I had cautiously flexed it back and forth without his noticing. Now I looked at the end of my stump. It was sore and bleeding, such had been the force of the blow.

The task now was to get out of the bathroom before Peter came round and finished off what he'd started.

I tugged at the handcuffs on my right hand. I twisted and pulled, I jerked and heaved but made no impression whatsoever on the metal, I simply tore and chaffed my wrist until I was bleeding on both sides.

I trod on my arm battery that was lying on the floor. How do I pick that up, I wondered? I kicked off my shoes and used my left big toe to pull the sock off my right foot. I tried to pick up the battery in my toes but it was too big to grasp.

Peter groaned again. I was getting desperate now. I bloody refused to be still attached to this bloody towel rail when he came round.

I went down on my knees and tried to get my mouth down to the battery but it was too far. I used my toes to pull the battery a little closer and, between my right foot and left stump, I managed to upend it so that it sat vertically on the floor. I hung down with most of my weight on my sore handcuffed right wrist, but I didn't care. I stretched my body down and forward as far as I could reach and put my mouth over the end of the battery.

I could feel a tingling on my tongue as it touched the battery electrodes. I had freshly charged it the previous night.

Peter groaned again and this time more loudly. I looked at him in alarm. He was being sick. I could see the vomit as it came down his nose and out of the corner of his mouth. I hoped he'd choke on it.

I knelt on the floor again and tried to use my mouth to push the battery into its holder in the fibreglass shell that stuck out rigidly sideways from the mechanical hand that was firmly gripping the towel rail. It was simple really. Place the lower end of the battery under the lugs at the wrist end of the holder and snap the upper end in under the sprung plastic clip. A task I performed day in, day out, hundreds of times a year. But always with my dextrous right hand. It was not so easy with a tingling mouth and when my life depended on it. Eventually I positioned the battery at the correct angle under the lugs and used my nose and forehead to push the other end in. It snapped into place. Hallelujah!

Now I had to get my bruised and bloody stump back into the fibreglass shell before it swelled up too much to fit. I stood up and eased it in. Normally I used talcum powder to help as the fit was tight even at the best of times, and a little moisture can cause the real me to stick to the plastic, making things impossible. This time I had no available talcum powder and there was masses of moisture, both blood and sweat.

I managed it after a fashion although the elbow seal was far from perfect. I sent the impulses but the thumb refused to budge. Bugger. Maybe there was blood between my skin and the electrodes. I tried again and then again.

The thumb moved a fraction but still refused to swing open fully.

I kept sending the necessary signals and slowly, little by little, the thumb moved enough to allow my hand to unclasp the towel rail.

But I was still firmly attached on my right-hand side.

My normally strong mechanical left hand was letting me down. The hand that this morning could have crushed not only eggs and fingers, but also apples and tennis balls, would have had trouble now with a soap bubble. Nevertheless, I used it to attack the handcuffs. But I had no success. I wished I had a cutting tool on the hand like that character in the James Bond movie. I would have cut myself out of trouble in no time.

Peter coughed. Perhaps he was indeed choking on his vomit.

I wondered if I should shout for help. But wouldn't it rouse Peter? And would anyone else hear me anyway? My building was predominantly

343

occupied by businessmen. Would anyone be in their flats to hear me at one thirty on a Tuesday afternoon? The porters/security were safely behind their desk, four floors down. They may as well have been on the moon.

I looked closely at the handcuffs. The cuff around my wrist was annoyingly tight. Too tight for me to slip my hand through, I'd tried that. The other cuff around the rail bracket was not so tight. I put the thumb of my false hand through the ring and tried to use the arm as a lever to break the lock.

I couldn't move it far enough so I eased my forearm once more out of the shell and used my left elbow to push the prosthetic arm down. I am sure that the boffins at the Roehampton artificial limb centre would have loved to know that I was using their highly expensive pride and joy as a crowbar.

But it worked. The thumb on the hand was stronger than the lock that resisted for a while but finally gave way with a crack. My false arm fell to the floor but it had done its job. I was free from the towel rail although I still had the handcuffs dangling around my right wrist.

I wasted no time. I leaned over Peter in the bath and took his gun. I held it in my right hand and pointed it at him. Should I shoot him? I asked myself. Indeed, could I shoot him? I had never been one to shy away from a bit of violence if it were necessary, but shooting someone seemed a bit extreme, even terminal. Especially someone who was unconscious.

I wasn't sure that I could bring myself to shoot Peter even if he woke up. Perhaps I would threaten

344

to do so but then not have the resolve to carry it out. If I wasn't going to use the gun, then no one else was either. I removed the bullets from the cylinder and put them in my pocket.

I left Peter where he was and went into the sitting room to call for reinforcements from the police. I put the gun down on the table and dialled 999.

'Emergency, what service?' asked a female voice.

'Police,' I said.

I could hear the voice give my telephone number to the police operator who then came on the line.

'Police emergency,' he said.

'I need help and fast,' I said. 'I have a gunman in my flat.'

He asked for the address. I gave it. He asked if I was in danger. Yes, I said, I was.

They were on their way.

'Tell Superintendent Aldridge that the gunman is Peter Enstone.'

'Right,' said the police operator, but I wondered if he would.

I walked into the hallway and used the internal telephone to call down to the reception desk.

'Yes, Mr Halley?' said a voice. It wasn't Derek. It was one of the new staff.

'Some policemen will be arriving soon. Please send them straight up.'

'Certainly, sir,' he said somewhat uncertainly. 'Is everything all right?'

'Yes,' I said. 'Everything's fine.'

I went back to check on my unwanted guest in the bathroom, but the bath was empty.

Oh my God! Everything was far from fine.

I should have shot him while I'd had the chance.

I spun round but he wasn't behind me.

Now what should I do? Should I go and get the gun? Should I reload it?

And where was he? There weren't many places to hide in this flat. I went back to the kitchen door, picked up the internal telephone to push the buzzer to summon help from Security downstairs.

I never got the chance.

Peter came charging out of one of the bedrooms straight at me. His lips were drawn back, revealing his teeth in some evil grin, and there was murder in his eyes. This wasn't to be the cold-blooded, almost sanitized killing he had planned, this was going to be uncontrolled and furious. He was in a frenzy and a rage. That made two of us.

He dived at me as I tried to side-step into the kitchen and he used my own false arm as a club to aim a swing at my head.

That's a bit cheeky, I thought. That was usually my game plan.

I dodged and he caught me only a glancing blow on my shoulder. I shoved him and sent him spinning across the hall on his knees. He was quickly back up on his feet and bunching for a fresh attack. I dropped the internal telephone and retreated into the kitchen and tried to close the door.

He stuck his foot in the gap and pushed hard. I leaned on the door to keep him out but he had the strength of the demented, as well as two good hands.

I looked around for a weapon. I had a pocket full of bullets but no gun. Too late to discover that

I could have gladly shot him dead.

There was a pine block full of kitchen knives on the worktop on the far side of the room near the cooker but it would have meant leaving the door to reach them. Did I have a choice, I asked myself. I was slowly losing the battle to keep him out anyway.

Again, I asked myself the question. Even if I reached a knife, would I use it? I had once known a particularly nasty villain who had told me that killing with a knife was an experience not to be missed. He had described with relish how he liked to feel the warmth of his victim's blood on his hand as it spurted out from the wound. It was an image I had often tried to remove from my consciousness without much success. Could I stab Peter and feel the warmth of his blood?

He heaved at the door and sent me sprawling across the floor.

I jumped up and went for the knife block.

He tore at my collar and tossed me away from it. He stretched for it himself. I grabbed at him and put my right arm round his neck and pulled him backwards.

But I was losing this fight. Hand-to-hand combat is somewhat tricky when your opponent has twice as many hands and no scruples about using his nails and teeth as well.

He dug his nails into my already sore wrist and used the still-dangling handcuffs to pull my hand up to his mouth where he bit it. But I refused to let go and went on hauling him away from the knives. He bit me again, this time using all his might to sink his teeth into my thumb. I thought he would bite it off completely.

I gave up my neck-lock, and tore my hand free of him.

He went for the knives.

I picked up the only thing I could see. My trusted one-handed cork remover. The spike sat ready for action on a shelf next to the wine glasses.

I tried to stab it into his back but I couldn't get it through his coat.

He chose a long wide carving knife from the block and turned around. I knew the edge was sharp. I had honed it myself.

So it was to be my blood warming his hands.

He was still smiling the evil grin and if anything his lips were even further back than before. There was something horrific about what such hate can do to a human being.

He stepped forward and I stepped back. In two strides I was flat against the wall.

As he lunged at me, I stabbed him with the cork remover. I drove the spike deep into the soft tissue between the thumb and first finger of his right hand.

He screamed and dropped the knife. The spike had gone right through. The sharp point was clearly visible sticking out of his palm. He clutched at it.

I pushed past him. The front door to my left was no good, it was locked and the key was in Peter's pocket. I went right and fairly sprinted down the hallway to the bathroom. I locked myself in.

A moment later, I could hear him walking about.

'Sid,' he said. He sounded quite calm and also very close. 'I have my gun back now and I'm going to come in there and kill you.'

Not if I could help it.

Where were the bloody police?

I heard the gun go click. Then click again, and again.

'Oh, very funny,' he said.

I hoped to God he hadn't brought more ammunition with him.

'Well, Sid, what shall we do now?' he said through the door. 'Perhaps I'll wait here until your girlfriend comes home. Then you'll come out.'

*   *   *

I wasn't sure whether it dawned on me or Peter first that Marina was not coming home.

I had been in the bathroom for well over an hour. I wasn't coming out and Peter hadn't been able to get in. He'd tried a few times. At first, he had attempted to kick the door down. I had leaned against it and I could feel the blows through the wood. Thankfully, the corridor outside was so narrow that he couldn't get a run at it and the lock had held easily. Next, he had tried to hack his way through with the carving knife. I know because he'd told me so, but wood doesn't cut very easily with a knife, even a sharp knife, and I reckoned it would take him all night to get through that way. I was glad I didn't have a fire axe in the flat.

The phone had rung several times. I could hear my new answering machine picking up each time after seven rings, just as I'd told it to.

I'd worked out that the police must be somewhere outside and it was probably them on the phone. They must surely have stopped Marina from coming back. By now they must have also intercepted the real Charles Rowland.

I wondered how long they would wait.

A long time. They would have no desire to walk in on a loaded gun.

The phone rang again.

'Answer the phone, Peter,' I called to him through the door.

There was no sound. He had been quiet for a long time now.

'Peter,' I shouted, 'answer the bloody phone.'

But the machine did it for him, again.

I wished I had my mobile. It was on its charging cradle in the sitting room and I had heard it ringing, too.

I sat on the edge of the bath in darkness. The light switch was outside in the corridor and Peter had turned it out long ago. The only light came from the narrow gap under the door. I had several times lain down and tried to look under, but without much success. Occasionally I had seen a shadow as Peter had walked past or stood outside the door. But not for a while now.

What was he doing?

Was he still there?

I stood up and put my ear to the door. Nothing.

The floor was wet. I could feel it on my right foot, the one without the sock.

What was he up to?

Was he pouring something flammable under the door? Was he going to burn me out?

I went down quickly on my knees and put a finger in the liquid. I put it to my nose. It didn't smell of petrol. I tasted it.

I knew that taste. When one was accustomed to eating grass at half a mile a minute it was seemingly always mixed with blood from one's mouth or nose. And blood is what I could taste now. I found I was paddling in the stuff and it was coming under the door. It had to be Peter's but the wound I had inflicted on his hand would not have produced so much.

Gingerly I opened the bathroom door and peered out. Peter was seated on the floor a little to the left, leaning up against the magnolia-painted wall.

His eyes swivelled round and looked at me.

I was surprised he was still conscious. His blood was all down the wooden-floored corridor and there were splashes of it on the paintwork where surges of it had landed.

He had used the carving knife with its finely honed edge.

He had sliced through his left wrist so deeply I could see the bones. I had seen something like that before.

I stepped towards him and used my foot to pull the knife away, just to be on the safe side.

He was trying to say something.

I went down and put my ear close to his mouth. His voice was so weak I could barely hear him.

'Go back in the bathroom,' he whispered. 'Let me die.'

EPILOGUE

Three weeks later Marina and I went to Huw Walker's funeral outside a rainy Brecon.

The service took place in a small grey stone chapel with a grey slate roof, and every seat was filled. Evan Walker was there in a starched white shirt and stiff collar under his best Sunday suit. Chief Inspector Carlisle represented the police and Edward, the managing director, was there on behalf of Cheltenham Racecourse.

Jonny Enstone had sensibly stayed away. The turbulent relationship between father and son had been much reported and dissected by the media with little credit falling at his feet. I wondered if he still worked the dining room at the House of Lords.

However, it was the turnout from the rest of the racing world that would have pleased Huw most. Chris Beecher had unashamedly been using his column in *The Pump* to restore Huw's reputation and to cast him as another victim of the Enstone conspiracy. It was the least he could do.

I wasn't entirely sure whether so many had made the long journey to South Wales out of genuine fondness for the man or, like Chris, due to their guilty feelings for having initially condemned him so easily as an out-and-out villain.

It didn't matter. In his father's eyes, it was a vindication of his son.

We stood under umbrellas in the muddy graveyard as Huw's simple oak coffin was lowered into the ground next to his mother and his brother, and then we retired to the pub across the road for a drink and to warm up.

'What news?' I asked Carlisle.

'We caught the child killer,' he said. 'So my job is safe for a while longer.'

'Great,' I said, 'but what news on this front?'

'Juliet Burns has been charged with aiding and abetting a felon, and with being an accessory after the fact.'

'And what does that mean?' I asked.

'About eighteen months, I suspect,' he said. 'Less if she plays her cards right. It will be up to Thames Valley and the Crown Prosecution Service.'

'I thought that plea bargains didn't happen in this country,' I said.

'Oh yeah,' he said. 'Like euthanasia? It's just called something different. How about you?'

He pointed at my left arm, which I had in a sling.

'I split the end of my ulna when I punched Peter Enstone,' I said. 'I haven't been able to wear my false arm since. But it's mending.'

In truth, I had been much more comfortable with my left arm these last three weeks than I had for ten years, since my racing disaster. I was aware that, in spite of its truncation, it was a part of me as a whole. It had saved my life. It was my friend again.

'And your girlfriend?' he asked, nodding towards Marina who was talking to Evan Walker.

'My wife,' I said smiling, 'is just fine, thank you.'

Marina had found that she had thought about an engagement for long enough while she had waited outside the flat with the police. She had told both Charles and Jenny that if I came out alive she would marry me at once. 'At once' had actually been two weeks because her parents had been away on a safari through the African bush. They had remained blissfully unaware of their daughter's fight for life until after the drama was over. We had waited for them to return and then had done the deed in a West Oxfordshire register office followed by a small reception at Aynsford. Jenny had been there all smiles, her guilt forever purged.

'Congratulations,' said Carlisle. 'So what's next for you?'

'I'm still working on the internet gambling investigation,' I said.

As I'd predicted, make-a-wager.com had taken a nose-dive. The Jockey Club had initiated an enquiry into the running of the exchange and Chris Beecher had publicised the fact at full volume in the paper. George Lochs had so far avoided being charged with any actual crime but in the meantime he had been declared *persona non grata* on any racecourse. It was rumoured that all his assets had been held in his company's name and he was now going down the tubes quicker than Enron.

Frank Snow at Harrow would be pleased.

Marina came over to me with Evan Walker in tow.

'Mr Halley,' he said, 'thank you for what you've done for my Huw. I will expect to receive your bill in due course.'

'There will be no bill,' I said. 'There's nothing to pay.'

'I can afford it, you know,' he said, somewhat stiffly. 'I don't need your charity.'

'Mr Walker,' I said, 'I wasn't offering you charity. The costs of the investigation have been covered by *The Pump.*'

'Conscience money.' He chortled. 'OK, I'll take that.' He went off to talk to a group near the buffet.

'Are you going back to Cheltenham tonight?' I asked Carlisle.

'No, I'm taking the train to London,' he said. 'It looks like Peter Enstone will survive after all, thanks to you. I have to go and formally arrest him at St Thomas's for the murder of Huw Walker.'

I'd heard that he had lost the use of his left hand.

He was crippled, just like me.